# Praise for the *Masters*

### Club Shad

"*Club Shadowlands* is a superbly crafted story .ll dazzle any BDSM fan and have them adding it to their must read list!"

— Shannon, *The Romance Studio*

### Dark Citadel

"*Dark Citadel* is a decadent delight and an immensely satisfying read."

— Priscilla Alston, *Just Erotic Romance Reviews*

### Breaking Free

"A riveting tale, *Breaking Free* is a book I highly recommend."

— Jennifer Bishop, *Romance Reviews Today*

### Lean on Me

"Ms. Sinclair's stories are rare gems that continue to haunt the reader even as the last page is read."

— Dawn, *Love Romances and More*

### Make Me, Sir

"*Make Me, Sir* was a gripping story that kept me entertained all the way through to the end."

— *Whipped Cream Erotic Reviews*

### To Command and Collar

"Get ready for the most emotionally wrenching MASTERS OF THE SHADOWLANDS book to date."

— Lily, *Romance Junkies*

# LooseId®

ISBN 13: 978-1-61118-983-4
TO COMMAND AND COLLAR
Copyright © July 2012 by Cherise Sinclair
Originally released in e-book format in November 2011

Cover Art by Christine M. Griffin
Cover Layout and Design by April Martinez

Printed in the U.S.A. by
Lightning Source, Inc.
1246 Heil Quaker Blvd
La Vergne TN 37086
www.lightningsource.com

# TO COMMAND
# AND COLLAR

## Cherise Sinclair

# Acknowledgement

*I'm a writer, and words are supposed to come easily to me, yet there's no way to adequately express my appreciation to the people below.*

*I'm blessed to have the sweetest, most enthusiastic readers in the world. The long hours at the computer, the blurry eyes, the dirty house, and the frozen dinners—you make it worthwhile. Please realize that without your stubborn insistence (that's a polite way to say nagging <g>), Master Raoul wouldn't have a story. Truly, I adore you all.*

*A book is a team effort, and I'm very grateful for all those who helped get this story into your hands. A special shout-out:*

*To my Erotic Romance Authors critique group, who kicked the beginning of this book into shape. To Bianca Sommerland and Cari Silverwood, who beta-read it...and made me rewrite the ending again and again.*

*To G.G. Royale, my wonderful editor, who keeps the story on track—and made me lighten up the torture on the boat—and to the excellent line and proofing editors who made this book readable. To the Loose Id Quad who kindly ignore the way I tuck extra characters in...and how long these books have gotten. To the supremely talented artist, Christine Griffin, who's created each Shadowlands cover and captured the ambience so well.*

*To Suede, who enthusiastically shares tales and answers questions. A big hug to you.*

*I'd like to thank Kane and careena at the Lair de Sade in Los Angeles for your warm welcome and for the tour of your huge dungeon...especially that sinister jail cell in the basement. Thanks to the generous Doms, Masters, submissives, and slaves there who shared their stories, and a special thanks to the awesome Dom who did the fireplay scene. Many hugs go to Fiona Archer from Australia, who joined me on the late-night dungeon jaunt despite an early flight. That's friendship above and beyond the call of duty.*

*To my wonderful, creative, loving children, real and honorary, who put up with a mom who disappears for hours at a time. And last but never least, to my good-natured husband for his patience when I say "uh-huh" without hearing a word. You're the reason I can write about love.*

*Bless you all.*

*Cherise*

# Author's Note

To my readers,

This book is fiction, not reality and, as in most romantic fiction, the romance is compressed into a very, very short time period.

You, my darlings, live in the real world and I want you to take a little more time than the heroines you read about. Good Doms don't grow on trees and there's some strange people out there. So while you're looking for that special Dom, please, be careful.

When you find him, realize he can't read your mind. Yes, frightening as it might be, you're going to have to open up and talk to him. And you listen to him, in return. Share your hopes and fears, what you want from him, what scares you spitless. Okay, he may try to push your boundaries a little—he's a Dom, after all—but you have your safeword. You *will* have a safeword, am I clear? Use protection. Have a back-up person. Communicate.

Remember: *safe, sane* and *consensual.*

Know that I'm hoping you find that special, loving person who will understand your needs and hold you close. Let me know how you're doing. I worry, you know.

Meantime, come and hang out with the Masters of the Shadowlands.

—*Cherise*

# Chapter One

Kimberly Moore kept her eyes focused on her long, transparent skirt. The silky material provided no cushioning for her knees on the cold tile floor. But she should be used to misery—since the day she'd been kidnapped, her life had held no comforts, just pain and abuse. And it looked about to get worse. *Don't move. Don't tense. Don't show anger.*

The Overseer stepped closer, his boots—black like his soul—entering her field of vision. "The three buyers are in the living room. Serve them drinks, hors d'oeuvres. Use your bodies to please them. I suggest you all do your best. If you're not bought, you'll entertain the staff in any way they choose, and then be auctioned off next month."

*A new owner.* Trembling started deep in Kim's center, and bile rose into her throat. She tried to swallow, but her collar seemed to tighten, choking off her breath, choking off her life. Forcing a slow inhalation, she kept her hands still. *Don't try to rip it off.* A scar ran up her neck from the first collar she'd cut off, slicing herself in the process.

Lord Greville had beaten her until she'd vomited from the nightmarish pain. As her hands had smudged the blood on the concrete, she'd futilely wished her knife had sliced deeper—an artery and not merely her skin.

*Endure. Be silent.* She tightened her stomach muscles and made herself into a statue. The Overseer's boots remained in her vision for another moment before he walked out of the kitchen and into the living room.

The sound of his footsteps had faded completely before Kim dared look up. She could keep her face from betraying her, but not her eyes. Any slaver seeing the hatred in her eyes would beat her.

"Buyers," Holly whimpered.

Kim reached over to squeeze the nineteen-year-old blonde's hand. "Shhh. It'll be fine. Maybe there's a nice one here tonight."

"Do you think so?" Hope filled Holly's sweet face.

"Who knows?"

The third slave in the kitchen took Holly's other hand. "Be strong, honey. We'll get through this." She shook her head at Kim, disapproving of giving the younger woman false expectations. They both knew nice men didn't buy kidnapped women.

Kim only wanted to be purchased, to get away from the Overseer. After that, somehow—somehow she'd get free. She remembered for an instant the surge of the ocean under her boat, the scent and taste of a briny breeze, the camaraderie of the other Georgia biologists. *Keep those memories, but bury them deep, where whips can't reach.* She'd get home again. Somehow. Maybe tonight. Any change in routine presented opportunity for escape, especially during transportation. She'd learned the hard way chances decreased once a buyer got her home. Slaves were put into closets or basements when the masters weren't using them. A shiver ran over her skin. Or *cages.*

She swallowed. Her defiance had broken against the heavy steel of the dog-sized cage. On hands and knees, unable to stand, to move. Pissing down her legs. Panicking and screaming until her voice gave out.

Her master hadn't liked it when she'd tried to kill him.

*And did you learn anything from your experience, Kim?* her inner cynic asked. She scowled. *Next time, I'll stab him faster.* Yet she knew in her gut that she'd never have the courage again.

With a sigh, she rose and hauled Holly and Linda up beside her. "Well, ladies, let's go entice some buyers."

Silently, she led the way into the formal parlor. She studied the two men conversing quietly by the fire. One was overweight, thirties, with a cruel twist to his fat lips. The other was gaunt and older. Which would be more careless?

The third buyer... Across the room, a man stood in the hall doorway. Only around six feet, but so muscular, he appeared huge. His white silky shirt set off his dark tan and even darker eyes. Expressionless face, unreadable gaze. He studied Linda and Holly before turning his attention to her, and his impersonal regard blew like a winter wind across her naked skin.

She shivered. Not him. Please, God, not him. *I'm ugly. Clumsy. Bad slave. You don't want to buy me.*

STANDING IN THE doorway, Raoul Sandoval breathed in the humid Florida air coming from an open window. The dark Victorian parlor with regal blue floral wallpaper and Oriental carpets seemed an appropriate setting for masters and slaves. The other unnamed buyers occupied tapestry-covered chairs. He gave each an indifferent nod, catching sight of himself in the ornate mirror over the fireplace—tailored slacks and silk shirt, his black hair shortened to collar-length and styled. He looked more like his sleek friend Z than himself, but that was the point. He needed to appear rich enough to buy a slave girl. And not a third-world female with broken English, but a well-educated, well-brought-up woman from the US. Only the finest slaves for the richest men.

Across the room, a dark wood buffet held an array of liquor bottles where three slave girls made drinks, supervised by the tall, pale man labeled the Overseer. *"Call me Dahmer,"* he'd said, and Raoul had to wonder what kind of psychopath named himself after a serial killer. He appeared average enough. In fair shape, straight brown hair starting to thin, narrow-set eyes the color of mud. A long upper lip with a dent, mouth with a cynical twist. Not the appearance of a person who kidnapped and sold people like cattle.

Taking his time, Raoul checked out the women. A terrified young blonde; a tall, lush redhead; and a pretty, black-haired female who quickly dropped her gaze. All were dressed in matching silk skirts and nothing else.

"Any preferences, gentlemen?" Dahmer asked. He handed the blonde a drink and nodded toward Raoul.

The short, overweight buyer pointed. "That one's on the old side, but I like redheads. For some reason, they're more fun to fuck."

When the redhead paled, Raoul had to tighten his control over his emotions.

The balding older man barked a laugh and leered at the youngest woman. "I prefer blondes."

The little blonde startled, her arm jerking.

Raoul caught the glass of wine before it spilled on him. "Easy, *chica*," he said.

She cringed, obviously expecting a blow. Anger spiked inside him. Keeping his expression calm, he took a sip of the drink.

His nod of approval cleared the worry from her face...until the Overseer directed her toward the old man. Her expression of dismay showed clearly.

The remaining slave had more control. She stood beside Dahmer, eyes down, hands clasped in front. He wouldn't call her beautiful, but she was pretty enough to please any man. Her skin held a bronze-red tone a few shades lighter than Raoul's, perhaps from some Native American in her ancestry. Her high breasts sagged slightly, her cheeks were hollowed, and she was slim to the point of being gaunt. She'd obviously lost weight in captivity.

The Overseer nodded at Raoul. "Will this one be adequate for now, Master R? Of course, switching around is easy enough, or if none pleases you, then simply enjoy the evening, and we'll arrange another selection at a later date."

That was the plan. Refuse them all and score an invitation to the big auction. Where there would be more kidnapped women. Where the FBI could net the entire bunch of bastards. *Don't think about the future. Buyer. You're a buyer, Sandoval.* He strolled across the room to stand in front of the unchosen woman. She kept her gaze on the floor. "Turn," he ordered, keeping his voice clipped and rough to hide his pity.

She rotated in place. Long hair so dark as to be almost black hung in waves to the hollow of her back. Under the blue-tinted skirt, her hips curved outward in a pleasing manner.

"Skinny." He glanced at Dahmer.

"Ah." Dahmer said in his slimy voice, "The slave got herself hurt. She's fine now but hasn't regained the pounds she lost. She hasn't had much training, and she bears some scars, which is why we're offering her at a bargain price."

The tiny muscles around the woman's mouth barely tightened, but no other reaction showed. Very good control.

"She'll do. For now," Raoul said. The two FBI agents running the show had recommended he present an aloof personality.

Raoul threaded his hand in the girl's black hair, the weight like heavy silk, and used it to pull her closer.

She didn't fight him, silently compliant.

"Look at me." When she didn't obey, he tightened his grip and pulled her head back...gently, although it hopefully appeared cruel.

Her gaze lifted to his, and he froze for a long breath.

Startling clear blue eyes, the color of antique glass. He'd seen those eyes before...when Marcus's submissive had shown him a picture and begged for him to watch for her friend. This had to be Kimberly.

*Madre de Dios, what a fucking mess.* "The coloring is an asset," he said to the Overseer, then opened his hand and released the...slave. Not Kimberly. For tonight, she was nothing more than a slave, there to serve him. He had no other choice. "Bring me something to eat," he snapped and walked over to sit with the others by the fire.

Stretching his legs out, he sipped his wine and idly watched the old fart fondle the young girl's breasts. Rage simmered in an ugly stew in his guts. *No, Sandoval. Control.* Perhaps someday he could feed the lecher a knuckle sandwich, but not today. Raoul forced his fist to open.

Thankfully, the black-haired slave appeared and knelt at Raoul's side, holding up a plate of tidbits. Her submissive silence reminded him of his first slave, but Antonia had served him in love and joy. There was no comparison to this abused woman. "Very nice," he murmured to her, startling an upward glance from those beautiful eyes. And a hint—only a hint—of pleasure before it was drowned in fear and control.

He selected a cheese-stuffed mushroom, appreciating the effort someone had put into making the food, although it tasted like straw right now. He ate another, then held a piece of melon in front of the slave's mouth. "Eat, chica."

Her eyes lowered, but not before he spotted the icy flash. She took the morsel, her soft lips grazing his fingers. He fed her several more, alternating with his own meal, then held his fingers for her to lick clean. He noted the pause before she obeyed. Although she subdued her body language skillfully, the tiny muscles around the eyes and mouth were difficult to control, and her eyes were an open window to her emotions. He could see she'd hated taking food from his hand. Hated him.

He needed to get with the program. *"Behave as if you're interviewing her for a job,"* Special Agent Kouros had coached, obviously doubtful Raoul could manage.

"What talents do you possess?" Raoul asked, taking the plate and setting it on the end table.

She shifted her weight on her knees. "I don't have any skills, Master," she murmured, almost inaudibly, as if she didn't want the Overseer to hear.

No talents? Doubtful. Perhaps she hoped he wouldn't buy her? Was it him she disliked or all the buyers? Did she hope to remain here? "What happens if you're not bought tonight?"

She couldn't control her flinch. So her aim wasn't to remain with the Overseer. She preferred one of the other two buyers? Raoul glanced over. Perhaps she hoped she might escape more easily from a fat or an old master? Clever girl.

But both buyers were sadists. Not good. And he could tell from her flinch, something bad happened to girls who didn't get sold.

How could he leave this young woman here to suffer? *Gabi's friend.* He couldn't.

Some of the foul taste left his mouth. At least he could save one girl. The agents would go ballistic, but they'd find an alternative plan.

And if they couldn't?

He rubbed his hand over his mouth. In buying Kimberly, he might doom the others. His gut tightened. There were no easy solutions to this nightmare.

"Can you cook?" he asked.

"Yes, Master R."

Not going to expand on the answer, was she? He

chuckled. "Must I drag the information from you?"

She went white with fear. "No, Master. I'm sorry, Master."

His anger at the slavers rose so hard and hot that his hands clamped on the chair arms. He forced himself to lean back. "Bring me a fresh drink." *And let me get past wanting to strangle every bastard in this place.* He damn well wanted this evening over with, but no chance of that. No buyer would spend this much money without a test-drive first, and if he offered for the girl too soon, Dahmer would make him for a fraud. *Play the part, Sandoval. Even if you terrify her.*

She returned, knelt silently, and held the glass up.

As he sipped his drink, he studied her, learning how she breathed, how she shifted her weight as her anxiety grew. In her late twenties or early thirties. Average height, skin slack rather than taut, so she was normally rounder. Softer. Her nipples a pinkish brown and large. A long, almost-healed red scar wound along her left rib cage, reminding him of his gang-member days. Knife scar.

Tracing a finger over her scarred remnant of violence, he saw the momentary vulnerable quiver of her lips before her mouth flattened. Gabi had described her friend as exuberant, and he could see lines of past laughter bracketing her mouth and veeing out from the corners of her eyes.

She was joyful no longer. Grief at the loss was a smudge on his soul.

"She dances, you know," the Overseer said, stopping at Raoul's chair. "Intelligent. An excellent cook. Not a particularly good singing voice, but you forget that when she dances."

Raoul glanced down at her. "Dance for me then, slave. Something seductive."

She rose gracefully. As she hurried away, he noticed

whip scars on her back. "Tell me more."

"A marine biologist from Georgia, middle-class background. Healthy, single, no children. A lightweight in the lifestyle before."

"Whip marks. A recent knife cut. Was she sold before?" Raoul asked.

"Well." Dahmer cleared his throat, smoothed his black suit. "She was picked up for the 'rebellious slave' auction."

Raoul raised his eyebrows as if confused, although he knew exactly what Dahmer was talking about. His best friend's submissive, Gabi, had been one of those kidnapped to be sold.

"Ah, each sale event has a theme. The last one featured feisty slaves with prior BDSM experience. Sassy. Bratty. Designed to give a master a challenge. I'm afraid she didn't live up to her promise. The owner was displeased and requested a refund."

The buyer had obviously taken his displeasure out on Kimberly. "So she's used merchandise. What's wrong with the other two?"

"The blonde is...awkward. She would do well in a comfortable environment, but she exhibits poorly." The Overseer turned, and the young woman cringed at his frown. "The redhead is older. She wasn't on our list, but since she witnessed a pickup being made, the deliveryman Tasered her and brought her along as well. She has a few sellable talents, but her age puts her in a lower price range."

The bargain basement for slaves. Exactly as advertised. Since he hadn't known if the slavers investigated a buyer's financial status, Raoul hadn't tried to fake extreme wealth. Instead during the interview, he'd asked about lower-priced slaves, figuring it would consolidate his story.

"Well, Blackie has possibilities," Raoul said.

"Excellent." Satisfaction oozed from Dahmer's voice.

"But test her out thoroughly this evening. We've found that buyers make better choices and are more satisfied if they take their time and put the merchandise through their paces."

"Makes sense." He thought about playing with a nonwilling participant, and his gut tightened.

Raoul looked up as Kimberly reentered the room, now covered in veils. "Well..." he let himself say with an appreciative murmur.

Dahmer laughed. "She belonged to a modern dance group that put on shows for charity. I had an experienced slave give her lessons in erotic dancing and... You'll see."

The music started.

CONCENTRATING ONLY ON the Middle Eastern music, Kim walked in a slow circle as the chiffon material trailed behind her. The other veils covering her body fluttered delicately against her skin. Barefoot, she turned slowly, presented a hip, rotated, letting her hair swing. Slow turns. Arms moving to emphasize her body's curves. She let the scarf in her hand float away and replaced it with the one covering her face.

Knowing her stamina was poor, she'd chosen a short tune. To heck with Hollywood's Dance of the Seven Veils— she was doing four, and that was that.

As the beat picked up, she began the undulating movements, ignoring the painful pulling of the barely healed muscles over her ribs. She concentrated on the dance, trying to ignore the men watching. All of them. The Overseer's face had flushed with lust, and she concealed a shudder. *Music. Think of the music.*

One more veil and her breasts were bare. She shimmied as her teacher had taught. The middle-aged buyer swallowed and leaned forward. She turned her gaze away.

Her body wanted to dance; her soul needed to flee. Her brain knew better and took control, forcing her feet closer to the darkly tanned buyer. Eyes down, she managed to smile appealingly and not grimace. Another spin. *Move closer.*

She lifted her head finally. Her eyes met his, and he trapped her gaze as tightly as he'd gripped her hair earlier. Yet his look was warm, so warm, and when he released her, he seemed to have taken off all the chains binding her muscles.

The music poured around her, rocking her in its embrace. She floated through the dance, the beat of the *dumbek* ruling her hips, the song of the *mizmar* moving her arms and shoulders. Each foot came down exactly right, the feeling indescribable.

Removing the last veil bared her completely, but the sound increased, pulling her after until it slowed and stopped.

She realized she'd knelt in front of Master R instead of in the center of the room. As if he'd keep her safe from the others. The murmur of conversation came from the other two buyers and the Overseer.

Her chest heaved as she tried to catch her breath. Out of shape. She hadn't danced since before Lord Greville had... Since before. A film of moisture dampened her body, and the breeze was cool against her skin. *Naked.* She hated the feeling of being unclothed in front of men. Why hadn't it seemed a problem in the clubs she'd visited in the past?

Because it had been her choice then. And she'd stripped to please and arouse whoever she was playing with. Right now, the thought of arousing anyone wasn't at all appealing. Yet if she didn't, the consequences...

She'd still been recovering during the last private sale—thank you, God—but after the buyers had left, one slave had remained, unwanted and unsold. The Overseer had given her to the staff. The woman's shrill screams had eventually died, sometime late in the night, and the next day, she'd returned to the locked room. Not a person anymore; nothing lived behind her blank eyes. The Overseer had fined his staff a week's wages for ruining the merchandise. And the slave had...disappeared.

Kim swallowed hard.

Sure fingers cupped her chin, lifting her face. The brown eyes that had been so cold at first now held the desire she wasn't sure she wanted...and something else. Concern? "What is wrong, *chiquita?*" he asked softly.

The question, the gentleness brought tears to her eyes. She tried to pull back, but his fingers tightened, keeping her face exposed to his scrutiny. To her horror, she realized she was close to crying. *No.* "Please. Don't."

His frown grew. Then he released her and looked away. When he turned back, his eyes were remote, his face like stone, chilling her inside as well as outside. For a moment, he'd almost seemed human.

*Haven't you learned anything, Kim? You really are a dumb slut like Lord Greville said.*

"Gentlemen, if you are ready, the dungeon is waiting," the Overseer announced.

The fat one made a pleased sound, face filling with lust.

The older one snapped, "About time." He rose and grabbed Holly by her hair, dragging her behind him. She was half-bent over. Crying.

Kim's wish to kill the cruel man almost...almost outweighed her common sense. But she'd learned. Painfully. Interfering meant the slavers would beat her—and the woman she tried to help as well. *The short whip slicing across her back, then the shocking explosion of pain. The screaming of the other slave.* Her hands flattened on her thighs. *Don't speak; don't look.*

Master R rose. "Come."

She started to gather her discarded garments, and he shook his head. "You are dressed appropriately for the dungeon."

When she was on her feet, he grasped her by the back of her neck, his grip firm but not painful, his fingers calloused. Pushing her in front of him, he followed the others to the dungeon, a converted living area with hardwood floors, chains dangling from the rafters, a couple of St. Andrew's crosses, sawhorse benches, a bondage table. Implements hung on the dark paneled walls between the bloodred drapes covering the windows. Even in silence, the dimly lit room seemed to echo with the sounds of pain.

"Go ahead and put your prospective slaves through their paces," the Overseer announced. "Since you have provided medical papers, no condoms are necessary. All three women have birth control implants and are certified disease-free. I remind you not to inflict permanent damage, but anything that'll heal in a few days is fine: welts, stripes, bruises."

The pudgy one headed for the St. Andrew's cross on the right wall, picking up a single-tail on the way. The older man shoved Holly to her knees beside him as he examined the rack of canes.

Kim's stomach tightened as she remembered her words earlier. *"Maybe there's a nice one out there."* There were no nice ones in this world. *Oh Holly, I'm sorry, honey.*

"And you, sir?" The Overseer turned to Master R. "I heard you enjoy dispensing a good beating."

The hand gripping her neck flexed slightly. "I'll use a flogger."

Staring at the floor, Kim breathed out, trying to tell herself a flogger wasn't as bad as other stuff. Like a whip. Or a cane. Unless he picked one of the nastier kinds. Her nerves were jumping with her need to yank away and run, but she wouldn't even get out of the room. And then she'd pay and pay and pay. *I can endure this. It's only pain.*

Somehow she could feel the buyer's attention on her like a warm breeze. His thumb stroked the side of her neck. "Dahmer, you've got a pretty setup here."

"Thank you," the Overseer said, his voice with that slick, sharp edge to it. "Although pulling everything down and setting up in a new house becomes tedious."

"I can imagine. How long have you been in this...line of work?"

"The Harvest Association hired me about seven years ago." The Overseer's laugh made Kim's skin crawl. "The side benefits are great—like training the merchandise."

"I daresay. Do you choose the women?"

"Our watchers select potential slaves according to what we're looking for at the time." The Overseer nodded to Holly. "That one was picked up for our annual 'Blondes are more fun' auction. In the Southeast quadrant, I select from the list and contract the appropriate people to make the pickups."

"Quite a few layers in your group. That's reassuring."

Layers upon layers. *Drown the bastards and let crabs eat their bodies.* Kim bit her tongue until she tasted blood. Early on, the Overseer had explained how long the Association had been in business, and the impossibility of their families ever finding them. One despairing slave had tried to commit suicide that night, but the torn plastic cup couldn't cut her skin deep enough.

"The safety and anonymity of the association and our buyers is our primary concern." The Overseer stopped. Kim glanced up to see him gesture toward the floggers on the back wall. "I think you'll find something there that fits your needs."

"How much time do we have?"

"Long as you want." The Overseer's eyes met Kim's. "According to her last owner, this piece of goods doesn't break down quickly."

Her skin went cold; her hands started to tremble. Lord Greville had never stopped until she'd broken, and then he'd...

Master R snorted and pulled her back against his body, his arm around her waist, one wide palm covering her breast. "Any ham-handed idiot can make a woman scream. I prefer to assess...responsiveness." His powerful hand caressed her, his touch light. Not somehow repugnant, but still...touching her, as a reminder that her body was no longer her own. She tried to move, but the iron band of his arm held her easily in place.

The Overseer tipped his head. "It's a pleasure to have an experienced dominant."

As if he'd recognize experience if it bit him on the butt, Kim thought, but Master R was a dom. She could tell. As the Overseer left at a hail from the fat buyer, Master R turned her around. His face held no expression she could read, and a tremor ran through her. What was he planning to do?

Did she want to try to get him to buy her or not? He hadn't been cruel—not in the way the other two buyers displayed. Her stomach sank when she saw Holly restrained on a bench, enduring the slash of the cane, whimpering with each blow.

On the St. Andrew's cross, Linda was silent, but tears streamed down her face as the whip left red stripes on her breasts and stomach. The older woman had admitted she was a masochist—actually liked pain—but not like this. Never like this.

Kim didn't want either of those sadists, yet this man was...observant. Too smart to get away from. She flinched as Holly's buyer changed to a leather strap, the sound loud in the room. Should she chance the cruelty in hopes of escape? How badly would she be damaged before she could get free?

"You're thinking too much, little slave. Keep your eyes only on me."

Her attention jerked back to him at the soft command. His veil of remoteness had dropped away again. Folding his arms over his chest, he studied her, his dark gaze skimming over her face, her shoulders, her hands, her legs. Under the discomfort of the heavy silence, she shifted her weight as the flutters in her stomach increased. An experienced dominant. She saw the signs in his posture and in the way that sometimes she reacted to him as a dom—not a monster.

*He's a monster. Never forget that.*

"What is your real name?" he asked softly.

*My name. Part of me. Not answering this.* His chin lifted and under his gaze, her defiance that had infuriated Lord Greville bent as inevitably as a palm tree in a tropical storm. "Kimberly. Sir."

"Thank you." When his face softened in approval, her muscles relaxed even though she knew—*she knew*—he was a slaver. And he—he wanted to use a flogger on her.

He grasped her shoulders and turned her so her back was to him. Why wasn't he being rough with her? As he traced lines down her back, his fingers were warm, the calluses scraping lightly. "You've been whipped. Was it before or after your slavery?"

Her throat went tight. *Slavery.* Why did hearing the word send disbelief through her every time? *This can't be me. Can't be happening.* "After." *Lord Greville's eyes, crazy mad, the pain, falling to her knees, blood everywhere.*

He grunted. "Assholes."

*What?* She forced herself to stillness.

"You are not going to escape this evening without

some pain, chiquita." Even as she stiffened, he pulled her back against him again, his body like a brick wall, his arm circling her waist. He fondled her breasts, his gentleness disconcerting. His breath teased the curls at her temple. "Did you enjoy being flogged before all this happened?"

That was a different life, no relation to the one now.

"Kimberly?"

She should never have told him her name—hearing it now, used in a master's authoritative voice, shook something inside her. *My name. I'm real. I'm still me, Kimberly Elizabeth Moore.* She swallowed, remembered the question about BDSM clubs and play parties. *Before.* "I— yes."

"Good girl." His resonant voice relaxed her, even as she tried to keep herself defended. "And restraints? Do they bother you?"

This seemed like before somehow, the dance of negotiations, while finding a partner who liked what she did. *But it isn't, Kim. You're a slave. A fuckhole. A slut.* She stiffened.

He nipped her earlobe, making her jump and raising the oddest tingle inside her. "Stay in the present with me, Kimberly," he said, his voice so very different than earlier. Low and rich and smooth with a hint of a Spanish accent. As unexpectedly warm as a sunny day in the spring. "Answer me now. Do restraints bother you?"

"No. Not really." Not like enclosed spaces, hoods, cages. Her stomach turned over, and her chest constricted.

"Something bothers you. What?"

As if she'd give him a weapon to use against her. To punish her with like the Overseer had. Her mouth compressed into a thin line.

"No?" He sighed and turned her to face him. As he regarded her, he massaged her upper arms, his grip powerful, controlled...warm. "I am going to restrain you and flog you. I will use my hands on you, perhaps my mouth. I know you don't have a choice in this"—his eyes chilled for a moment—"but you might find it easier, knowing I won't exceed those boundaries."

He—he was right. He planned nothing she hadn't enjoyed at one time—nothing she hadn't survived since. No cages. The relief blanked her mind, and a thank-you escaped before she could pull it back.

One corner of his mouth tipped up. "I like hearing gratitude." He ran his knuckles over her left breast. As always, since soon after her capture, she felt nothing. No pain, no revulsion, just...nothing.

His eyes narrowed. He stroked over her breast again slowly, this time studying her face as he did. Without lifting his hand, he stroked upward and over her shoulder. Her neck.

The skin on his fingertips was a little rough. His palm melted the ice under her skin the way the heat from the sun would dissipate morning fog on the water.

"You will need much work, chiquita," he murmured, "but this is not the night."

"What?" Shocked that the word had escaped her, she took a hasty step away, tensing in preparation for his blow.

Ignoring her mistake, he jerked his chin at the rack of restraints. "Pick out comfortable wrist and ankle cuffs, then return to me."

She hurried, relief making her knees wobbly. He hadn't hit her for speaking without permission. Either time. But what had he meant by work to do? She shook her head and concentrated on doing as he ordered.

Once the cuffs were on, she returned.

He nodded. "Hands laced behind your neck. Open your legs farther. Eyes on me."

She followed his orders, spreading her feet apart slightly wider than her shoulder. Other slaves had been taught this position, she knew. Her experience had been... other. The restricted sensation from the cuffs started her stomach roiling.

"Very nice." He checked the fit of her cuffs. To her surprise, he loosened one overly snug ankle cuff.

He eyed her for a moment. "You're a lovely woman, Kimberly." He strolled around her, inspecting her, and somehow, perhaps because of his light touch, she didn't feel the usual nausea and fury. He explored the marks on her back where Lord Greville and his staff had whipped her bloody, then the bruising on her hips from when the Overseer... Her mind winced away.

Again his finger ran over the knife scar, giving her the odd sensation of tingling and numbness from damaged nerves. He frowned at the purple bruising on her foot left by the Overseer's boot from when she'd spilled a drop of his coffee.

After running his hands over her hips, he touched her pussy. Bare. Smooth. She'd become adept at shaving in the past weeks. She felt the stroke of his hand, but it brought nothing but memories of other hands and cocks.

"*Pobrecita*," he said under his breath and looked her straight in the eyes. "I am going to check you more closely, Kimberly. I need to know if there are any problems."

More closely? Understanding hit in a dizzying wave when he moved to the table and squirted lubricant over his fingers. *Oh God.* She closed her eyes and simply waited. *Don't tense. I'm not here. It's a good day to visit the beach. Grains of sand under my feet, the ocean breeze...*

To her surprise, she felt only the heat of his body, the brush of his silky shirt against her breasts, his breath on her cheek. "Look at me," he said, ever so softly.

*I don't want to.* She raised her gaze. His face was close

to hers, his dark brown eyes filled with such understanding she almost whimpered.

His hand cupped her mound.

*No.* She turned her head, only to have him give a warning sound from low in his throat. He'd given her an order. Expected her to obey.

She raised her eyes to his.

His lubricated fingers slid over her in a way she hadn't felt in a long time. He watched her silently as his fingers touched her clit, then separated her labia. He pressed one finger inside her, and she couldn't help the instinctive cringing away.

"Shhh, chiquita." His other hand cupped her bottom, holding her in place. He kissed her lightly as if to reassure her, then slid a second finger into her, pressing upward. She tried to close her thighs and realized his feet were inside hers, keeping her legs open. After a moment, he slid his fingers out.

Not done, though. He stepped back and took a latex glove from the box.

*I hate this. Hate you. Hate you all.*

"Bend over and spread your cheeks, girl." His voice was cold. Cruel.

She blinked at the change, then noticed the Overseer approaching. Did the dom's manner change to chilly because of the Overseer? The thought was...

"Now, girl."

Her mind blanked as her body tensed. He'd touch her...there. Gritting her teeth, she bent, arching her bottom up and opening herself for his inspection.

A lubricated finger circled her rim. "She has been taken anally?"

"Oh yes. Unless a buyer requests an anal virgin, we feel it best to have each slave prepared."

The dom's thick finger pressed against her anus. She wanted to escape, and as if he could tell, he gripped her hip in warning. Then his finger breached the ring of muscle, sliding inside her. In and out before the shudder had even left her body.

"Mmm. Not bad." He moved away to toss the glove into the waste. "I'd probably have to train with a wider plug to keep from tearing her up, though."

The thought made her cringe, and anger rose to replace the fear. As if he was that big. But a quick glance at his slacks indicated he told the truth. He could hurt her. Badly.

Grasping her nape again, he guided to where chains hung from the ceiling, between the ones attached to bolts in the floor. He put her into an upright, spread-eagle position, legs restrained widely apart, then tightened the chains on her arms, ensuring she couldn't move.

She closed her eyes, trying to get to the place where it wouldn't hurt as much. Not subspace...hardly that. This pain she'd simply endure, going as far away as she could. *The boat pushed off from shore, waves splashing on the sides, wind whipping her hair...*

After a brief survey of the wall, he chose a flogger and a cat-o'-nine-tails and returned. To her dismay, he ran his hands over her shoulders, her arms, her torso, her legs. Bringing her back to the now, damn him. His palms were rough, his fingernails cut short.

Her body warmed under his touch. Her skin did; her core stayed icy. He repeated the process, rubbing the strands of the flogger over her. He'd chosen medium weight, deerskin leather, not one with knotted strands, thank God.

He flicked the ends, and they pattered against her back like fat raindrops. She jumped, then relaxed as the rain of the flogger continued, even and smooth. Almost comforting.

He moved to her front, hitting her lightly. "Where are you from, Kimberly?"

*Doesn't matter. I'm in hell now.* She stared over his shoulder at the wall of whips and floggers.

"Kimberly?" he repeated in a deeper voice.

Her words stuttered out as if dredged from the ocean depths. "I...from Atlanta." *No, that was wrong. Mom's in Atlanta. Why do I feel so lost?* "I work in—"*Savannah.* The strands hit her breasts, and she jumped, feeling something unwelcome bloom inside her, something more than pain.

"You do have a little bit of a Southern accent." He stopped and studied her for a minute. His eyes... How did he make them change from gut-chillingly mean to snuggly kind? He stepped forward, again close enough for her to feel the heat he radiated, and then stroked a hand down her hair. "Little slave, I'm going to ask you a question. Whatever you answer, there will be no judgment or anger on my part. I simply need to know how you want this to go."

She frowned. Why did he keep wanting to talk? But she could answer a question—as if she had a choice. She nodded.

"*Bueno.*" He hesitated a moment, as if searching for words. "I think I can make you respond." He curved his hand over her cheek and brushed her lower lip with his thumb. "Make you enjoy the flogging. Make you come. Or I can simply flog you until you scream in pain. I... That is not my way." His eyes darkened, his jaw tight with anger—but not at her, somehow she knew. "You have had much taken away. To be *forced* to respond might be more damaging than enduring the pain. So I will let the choice be yours. Which would you prefer?"

She hadn't had an orgasm since her capture, but his touch and the authority he wore so comfortably yet used in an almost...caring...way were drawing her. A prisoner effect, undoubtedly, to cling to the one man who treats you like a person. As he waited, so horribly confident in his skills, she had the gut-twisting suspicion he *could* make her come. *Here*. Make her reveal her inmost self in front of the slavers. The Overseer. She shook her head and whispered, "No."

"No to what?"

"Don't make me... Just hurt me, okay?"

"You don't want an orgasm. You'd rather have the pain." He waited for her nod of confirmation, and his mouth twisted as if he tasted something foul. "Then I will ask this of you. When it truly hurts, please scream. It'll get us both out of here sooner."

*No.* She wouldn't make a sound. Begging, screaming, whimpering was admitting defeat. With each beating, she hung on until the pain overwhelmed her and flattened her mind into pure instinct. Now he ordered her to give in early?

The little piece of her that was still Kimberly said no. *Never.*

Yet he'd given her this choice, tried to make this easier for her.

Or was his kindness a trick?

She couldn't keep her own arguments straight. "Okay."

He lifted an eyebrow.

"Yes, Master. I'm sorry, Master," she added so quickly her tongue faltered.

"Very nice." His mouth curved before he kissed her again, his lips warm against her cold ones. When he stepped back, his posture altered: Clark Kent to Superman. The concern he'd shown disappeared from his face.

Why had she revealed so much—told him anything? He'd played her for a fool.

He moved with controlled power as he shook the flogger out, then disappeared behind her. Blows hit her upper back, on each side of her spine, on her bottom. The tails thudded lightly across her skin in a steady slow rhythm. Then faster.

All too soon, her back and bottom began to burn. He remained behind her, building up to a thorough flogging.

"You're damn good at that, Master R," the Overseer said, his oiled, knifelike voice making her cringe. "But I'm surprised you're not fucking her, like the other two."

"Please, call me Raoul," he said, never missing a stroke. Everywhere he hit was starting to really hurt.

And then he changed his stroke so only the tips struck her skin, and the tapping sensation changed to stinging. Much, much worse. Her hands fisted.

"I rarely fuck in public," Master R said. "If she's not talented now, she can learn." His voice sharpened. "Right now, I want to hear what she sounds like when she screams."

Through the swirling redness in her brain she caught his slight emphasis on the word. *Scream.* He'd told her to scream.

*No. Never.*

"Let's try the cat." The blows stopped. Footsteps. A different swishing sound.

Her courage fled. *A cat-o'-nine-tails.* She tried to brace herself.

It hit, ripping across the skin on her upper back like claws. Left, then right. *Oh God!* Her jaw clamped shut, not letting the sound out. She stared at the wall, her shoulders on fire, and could almost hear his voice: *Do it.*

His next blow was harder. She felt the sting and burn of torn skin. *Scream, Kim.* Her mouth opened. Nothing came out.

He struck across her upper buttocks, and this time, as the pain exploded through her, she forced a shriek past her clenched jaw. Another two blows fell, ripping into her body like fire. The wall of silence broken, she sagged and screamed again. A trickle of liquid ran down her back. Her blood.

He stopped. *Oh God, he stopped.* Tears rolled down her face, splattering on the floor. Through the ringing in her ears, she heard him say to the Overseer, "Quite a melodic scream. I noticed she serves nicely as well, and that's important to me. The clumsy blonde would be unacceptable."

"I like a master who knows what he wants. Too many impatient idiots purchase blindly." The Overseer laughed. "But it makes for good return business. They break their toys and have to buy a new one."

Her knees had buckled, and she hung from her arms, her shoulders aching. Her back felt as if she'd lain on glowing coals. Kim swallowed against the dryness in her mouth. She'd been broken once—and found herself again. She didn't think she could survive another.

"Nice even marks," the Overseer said, his voice much, much closer than she wanted. The chains kept her from moving as he stood right behind her. A finger ran down her spine, and it felt as if a trail of slime followed his touch. *Get away. Don't touch me.*

"I hit what I aim at." Master R walked in front of her, tilted her head up, and inspected her coldly.

RAOUL COULD FEEL the little slave's pain—pain he'd given with no pleasure, no emotional satisfaction. Guilt shot through him, and the desire to maim Dahmer was so strong he couldn't move. One slow breath. He controlled his rage, sent it deep into his foundations, and stepped away from the girl.

"I like your professionalism," Dahmer said. "Are you still interested in auditioning to do a demonstration at one of auctions?"

"Possibly." Could he still get into an auction? Maybe buying Kimberly wouldn't ruin the FBI's plans after all. Raoul tossed the cat with the cruelly knotted falls on a bench and forced a grin. "I'd like to attend one for the fun of it."

"I'm afraid the events are open only to active buyers and performers." Dahmer cleared his throat politely. "And you indicated your funds were limited."

"True. I won't be up to buying another slave for a while. But I could certainly do a demonstration."

"Bear in mind, the scenes have to be...carnal...in one way or another."

Fuck some poor woman in front of a bunch of perverts? Raoul's stomach turned over. "Of course. What's the point otherwise?"

Dahmer laughed. "That's the spirit. There's a long list of performers waiting already, so I'm not sure when you'd be scheduled. But you could audition during your follow-up visit and get on the list."

*What the hell?* "Sounds good, but what follow-up visit?"

"The info is in the paperwork you get when you buy. But basically it's for our refund policy—and a way to ensure buyers conform to the Harvest Association policies." The slimy *cabrón* chuckled. "After a few weeks, I stop by and watch you with your merchandise. It's so I can answer any questions that have arisen about training, and if a slave has proven unsatisfactory during the trial period, I remove her then. You get a refund, and we arrange for you to buy a new one."

That sounded totally impossible. But no matter now. Raoul frowned at Kimberly, every cell wanting to remove her restraints and care for her. "All right then. This slave is adequate. Let's do the paperwork."

"Good." Open satisfaction showed in the greedy bastard's eyes. "I think she'll do well for you."

Raoul glanced back at Kimberly, saw blood drip onto the floor, and covered his wince with a cold jerk of his head. "Have someone hose her off and dress her, please."

# Chapter Two

Raoul cradled Kimberly in his arms, watching the slaver's van pull away from his home, its headlights illuminating the splashing fountain, then the bronze statue of a heron at the end of the drive. He hated them knowing where he lived, his background…anything to do with his life.

Nonetheless, this was what he'd signed on to do.

As the sultry night air wrapped around him, he took his first decent breath of the evening. *Home.* The lights bracketing the front door tried to dispel the night's darkness but didn't touch what had lodged in his soul. A long, long time would pass before he'd get over his sense of helplessness and guilt at having to abandon the other two women.

But he'd saved one. "Don't worry, chiquita. I'll take care of you."

Her eyes opened, hazed with the sedative the Overseer had administered to ensure an uneventful trip. "Take care of myself," she mumbled yet curled closer into his arms.

Indomitable spirit—fragile, scarred body. The Feds wouldn't approve of him choosing emotion over logic, but he'd never have any regrets. Her head lolled against his chest, and his heart squeezed as he carried her into the coolness of his home. His boots thudded on the tile of the small foyer and echoed in the empty house.

As she slept on the couch in the great room, Raoul

texted the number the FBI agents had given him. The message was *1*, reporting he'd returned home.

In the morning, he'd inform them he'd screwed up the operation.

He tried to call Gabrielle. The thought of telling the sweet submissive that her best friend was freed lightened his heart. But no one answered at the house she shared with her dom, and Marcus didn't answer his cell phone. Was this the weekend the two planned to go sailing? Growling, he texted them also, telling them to come to his house tomorrow morning.

Raoul scowled. Apparently he had himself a slave for the night.

*Slave.* The word sandpapered his nerves. He rubbed his face. Even after three years, the remnants of the ugly fight with his mother and sister still echoed in his memory. *"You kept a woman as a slave? You're a monster, Raoul."* His fun-loving sister's voice had been so cold. Distant, as if she'd already cut him from her life. His mother's lined face had grown more careworn, and the brown eyes which matched his own had filled with tears as she whispered, *"How could you, my son?"*

*They should meet Dahmer and see what real monsters look like.*

*Now what?* He frowned at the little slave on his couch. At least she wasn't really his, even if he was stuck with her longer than he wanted.

Pretty little slave, somehow both innocent and sensual in the pink sweat pants and tank top the Overseer had provided for her. She slept heavily. Her thick black lashes lay against her pale cheeks, her breathing slow. Even if he managed to wake her, she wouldn't be capable of understanding any explanations.

He sighed. His body ached as if he'd been the one to be flogged, and he was exhausted in a way he'd never felt after doing a scene at the Shadowlands. He needed sleep, or he'd be incoherent when Buchanan or Kouros arrived, expecting a detailed report.

Sleep it was.

In the upstairs hallway with Kimberly in his arms, he started toward the guest room and then remembered the fury in her eyes. If she woke, she'd try to run, no doubt about it. As much as the thought disgusted him, she'd have to be secured against escape...but he never left a restrained sub unattended.

He turned and headed for his own room.

When he laid her down on his bed, her eyes popped open, and she hit at him.

He caught her small fist. "Shhh, Kimberly, no one is going to hurt you here."

Even drugged as she was, the twist of her lips showed her disbelief, but she couldn't maintain her anger. Her eyes slowly drooped, then closed.

He stroked her hair back from her face, wishing Gabi had been available to take her friend home. Kimberly shouldn't have to live in fear a moment longer. *What a mess.*

No choice. He glanced at the ankle and wrist cuffs she still wore—freebies from the slavers—and ones she'd stay in for tonight. At least the master bedroom was already set up for bondage with chains on the heavy ironwork. He secured the lower bedpost chain to her right ankle cuff. *No escape for you, little slave. Not tonight.*

After setting the multitool from his boot sheath and the padlock key the Overseer had given him on the bedside table, he moved them out of Kimberly's reach.

His shower didn't wash away the sensation of filth, but it helped. He rummaged in the dresser for a pair of loose cotton pants and pulled them on. She didn't wake as he rolled her over and checked her back. The attendants had put bandages over the places where he'd cut her skin and ointment on the welts. Everything looked clean. He'd seen— even done—much worse, but never to someone who wasn't willing.

Unhappiness stewing in his chest, he slid under the covers. Propped up on an elbow, he studied her, a little shocked at how different she was from Rachel, the healthy, enthusiastic woman he'd had in his bed last week. Kimberly had dark circles under her eyes, yellowing bruises here and there, and hollowed cheeks that made him want to feed her. Pamper her. But he doubted she'd agree or say two words to him, even after she learned she was safe.

She'd only remember that he'd flogged her bloody. Guilt stabbed through him again.

Well, he'd done the best he could. He sighed. Tomorrow wouldn't be a pleasant day. Special Agents Kouros and Buchanan would be furious. He was to have rejected all the slaves, essentially forcing the Overseer to invite him to the auction. Instead, he'd bought a slave.

One who had a wealth of anger simmering in her soul. One who undoubtedly hated the buyer who'd lashed her. He might wake to a fist in the face.

Better safe than sorry, he decided, and pulled her against his chest so he'd know if she moved. Her body was just the right size to fit within the curve of his, and when he slid his arm under her head for a pillow, her soft ass pressed on his groin. Ignoring the way he hardened, he kissed her silky hair and followed her into sleep.

\* \* \* \*

Pain woke Kim. Her back burned and throbbed. Her mouth tasted like putrid metal and was so dry she couldn't swallow. Her head pounded, and even her eyelids felt lethargic. Obviously, she'd been drugged. Again. The

Overseer did it every time they moved the slaves. Said it decreased the chances of anyone causing trouble.

*Where am I?* Lying on her side, she squinted at the painfully bright morning sunlight streaming in through French doors. *Wake up, brain.* The sale last night. Kneeling in front of a man. Dancing. The dungeon. Pain.

She stiffened. A heavy weight rested on her waist—not covers, but a darkly tanned, very muscular arm. A man lay behind her, his legs tangled with hers. The Hispanic master had bought her. The one who'd flogged her so cruelly her entire back still hurt like heck. His hard chest pressed against her, making the pain almost worse than the roiling nausea from the drugs and what she knew would come next.

And she needed to pee.

She must have moved, for his slow breathing stopped. His arm tightened around her for a second, and then he sat up.

Before she could react, he rolled her onto her back.

She tried to move and felt the drag of a restraint on her right ankle. She closed her eyes. *Welcome to your new owner. Time for a morning fuck.* Her hands fisted as she froze, waiting for him to start pulling her clothing off.

Nothing happened.

After a minute, she opened her eyes. He lay on his side, propped up on one elbow, studying her, much as he'd watched her last night in the dungeon.

She swallowed. *What does he want?*

He sighed. "I'm not going to jump on you, Kimberly. We need to talk."

"Talk about what? Master." *How he likes his blowjobs? How he—*

"If I told you that I bought you to free you, would you believe me?"

She gave a mental snort. He was into mind-fucking

like Lord Greville had been. "If Master wishes me to."

His dark brown eyes were unexpectedly soft. "That's what I thought. We'll wait then."

Wait for what? "Yes, Master."

"Call me Raoul."

Now that was strange. She'd never heard of a master welcoming such informality. And even if he did, she had no intention of calling him by his first name as if they were buddies or something. Never.

He undid the chain on her leg and helped her out of the bed. Her stomach twisted as she rose, her head spun, and she staggered sideways. His powerful hands closed around her waist, holding her up easily. Why did she have to get an owner who was so strong? How could she possibly escape him?

She would though. Probably not today—he'd be watching for an attempt.

And he did. Master R accompanied her into the bath. Dark wood, swirly tan marble, arched ceiling. Another rich bastard with the money to buy a slave. He pointed her to the walled-off toilet while he remained at the sink. She hid her scowl and studied the leaded glass window. She could fit. No problem.

She heard the water running, the sounds of him brushing his teeth, giving her the illusion of privacy at least. After peeing—major relief—she reluctantly joined him and washed her hands. Turning to hang up the hand towel, she winced when the movements pulled on her sore back.

"*Carajo,*" he said under his breath. "Put your hands on the counter and hold still, Kimberly."

*Yeah, here it comes. The fucking. From* my friend, *Raoul.* Her insides curled up in a tight ball as she followed his order. He pulled her tank top all the way to her neck, and she closed her eyes. Why didn't it ever get easier?

A pause. Then he sighed. "I'm not planning to rape you, chiquita. I need to tend to the damage I did." He met her gaze in the mirror, his sympathy obvious. "This won't feel good, but it will help you heal. As will time."

When he touched her back, she flinched. *God, it hurts.*

His left hand tightened on her shoulder, keeping her in place as he tugged off the bandages, going far more slowly than she'd expected. Rather than scrubbing her roughly, he gently washed her back. "I'm sorry, but I couldn't flog you lightly and still be believable." From a jar on the counter, he spread the ointment over her back.

Tears ran down her cheeks.

When he pushed her pants down, she stiffened, expecting—but he simply washed and lotioned, pinning her against the counter to prevent her involuntary attempts to evade him.

"All done." He pulled her shirt down and her pants up.

She couldn't move as the pain filled her vision with red streaks.

When she raised her head, he rubbed his finger on her wet cheek. "Pobrecita," he murmured and added at her confused expression, "Poor little one." After handing her a washcloth, he stepped out of the bathroom.

As she washed the tears from her face, as the pain died, she had to wonder: *Why is he being so nice to me?* The only answers she found were...ugly. She checked the window again. Too high to squirm through fast and... She glanced over her right shoulder at where he stood in the bedroom and met his knowing eyes.

He shook his head at her. "Come. Let's have breakfast before people arrive."

Everything inside her shriveled. Other men. He wanted to show off his new slave. Maybe share.

Before they reached the bottom of the stairs, the

doorbell rang. He glanced at the clock and grumbled, "No breakfast for either of us." He headed for the front door, his hand securely around her arm. "Prepare yourself, Kimberly. You're in for a pleasant surprise."

*Pleasant. Get real.* She managed to keep the sneer from her face but heard his amused snort.

Her owner opened the door. And let go of her, stepping back.

Kim stared at the woman, unable to move, her world shivering to a halt. Red hair with a streak of blue, creamy skin, big blue eyes. *Gabi?*

A shriek of joy split the air. "Kim. Oh, God, Kim!" Gabi grabbed her into a jumping-up-and-down hug.

Fiery pain ripped through Kim, and she yelped.

"*Dios!*" Master R pried Gabi off. "Stop it. Let go, Gabi. *Now.*"

The sharp command froze Kim in place.

Gabi scowled at Raoul. "Raoul, what are—"

"You're hurting her. I flogged her last night."

"What the hell did you do that for?"

The fury in her best friend's face panicked Kim. If Gabi was rude to him... She grabbed Gabi's arm. "Shhh. Don't make him mad."

"Kim," Gabi said, "you don't—"

"Shhh." She couldn't...couldn't let him hurt Gabi. She stepped in front of Master R. He'd have to go through her first.

He didn't even try. Instead, he slowly stroked her hair, ignoring the way she flinched away. His eyes seemed as gentle as his hand. "Brave chiquita. No one will hurt Gabi or you, Kimberly." He glanced at Gabi. "It was the only way I could get her out."

A man appeared on the doorstep. Styled brown hair,

sharp blue eyes, taller than Master R. He took Gabi by the upper arms and lifted her to one side so he could enter the house. Obviously a master with a terrifying self-confidence.

Oh God, they'd kidnapped Gabi too. As he greeted Master R, Kim swallowed and turned toward Gabi, whispering the horrible question, already knowing the answer. "You're a slave?"

Gabi's eyes filled, and she took Kim's hands. "Oh Kim, no. Neither are you, sweetie."

"What do you mean?" Kim stared at her, then at Master R. Her *owner*.

He looked down at her. "I'm no slaver, chiquita. I'm working with the FBI, but you wouldn't believe me—you thought I was trying to mess with your mind."

Kim shook her head. Her lips were numb. FBI? The air pulsed how around her, even though her face felt cold. Her knees sagged, melted into the floor, and the room whirled as she fell.

"Carajo!" Master R caught her and scooped her up, his arm like iron against her back, and she whimpered at the sear of pain from the welts.

"Shhh, chiquita." His smooth voice, velvety and warm, wrapped around her and eased her way into the blackness.

RAOUL SAT DOWN on the couch in the great room, not wanting to release the little slave in his arms, the need to comfort stronger than anything he'd known before. She'd survived horrors, and the aftereffects were going to be with her for a long, long time.

As the color returned to her face, she blinked up at him, her eyes huge. Before she panicked, he eased her down beside him, close enough she could lean against him. If she chose to. He hurt to know she wouldn't.

Gabi sat on her other side and took her hands. Did the

women even realize they were both silently crying ?

Marcus came from the kitchen with some juice. He squeezed Gabi's shoulder comfortingly as he handed Raoul the glass.

"I want you to drink this, Kimberly," Raoul said, holding the glass to her lips.

After taking a dutiful sip, she looked at him through drenched eyelashes. "Really? I'm free?"

"Really." He frowned. "But there might be a few problems."

"That is a definite understatement. What the *hell* did you do?" Buchanan walked into the house and slammed the door before stalking across the room. The big man had played defensive tackle in college and hadn't shrunk any in the intervening years. The Fed's Scottish complexion was turning an ominous dark red.

Well, he hadn't expected the FBI to be pleased, and at least he only had to deal with one of the pair. Raoul smiled. "Buchanan. Meet Gabi's friend, Kimberly. She was up for sale last night."

"And you just had to save her?" The agent sounded as if his teeth were grinding together. Then he frowned. "Really? This is Kimberly Moore?" He muttered something under his breath—probably as well that Raoul couldn't hear it—and eased back. "Sorry, Sandoval. You were the one in the field. Hell, I'd probably have done the same thing." He squatted in front of Kimberly. "I'm Special Agent Vance Buchanan with the FBI. Raoul is helping with our investigation. Last night, he was supposed to leave without any slaves, but"—he gave Gabi a smile—"he knew how long Gabi's been trying to find you."

Gabi smiled through her tears and rubbed her shoulder against Kimberly's.

The little slave stared at Buchanan, Raoul, then

Buchanan again. He could almost hear her brain kick into gear. "An FBI operation? What does that mean?"

"Good question." Buchanan frowned at Raoul. "How badly is this operation blown? And how the hell did you get her out, let alone home?"

Raoul smiled. "Nothing is blown...very much. I bought her, and the hired help brought us back."

"Sandoval, you don't have that kind of money."

"Z set up an offshore account in case I happened to run across her."

Marcus snorted and dropped down in a chair, saying in his soft Southern voice, "That man is frightening."

"So you bought her." Buchanan rose to pace across the room. "This wasn't remotely in any of our contingency plans."

"No. But there's time to decide what to do. I told the Overseer I planned to use my mountain cabin to...break her in." Raoul looked down at Kimberly. Her blue eyes were like a rain-drenched sky. He used a finger to wipe the tears from her face, unaccountably relieved when she didn't flinch away from his touch. "I have a bridge construction in Mexico needing my attention. Gabi can take Kimberly home with her."

Buchanan nodded. "That'll work. But we want a full report before you leave."

"Of course." Raoul frowned at Marcus. "Make sure she stays out of sight until we figure out how much danger she'll be in."

Marcus nodded. Considering the hell the lawyer had suffered when the slavers had kidnapped Gabi, Raoul knew his friend wouldn't be careless with either woman's safety.

Raoul turned back to Kimberly, his heart aching. In volunteering after an earthquake, he'd seen survivors with the same shocked expression that showed they'd discovered how unsafe the world could be. Every dominant gene in his body said she needed to be cared for, protected, helped—and that he should be the one to do it. But a master was the last thing she wanted. "Give me your wrist."

She hesitated a long moment, then held one arm out. After taking his keys from his pocket, he unlocked and removed her ankle and wrist cuffs. Finally the collar.

When he pulled it away, the relief on her face almost broke his heart.

A second later, her expression changed to fury. She plucked it from his fingers and threw it across the room, then cringed. "I'm sorry." Her shoulders stiffened as she braced for him to hit her.

"Relax. I understand." He glanced at the collar, lying like a dead thing on the floor, remembering the first time he'd collared a woman. She'd had tears of joy, of gratitude in her eyes. She'd kissed the leather and then his hands as he'd buckled it around her neck. He'd been humbled by her trust, determined to never let her down, to love and cherish her. The collar he'd given his first slave had been padded on the inside, gentle on her skin.

He traced a finger over a scar and raw marks left on Kimberly's neck from the rough leather, before realizing she was forcing herself to hold still. No, he wouldn't go get his healing ointment. *Not mine to care for.* "Will you be all right, chiquita?"

She looked at him uncertainly, as if waiting for his anger, but all he had to offer was sorrow. She touched her bare neck, and determination filled her face. "I'll be fine." As she looked past him at the ocean, the storm in her eyes settled. "I will."

# Chapter Three

Gabi had invited over two friends, and Kim had hidden in the bathroom. Hoping to stall for another minute, she stared into the mirror. The blue sleeveless top Gabi had lent her fit fairly well since she hadn't regained all the weight yet. Eyes clear, nose and cheeks a little sunburned. Almost healthy looking, at least on the outside.

Faith, the psychologist, kept insisting self-assessment was a necessary part of recovering. Easy for her to say.

The past week had been...bad. Real bad. But—she nodded at herself—now she no longer cried so violently she'd end up in the bathroom puking, although the tears still hit without warning. Her bouts of terror had lessoned, and hey, sometimes she even managed to talk herself out of one. The feeling something horrible would happen had gone from every second to oh...every few hours. Little victories. Of course, she had help from everyone, including a counselor.

*Thank you, Master R.* Even though he'd never visited, she felt he was watching over her. Maybe it was the way a doctor had shown up soon after she'd arrived at Gabi's house, then Faith that evening and daily after that. Gabi and Marcus had been surprised; Master R—*Raoul*—had arranged it without any consultation.

Yesterday, she'd gotten back the results of the tests the doctor had done. No nasty diseases. No pregnancy.

She patted her chest, smiling. Today, the elephant-on-the-chest sensation was gone. *Yes, I'm getting better.* The counseling definitely helped. So did Gabi, with her years as a victim specialist and her own history of rape. Kim could share with Gabi things she couldn't tell Faith—and vice versa. The two women gave her sympathy, hugs, and an occasional hard dose of reality. Gabi, especially, would shake her head and say, *"Yeah, of course you're having panic attacks and nightmares. They might not ever go away completely, but they'll subside."*

That helped a lot, knowing Gabi had gone on to have a life. To find love. And what a sweetie she'd found. Kim sighed. Marcus couldn't disguise he was a dominant, but he kept his distance, never asking Kim to do anything, usually letting Gabi do the talking. Seeing his tenderness toward Gabi and the love he openly showed her had been healing in itself.

*Why couldn't I have found someone like that? Why did the slavers choose me anyway?* Other women liked BDSM, went to the clubs, didn't get Tasered and kidnapped. Chained and beaten. *Why me? Because I'm a slut?* Kim peered into the mirror. Did it show on her face maybe?

Gabi had stopped visiting BDSM clubs years before. *I kept going, even drove back from Savannah to visit the Atlanta club.* So maybe Kim deserved everything she'd gotten. Maybe she really was a slut and a fuckhole as Lord Greville had said.

Laughter came from the other room, breaking into her thoughts before the darkness overwhelmed her. With a shuddering breath, Kim pushed the bleakness aside and tried to remember what Gabi and the counselor had said. *I'm not a slut. Not.*

"Kim, get out here," Gabi called. "The cookies are out of the oven. Jessica and Kari are hungry."

Enough already. Recovering would take time. Eventually, the FBI would give her permission to go home. *I can do this*. After splashing cold water on her face, Kim joined Gabi in the kitchen where the comforting fragrance of just-baked cookies filled the air.

The phone rang, and Gabi made a sound of exasperation. "Here. Can you take these out?" She handed over the platter and turned to answer the phone. "Hello?"

As laughter came from the two women in the living room, Kim stood still, having to fight the urge to retreat into solitude.

Once she joined Jessica and Kari, she knew—*knew*—they would lighten her mood. That was something else that Gabi had done. When Kim had started to retreat from people, Gabi'd brought in a couple of her submissive friends. Being in the lifestyle, they had a good idea of what had happened and how a person might react. Their understanding, without Kim having to explain, was wonderful. She liked them.

The only light during her captivity had been her friendship with the other slaves. Like Linda, the older woman who—Kim swallowed—who that fat scumbag had beaten. As the attendants had been bandaging Kim's back, she'd heard the bastard refuse to buy the redhead, saying she was too old. God, had Linda survived what the Overseer did to slaves who didn't sell?

Kim hauled in a breath. Fretting wouldn't help, or so the counselor kept telling her. Only it made her so…so mad. And guilty, like she'd abandoned Linda without doing anything to save her. But what could she have done? Maybe she—

Gabi cleared her throat and made a fist, gesturing in the way that meant *full speed ahead*.

*I should never have taught her those old tugboat signals*. Kim nodded and headed into the living room.

"You've got the cookies!" Jessica trotted over. After one bite, the short blonde moaned in delight. "Kari, this is the best recipe." Another bite and she took a second cookie, sending a frown to the woman across the room. "And hey, thanks for *not* helping me lose weight."

"Z likes you round," Kari said. "I'm just doing him a favor."

As Jessica curled up in a chair to nibble, Kim set the platter on the coffee table for Kari and tried not to laugh.

The very pregnant, sweet-faced schoolteacher was trying to lower herself into the other overstuffed chair. Finally, arms giving out, she dropped the last foot with a bounce and a squeak. After a squirm to settle, she gave Kim a composed smile. "Made it."

"Uh-huh. God help you when you want to stand up again. And you still have another month?"

"If I survive that long." Kari leaned forward to get a cookie and was stymied by her stomach. She giggled. "Help?"

No one could be grumpy around these two. Jessica was intelligent, logical, and assertive. Kari almost beamed with joy at the new life inside her, despite being so short and round she resembled a bowling ball. Kim handed her a couple of cookies. "Are you having a girl or a boy?"

"Dan doesn't want to know, and I let him have his way. Though he's getting ahead in winning arguments."

Kim smiled. Yesterday, when Kari's husband had dropped her off for a visit, she'd been spitting mad. Apparently Dan had seen her trying to adjust the driver's seat to accommodate her stomach, but not so far she couldn't reach the steering wheel. The dom had taken her car keys away.

Kim might have been angrier, except the man had driven Kari over himself. Hard-faced with cop's eyes, he looked really mean, yet he touched his wife as gently as Marcus did Gabi.

It was nice to be shown that all men weren't the enemy. *But some are.* Shoving the thought aside, she snatched a cookie and sat on the couch.

Gabi walked in, brows drawn together. She squeezed Kim's shoulder before sitting beside her. "That was Vance—the guy from the FBI. He's coming today."

"Really? Good." Kim's anticipation surged. They'd asked her not to call her mother until they figured a few things out. *Mom must be going crazy with worry. I need to go home.* "When will he be here?"

"Right away."

Jessica wrinkled her nose. "There's a typical man. He probably smelled the cookies baking all the way across the city." She leaned forward and picked up her glass of iced tea. "Speaking of which, can I take some home to Z? He loves chocolate chip cookies."

"Who doesn't?" Gabi said. "But sure, we made tons."

"Eat up, Kari, and we'll leave before Vance shows up. Otherwise I'll question Mr. Close-mouthed Special Agent about what's going on, and he won't spill, and I'll get mad and be rude." Jessica rolled her eyes. "He'll tell Z."

"And you'd love it." Gabi snickered. "We all know you act out just to see what creative torture Z will use on you."

Jessica pointed her cookie at Gabi. "Takes one to recognize one."

"This is true." Gabi's satisfied smile looked exactly like her young cat's after it had snatched a chicken wing from the table. "I'm not sure who's more inventive, your dom or mine."

Kim shuddered. *"Don't worry, fuckhole. I'm quite inventive at finding ways to break slaves."* The whippings. The cage.

"Kim."

Kim jerked her head up at the sound of her name.

Worry darkened Jessica's green eyes as she said, "I'm sorry."

"Hey, I'm glad I've recovered enough that you forgot," Kim said, remembering all the times she'd dissolved into tears. "Besides, it's nice to be reminded there's such a thing as teasing a dom for fun."

Kari grinned. "In that case, you should have been at the last barbecue when Gabi called Marcus a cretin and asked him if he'd had an extra bowl of stupid that morning."

Kim felt the blood drain from her face. What had he done to her?

"Easy, girl. He didn't beat on me or anything." Gabi bumped her shoulder against Kim's. "I'd rather have had the beating. Would you believe the butthead threw me in the pool after I'd spent an hour on my hair and makeup? And I'd done some really cool temp tattoos around my arms too."

Kim sputtered a laugh; the knot in her stomach eased.

"You looked so funny." Jessica rose and hauled Kari out of the chair with a grunt of effort, before grinning at Kim. "She kept cursing him, and he pushed her back in—I think about four times before she cooled down enough to beg forgiveness. And then she hugged him."

Kari snickered. "You deliberately got his clothes all wet. He didn't know whether to laugh or curse."

"Teach him to try to drown me." Still smirking, Gabi walked with the other two women to the front, exchanged good-byes, then returned to sit beside Kim. "Hey, Jessica forgot Z's treats—more for us." Before she got a cookie to her mouth, the doorbell rang. "Well, hell."

*Someone from outside.* Heart rate increasing, Kim grabbed her hand. "No, it might not be Vance. I hear another man too. You don't know who it is."

"I recognize the voices. It's okay, girlfriend."

After a couple of slow breaths, Kim managed to let go of Gabi's hand. "Sorry."

"Been there, done that. It takes time." Gabi hurried to the door and opened it.

The agent walked in first, followed by...*Master R?* In jeans and a white shirt, he nodded at Gabi, and then his dark gaze went straight to Kim. Intent, powerful.

Her head spun, and her face burned, but the pit of her stomach felt as if she'd swallowed ice cubes. Dizzily, she scrunched into a corner of the couch and pulled her legs up.

His mouth flattened into a straight line, and he said something to Vance too quiet to hear.

"We'll see." In khakis and a blue short-sleeved shirt, Vance walked into the living room and took the chair directly across from the couch. "How are you doing, Kim?"

She swallowed. *These are friends, not the enemy. Master R—Raoul—got me out.* That was the only reason, she realized, she hadn't run for her bedroom. He'd saved her. "Not good, but better."

"Lots better," Gabi said staunchly and dropped down beside her.

Disconcertingly, Master R kneed the large ottoman closer to Kim and sat on it. Within touching distance.

Kim barely kept herself from shrinking away. She'd forgotten how muscular he was. The sleeves of his polo shirt strained to fit around his thick biceps.

"You said you needed to talk about problems," Gabi prompted.

"Problems, definitely. Our operation is..." Vance's jaw tightened. "The Harvest Association auctions are big events with many buyers, lots of slaves, and a large number of the association's personnel. We've wanted to raid one for some time, but they change the locations and give out the date and time of the auction only at the last minute. The buyers are transported in windowless vans with anti-tracking technology. Sandoval was to have refused the slaves, so he'd get invited to the next auction. Instead..." He gestured toward Kim.

*Instead he bought me and won't get an invitation.* Kim wet her dry lips. "I'm sorry."

"I'm not, chiquita," Master R said softly. "We'll figure something out."

"But the FBI is angry and—"

Vance smiled slightly. "We can't be mad at him. He got referred as a buyer all on his own and was generous enough to let us in on the action."

"I didn't know that," Gabi said. "You weren't recruited? But why?"

Master R flashed her a grin. "My *mamá* named me after Raoul Wallenberg. How can I not help?" His mouth straightened. "Gabi, it's a dom's job to protect his submissives, not sit back while *they* volunteer to get kidnapped." He gave her a stern stare.

Kim gripped her friend's hand. Gabi had done insane things trying to rescue her. What if the slavers had actually succeeded and if—

"Stop imagining," Gabi muttered to her. "What happens now? Can Kim go home?"

Vance hesitated, and Kim couldn't bear the silence. "I know it's probably not good news. Just spit it out, okay?"

He smiled. "If you can speak to me like that, you're doing better than I thought."

Master R growled. "She is very strong, but she has been very hurt. This is not—"

Vance broke in. "First, going home isn't a good idea." He rubbed the back of his neck, his voice tight. "We've discovered at least two slaves escaped."

"Really?" Gabi leaned forward. "Then they can

identify, testify—"

"They can't," Vance said flatly. "They're dead along with anyone they talked with."

Kim felt her skin go clammy. Going home would put her mother at risk?

"I'm sorry, Kim." Vance started to say something and then stopped. Waited.

*Can't go home.* God, by staying here... She swallowed and edged away from Gabi. "They might come after Gabi and Marcus?"                                                    •

Gabi broke in. "Don't you even start thinking like—"

"It might not be a good idea to stay here," Vance interrupted.

If she ran, where would she hide? The Overseer claimed they had people in every state. She had no money. Her arms wrapped around her legs. The tide was coming in, and it was black.

"Kimberly," a low, resonant voice said. *"Kimberly."* Master R's voice.

She shuddered and looked at him.

His eyes held hers. "Better. You will listen to everything before you panic. You have options, chiquita." His intent gaze stayed on her as he prompted, "Buchanan, go on."

"We are trying to accomplish two things," Vance said. "To keep you safe and to continue with the operation of shutting down the slavers in the Southeast quadrant. You have a couple of choices." He waited for her nod. "We can put you into a witness-protection program. Sandoval will report you died—we can't risk saying you escaped, in case they go after your family—and he'll ask to buy another slave. The downside is your death would have to be public enough they'd know it was true. Your family would... It might be difficult for them."

Kim stared. *Have Mom think I'm dead? Is he insane?* "What's the other plan?" It must be better.

"We give up on having Sandoval attend the auction. Instead he'd refer someone else."

"That sounds good," Gabi said.

"It would be except for the Association's fu—damned precautions. The only way to talk to the Overseer is at the follow-up visit." Vance frowned at Kim. "The visit where he finds out if the customer is satisfied. Where he'll expect to see you, Sandoval's slave. A good slave, since otherwise you get returned."

Kim felt the ground drop away. *Be a slave. Meet the Overseer again?*

"God, no." Gabi scowled. "She can't handle that."

All the feeling had receded from Kim's fingers. How white they'd gotten. Did she have any blood left inside her? "How long is the visit? How long would I have to pretend?" She'd have to see the Overseer. Deep inside her body, her bones shook like a Halloween skeleton in a cold wind.

"I'm not sure. Probably a couple of hours at least, maybe an evening." Vance shook his head. "But, Kim, the problem is this: the Overseer doesn't make contact for a few weeks. At that point, he'd expect to see a fairly well-trained slave. One who knows Sandoval—his habits, his protocols."

"She could fake it."

Vance snorted. "Don't play stupid, Gabi. This isn't something a slave picks up in an hour. When Marcus nods at the floor, does he mean strip and prostrate yourself, suck his cock, or present yourself doggy-style, or maybe kneel with your hands on your thighs? Or does he prefer your hands behind your head?"

With a sinking feeling, Kim saw Gabi's understanding nod.

"But maybe she could be…well, kept in a separate

room. Like Raoul only uses her for sex or something?" Gabi asked.

Master R shook his head. "During my interview with the Overseer, he asked what functions my slave would perform. I said I wanted service as well as sex. I never imagined being caught in this kind of situation."

"Who could?" Vance asked. "So Kim would be expected to serve and be present in the room. Having her cringe if her master's displeased wouldn't be unusual, but cringing whenever he touches her—or even looks at her? No. Not knowing what to do when he motions for something?" Vance's gaze turned to Kim, pity softening his blue eyes. "You can't fake this kind of slavery, sweetie. You'd have to live with Sandoval starting now and actually be his slave, in order to act like one in front of someone as experienced as the Overseer."

"I already told you no. I won't have anything to do with this," Master R said in a hard voice. "She can't do it."

The tiny amount of pride left in Kim flickered at how easily he'd dismissed her. She could do whatever she put her mind to. But the rest of her agreed. Go back to being a slave? *No way.*

But to have them tell her mother she was dead? Would Mom survive such a devastating blow? *No.*

"I don't see any other choice," Vance said. "Not if—"

"I bought her to free her, not to torment her further." Master R interrupted. "She has enough nightmares without me adding to them. What if she panics when he's there?"

"Not a deal-breaker," Vance said. At the deadly look Master R gave him, he shrugged. "To still be struggling with her problems would be normal enough. So would jumpiness. But she can't fake training she never gets. Most masters do some instruction, even for a sex slave. The kicker is that you not only asked for a service slave, you're also known in the lifestyle as being an excellent teacher. I'm sorry, Raoul.

You'll have to train her—and you'll have to touch her as well."

"Maybe I could go and be there with her? It would be easier with…company or something," Gabi offered.

Kim looked up. Maybe that—

Vance shook his head. "They do an extensive background on the buyers, so they know Sandoval lives alone. They might do some monitoring after the sale. For him to bring in another woman right after he buys a slave would be downright unlikely and would probably send up a warning flag." He scowled. "They're paranoid bastards."

*Warning flag.* Ice water trickled into Kim's core as she remembered… She closed her eyes, took a breath. She had to tell them, but her words stuck to her tongue. "Vance."

Master R was still fighting to keep her out of it. "There's always the demonstration. I could get into an auction that way."

"Maybe," Vance said. "But that only gets you on the waiting list for God knows when in the future. Besides, the Overseer would still expect to see Kim since your audition is during the follow-up visit."

"Vance," Kim said, raising her voice. Their attention shifted to her. "The gossip in… I heard from the other slaves that if a buyer kills a slave, they don't contact him for quite a while in case he didn't cover up well enough, or the body's found or there're witnesses. Repercussions."

"Hell." Vance scowled. "Then pretending you died won't work. At least not for getting Sandoval into an auction in the near future, either as a buyer or doing a demo." He cursed under his breath.

Silence. The number of eyes on her made her shake, and she stared at her hands. *Such white fingers, all twined together in knots.*

Master R's voice. "It doesn't matter." She looked up

into compassion. Worry. "Go into the witness protection program anyway, Kimberly. Stay safe and out of sight."

How incredible it felt to have someone on her side. In slavery, each woman stood alone, for if one tried to protect another, both were beaten. She winced as a lash cracked across her memory. But now... She wasn't at their mercy, and the man beside her, like a massive tank, was so, so not helpless.

How could she find a plan that would work? At one time, she'd been good at solutions. Back...before. But now... Pretend to be dead and be safe, but her mother would suffer, and she'd have ruined any chance of getting the FBI to the auction. Be a slave and...oh God, she couldn't.

"What about the other slaves still in their grasp, Raoul?" Vance asked, his voice edged with pain. With pity. "Can you abandon them so easily?"

The question was a blow straight to Kim's chest. She watched as Master R turned his face away, the skin taut over his cheekbones. He'd planned the whole thing to rescue *all* the slaves and abandoned it to save her. Just her. While the rest—Holly and Linda and the others—were still there. They'd never get out. *Because of me. Because he rescued me.*

Guilt settled in her belly, cold and leaden, and with every breath she could hear Holly's terrified screams, as if the dungeon were only a few feet away. *I can't. Can't be a slave.* Her throat felt as if a rope bound it, contracting to keep the words from escaping.

But to leave them there? Linda had changed the bandages on Kim's stomach, her hands gentle and careful. She'd told jokes to make Kim laugh, diverting her from memories of how Lord Greville had... *I can't do this.* But then Linda would be never get free. She'd live in pain. She had two children in college. Talked about being a grandmother someday. Held Kim when she cried. She'd been so strong, but eventually everybody would break, even

Linda.

*Is it worth it to live if I betray...everyone?* She looked at her wrists. The bruises from the cuffs had faded to a faint yellow. *I endured before. I can endure again.* No, she probably couldn't. She'd die if she was a slave again. *No no no.* She looked at Master R, who still stared out the window. He'd tried to soothe her fears. He'd held her, not hurting her, but—she shivered—not letting her go either. He did as he thought best. He was a dom.

*I can't do it, can't even pretend to be a slave. No.*

Holly had cried herself to sleep every night. Every night.

*I have to do this.* The nausea came fast, choking her, and she inhaled through her nose, forcing it back. *I'm me. Not a slave, even if I choose to pretend. And I will do this. Because I'm me. Not broken.*

A warm hand closed on her upper arm. "Chiquita... Kimberly...look at me."

She heard him sometimes in her dreams, his voice breaking through the storm of screaming, and everything would calm, the slow smooth baritone as comforting as the ocean rocking a boat. She looked up at him. "I'll be your s-slave."

\* \* \* \*

Had he ever seen anyone look so terrified and still manage to move? Raoul leaned against the door frame and watched Kimberly enter his home. Her dusky complexion was a grayish pale, her cheekbones standing out above a clenched jaw. She walked as if the tile floor was covered with sharp spikes.

He sighed. She was incredibly brave, but he had doubts she could maintain her courage. Gabi might get a call this evening begging for rescue.

Kim saw him watching and took a step back. "What would you like me to do now, M-master R?"

*Stop looking at me as if I plan to slice you into inch-sized chunks of flesh.* He glanced at his watch. "It's almost suppertime. Why don't we sit on the patio"— *where you won't feel as cornered*—"and talk? Then we can figure out what to do for supper."

She gave him a jerky nod.

He led the way through the great room and out the French doors. Sun sparkled off the wide expanse of water. On the shore, waves lapped quietly on the sand. Behind him—silence. He turned.

She was on her knees, hugging herself, staring at the beach, at the waves rolling in. The breeze ruffled her hair back, and the setting sun glinted off the tears on her cheeks. She cried as silently as anyone he'd ever known.

Very slowly, he dropped to one knee and touched her cheek with his fingertips to get her attention. He could feel tiny shudders running through her. "Kimberly, can you tell me why you're crying?" Should he call Gabi now?

To his complete shock, she rubbed her cheek against his hand like an overwhelmed kitten, and her blue, blue eyes looked up at him. "I forgot. I didn't even remember…"

He cupped her cheek and rubbed her shoulder, feeling the fragile bones. "What did you forget, *gatita?*"

"You live on the beach. On the gulf." Her eyes were wide—not with fear, but with joy. "I can breathe again. Thank you."

He laughed and rubbed his knuckles over her curving cheek. Perhaps this was not such a forlorn hope after all. If she could share happiness with him, then the rest would come.

\* \* \* \*

The next day, Kim stepped out of the guest room onto the long balcony overlooking the gulf. Master R had an interesting place in a beach-house-meets-hacienda way. It was two-story stucco except for a small third story, like a tower, and curved in a C shape around the patio up from the sandy shore. With huge arched windows and balconies everywhere, the inside seemed to merge into the outdoors.

She squinted against the bright sunlight that reflected on the water. Almost noon. She'd hidden in the bedroom since breakfast.

With a sigh, she dropped onto the dark red cushioned chair. Bare feet on the iron railing, she leaned her head back, immersing herself in the feeling of the moisture forming on her skin, the ocean breeze, the heat of the sun. Waves lapped quietly on the sand, the gentle gulf surf nothing like that of her energetic Atlantic. A gull circled, screeching.

Oh, she'd missed the ocean. The rhythm of her life had been marked by the tides, starting on her father's fishing trawler to her work as a marine biologist. But slaves were shut inside, never to see the sun or hear the surf. Worse than any drug addict, she'd craved the sound and smell of the shore.

She'd probably scared Master R with her reaction last night, but apparently he'd understood. He'd laughed.

*He can laugh.* He had a great laugh. Braced by the knowledge, she'd made it through yesterday evening without panicking. She'd been quite proud of herself.

A noise came from the room behind her, and she glanced over her shoulder. Sitting with her back to a door felt as if she asked to be attacked, but she forced herself to stay. To try to relax. To ignore the certainty a stranger would come out of nowhere and grab her. Knowing Master R was in the house helped...at least with the *stranger-abduction* fear.

It sucked to have so many fears she had to name them.

Would Master R create more terror than he eased? A tremor ran through her. *I don't know him at all.* Aside from insisting she eat supper with him, he'd left her alone last evening, letting her get used to his house, to losing Gabi's support...although Gabi had called about every half hour to check on her. Kim smiled. Sweet Gabi.

But Master R apparently realized how terrifying his presence was—not for anything he'd done, but because he was male. A dom.

He was even more careful with her than Marcus had been. Like last night when she'd had a nightmare. Nothing new. Usually Gabi would hear her screams and wake her up. This time it had been Master R.

*"Kimberly."* His voice had entered her dream, where she was pinned down, unspeakable things...pain... *"Kimberly!"* Such a smooth voice. The horrors reverberated through her in the slaps, the burning. *"Wake up, chica!"* A sharp command. A master's voice. Her eyes had snapped open. A man in the doorway. Another scream, awake now, but the lights were on, and she saw—after a minute—the man who had bought her. Freed her. Master R.

He'd waited until she said his name before entering, then fetched her a glass of water from the bathroom. Pulled up a chair. Let her drink and shake. He hadn't touched her once, and his presence had turned comforting. Did he know if he'd loomed over her, she'd have gone into hysterics? That she couldn't stand being touched right then, not after the nightmare of so many men?

He'd watched her, patient and quiet, then picked up the book she had on the bedside table and simply read to her in that voice, dark with a twist of accent. No nightmare could compete with Raoul Sandoval reading *Huckleberry Finn.*

So she really was better. Maybe the spark of her very self hadn't gone out. Maybe she wasn't filthy inside, deserving of everything done to her and more. Only she felt dirty. Ugly and ruined. She blinked against the welling tears. Would *"filthy slut"* echo in her mind forever?

The psychologist hadn't made much progress with her feelings of self-loathing. Or with helping her to figure out what came next, after this was over. How could she go back to her job, knowing someone might grab her again? That—

She heard a footstep and jerked around, heart jackhammering against her ribs.

"Easy, gatita." Master R stopped. Waited, his eyes steady on hers.

"Sorry."

"You have the right to be jumpy." He squatted beside her chair, tilting her chin up to wipe her cheeks with his fingers. "And to cry. No matter how strong you are, I think you will be in tears often for a while."

"Are we going to start...?" She couldn't finish, hated how pitiful she sounded.

"When you are ready, Kimberly, come downstairs and we'll talk."

"Kim. Everyone calls me Kim."

He smiled, and for a second, she saw the dom he was. Self-confident. Powerful. He would do what he wanted.

A shiver ran through her. "You really are a dom, aren't you?"

"Yes, I am." He released her chin and brushed his knuckles down her cheek. "But you're safe, chiquita. The only slave I want is one whose dearest wish is to be mine."

He wanted to own a slave? A chill settled deep in her bones.

*  *  *  *

An hour later, Raoul pushed his keyboard to one side and rested his forearms on the massive oak desk. The design for a new waterfront area in Belize couldn't keep his attention.

Could Kimberly tolerate being a slave? He wasn't a harsh master, but he wasn't a pushover either, and since he'd acted like a cold bastard for the Overseer, turning into a hearts-and-flowers master wouldn't cut it. Honesty would serve both him and Kimberly best. After all the upheavals in her life, she'd need the stability—the reassurance—of consistency.

He looked up at a sound from the door.

She stood there, her face pale, but chin up and standing straight. Brave little subbie. Satisfaction welled in him as he noted her cheeks had started to round out. Gabi's cooking and pampering had put some weight on her.

"I'm ready to talk," she said. "Is this a bad time?"

"This is fine." He rose and saw her force herself to stand still.

In the doorway, he put his hand on her back, touching her as he'd avoided doing before. He felt her tremble. His brows drew together as he realized he was seeing her in two ways: as a hurt woman and as a willing sub. How had his mind ever received the impression she was willing? Yet there had been times in the slaver's dungeon, when their rhythms had come together, and she'd unconsciously accepted him as dominant.

He paused, then turned toward the stairs, steering her up past the second floor to the third and into the tower room. Their discussion should be in a private place. Intimate. Not his office. And the great room was for guests.

Here, the steeply angled roof formed two sides of the square room, but the front and back walls were all glass, giving a breathtaking view of the sea to the west and his gardens to the east. The floor was a rich brown pile, the off-white sectional soft and welcoming. The toys for bondage and play stayed hidden inside the sturdy ottoman and bombé chest by the wall.

"This is beautiful," she said, walking to the window with the ocean view.

*So are you, little submissive.* The light of the afternoon sun glinted off her straight black hair, bringing out brown tints, and silhouetted her slim figure. Under the loose-fitting clothing, she had a pretty body, he recalled. So thin, yet still graceful with nicely curved hips. He pointed to the sofa, saw her hesitation, and patiently waited for her to take a seat.

What should have been eagerness to obey—and probably had been once—was fear instead. His heart ached that anyone could treat a woman so harshly. He sat on the sturdy square ottoman, knee to knee with her, the sofa back keeping her from retreating farther. "We're going to talk about what I expect and what you will do. And we'll get to know each other, gatita."

"What's gatita mean?"

"Little cat. Kitten." He tugged on her black hair. "Baby cats often have blue eyes, and when I was young, I had a black kitten with big blue eyes."

She smiled. "You called me chiquita."

"Little girl."

She didn't like that. "You said pobre-something means poor little baby."

"Yes."

Her eyes narrowed. "That's an awful lot of *littles*, don't you think?"

"Perhaps." He displayed his hand. "Big." He set hers next to his, so small and delicate contrasted with his thick, blunt fingers. Why did holding her fragile hand raise every protective instinct he had? "Little."

When she huffed in exasperation, he captured her other hand and leaned forward. "Now, tell me what happened when you were a slave."

HIS UNEXPECTED QUESTION felt like a kick to the stomach. *Talk about it? No way.* Kim attempted to withdraw, and his fingers tightened. "Excuse me?" Her mind shifted, trying to detach from her body.

"You heard me, Kimberly. Until this is over, I will be your dom—your master. I will expect you to follow orders. Your body will be available to me—"

She froze.

"No, not for sex," he added with a sigh. "But my hands will be on you at times. You need to become accustomed to my touch so you're not jumping."

She managed a nod. *I knew this. I did.* Why did it seem much more intimidating when she was looking at those powerful hands?

"I expect you to tell me when something bothers you— and things will. I need to know what to avoid, and I can't help you if you can't share what happened."

*Go into it? Talk about it? With him?* His fingers were hot against her skin as the ice crept into her hands.

"Share with me, Kimberly." His voice was a grave baritone, the slight Spanish accent softening it. "When did they kidnap you?"

"A-about maybe seven weeks ago." The pain, horrible pain from the Taser, then a sting. The world going fuzzy, then she awoke to terror. A nasty kick when she threw up, a slap when she cried too loudly.

"I'd forgotten it was so long. Did they hold you for a while before they auctioned you off? What happened during that period?"

"They...didn't do much. I was penned up with the others for...I think almost two weeks?" The time was blurry, crying women, leering men, nothing to do. The days ran together. "Our 'rebelliousness' was a selling point, so we got no training." She swallowed, remembering how scared she'd been. If she'd known what would come after, she'd have jumped overboard right then. "I didn't go to the big auction though. Lord Greville bought me a while before."

"The owner who sent you back to the Overseer?"

She nodded, blinking furiously. *I won't cry.*

Master R's hands squeezed her fingers. "Tell it all."

He needed the information. But it was hard. "He took me to his house." Cold with white walls and furniture, no comfort anywhere. "He had his servants hold me down, and h-he raped me." She forced the word out. After a week of talking with Gabi and Faith, she could say it now—say it without vomiting. "I fought them. He beat me until I passed out. And raped me again." And again and again.

"Was he the one who used a whip on you?" Master R asked, his voice even.

She nodded, looking at their entwined hands. "Each time, each day. The pain—" So much pain that every breath had hurt, until it billowed in her head, made her vision waver. Until all she could think was, Make it stop. "I couldn't quit fighting, even...even though..." Blood in her mouth, on the floor, the stink of sweat and sex.

"It's why the bastard wanted you—because you'd fight back." His fingers massaged hers. "So you've had both physical and sexual abuse. How about mental? Did he call you names?"

"Yeah." *Slut, cunt, dirty whore.* Did the filth inside her show? Could Master R see the darkness? She tried to laugh. "Even some words I'd never heard of before. He said I deserved everything I got because I was a slut. Bad. Filthy. He locked me in a cage during the day—put my water and food in bowls because I was an animal." She dared to look up, had to, and saw his black frown. "That's why he gave me to his friends." Her throat clogged as her stomach turned over.

He cursed under his breath and gripped her chin with those strong fingers, pulling her head up. "Look at me, chiquita."

Her gaze came up to meet his dark brown eyes, patient. Firm.

"Good. Now take a breath. Yes. Let it out slowly. That's a good girl."

The memories retreated, pushed away by his anger... for her. Her nausea eased.

After she'd managed a few breaths, he sat back, taking her hand again. "Others used you. And?"

"I stabbed him afterwards."

He stared at her, then burst out laughing, and with the sound of his hearty laughter, open and pleased, the darkness in her head shrank. He kissed her fingers. "Good for you. But...I think this is why you were hurt so badly?"

*Badly.* She couldn't answer, just started to shake.

A growl came from him. He plucked her up like a dandelion and sat down with her in his arms. Warmth and strength enfolded her, not frightening her. Somehow. How did being ordered to talk make her blurt things out like that?

He waited, simply holding her, one hand running up and down her arm. As her trembling slowed, he said, "I know something of trauma. I have friends who were in war. Others survived the gangs. You will continue with the counselor—she and Gabi can come here—but even so, things will set you off. Panic you or make you cry. I expect that."

Gabi? And Faith? Not alone, not abandoned. "Thank you."

"But if simply talking does this to you, then I need to know the rest, so I can help you through it. Or avoid it. Do you understand?"

She felt dirty. Weak and useless and ruined. But he was right. She bit her lip and nodded.

"How did you manage to stab Lord Greville, and what did he do afterward?"

"As the...men...were leaving, I hid a knife in my dancing scarves." *Crawling to the veils, pulling them around her, knotting one over the blade. Her blood staining the delicate fabric. Trying to stand. Falling. Pushing to her feet. Blood trickling down her legs like warm water.* "When he returned for me, I stabbed him." She swallowed. *The blade punching through his shirt, then his skin, his flesh resisting.* "He jerked away as I did. Enough that I got his shoulder and not his heart. He hit me." Knocked her across the room.

"I'm sorry you were not more accurate," Master R said mildly. "And then?"

"He yelled, and his staff came. He was crazy mad." Blood everywhere, yelling, insanity in his eyes. "He whipped me and then got the knife I'd used." *"I'll cut you into pieces. Scream, slut."* She touched her ribs where the long slash had opened her to the bone. The pain had bloomed and grown and grown. "But he'd lost enough blood that he passed out." She'd hurt so much, too much to glory in it. "They tied a bandage around my ribs and put me back in the cage. The little one." Not the kennel. Made for a medium-sized dog and so small she couldn't straighten her legs, couldn't stand up. Couldn't move. Couldn't... Her lungs spasmed like a fish on dry land, suffocating with air all around.

"Shhh, shhh." A big hand stroked her hair. "You're here, gatita. No one will hurt you."

*Here.* She blinked away the darkness at the edge of her vision. "They left me... I don't know how long." In the dark. Never let out. Bleeding. Hurting. Peeing on herself, her legs wet and stinking. The cage stinking. Her voice had broken from screaming. "Eventually they came and got me." When the door opened, she knew she'd die and felt only relief.

He shook her gently, breaking her from the nightmarish thoughts. "Breathe for me, Kimberly."

Slow breath. She stared out at the waves. The small windows lining the huge ones were cracked open, and the ocean's shushing sounds rolled over her, drawing her memories away, grain by grain.

"Look at me." He drew her back to the present. "They took you out and...?"

"The Overseer was there. They made him take me back."

"Pobrecita," Master R murmured.

Too tired to be afraid, she laid her cheek against his soft shirt. Beneath the thick muscles of his chest, his heart beat slowly, evenly, his breathing pulling hers into a matching rhythm. Under the influence of the even pace, she found her voice again. "The Overseer was furious because he said I was damaged, but he gave them a refund since Lord Greville'd brought in a lot of referrals. One of the Overseer's slaves sewed me up, and I didn't do anything for a while. After the stitches came out, I helped out in the kitchen for another week. And learned to dance."

"No hospital?"

She managed a laugh. "Hardly. Although I got anti-biotics. I think they were for dogs from a feed store." *I'm an animal.*

"Well, I see why you were a bargain," he said, breaking up her thoughts. "Almost killing your owner would definitely lower your value." He tapped a finger on her nose. "Good job."

She blinked, startled. A trickle of warmth crept into her at the open approval in his voice.

"Aside from being kidnapped, which would leave you insecure, most of what terrifies you happened at this Greville's house? Rape, cage, beating. The way they treated you, being called names—you feel as if they're right? That you're what they called you?"

Why did it help when he...listed...things? Because it sounded like a set of problems she could deal with instead of an overwhelming chasm she'd fall into? "I... Yes."

"Mmmmh. You get counseling already. I'll add in some self-defense, so if you have to stab someone, you'll do a better job." He waited for her nod. "Getting over being raped will take time, but since you're here in my arms, it might not be the worst of your problems. But you suffered enough that things will set you off. Unless your counselor says otherwise, we'll stop, go through your fear so you handle it, and if possible repeat the trigger until it doesn't work any longer."

Maybe she could survive. Except... "Not the cage."

He shook his head. "No, that one is for your counselor to deal with. You and I will stick with what causes you problems in your slave training."

Slave. The word made her want to retch. "I'll do my best."

"I know you will, chiquita."

As his arms tightened around her, she felt fear and safety mingle inside her as she was comforted...by her *master*. God had the oddest sense of humor.

\* \* \* \*

With a low groan, Raoul pushed the weight slowly

upward, his arms shaking with the strain. At the top, he dropped the bar into the rack, the clank loud in his empty weight room.

As he sat up on the bench and shook out his arms, sweat plastered his tank top to his skin, and his pecs and triceps burned. His body made the shadows on the wall dance. He'd deliberately left off most of the lights, the darkness suiting his mood.

He'd managed to keep from showing his fury when Kimberly talked about her kidnapping, but, *Dios*, it had been difficult to hear her voice tremble, feel her scarred body tremble.

An hour of lifting weights, of pushing himself to exhaustion and beyond, had restored his control. Leaning forward, he set his elbows on his knees and stared at his forearms. His skin was taut over the pumped muscles. His veins bulged. Yes, he was fucking strong.

Uselessly strong. He'd been too late to save his brother from dying in a filthy alley, too late to rescue this little slave before her abuse. Even worse, next time he saw the Overseer, he couldn't beat him into the ground. Not yet. His jaw tightened until his teeth ground together. Hopefully later.

For now, his task was to heal the damage to Kimberly's soul...and train her as his slave. He dropped his head into his hands, despair edging through his defenses. A slave. Here, in his house, the one he'd built after his divorce, not wanting to live with any memories of Alicia and their failed Master/slave relationship.

Now he would bring it back into his life.

# Chapter Four

That evening, Raoul made Kimberly fix stir-fry while he sat on a tall chair at the kitchen island, sipping a beer. The way she moved was as beautiful as the way she danced. No motion wasted, everything in order. But the multitasking was making his head hurt. When he cooked, he'd fix one part; when it was done, he'd prepare the next. The little slave had several different preparations going on at once.

The slight smile on her face pleased him. Cooking was a comfort to her. He'd remember that.

Once the meal was on the table, he took a chair, holding up a finger to stop her before she sat down. As she stood beside the table, he helped himself to a bite. The flavors were excellent—strong and well balanced. "Very good, chiquita."

"Thank you, Sir," she said in a distant voice. She'd withdrawn emotionally from him since their talk. He understood. He tended to do the same, but it couldn't be permitted. If she bottled up her anger and fear, he wouldn't be able to read her or help.

"You sound unhappy." He rested his arm on the back of the chair, deliberately letting his gaze wander down her body, the loose blue T-shirt, the baggy shorts. She'd put her hair into a long braid, and he missed seeing it free. "I think I have been a tolerant master so far. I even let you wear clothing while you were cooking."

When her eyes widened, he frowned. At the sale house, she'd shown skill in serving drink and food. In dancing. She'd kept her eyes down, knelt gracefully, spoken only when told. Had she received more training than that? She'd said she was left alone after her kidnapping and then was sold to a sadist to be used for whippings and sex. After her return to the Overseer, she'd spent most of the time healing.

She not only had received little training, she might have no realization at what being a true full-time submissive entailed. He rubbed his cheek thoughtfully. If she hadn't been so emotionally fragile, he'd probably enjoy this. He loved teaching.

He'd loved being a master, at least until a while after he'd married. His mouth tightened. That was in the past and nothing to be repeated.

When she took a nervous step back, he wiped the anger from his expression and his mind. *Eyes on the job, Sandoval.* He pointed to the chair beside him. "You may join me this evening at the table."

As she sat down, her face was easy to read. Yes, she had much to learn.

"There may be times I prefer to feed you myself, and then you will kneel beside me and take food from my hand." When a shudder ran through her, he studied her for a minute, trying to read her. Too many emotions there. Fear. Disgust. But was that a hint of anticipation? "The Overseer said you were in the lifestyle before this. Do you know anything about Master/slave relationships in real life?"

"Uh, not much. I dated a few doms, but that was mostly...uh, sex. Fun. Nothing else. I always thought women who wanted to be slaves... Well, it'd be like wearing a sign that said KICK ME. It's disgusting." An odd combination of revulsion and pain twisted her mouth.

If she had no experience, why such disgust? From

someone else's past? "So...before all this...you liked giving up control during sex. Perhaps to completely enjoy it, you need someone else in charge?"

Her cheeks pinkened delightfully. "I guess."

He smothered his smile. "Some women enjoy giving up control for longer periods, not just in the bedroom. There are those who find that making others happy, especially their doms, fills a different kind of need."

From the cynical twist of her lips, he saw she stuck to her opinion: slave equaled doormat.

"A good relationship is a two-way street, gatita. Submitting and serving is equaled by a master's need to take control, to protect, to make someone happy."

She not only didn't believe him, but she also dropped her gaze again, shielding herself from him. Something else he would not permit. He set his fingers under her chin, lifting her face to his scrutiny, feeling the way she wanted to pull back.

This wasn't going to be easy for either of them, especially if she wasn't honest with him. Even worse, if he happened to misread her body language during a scene— assuming the Overseer required one—they could have a major problem. "A purchased slave would not have a safe word to stop an activity because they're afraid, but I am uncomfortable without one. So, if you should say 'cramp' or complain of one, I will know you need a break or are having problems, and we will talk." He grinned. "Yet it won't look like I'm giving in to something most owners would ignore."

The relief in her eyes appalled him. To feel grateful for the most basic of BDSM considerations. Well, they definitely had much work to do. He released her.

As he ate, she pushed her food around, her nervousness obvious in the way her eyes checked him constantly and her muscles tensed each time he moved.

Once finished, he leaned back, stretching his legs out before him. "I have two basic positions I wish you to know right away. We'll work on the others later. The first is *kneel*, and you did very well with that one. The next is called *display*, and it's what I requested you to do in the dungeon." He raised an eyebrow.

She shook her head. "I'm not sure I remember."

"Stand up."

After a second of hesitation—something else to work on—she rose.

"Good." Leaning forward, he tapped her inner thighs to have her open her legs farther, and stood to adjust her position. "Hands laced behind your neck." He waited for her to comply.

Under his touch, she trembled, and her gaze dropped away. Curling his hand lightly over her shoulder, he waited to see if she was still with him. After a few seconds, her blue eyes cleared, and she looked directly at him.

The trusting had begun. He stroked his hand over her cheek. "You're very lovely, gatita."

Her brows pulled together, and she gave him a skeptical stare.

"Do not look at your master as if he's an idiot."

A surprised smile flickered over her lips.

Raoul drew his finger down her jawline. "Your skin is beautiful and very soft. Touchable." He continued down her neck to above her breasts. "Your breasts are beautiful—full and high."

Her breathing stopped, her lips pressing together. But she maintained her stance.

He trailed his finger between her breasts, not pressing at all, so the fabric of her shirt kept his touch from her skin. When he reached her stomach, he felt the shiver even through the khaki material of her shorts and knew she was aware of him...as a master. As a man.

He said softly, "Your waist curves in and then out to hips that were made to cradle a man, soft thighs to hold a man between them."

The color rising in her cheeks wasn't entirely from fear, yet it was far too soon to even attempt to touch her in any sexual manner. "You may relax. Hands at your sides, palms forward."

In all reality, pretty as she was, he'd prefer to avoid it altogether. Nonetheless, every dom instinct in him wanted to act, to try to heal the damage, and as she was under his care, he must do what he could. So he would move slowly with small touches, verbal play.

"Now, you will remember to ask to speak, no? If we are having a conversation, permission is understood. Address me as Master or Master R or Sir. Nothing else. This, I saw, you have already learned."

He noticed she'd never called him Raoul either, even at Gabrielle's home. Did she think of him as the enemy then? Or as her master?

She nodded.

"Most of your responses should be simply, 'Yes, Master', but if you're particularly enthusiastic, you may say, 'It will be my pleasure, Master.'"

Her expression showed doubt that anything he suggested could ignite her enthusiasm.

"You are to care for the house and meals. A housekeeper comes in on Thursdays to stock the kitchen and do general cleaning. I'll introduce you, and you may take on overseeing her."

"I'll oversee someone else?"

Her incredulity made him grin. She was so very unused to the dance between dominant and submissive. His lips tightened. And that was because she had experienced only the raping away of her power rather than the joy of giving it into loving hands. "A slave might have clothes or not, speech or silence, no responsibility or much. Nothing is set in stone."

He held her gaze with his and could see her yield to his voice, his authority. Something constricted inside him— she feared his control yet wanted it. How deep did her need run? Light submission...or complete? "The only consistency in the relationship is this: the master decides."

"But—" Her shoulders hunched defensively.

"That makes you anxious, gatita. Why?"

"I won't know... I need to know what—"

Did she fear arbitrary punishment? "We'll go over what I expect from you. The rules. I will never punish you for something you didn't know or didn't understand, Kimberly. That isn't my way."

Some of the worry faded from her eyes. But not all. Her gaze was focused on the floor.

He considered what he knew of her. Not nearly enough. *"I need to know..."* she'd said. Needed to know what to do? Some people—and a high percentage of submissives— wanted clear-cut rules. Preferred their duties laid out, liked schedules and lists. He was somewhat that way himself, as were many engineers.

"I think I understand," he said. "Tomorrow I'll list out your responsibilities."

The tensed muscles of her shoulders eased. The whiteness around her mouth started to pinken.

Much better. He added, "At breakfast every morning, we'll plan out your day."

There it was. He'd won an actual smile.

\* \* \* \*

Kim had been left alone to clean the kitchen—*thank you, God*—and the time putting dishes in the dishwasher and wiping down the dark granite counters helped settle her nerves. She scrubbed at a stubborn stain, still a bit shaken by her reaction to Master R. When he'd talked to her in that dark rich baritone, telling her she was lovely, talking about her breasts, well... Apparently her hormones hadn't gone into hibernation after all. Only she wished they had.

The thought of having sex ever again filled her with ice. And panic.

*I'm fine. Just keep my emotions calm and cool.* She imagined picking up a heavy shield, like something Lancelot would carry. Nothing could get through it.

She stopped in the doorway of the TV room. Like the rest of the house, it had creamy stucco walls and terra-cotta tile flooring. The end tables and entertainment center were of dark wood, a waist-high brick red vase stood in one corner, and throws in autumn colors made the room cozy. A painting of a gorgeous old world sailboat hung over the leather couch where Master R was reading a technical magazine.

He glanced over and smiled. "Barring any other instructions, when I am sitting, you will join me by kneeling at my feet, half-facing me, eyes down."

That's disgusting, her cynical part said. But her inner self...was silent. That wasn't right. Shouldn't everything in her disagree with subservience? A tiny shiver went through her as she knelt, grateful for the softness of the Oriental rug.

"Very, very pretty, chiquita," he said softly. "I'd never planned to have a slave in this house"—he hesitated, and his jaw tightened for a second—"so most of the floors are tile and will be uncomfortable for you. If there is no carpet, you may use a pillow."

Had he owned a slave in a different house? She looked

up, almost spoke. "Permission to speak?"

"Good. Add Master onto the end, please."

"Permission to speak, M-master."

He leaned forward and cupped her cheek, his brown eyes frighteningly serious. "It pleases me when you call me that, Kimberly. I thought you should know." He held her gaze, his look reaching deep, deep into her, melting the ice in her center.

She swallowed past a dry throat.

He waited, still touching her, his thumb stroking her jaw.

"Did you have a s-slave before?"

"Mmmhmm. After college, I had a slave for about two years before I moved here. She preferred to stay in that city, so I helped her find a new master." The movement of his slightly rough thumb stroking her skin lulled her into relaxing...until his expression hardened, the warmth in his eyes disappeared. "The woman I married was my slave as well."

Kimberly pulled away. "Married? But—"

"I'm divorced, gatita, for almost three years now."

The bitter twist to his lips made her want to pat his hand in comfort. "What happened?"

He leaned back, putting more distance between them. "The usual things that break up a marriage." His voice made it clear the subject was off-limits. Pretty unfair considering the way he'd probed her life.

She had one last question. "Did your wife do all right once you let her go? After being a slave, could she still function?"

The humor returned to his face. "Because a woman places her power in my hands doesn't mean she'll give it to anyone else. My wife was CEO of her own company. She ripped young executives apart without ever raising her voice."

*Wow.* That was... He was screwing with all her preconceptions. Pretty rude. "And your first slave?" Slave— the word sickened her.

"She makes an excellent living as a real estate agent, specializing in million-dollar-and-up properties."

Not comforting to know he apparently had liked being a master and having a slave. But, oddly enough, it was reassuring that two women had willingly given themselves over to his care...without being kidnapped. Sold. "They cooked and cleaned your house too?"

"No, gatita, that's what housekeeping services are for. I only assigned you those responsibilities since you have nothing else to do. As it happens, I enjoy cooking and will take a turn on weekends, as I used to do." Amusement danced in his eyes. "And when I didn't want to cook, then my slave did, wearing only an apron. As will you."

*Oh boy.*

"Now, fetch the book you were reading earlier, and you may join me on the couch."

When she came back with her book, he didn't look up, just murmured, "Remove your shirt and bra first, please."

She stared at him.

He turned a page.

She'd agreed to this. He hadn't wanted her to do it. But clothes were a...a defense. Her own kind of chain mail. *I don't want to.*

He appeared so relaxed, his attention on his reading. Another page turned.

Swallowing down tears, she pulled her T-shirt off, then her bra, and stood waiting.

He looked up then. His gaze ran over her, nothing in his expression except approval at her obedience. "Good, gatita. You took a big step. Now come and sit beside me." He patted the couch.

She sat gingerly beside him, stiffly upright until he pulled her to his side. Her fingernails dented the cover of the book as she waited for the inevitable groping, the attack...

His heavy arm settled on her shoulders, and his fingers curled around her upper arm. He shifted, settling her against him more comfortably, and then picked his magazine up.

After a minute or two, he sighed. "A *slow* breath, please, Kimberly. You are not running a race."

*Oh.* Her pulse pounded, but she managed to even out her breathing, from racing to maybe a jog. After another minute, she lifted her book. The room was cool enough that where his body touched hers felt...nice, warm against her bare skin. His hand occasionally stroked her arm.

Another minute or two, and she actually read a few of the words in her book.

WHEN THE LITTLE subbie leaned against him in earnest, her head nodding, Raoul sighed. He'd known this would be difficult for both of them. He hadn't realized how terrifying it would be as well. He'd dealt with emotional trauma before, since scenes tended to open a submissive to bad memories, and it was a rare human who reached adulthood without picking up a problem or two.

But she'd experienced way too much trauma, too recently. Even worse, much of her turmoil was related to being enslaved, and everything he did would bring back those memories.

This wasn't going to be easy. During the afternoon while Kimberly napped, Raoul had a conference call with her counselor, Gabi, and Z, the owner of the Shadowlands BDSM club. Since Z was also a psychologist, he knew the emotional problems associated with the lifestyle.

Gabi, Z, and Faith had all had qualms over what might happen, but also some hope. The counselor thought patients with PTSD did better if they learned what caused their panic attacks and had help working through them. Gabi agreed and said that, in her experience, having a purpose—like defeating the slavers—was a strength and spur to confronting fears.

Unfortunately, they also agreed this FBI operation was moving too fast, especially since Kimberly would have to face the Overseer again.

Raoul sighed. He not only couldn't protect her, but would, in fact, often be the one giving her nightmares. Yet this was what she'd chosen, so they had to make the best of it.

He shook her lightly. "Kimberly, it's time for bed."

She jerked away, the blank panic on her face tightening his throat.

"Easy, gatita. You're safe."

"Oh." She blinked. "Bed. Right. Okay."

He cleared his throat.

"I mean, yes, Sir." She hadn't cringed this time, and the way she peeked out from under her long black eyelashes made him grin as he helped her to her feet and up the stairs. Resilient little chica, wasn't she?

*Bed.* Dios, another problem. He'd have to do this in stages as with everything else. He let her go to her bedroom but waited in the hallway until he heard her return from her bathroom. The bed squeaked. He tapped on the door.

Her sharp inhalation sounded clearly. "Y-yes?"

"Open the door, please."

"Oh God," she whispered. The door opened. When he saw the terror in her wide eyes, he almost gave up then and there. But she possessed more courage than he did, and after a hard breath, she lifted her chin. "I bet I'm losing my bedroom, aren't I?"

The lump in his throat made his voice hoarse. "I'm sorry, but I think it best."

She nodded, and her mouth firmed. Her hands fisted with her struggle to step forward.

So brave. He moved close enough to rub his hand over her lower back. Soft cotton pajamas. Comics, no less. Had Gabi chosen them? "I see Wonder Woman looks worried also."

Kimberly gave him a confused look, so he ran a finger over the graphic at her waist. With her surprised laugh, the tight muscles under his fingers eased. For the moment.

In the master bedroom, he motioned to the bed. "Tonight, you may leave your nightclothes on. Tomorrow, you will wear nothing to bed." He paused. "What do you say to me?"

She swallowed. "Yes, M-master." Another hesitation before she jumped up and onto the high bed. Raoul had bought it because it was the perfect height to take a submissive leaning over the bed. Not a fact he'd share with her.

Kimberly buried herself under the covers.

In his bathroom, he cleaned up and donned a loose pair of cotton pants. After flipping the bedroom lights out, he joined her in the bed. Curled into a defensive ball, she was a huddled mass of misery, watching every move he made. She'd never get any sleep that way.

He rolled onto his side and propped his head up with his hand. Would Z's suggestion work? "On a scale of one to ten, how frightened are you?"

KIM FROWNED. THE moonlight streamed through the balcony doors, a pathway of light, falling over Master

R's face. No lust, no anger. He simply watched her with those quiet, steady eyes. She was grateful for how her loose hair fell forward and screened her face. "When my mom had surgery, they had her rank her pain that way. You want me to use the numbers for how scared I get?"

"You will do so, yes." He reached out as carefully as if she were a wild animal and, using one finger, pushed her hair out of her face, behind her ear.

So much for her shield. She barely kept from glaring at him.

His firm lips curved slightly. "You will not hide from me, gatita." He gave her hair a tiny tug. "So. I think you will show me your scale with your fingers. One finger tells me you are fine; all ten fingers extended means you're going into a panic attack. Use this starting now, so when we...entertain...you will not have to think, and we'll have worked out the best response."

"Response?"

"Yes. If you get to—we'll say seven for now—I'll stop and hold you until you are steady again."

"I—" His plan shouldn't sound good at all, yet it did. Knowing he wouldn't ignore her fears helped. And she'd already learned he had a comforting hug. "Sounds good." He deserved more than that. "No, it helps...M-master. It helps a lot."

He tsk-tsked and ran a finger over her cheek. "There will come a time when your tongue does not stumble over the word."

She sincerely doubted that, and her doubt probably showed in her face since he grinned, that mesmerizing flash of white against his bronzed skin. "Do you usually sleep on your left or right side?" he asked.

"Huh?"

Silence.

*Darn it.* "On my right. Sir." Especially after she got stabbed when her left ribs had been so tender. When his hand closed on hers, she realized she was tracing the wound.

"The right. Then turn over," he said. Ordered.

Her body stiffened until she felt like an unbending board as she rolled onto her right side. *No. Oh no.*

His arm slid under her head as he pulled her against his body, spooning around her. His bare chest warmed her back, his groin—and a thickening erection—pressed against her bottom. Her breathing hitched. *No, oh God, please no. I can't.* She couldn't move, as if whatever she did would incite him to attack.

A laugh rumbled through his chest. "No sex, Kimberly. However, before the Overseer visits, you must be comfortable with me touching you. And so your lesson is merely to accustom yourself to my arms, to being against me." A pause. "You will sleep better if you are not so tense though."

An awkward gasp jolted from her. As if she could control that?

"Breathe when I do."

The man was breathing way too slowly. But she tried.

A minute later, he said, "Very good. Now think about your toes. Relax the muscles in them. Let them go limp."

*Toes? Get real.* But he was being so kind. No sex. She wiggled her toes to remind herself where they were, to take her attention from the huge thing pushing against her bottom. *Toes.* Then she let them still, relax.

"Good girl. Now your lower legs—ankles and calves. Let the tenseness drain out onto the mattress, onto the floor. The bed will hold you up."

The exercise had her attention now. *Right ankle. Left ankle.*

"Good. Feel how heavy your legs are, how they sink down into the mattress."

By the time he reached the top of her head, she was just awake enough to feel a gentle kiss on her hair, the soft exhalation of his breath, the firm arm holding her against him. And she let herself fall into sleep.

# Chapter Five

Raoul woke, feeling the pressure of time. The auction, according to the Feds' best guess based on their tracking of kidnapped women, would be in about three weeks. Sam needed to be referred before then and in enough time to get approved. When the Overseer made his follow-up visit, Kimberly needed to be well into the slave mindset, comfortable with him touching her body, comfortable with submitting to his will. If the Overseer had doubts, Sam's referral would get nowhere.

At least, Kimberly wasn't an inexperienced submissive, even if she'd never gone further than light erotic submission.

He smiled, inhaling the faint citrus scent of her hair, the fragrance of her feminine musk. But no perfume of arousal filled the air.

Kimberly was solidly asleep, her arms curled around his forearm like a stuffed toy, and... He frowned, realizing his hand had cupped her right breast during sleep. *No, Sandoval.* He released her—regretting the loss of the soft roundness in his palm—closed his fingers, and resettled his hand between her breasts. His cock ached like a torn muscle, and he sighed. This was going to be a long few weeks. And a very long morning.

At least they'd both slept well. Her shivering had woken him once, but he'd been able to soothe the nightmare away before it took her over. Better than the first night when her gut-wrenching screams had dragged him from sleep. So much pain yet willing to face the Overseer, to save the other women. Her courage awed him.

He squeezed her slightly. "Kimberly, time to get up."

Her arms tightened around his, and her breasts enclosed his hand in softness.

"Dios," he said under his breath. He pulled away slowly and slid out of the bed.

She muttered and woke, pushing herself to sit in the bed, frowning at him.

"Sorry, chica, but I have work to do, which means you get up also."

Her frown deepened.

"Use the bathroom to take care of business and brush your teeth, then call me."

She was wide-awake at that point, fear edging into her eyes. But she didn't argue, just moved into the bathroom.

He entertained himself by picking out the clothes she'd wear today.

A few minutes later, she reopened the door, and he walked in.

After removing his loose pants, he stepped into the walk-in shower and turned on the water. The dark green tile steamed up immediately. Turning, he motioned her in. Her hands fisted at her sides, and she'd started to tremble.

"Show me a number," he said firmly, snapping her out of panic before it could take hold.

OH GOD, HE was naked. And fully erect, his cock huge and pointing toward her like a weapon. Her gaze dropped away immediately.

He'd rape her now... Then Kim heard his voice, and a second later the words registered. *A number.* Ten, twenty, a hundred! With the exaggeration, her brain clicked back on.

He wasn't hurting her. Not even touching her. Really, she'd been more scared than this, hadn't she? *Yes. And she was with Master R, not...a monster.* With the thought, the fear edged down further, and she forced her hands open to show him six fingers.

"Good. You did very well at making yourself think."

The approval in his voice warmed her far better than the steam from the shower. She forced herself to lower her head and wait for his command.

"Look at me, gatita. This morning, you may remain in your pajamas...although you will join me in here. Today you bathe me." Silence.

Relief eased her breathing.

"Tomorrow we bathe each other. Understood?"

A reprieve, not a stay of execution. But it still helped. A lot. "Yes. Yes, M-master."

He snorted. "If you are with me long, I will begin to spell Master with two *M*'s." He held out his hand. "Come, chiquita. Wash me so I can get some real work done today."

The brisk tone had her moving forward. His blunt fingers closed around hers, pulling her under the water. Warm spray soaked her pajamas, and they clung to her skin, hiding very little. He said nothing, simply handed her the soap and turned his back.

*Well, okay.* She worked up some foam and started. Impossibly wide shoulders, down the muscled planes of his back. Skip over his butt. His thighs were as thick as her waist, with light coarse hair. His ankles and feet solid. She stepped back—the metallic taste had disappeared from her mouth—and looked at him. There was nothing graceful about this man; he was sheer blunt power and strength.

His ass remained...and he didn't turn around. She eyed the soap. "Um..."

"All of me, Kimberly."

Dammit. Biting her lip, she washed his tight buttocks and between. So intimate, touching him there. "T-turn, M-master."

His laugh echoed through the shower. "Is this going to give you a permanent stutter?" When he faced her, she could see the amusement in his eyes. Her tenseness retreated a step. At least until his erection bumped her stomach. She jerked back so quickly her feet skidded.

His firm grip on her arm held her up, but he released her as soon as she caught her balance.

"Wash my face, please," he said gently, the command forcing her to pay attention. The understanding in his expression made tears burn in her eyes.

"Yes, Sir." She soaped over his forehead, the hard cheekbones, and the blunt angle of his jaw. His morning stubble rasped her fingers. "Rinse, M-master."

He stepped under the spray and back, wiped his eyes, and stood quietly as she soaped his corded neck, the steely muscles of his arm, tracing the line between biceps and triceps, his thick, powerful wrists. After washing each broad palm, she worked on his fingers, scrubbing thick calluses and short fingernails.

She soaped the soft black hair under his arms, then the inverted triangle of dark hair over his pectorals that hid flat brown nipples. His chest was a solid wall of muscle. Mesmerized, she ran her finger across the ridges of his abdomen. *Damn, a real six-pack.*

"I like the feeling of your hands on me," he said softly, unsettling her so she paused to look up at him warily. "Continue."

She averted her gaze from his groin and washed the front of his legs, his feet, and ankles. Then... Oh God, did she have to do this? But he wasn't touching her, grabbing her, or forcing her. A shiver ran through her as he stood in place, silently waiting.

86 *Cherise Sinclair*

Why did he have to be...erect? She stared at the wall, frozen.

"Chiquita," He lifted her chin. "You are learning to control your fear. In exactly the same way, an honorable man will control his lust. My body desires you, yes. Any living man would, and I'm not dead, after all." A smile flickered over his lips. "But my body doesn't get everything it wants, or we'd still be asleep in bed, no?"

The logic made sense. He'd rather have slept in but didn't. He'd rather...fuck...her, but wouldn't. "Thank you," she whispered.

"You're welcome. Now wash me so I can begin work, and you can take your own shower."

*Wash his cock. Got it. No problem.* She looked down and gasped. How had she missed seeing *that*? "You have a piercing."

He chuckled. "So I do."

*Oh wow.* A silvery barbell with a ball on the top of his shaft went straight through to underside of the head. Straight through. "Didn't that hurt?"

"A bit."

Uh-huh. *A bit.*

He clucked his tongue. "Kimberly? You've been given a task."

*Right.* Although her fear had eased, worry constricted her chest. His cock was almost the same color as his skin, thick and long with a slight bend to the left. She gave him a quick glance as she touched it, tensing, half-expecting him to grab her and... But he just watched her calmly with a small smile. Her soapy hand slid around his shaft, slickly up...and she brushed over the metal on the tip. Circled it with a finger, then did the one on the underside. How would those feel...inside?

"Most women like it. A few don't," he said, answering

her unspoken question. "I remove it if it's a problem or sometimes for oral sex." He grinned. "Stop playing."

Realizing she was fingering the silvery piercing, she flushed. But now it wasn't as impossible to finish, from the head, down over the thick veins, to the springy trimmed hair at the base. He opened his legs. His testicles were large and heavy. Fascinating. She'd had shower sex before, but had she ever washed a man so thoroughly? With this much attention?

When she finished, his face was flushed, and the muscles in his jaw had turned rigid. She knew that expression. Her body tensed, ready to flee.

As she took a step back, he turned and rinsed the soap from his body. When he faced her again, his smile was easy. He lifted her chin with one finger and brushed a kiss over her lips. "Thank you, gatita. Your courage pleases me." He gave her an infectious grin, and her heart skipped a beat at how dangerously handsome he was. "Your soft hands please me as well."

Before she could worry about his words, he stepped out of the shower and toweled himself off. "I left your clothing for today on the bed," he said a second before the bathroom door closed behind him.

*He picked out my clothing? Excuse me?*

But she didn't really care...not right now. She stared at the door as the hot water beat on her back. *I did it.* Hadn't panicked. He'd even thanked her. She touched her tingling lips. *He kissed me.* It had been...nice. Not horrible at all.

She started to pull her pajamas off and stopped. What if he returned? But...he wouldn't. She just knew that.

\* \* \* \*

Raoul pushed away from his desk. His work was

caught up, and the afternoon was almost over. So far, it hadn't been a bad day.

At breakfast, they'd gone over schedules and expectations, then gone to their various chores.

After lunch, he'd tried gentling Kimberly in the same way he would a wild animal—start at a distance and move closer, bit by bit. While he'd worked in his office, she'd sat on a floor pillow beside him, close enough he could stroke her hair.

It had taken almost an hour for her to relax. When she'd tired, he'd leaned her closer, pressing her cheek against his thigh.

He'd planned the method to increase her trust in him; what he hadn't expected was his own peace at having her close. When her psychologist had arrived and taken Kimberly to the great room, his office had felt empty and cold.

But he'd heard Faith leave a while ago. Time for the next step. He rose and stretched, tucked his shirt neatly into his jeans, and went in search of his little slave. He found her still in the great room. Curled up on the couch, she appeared strained. The session must have been a painful one.

Maybe she'd enjoy his way of defeating stress. "Come, gatita. It's time for something more vigorous than sitting."

"Yes, Sir."

She followed him silently as he walked to the front corner of the house. He opened the door and stepped into the room, then realized she wasn't beside him. He turned.

Almost as pale as her white T-shirt, she stood frozen in the hall.

"What's wrong, chiquita?"

She moved a step closer, stared into the weight room, and sagged against the wall. "I thought you were bringing me to a dungeon."

"Ah." He shook his head. *Poor little slave.* "I have a dungeon, yes, but it's on the south side. After we finish here, I'll give you a tour of the house."

Color returning, she followed him into the brightly lit exercise room and wandered around, looking at the bench press, the squat machine, the pulleys. "If you didn't know what this stuff was, you might think you'd entered a dungeon." She eyed the cables.

"I suppose," he said noncommittally, not even tempted to tell her how nicely some of the equipment worked as restraints. Attach that pulley to a submissive's wrist cuffs, add weight... A couple of the subs he'd entertained actually preferred playing in this room to the dungeon. "We're going to build up your muscles and endurance." He eyed her loose shorts and T-shirt. Good enough for now. "In a couple of days, I'll start you on self-defense."

"I know a little. My father made me take karate classes as a kid."

"Really. Why did you stop?"

"I—" When she shrugged, her breasts moved in interesting ways, diverting him for a second. "I...didn't want to be a tomboy anymore." Her mouth firmed as if she were remembering old battles.

Odd. Something else to investigate.

"But at this point, I don't think I could learn quickly enough to worry even a ninety-nine-pound weakling," she added, her brows drawing together.

Had he ever seen a woman who was so pretty even when frowning? "With karate, no. I'm going to give you the benefit of my years of street fighting. We'll start with some of the nastier tricks—the ones they don't teach martial arts students, since explaining to a mamá why her son's eyeballs are on the floor is most difficult."

"Ew." She stared at him in horror.

"Or why his few fingers now bend the wrong way."

Her disgust turned to a speculative gleam as she undoubtedly envisioned slavers who could no longer grip a flogger. Exactly the concept he wanted in her head. She wasn't a victim; she was a survivor—and one who might do some real damage if the chance ever came.

\* \* \* \*

An hour later, Kim's legs wobbled when Master R helped her off the leg extension machine. His hard grip on her arm was all that kept her from flopping onto the rubber mat like a landed trout. "I won't be able to walk tomorrow," she moaned.

Dammit, why did he have to have such a great smile? "You will, although you'll groan all the way out of bed."

"Thanks a lot."

His laugh was deep, resonating in her bones. "Now I want you to be clear on the rules we discussed earlier. When working together like in the weight room or cooking in the kitchen, I don't expect you to be formal. Everywhere else, you will ask permission to speak. You will use my title and be respectful at all times. If I am sitting in a room, kneel before you speak to me, and wait for permission to sit anywhere except the floor or on a pillow."

"Yes, M-master." The same rules they'd gone over at breakfast. No contradictions. Did he realize how wonderful his consistency was? She winced, remembering she'd sat on the couch in the great room. He hadn't said anything. "I was on the sofa before."

"Ah." He frowned. "Many masters don't let their slaves on the furniture at all, but I found that awkward and unnecessarily strict."

*"I found."* Every time he reminded her that he'd had

slaves before, the pit of her stomach dropped away.

"If there are no doms in the room, use the couch or chairs and be comfortable. If I enter the room, you stand. If I sit, you kneel. Any questions?"

"No, Sir." So she should have stood up when he came into the great room.

"If you break the rules, you will be punished— probably with a spanking. Is that clear?"

"Yes, M-master."

"Very good." He rubbed his knuckles over her cheek, his gaze tender. "Is there anything you need now or want to say?"

Why would a master ask a slave something like that? And why did it make her feel…off balance? "No, Sir."

"No? Then let me show you the parts of the house you missed." He took her hand in his, leading her.

On the second floor were three guest rooms and the master bedroom. At the end, he opened a door and showed her a sitting room overlooking the ocean. "This is your private area for when you need a place to be quiet. If you're in here, I'll know you want time alone."

Before her relief had taken hold, he set a finger under her chin, lifting her face to give her a level look. "Having a space to use doesn't mean you'll be permitted to hide in here, Kimberly. As with all things, that is up to me."

"Yes, Sir."

"Good." His hand cupped her cheek, and gaze on hers, he lowered his head. A flutter like butterfly wings tickled in her chest, but she didn't move. A brush of his lips, a slide of his tongue on her lower lip followed by the nibble of teeth. Her mouth softened, and a tiny flicker of heat sparked to life low in her belly.

Not forceful. Gentle, teasing kisses from firm, velvety lips. His palm was warm against her cheek, his knowledgeable mouth on hers, but nothing else touched her. He didn't even try to push his tongue in, just led her, step by step, into responding to the kind of kisses she'd experienced as a girl, before French kissing had come along.

He pulled away as slowly as he'd advanced, his gaze still intent but...oh, so much warmer. As was she.

She stared at him, setting her hand over her quivering stomach.

The corners of his eyes crinkled, but he didn't speak, just ran his thumb over the moisture on her lower lip and then took her hand.

He led her downstairs to areas she'd already seen. The foyer and great room, dining area and kitchen, TV room. When he headed toward the south side of the house, her skin went cold. His dungeon. *No. I don't want to go there.*

Ignoring the way she hung back, he opened the door and flipped on the overhead light, filling the area with brightness, erasing some of the menace. "Walk around the room three times. Look at everything," he said in exactly the same tone as when he'd instructed her to do leg presses.

Every fiber in her urged her to flee, but she took one step through the door. Her knees shook as she forced herself to continue. He didn't follow. She glanced back.

He leaned against the wall, arms crossed over his chest, just watching.

*Okay then.* Hands fisted at her sides, she managed to get one foot to move, then the other. The taste in her mouth, the way her skin went cold—at age six, she'd gone in a Halloween haunted house. Screams and moans, cobwebs and skeletons. She'd frozen, unable to move until her furious and shamed father had dragged her out and yelled at her for being a coward. *"Moores are not cowards."*

*But they are sometimes.* Yet she pushed herself on, across the empty side of the room, then toward the equipment. Her feet stopped. *Breathe. Breathe.* She forced her legs forward, tasting blood from where she'd bitten her tongue. She made it past the St. Andrew's cross and a bondage table. Her stomach almost revolted when she saw whips—so many whips—coiled snakelike on a shelf. A glass-fronted cabinet displayed gags. Masks. *God. Pass that one quickly.* She came even with Master R.

He held up one finger. "Two more."

A throne chair with no bottom. A sink and counter. She detoured about chains dangling from the ceiling rafters. Then reached Master R.

*Two fingers.*

The room was well-equipped, nicer than some of the clubs she'd played in. Leather padding on almost everything. A sawhorse spanking bench. Master Raoul.

*Three fingers.*

She stopped in front of him and shivered, thinking of all the horrible things behind her. *Now what?*

"Kimberly, we're not going to play today."

*Oh, thank you, God.* Her shoulders loosened as the tenseness disappeared. "Thank you, Sir."

"However, I do want you on that. Facedown." He pointed to the waist-high bondage table, and she froze. He waited, then lifted his chin, his jaw hard.

*Don't make him mad.* She crossed the room, ignoring her inner coward that kept screaming, *Run, run, run.* After she climbed onto the table, she lay on her stomach, every muscle rigid with fear.

"Good, gatita. You're conquering yourself and doing very well."

He took her arms, laying them at her sides, and massaged her shoulders with strong fingers. As her muscles relaxed, she opened her eyes and craned her neck to look at him. No lust in his face, just the focused attention he brought to everything he did. "Sir?"

"Master, gatita."

"M-master, what are you doing?"

He snorted. "Massaging all your tired baby muscles. What does it feel like?"

*Oh.* "Nice." Except for the need to run away and hide. "Thank you. Master."

He worked his way down her body, and she knew he did it to get her accustomed to his touch, but it was effective. She tensed when he dug his fingers into the aching muscles of her buttocks, but he didn't do anything sexual at all. Down her legs. Her feet. She moaned when his thumbs dug into her arches.

"Turn over."

Her eyes popped open.

He didn't wait but rolled her onto her back and smiled down at her. "Such big eyes. Yes, I'm going to massage your front as well." His fingers curved over her shoulders, his thumbs digging into the muscles around the collarbones.

God, it felt good...but she couldn't relax, not with his hands so close to her breasts. He worked on her pectoral muscles, easing around her breasts, moving them out of his way. She tensed every time he touched somewhere new.

Finally he shook his head in exasperation. "Your worries are getting the best of you, chiquita. You're not going to fall into pieces if I touch your breasts." And then he put his hands directly on her breasts, curving his palms around them.

Her breathing stopped.

He didn't move as he looked down into her eyes. "Am I hurting you?" He waited. "Kimberly?"

She licked her lips. "No." Her feelings were too messed up to figure out. Fear—oh yes. But...pleasure? She'd always liked a man's hands on her breasts, but not now. Surely not anymore.

"Are we okay?" he asked. The firmness in his voice held the expectation that she'd get over this.

"Yes, Sir."

"Good girl." He moved down to her feet, working his way up. Leaving her shaken. Always friendly, polite, yet this solid immovable core. More than his self-confidence and ability to give a command, he showed his certainty she'd not only obey him, but that she wanted to.

And he didn't hide his satisfaction or even pleasure when she met those expectations.

His big hands squeezed one thigh and the other, moving higher until his fingers grazed the crotch of her pants with each movement. Her fear flashed and faded, leaving…anticipation. Warmth.

God, she wanted him to touch her. The realization slashed into her, more painful than a knife stroke. How could she live through rape and slavery and ever want to be touched again? What kind of slut was she? *I really am the dirty fuckhole that the—*

"Tell me what you're thinking," he said. He'd moved up the table to regard her closely with shadowed eyes.

*Not ever.* "Nothing."

"Gatita, I know when my touch heats a woman. Why does being aroused bother you?" He waited; then his voice deepened in an explicit command. "Tell me now, Kimberly."

The words spilled from her like a dam breaking, releasing a torrent. "I shouldn't ever want anyone to touch me. He said I was a dirty slut, and I am. *I am.*" Sobs broke from her. *A cunt, an animal, not worthy to be human.* She knew it. Like a sewer, filth filled her, running through her core.

"*Hijo de puta,*" Master R muttered and picked her off the bench. He cradled her to him as he carried her to the small living room.

He shouldn't touch her. She was not fit to be near a real person. Dirty all the way through. Tears streamed down her face, making her even uglier. *A f-fuckhole and a—*

He sat on the couch, leaning her against his chest. "Stop." He shook her lightly. "*Stop. Now.*" A master's voice. Her master.

She choked, pushing the sobs down.

"Better. You will listen to me. Do you remember how your memories work?"

Memories? "What?" She blinked, trying to focus on his face.

"When something horrible happens, your brain doesn't process the memories right. It stores everything—sounds, pain, smells, feelings—all mixed up. It doesn't matter if you believed it or it made sense; it gets stored. Did Gabi or Faith not tell you this?"

They both had. Kim nodded, her cheek rubbing on his chest. His scent came to her, clean as an ocean breeze.

"So if your memory is triggered, you get parts of the mess back—and maybe what you heard or felt at the time. Are you listening, Kimberly?"

"Yes, Sir."

"He told you over and over that you were bad. Made you feel dirty. So sometimes, when your brain accesses those memories—the ones you haven't thought about—you're going to hear those words and feel that way again. *Sí?*"

She hauled in a breath. He was right. She didn't normally think she was a bad person. "I guess."

"Gabrielle told me she was raped when she was a teenager. Is she a filthy slut?"

"No!" Wonderful Gabi, who cared for everyone and brightened any room she entered. "How can you—" She bit her lip. *Duh. And neither am I.*

"That's it," he murmured. He kissed the top of her head, then her lips, ever so gently. After picking up the TV remote from the side table, he said, "Let's watch something really dirty. Like football."

As the Saints took on the Packers, she fell asleep wrapped in comfort.

# Chapter Six

Each day came with something new. Over and over, Kim had to remind herself why she was doing this. For the others. For Linda and Holly. And really...for herself, as well. To have a part in hurting the slavers, in wrecking their business, would be healing, would show that she wasn't a nothing, but was a person who needed to be taken into account. She struggled on.

She managed the loss of her clothing—barely—although she doubted she'd ever get used to being naked when Master R was in jeans and a short-sleeved shirt. At least he allowed her to dress when other people visited.

Since he often conducted business at home, he and the FBI made Gabi and Faith wear shirts with his company's green logo so they'd appear to be his employees. Gabi bitched about the boring white shirt—and a matching green streak appeared in her hair beside the blue one.

Slowly, Kim got accustomed to Master R's hands on her body, washing her, massaging her, holding her. Each night, after receiving a good-night kiss that grew more demanding, she'd sleep in the nude, curled in his arms, and wake with his erection pressing against her buttocks. He terrified her and made her feel safe at the same time, and wasn't that weird?

Each morning they'd discuss her day and her tasks and anything else he expected. If she made a mistake in her posture or did something wrong—like the drawer where the silverware went—he'd calmly tell her how he wanted it done. He didn't yell, didn't call her names, was always polite.

When she'd broken a cup, she'd frozen, expecting him to yell, if not punish her. He only told her to put shoes on before she swept it up.

The only thing that brought her close to being disciplined was rudeness. Being disrespectful was definitely one of his crash-and-burn offenses. But even then, he stayed calm. Consistent.

If only he'd stop adding things she had to adjust to.

Yesterday, before lunch, the scum-sucking algae eater had buckled leather cuffs on her wrists. As she'd tried to remember how to breathe, he'd informed her he wanted tacos from his mamá's special recipe. By the time she'd figured out all the spices—*like what was wrong with the little envelopes of seasoning?*—and had the meal set out, she'd almost forgotten about the cuffs...until he clipped them together in front of her. Couldn't move, couldn't get away. Mega-claustrophobia. He'd had to help her to her knees beside the table.

But as she'd knelt beside him and he'd fed her, her shaking had disappeared. Why did taking food from his hand no longer make her feel humiliated, but cared for? Because he selected the best pieces for her? Because his attention was fully on her? Lunch hadn't been so bad after all.

Today, everything had gone downhill... First, he'd buckled the damned leather cuffs on her wrists after their shower in an automatic way that said she'd be wearing them a lot. Dammit.

Fifteen minutes ago, he'd given her his *I'm-going-to-be-mean-to-you* smile and clipped the cuffs behind her back, held her while she panicked, and then frowned at her. *"You will do squats until I tell you to stop. We'll build up both your leg muscles and your courage."*

In the empty part of the weight room, surrounded by the scents of rubber mats and steel, she managed a few squats. Bending her knees, she did another and straightened up slowly. That was seven. *How many more is he going to make me do?* She scowled at him as the first drop of sweat rolled down her neck.

*Ten squats...fifteen.* Her thighs burned with pain. *Drown him anyway.*

Over by the rack of dumbbells, Master R was doing biceps curls. His pumped-up arms were huge. The way his darkly tanned skin stretched so tightly over the muscles made her fingers itch to touch. Besides, anything would be better than this squatting garbage.

He glanced over where she stood, her legs quivering until she was afraid she'd fall. "You can do another, *cariño.*"

So not happening. "What does cariño mean?"

"It means sweetheart." His lips quirked. "Now stop stalling and push those spaghetti legs."

Yeah, drown him and let the crabs eat him, no matter how many affectionate things he called her. After hauling in a breath, Kim blew her sweaty hair out of her face, checked her balance, and bent her wobbling knees again. Down. She gritted her teeth and straightened. The cuffs didn't matter anymore, except if she fell, she'd not be able to catch herself. Her thighs burned, and sweat trickled down her back and between her bare breasts. She stuck halfway up. Groaning, she pushed determinedly and made it all the way to standing, sucking air like a landed fish.

A minute later, as her breathing slowed, he said, "Another."

"Damn you, I can't. Are you fucking blind or—"*Oh shit. Oh no.* Her breath strangled in her throat as his eyes chilled, and his jaw turned stern.

"That was very disrespectful, Kimberly. Do I swear at

you?" He didn't move toward her, but pointed to a bench. "Bend across the side of that."

*No.* She took a step back. Her heart had been fast; now it slammed against her ribs as if desperate to escape a cage. "No. Please. I'm sorry. Master, I'm sorry."

"I know, chiquita. You will still be punished." He picked up heavier dumbbells. His left arm curled up slowly, straining, then down, before he glanced over at her. "Do I need to repeat myself?"

*No no no.* Her feet felt as if he'd clamped weights around her ankles. One step. Another. Her wrists were still restrained behind her, and her legs shook, making her stagger like a drunk. As she tried to kneel, her knees gave out and hit the rubber matting with a painful thump. Fighting tears, she pressed her bare shoulders and face to the cool bench padding. Naked. Restrained. Her pulse was an ocean of sound in her ears.

She turned her head and watched his reflection in the wall mirrors. He didn't pay her any attention. At all. His right arm curled up, down. The other arm. His concentration remained on his exercise, as if she'd become invisible. She wished she had. *Really.*

The weights went onto the rack. *Clank. Clank.* Her stomach tightened.

He walked to her, his approach like the darkening atmosphere before a storm. Swinging a leg over, he straddled the bench beside her. She craned her head to see his face.

"If you are sent somewhere for punishment, you will take this position." He grasped her around the waist with merciless hands, sliding her forward until her hips met the edge of the narrow bench. Her head and shoulders hung down off one side; her knees barely touched the ground on the other.

His palm pressed firmly on her low back, and he set

his foot on her calves. Immobilizing her.

A whimper escaped her as she tried to struggle.

He merely increased the weight on her. "Only three this time, chica. Count them for me."

*Oh God, oh God, oh God.* She tensed and heard him sigh.

"I'm sorry, gatita, but we both must observe the rules." His incredibly hard hand slapped her left butt cheek, not gently at all, and the stinging pain burst through her.

She jerked and gasped...and wasn't allowed to move.

"Count?" he prompted.

"One."

Thickening silence.

"One, Master."

"That sounds much nicer, don't you think?" His next spank landed on her right butt cheek. Sheer burning.

She yelped, and tears filled her eyes. *It hurts.* Her shaking increased. "Two, Master." Only one more. She could handle another.

The third swat was over both her cheeks on the under curve. The pain sheeted through her in a hot wave, and she sobbed, tears spilling down her face. Her bottom burned as if she'd sat on coals.

Silence.

*Damn him.* "Three, Master." The fire started to fade.

"Tell me what you did wrong."

"I cursed at you and refused your order. I'm sorry, Master."

His hand rubbed her throbbing bottom. "Yes, I think you are." Then, to her horror, his palm moved between her legs and over her pussy, and when she tried to evade, she realized his foot and left hand still held her down. His ruthless fingers touched her, slid...*slid* between her labia, inside her and back out. "You're also wet, little subbie."

Her resistance disappeared like sand washed away on the shore. *Filthy slut. Dirty fuckhole. Not worth—*

A stinging slap on her sore buttocks knocked the thoughts out of her head.

"I recognize that look now," Master R growled. "You're a sensual, delightful woman, Kimberly."

The conviction in his voice smoothed the self-loathing away, but then his fingers ran between her folds again, teasing her entrance. "You're also submissive. I don't know if pain from the spanking turned you on today—we'll find that out—but we both know that being mastered is something you like. Something you need."

His fingers stroked her intimately, and a shudder ran through her as heat pooled in her lower body.

"We both know I will give you what you need." A pause. He cursed under his breath. His hand moved away, leaving her aching. He rose and walked across the room.

What had happened? With her hands still locked behind her back, she struggled to a standing position, grimacing at how her legs shook. He faced the blank wall, not moving. Was he mad? Had she done something? Only she hadn't. Like the tide coming in, anxiety flowed in and out, each time adding more.

When he strode back to her, his face hard with anger, she flinched...but held her ground.

His expression cleared. "Ah, chiquita, I am sorry. I'm not displeased with you. Not at all." He cupped her cheek, infinitely gentle, his big hand hot against her chilled skin.

She wet her dry lip. "Then what?"

"I'm angry with me." His mouth tightened as he met her gaze. "You are...appealing, gatita. You're submissive, brave, beautiful. You give of yourself without holding back."

*He really sees me like that? And yet...* "Is that bad?"

"I am supposed to push you, but only so you can perform for the Overseer. For that one time, you must show your training, be comfortable in the role of my slave, comfortable with my hands on you, no?"

She nodded, thinking back over the past week or so and... *Damn, look at me. Restrained and spanked. Naked. Seeing a pissed-off master and not running for the nearest door.* Her spine straightened a little.

His eyes lightened. "Yes, you've done very, very well, and I'm proud of you."

She felt as if she'd swum into a sunny patch of water in a cold ocean. Wouldn't last, couldn't see the bottom, but so warm... "Thank you, Master."

He winced, leaned forward until their foreheads met. "Yes, that is the problem. I forget you are not truly mine. Kimberly, I should not have touched you so intimately." He straightened, holding her gaze. "There is no need for us to have sex for you to handle a visit by the Overseer."

"No. There's not." Her surge of relief could have been expected, but not the regret. Yet she realized her body was coming back alive, belonging to her. Her pussy still throbbed, and under his controlling hands, she'd felt beautiful. Sexy. Not a thing or an animal, but a desirable woman. Sex with Master R would be...scary. Maybe wonderful.

"It is part of a dom's nature to push. To give you what you need, to help you past your limits. But I don't have the right to do that to you." He turned her around and removed her cuffs. "It will not happen again, and I hope you'll forgive me."

God, had she ever heard a man apologize so sincerely—let alone a master? He'd bought her, was trying to keep her safe. That he felt so guilty now seemed wrong. She turned and clasped her arms around him, resting her cheek on his shoulder to hide how her treacherous tears were spilling over again. "There's n-nothing to forgive."

He sighed and wrapped her tightly against him, holding her for a long, happy minute. No one in the world hugged as well as Master R. After a kiss on top of her head, he grasped her shoulders to frown at her tears.

Wiping her cheeks, she managed a gurgly laugh. "On second thought, you can apologize for walloping me. I'm going to have trouble sitting."

His quick smile was like glimpsing the sun on a cold, foggy morning. "You earned the punishment, chiquita. Now go swim a few laps in the pool to cool off."

"Yes, Master." As she started out of the room, he didn't follow. She hesitated. He hadn't even turned to watch her. His gaze had returned to the wall, and he looked…unhappy.

"Gatita, obedience is required," he said quietly without moving.

This time, she left.

* * * *

On Wednesday, Raoul walked into the dungeon room. At breakfast, he'd seen the calendar and realized it couldn't be much longer before the Overseer would call. The thought soured his day but reminded him not to let up on Kimberly. So he'd told her they'd play in the dungeon today.

What could he use that wouldn't terrify her? He opened the toy cabinet doors and frowned at the shelf where the gags were supposed to be. Empty. *Madre de Dios.* Eyes narrowed, he surveyed the shelves. In the row of nipple clamps, the wicked-toothed clover ones were missing. The next shelf had lost the midsize and larger anal plugs. The big dildos as well. The posture collar. In fact, anything that might cause a little slave some distress had disappeared.

His laugh broke the silence in the room and lightened his mood. Sneaky brat. Did she think he wouldn't notice the missing toys? Or had she simply not been able to deal with the nastier implements? He glanced at the wall. She hadn't removed any impact toys. Then again, he'd mentioned he wouldn't flog, whip, or paddle her.

When she needed punishment, he'd use his bare hand. As he had the other day.

Such soft skin. He remembered how his hand had left marks on her curvy ass, and his cock stirred. He shook his head. Touching her so intimately had been a mistake, not only in exceeding his promises, but also because he couldn't forget the silkiness of her bare skin and how wet and hot her cunt had been around his fingers. Her arousal despite her fears.

She'd submitted so sweetly. She hugged him after his apology, showing a nature both giving and forgiving.

*And not mine. Keep that in mind, Sandoval.*

However, it appeared he'd pinken her pretty ass again today.

He grinned. Warning her of his plans for dungeon time had been a mistake.

\* \* \* \*

Kimberly pushed a little farther back in the closet, feeling like a complete idiot. *What have I done?*

First she'd stolen some of Master R's toys and hidden them.

God, she'd only planned to check what was in the cabinets because he said they'd use the dungeon today, and she...she needed to know.

Only there had been an anal plug, a huge one, and maybe if she removed it, he wouldn't notice. A dildo had joined it, and then her inner coward had come unhinged. She'd filled a plastic bag with everything she didn't want him to use. And then hidden the sack.

How could she have thought he'd be blind to half-empty shelves?

That was bad enough, but to hide. Like, okay, on her first day here, she'd spotted this little corner closet under the stairs—so very Harry Potter-like—and also noted every single place a person might hide and all the exits as well. But she hadn't thought about any of them since.

Not until today when he'd said *"play in the dungeon."* God, with every passing minute, her dread had grown. After hiding the toys, she'd tried to clean the kitchen, to read, to do laundry, but her feet had carried her here as if she had no control over them at all.

Despair filled her as she heard Master R's footsteps. So distinctive. Not quiet or sneaky, but solid. Even. Unstoppable.

Get up, she told herself. *Go out and beg forgiveness. Do it now.* Her body didn't move. Her inner coward shrank further inside its cave.

He wasn't calling for her. Oh God. Was that good or bad? How mad was he? She started to shiver.

The door opened. Light shone through the spaces between the clothes. Surely he wouldn't spot her in the corner.

A grunt of satisfaction. His big hands grasped her arms and pulled her out of her hiding place.

She went limp, unable to stand, but he hardly noticed. He lifted her far enough to view her face and sighed.

Her trembling didn't stop, but tears brimmed in her eyes as she realized his disappointment in her. He wasn't mad, and that almost...almost made it worse. She firmed her knees, managed to stand, and earned herself a nod.

With one hand firmly curled around her upper arm as if he no longer trusted her not to run, he led her to the tower room. The place he liked to use for their talks.

He took the chair, pointed to the floor.

Blinking away tears, she knelt clumsily and lowered her head. Her throat clogged as the silence turned thicker. Heavier. A tear escaped. Another.

And then, as if a storm surge sent waves crashing over her barriers, she started to cry. "I'm s-sorry, Master. I…couldn't." Why didn't he hold her? The need for his arms pulled at her, shaking her like a loose sail in the wind.

He gave her only a touch, his finger lifting her chin. He leaned his elbow on his thigh and studied her. "Couldn't what?"

*Couldn't face the dungeon, talking about it, seeing your disappointment.* "I—" She cried harder, unable to say any of it.

"*Carajo,*" he muttered, and she flinched at the Spanish *F* word. "Tell me—clearly—why you hid from me." He waited, offering nothing more as she struggled for control.

Her breath hitched, but she managed to whisper, "I was scared."

"I realize that. Why didn't you talk to me?"

Talk to him? Her brain stopped as if it had floated to the end of an anchor line. "I-I don't know."

His finger stayed under her chin, keeping her face exposed to him. She blinked the water from her eyes, needing to see his expression. Hard…but not cold. He had on the *you-screwed-up* dom face, but he wasn't angry. *Why isn't he angry?*

"Have I asked you to let me know when you're getting too afraid?"

She tried to nod.

His eyes chilled.

"Yes, Master."

"I make you so fearful you cannot speak with me?" She

heard his unhappiness in his tone, in the slowness of his phrasing.

Her tears started up again. "No, Master. I'm sorry, Master."

This time, he framed her face between his hands, using his thumbs to wipe the wetness from her cheeks. "Then talk to me now. Explain so I can understand." Releasing her, he set his forearms on his knees and waited.

Why *hadn't* she gone to him? Talked to him before she got too crazy in her head? He always listened. He'd hold her during panic attacks. He'd go slower if she was really scared. But... "I wasn't thinking. I just hid." Had he maybe not seen the missing toys? God, let her have a chance to put them all back first.

He frowned at her. "When you were little and scared, who did you run to?"

"Mom." What did that have to do with anything?

"Not your father?"

*Like he would have helped.* Her laugh sounded...odd. She shook her head.

"Why?"

How to explain their family? "He... When I was younger, he treated me like a son. Boys don't get scared."

"No?" His mouth twitched. "Thank you for letting me know."

Her mouth dropped open, and her brain started to kick in, erratic as a motor with some salt water in the fuel. Other fathers hugged their children...both sons and daughters. They'd comfort them and hold them if a baseball smashed into them or when a big dog chased them. Her father hadn't been...fatherly.

"At first, he treated you like a son. What happened when you grew older?"

Her own fault. Her own choice. She didn't regret it. "I

decided I was female and started dressing like one. Helping my mother. So I was...nothing to him."

Master R was frowning again. "You would have been a beautiful little girl. How could any *papá* not be proud?" His knuckles stroked her cheek, and she...yearned.

"I guess you had a good father," she said.

"I did." His fingers ran through her tangled hair. "Kimberly. Terror can make us like children. If you didn't run to your father—a man—to comfort you, and considering your experiences with men recently, I understand why you hid." His level gaze held hers. "But, chiquita, you must understand that while you are here, I expect you to come to me and share your fears. Even if I am the one causing them."

Why did his uncompromising look make her heart stutter? "Yes, Master."

The corner of his mouth curved. "I like all the Masters I'm hearing right now, slave."

She flinched, chilling as if arctic water was seeping into her core.

His eyes narrowed. "This is the type of thing we discuss." He paused. Then his voice hardened. "Slave."

He rarely called her that horrible word. Surely he couldn't understand the effect on her. How could he?

Now he expected her to talk as her insides shriveled like a jellyfish on dry sand. *Can't talk.* She pulled in a breath. *Must talk. I'm braver than this.* Her shoulders straightened a little. Gabi would tell her to pull up her big girl panties and spit the words out. "The word. Slave." Could she bleach her mouth out? "I never liked it even...before. Now it makes me sick to my stomach. Ugly." She bit her lip and forced the rest out. "When *you* call me that, it's...worse." As if her security blanket had a snake on it.

"Mmm." He picked her up, tucking her easily onto his

lap and against his chest.

Every muscle in her body relaxed at the enveloping comfort of his embrace. A reward. He was rewarding her for her honesty. Manipulative? Kind of. But she'd take it.

"You don't look sick when you say master."

"It's not the same—not ugly." She rubbed her cheek on his chest; his faded T-shirt was soft over his solid pectorals. His masculine scent mingled with that of the laundry soap and had come to mean safety. "I like the master word." She considered and added, "Although sometimes I want to throw things at you when you make me use it."

His laugh sounded different, deeper, when her ear was pressed to his chest. "Bueno. Is submissive better than slave?"

"I guess." She tried to imagine him calling her that. "It's kind of blah."

"Mmm. Perhaps *sumisa*—or even *sumisita*? It means little submissive in Spanish." He shifted her so her face snuggled into his neck. "Someday we'll discuss why I think the word fits you."

*Sumisita.* It sounded...sweet somehow. He'd called Gabi *chiquita* a couple of times, so that term didn't seem very special. Gatita was...more hers. And sumisita was more...ownery. His way of saying "mine." "I like that, Master."

"Good." He tipped her face up. His approving kiss made her feel as if her boat had entered the harbor.

"I put a blank journal in your sitting room," he said. "And a limit list as well. You know what that is?"

A list of BDSM activities where a submissive could check off what she might be interested in trying...and what she absolutely wouldn't do. Sometimes a club dom would hand her one. She nodded.

"Fill out the list, and we will discuss it." He tapped her

nose. "I doubt we'll actually play much, but we have reached the point where I need to know more about what bothers you."

"And the journal?"

"Is mostly for you. Faith agreed you should use it." He paused. "I want you to write one page for me every day, and we'll read it together each night. The rest is only for you; I won't ask to see the other pages."

A journal. *Bleah.* "I get Faith's reasons. But why a page for—to—you?"

"To avert problems like today." He stroked her hair gently. "There will be things you need from me. Thoughts you can't speak but might be able to write. So. You will fill the page, even if your words seem foolish to you. Clear?"

"Yes, Master." Homework. Frigging *what-I-did-on-my-slavery-vacation* homework.

"Such a pout," he murmured and kissed it right off her lips. His lips were warm, firm, controlling. His hand tightened in her hair as he took her mouth, punishing before he finished in gentleness.

Her head swam as if she'd downed three quick drinks.

When he pulled back, his gaze smoldered with as much heat as she had simmering inside. His expression hardened. "Now about what you took from the toy cabinet..."

She buried her head in his neck. *Oh God.*

"Bring them here and lay out everything neatly on the ottoman. For your punishment, you will pick one of the toys—just one—which I'll use on you sometime in the next few days."

"When?" she whispered.

"Wrong response. Try again, sumisa."

"I'm sorry, Master." *More.* She should say something more. "Whatever Master wishes."

"Very pretty." He kissed the top of her head and set her on her feet. "Off you go now...and, Kimberly?"

Trying to remember what all she'd taken—*that huge dildo, definitely don't want to pick that*—she turned. "Yes, Master."

His lips quirked as if he was trying not to smile. "Next time when I say we will play, I do not mean hide-and-seek."

# Chapter Seven

A few days later, Raoul practiced in his dungeon with the door locked. Using a whip was a skill a dom couldn't afford to let grow rusty, not if he didn't want to mark up the bottom.

He'd watched from the tower room as Kimberly walked on the beach with Gabi. The sun had glinted off his sumisita's dark hair. Her tan had darkened from her frequent walks, and her skin glowed with the return of her health. Kimberly had shoved Gabi into the frothing surf, her face alight with laughter. To see her so carefree lightened his heart.

And having her out of the house meant he could practice. Although the crack of the whip probably couldn't be heard outside the dungeon, he'd take no chances. She didn't need to know how much he enjoyed bullwhips.

After stretching up until his arms and shoulders were loose, he started. An empty space on the wall held various practice targets—today newspapers were between the wide clamps. He worked on slicing delicately through only the top layer of paper. At intervals, he'd lash the adjacent piece of suede, checking that the cracker on the end barely raised the nap.

What was there about the crack of a whip that was so erotic?

His phone rang. After finishing his swing—only a fool pulled a stroke—he took the cell from his pocket. A private number. His gut tightened as he answered. "Sandoval."

"Raoul, it's nice to hear your voice. This is Dahmer...the Overseer. Is this a good time to talk, or should I call back?"

"Your timing is excellent." Raoul reminded himself of what must be brought up. The location. Referring Sam.

"How is the merchandise working out? Any problems?"

Raoul forced a laugh. "Well enough, although buying...used...wasn't my smartest choice. The previous owner left some dents."

"Not surprising. The prior owner has a temper. But I'm happy everything else is good."

"Yes. In fact—"

Dahmer cleared his throat. "Phones are—"

"Not a problem." Paranoid bastard, as Buchanan had said. "I have a friend who admired the merchandise. He's rough on his playthings and hopes to purchase something sturdier."

"Well." A pause. "We do have an upcoming event. Perhaps if he qualifies, he might attend."

"He'd enjoy that."

"As I did with you, I'll need to see your friend in action. It decreases the chances of...ah...unexpected visitors."

He meant cops. "Speaking as a buyer, I appreciate the precautions."

"Is there a location you prefer? Your house or a Tampa club?"

Raoul didn't want to foul his home with Dahmer's presence, yet taking Kimberly to a regular BDSM club with no safeguards in place was totally unacceptable. A few days ago, he'd discussed an alternative with Buchanan and Kouros...and then Z. "Since public clubs are noisy, perhaps you would be my guest at the Shadowlands?"

"The Shadowlands." Dahmer paused. "I'd like that. The club has an amazing reputation."

"Well deserved."

"About the audition scene you planned to do at this visit…"

"Yes?" Raoul's hand tightened on the phone. He'd hoped Dahmer would have forgotten. How to blow him off?

"The master scheduled to do the fireplay demonstration this month is unavailable, and I've had difficulty finding fireplay scenes erotic enough for our buyers. Someone mentioned you give a fine show."

*Someone.* Would that be the bastard who had scoped out submissives from the Shadowlands for the slavers to kidnap? Raoul's jaw clenched. "Good to hear."

"For your audition, I'd like to see a fireplay scene with your new toy. If you do as well as I've heard, I'll book you for the coming auction."

*The coming auction.* Raoul paced across the room, thinking. He wouldn't be on a waiting list. Since Sam might not be cleared as a buyer, this might be the best chance to get a person into the auction. But what about Kimberly? Raoul stared at the bullwhip and wished Dahmer was close enough to serve as a target.

If Kimberly could manage the scene in the Shadowlands, the FBI could find an agent to play his submissive at the auction. It might work. *Agree now; back out later if needed.* "A fireplay scene it is. The Shadowlands is open Friday and Saturday. Which night suits you?"

"Let me check my calendar." Silence. "Next Saturday would be good. Ten o'clock?"

"Fine. We'll meet you in the parking lot and go in together." Raoul punched the Off button. He tightened his grip on the bullwhip. A crack, and he slashed through every layer of newspaper.

* * * *

Master R had been awfully quiet since yesterday, Kim thought as she took her beach walk. Was something wrong?

Had he gotten upset that she'd retreated to her private sitting room right after Gabi's visit? But after talking some fears over with her friend, she'd needed to regroup. Maybe Gabi had told him to give her time alone?

He hadn't seemed upset at supper last night. Just silent.

Still, before bed, he'd read "his" designated page in her journal and laughed at her insulting description of his temper. He'd hugged her for sharing how she felt like a piece of meat in the *inspect* position. So he probably wasn't upset with her. If anything, he'd been gentler than normal. Sweeter. Snugglier.

Okay, she wouldn't worry until he told her she needed to. Instead, she took a breath, enjoying the tang of the salt air. In the distance, laughing gulls circled over something on the shore, squabbling and diving. Farther out, pelicans flew in a line, probably heading toward Clearwater.

The air off the water tugged at her T-shirt, blew her hair in her face, and lightened the humid heat a little. The wind off the Atlantic in Savannah was much more effective. She remembered the welcome ocean breeze when she'd go out on the trawler with her father. Her father…

She frowned, remembering Master R's questions about him. Had she ever run to Father for comfort? Hardly. He'd been a gruff man, dark in both nature and appearance. His Native American mother had gifted him black hair and wide cheekbones; his father had left him the fishing boat.

She shoved her hands into the pockets of her shorts. His life had revolved around the trawler, and until her rebellion, so had hers. But she'd hated how horribly he treated Mom. *"Fat cow." "Can't do anything right." "Stupid as a stump."* Mom had worked like a…a slave for him, and he never said thank you. Never noticed unless something wasn't perfect.

One day, Kim had yelled at him for calling Mom names. He'd backhanded her into the wall. After that, Kim stopped pretending to be his *son.* She'd gone out for cheerleading, worn makeup and pretty clothes. He'd called her a whore and a stupid slut. God, she'd hated him sometimes.

She stopped and frowned at a small sand castle. A red bucket lay nearby. High walls, a moat around it. No bridge. Smart kid. Keep the world out and stay within. Much safer that way.

Kim turned and headed back, shaking her head. Odd how she'd hated her father, yet her mother never had. It had taken Mom years to regain her independence and stop doubting everything she did. They'd both worked their asses off after he'd died, drunk, in a car wreck. The stab of pain hit her unexpectedly. His life had been the stupid trawler, and when the boat had died, so had he. Mom hadn't been enough to live for. Neither had Kim. Hell, they were only women. Slaves.

*Not slaves.* Mom was an office manager at a real estate firm now, and Kim was a marine biologist. *So there, Father. We're better off without you.* That hurt too. Mom should have…have left him, shouldn't have taken his abuse.

How could a wife suffer as many restraints as a collared slave?

Kim snorted. *And gee, look at me now. I'm a slave, just like you were, Mom.*

When she returned to the house, Master R would put those cuffs on her wrists. And she'd feel torn. Like she wanted them. Hated them.

She sometimes hated him too, but she was starting to want him more. Need him. She worked to win his smile, loved it when he laughed.

*Don't go down that liking path, Kim.* First, he was just doing what had to be done to get the slavers. Second, he'd want his girlfriend to be a slave. *That's so not me. So, Ms. Romantic, do not get attached. He's another team member like the FBI agents. Clear?*

She looked up at the house and stopped.

Master R stood at the foot of the steps to the beach, leaning back on the railing, arms crossed on his chest. Just watching her.

That was nothing new, but the way her heart leaped... Now that was a problem. *Dammit, heart, didn't we just have a talk? Weren't you listening?*

She detoured around the weathered chair on the shore and paced toward him, trying to ignore the delight fizzing in her veins like frothy surf. When she reached him, she dropped to her knees, in exactly the correct position, and bowed her head.

"*Muy bonita*," he murmured, stroking her hair. "You are so very pretty." He grasped her arms and lifted her to her feet with that effortless strength that took her breath away. "Now, I need to talk with you."

Wasn't that what a man said to his wife when he was going to ask for a divorce? *Honey, we have to talk*? She grinned. At least, not being married, she'd sidestepped that one. "Yes, Sir?"

"The Overseer called yesterday."

"The—" Her knees buckled. He tightened his hands on her arms and held her up, his brown eyes steady on her face. A cold sweat broke out over her skin, and her heart raced until her chest hurt, hurt bad. Maybe she was having a heart attack, and her air was all gone and—

He shook her once, making her head jerk on her shoulders. "Kimberly!"

She gasped in a breath, then moaned as her eyes fixed on the house. *He'd come here. Maybe he was already here.* Her lungs squeezed down again.

"Look. At. Me." Each word was accompanied by a ruthless shake.

Her gaze returned to his face.

"There. Much nicer." He smiled, the tiny lines beside his eyes crinkling. "Did you know your nose is pink?"

"Have you gone crazy?"

"Have you gone crazy, *Master*." Still gripping her arms, he bounced her, obviously testing if her legs would hold her up. "I'm perfectly sane, thank you. Kimberly, we meet him at the Shadowlands next Saturday for drinks. For a civilized conversation. He's not going to run amok and slaughter the club members like chickens."

His bland tone made her choke on a laugh, but she gave him a dark look. "So little you know." Her legs started to work, and she stood under her own power.

He leaned against the railing again, clasping her waist and pulling her between his long legs as he liked to do. Why did that make her feel safe instead of trapped? His eyes were level. Intent. "There's something else, gatita. We will do a scene at the Shadowlands. A fi—" He broke off and said, "An erotic one."

She was the *Titanic* hitting an underwater iceberg. Hulled. Sinking into the freezing water. "A scene?" In front of the Overseer? The burn of anger—of betrayal—drove the ice away. She hit his wide chest, once, then over and over. "No. No. No!"

His hands were still around her waist; he didn't move as she pounded on him.

Her fists slowed. "No," she whispered. She'd agreed

only to pretend to be his slave, not to do a scene with him. But then she saw the tightness of his jaw. Not anger— unhappiness. She pulled in a shuddering breath. "Tell me why."

He curved his hand around her nape in support. Comfort. "During my initial interview, Dahmer said they bring in people to do scenes for the entertainment of the buyers, and I thought that might be another way to get into an auction. The night I bought you, I agreed to an audition during the follow-up visit."

"I vaguely remember hearing you." But she'd hurt badly enough that their conversation was a blur. Vance had mentioned it at Gabi's house too. "There's a waiting list though."

He sighed. "That's the problem. He wants someone for this coming auction. If Sam's referral falls through, this might be the only chance to get in. I'd use an FBI agent at the auction, not you. But next weekend"—his jaw tightened—"Dahmer expects to see you."

*Me. Do a scene. With the Overseer watching.*

Master R started to speak, and she pulled away. "Just...just give me a minute, okay?"

He nodded, and she walked toward the waves. A few tiny plovers skittered in front of her, their bird feet leaving shallow tracks on the sand.

*Okay, Kim, put it all in order.* Neatly. First, he wanted her to do the scene this weekend but wasn't planning to make her attend the auction. Good.

The original plan had always been for the Overseer to see her. That was the point of the follow-up visit. Doing a scene with Master R wouldn't be that different, would it?

Only he'd said *erotic.* That meant...his hands on her. Arousing her. She hugged herself against the cooling breeze. He'd been touching her, washing her. Intimate but never sexual. He often kissed her. *I do pretty good with all that.*

Actually, sometimes she almost wanted more, but then she'd freeze. Really, she just wanted to stay celibate and icicle cold for a while. A few years.

If Master R refused to audition, how could he justify it? They'd be at a BDSM club. And she'd be there. No excuse came to mind, since no slaver would care if his property had the jitters.

She scuffled the sand over her toes, letting the warmth sink into her skin. Could she do this?

Well, a lot of her fears concerned the Overseer, but she'd put those in a mental box. *Stay closed, box.* So what was really bothering her?

She stared at the rain clouds forming into a mass. Her nerves were because Master R would be touching her. Deliberately trying to arouse her. In front of people. The Overseer.

He'd never gone sexual on her before—what if she panicked? Let him down? It'd almost...almost be easier if he'd actually done some of that intimate stuff, like that day in the weight room. She shivered, remembering the feel of his fingers between her legs, pushing inside her. She'd been wet.

The waves lapped at her toes as she walked. She watched how the water gave way to her feet, and yet the same substance carved canyons in the earth. Strength could be found in the determination to get where a person needed to go. In just keeping on.

*I need to go home, and that means I need the slavers in jail.* She had to keep on.

Master R was still waiting when she walked back to him. He waited even longer for her to speak.

"I understand why we should do the scene." She swallowed, tasting the briny air. "I'm scared I might panic."

His eyes filled with tenderness. "Is there anything that would help?"

"I think you'd better...touch me some. Before." Her face heated, her blush a dead giveaway as to what she meant. Six days until then. Maybe she'd be ready.

"I think you're probably right." His lips curved, and he stroked a finger down her hot cheek. "It will be my pleasure."

*Oh boy.*

\* \* \* \*

Kimberly bent over, trying to catch her breath, sweat dripping from her face and trickling between her bare breasts. Her sadistic, nasty master had increased the length of her workout today, for which she was maybe a little grateful. Since yesterday when he'd told her about the Shadowlands scene, the hours dragged as if to build her dread to a mountain she couldn't climb. Over breakfast, Master R had assigned her a long list of tasks and complicated meals. He obviously planned to keep her too busy to think. He'd even put her to work in his home office this morning.

Major eye-opener. With such a beautiful beach house, he couldn't be poor, but the dom owned an international engineering company. When she wondered how he could take so much time off, he smiled and said if employees couldn't handle the work, why hire them?

She was grateful he worked from here. Knowing he was in the house let her relax.

His calmness helped too. He never got frazzled. Not that he was particularly easygoing—his Latin temper showed, especially when they talked about the slavers.

But he didn't worry about little stuff or things he couldn't do anything about.

She was a worrier. And worse, she wanted to do things perfectly so she could get approval from—she scowled—from her father and everyone else.

Master R didn't expect perfection from her. Just her best, and he'd push her until he got it.

In his office, he had a framed calligraphy on the wall. *"Strive for perfection in everything you do. Take the best that exists and make it better. When it does not exist, design it."* *Sir Henry Royce.* Yeah, that was so her master who was also an engineer.

He never made her guess if she'd pleased him. If she did, he showed it. If she didn't, he told her how to do better. She never had to worry about clothes or her performance or even what to do next.

Or how to deal with...interpersonal relations.

Dating had always been a nightmare. From questions of clothing: *What should I wear to look pretty but not like a slut. Should I dress up? Or would it be better to look casual?*

To behavior: *Should I touch him? Let him hold my hand? Ask him in for a drink, or would he think I'm easy? Sleep with him on the second or third date or not? Let him grope my ass on the dance floor, or does that make me look like a slut?*

But here, Master R picked out her clothes—or made her stay naked. Choice over.

For behavior? He decided what he wanted from her and said so. No decisions to make. That was so restful.

And boy, he definitely decided how interpersonal stuff would go. Last night, he'd pushed her into the pool. When she'd surfaced, trying not to spit curses at him, he'd said they'd play tag. Every time she caught him, she could claim a kiss. If she took too long to catch him, he'd spank her. *Great incentive.*

Chasing after him—and he didn't make it easy—made

touching fun. Not scary. After she caught him a few times, she was definitely aroused. Damn, the man could kiss. Then he upped the stakes to "copping a feel," only whenever she put her hands on him, he duplicated her movements, putting his hands on her. She was giggling and hot and—

"Stop daydreaming and do it all again." Master R's sexy baritone made her straighten.

He was lying on the weight bench and not even looking at her. His dom radar always told him when she slacked off. *Drown him in high seas anyway.*

She watched him push the bar up. Giant metal plates clanked on each end, and his chest muscles and biceps bunched and turned to granite under his tank. God, she could almost see testosterone oozing from his pores instead of sweat.

"Kimberly."

"Yes, Master." She launched into the last street-fighting combination he'd taught her. Block, knuckles to the Adam's apple, other hand—fingers to the eyes. One-two. She saw the fat guard on the floor, screaming in pain. She did it again. And again.

Until she tripped and landed on her hands and knees. "Suck water," she muttered.

"The last move appeared a bit clumsy." Lying on his back, he was watching.

She giggled and sat her bare butt on the rubber matt, pushing back the hair that had escaped her braid. "How come you're so good at all this? You said from street fighting?"

"You're stalling." But he sat up, wiping his forehead with the towel. "We lived in a rough area when I grew up. When my brother joined a gang, he taught me what he learned from them."

*Brother*? She frowned. He'd talked of a sister and his

mother. "I don't remember you mentioning a brother."

His face—so sad. Before she considered, she'd joined him on the bench. She put her arms around him and then froze, thinking she'd overstepped her bounds.

But he pulled her in, holding her tightly, his cheek against the top of her head. After a minute, he sighed. "Thank you, gatita. I needed a hug."

"What happened?" She stayed, not letting go.


RAOUL DIDN'T WANT to talk about the past. Not in the least. The ache of loss—of guilt—never went away.

"It still bothers you." She rubbed her head on his shoulder. Naked little submissive trying to comfort her master—she awed him with her courage and care. "Share with me, Master."

*Share.* She wanted openness. Honesty. They might be doing this to capture the slavers, but the bond of trust between them was real. He'd required she share her emotions and had pushed her to tears when needed. He could give her no less in return.

"He died." His arms tightened for a second, before he regained control. "He was only fifteen. I was twelve and thought he was God and followed him everywhere." Mamá had yelled at Manuel, told him gangs were bad. "His gang was outnumbered in a street fight with another gang. Manuel told me to hide." Raoul had obeyed, then peeked out from the pile of empty grocery boxes, the stench of rotted fruit surrounding him, his heart hammering enough to choke him.

"Twelve. God, you were a baby."

He frowned. "Old enough. I should have"— *forced Manuel to leave, gotten the cops, fought beside him*—"Three of them attacked Manuel." They seemed huge, knives flashing, yelling curses in Spanish. A knife opened Manuel's arm, his T-shirt ripping, red running down his wrist. Raoul hit the knife-wielder from behind, knocking the boy to his knees. But another backhanded him like a fly into the garbage. "I tried. Dios, I tried to get them away from him." Scrambling up, punching, kicking, it was as if he wasn't even there. They'd surrounded Manuel, cutting him from behind every time he turned to fight one. Raoul yelled, grabbed a gangster's arm, bit down. "They knocked me away, concentrating on him. Nothing I did helped."

"You couldn't have been that big, not at twelve."

"Skinny. Weak. I liked books. I was useless to him." He'd crawled back the last time, crying, grabbing one's leg, and hanging on. Manuel had stabbed that one. Raoul had felt the blow through the gangster's body, the shudder of pain. When he tried to scramble away, a brutal kick in the gut laid him out. He couldn't breathe. More came, stepping on him on the way past. He'd heard his brother scream. That high scream—not a man's voice. So young. Too young. "By the time I got to my feet, Manuel was dead."

"Oh, that's horrible. You were only babies. But you tried to help."

Blood everywhere. So many cuts. He'd failed his brother. Been useless. Weak. *Never again.* Once his injuries had healed, he'd traded his bike for a set of weights.

Her arms clamped around him, holding him as if she could keep him together, her fears pushed aside. Sweet gatita. He rubbed his cheek in her soft hair and said, "So I know how it feels to be weaker, sumisita, and not able to fight back. When I got my first job, my money went for self-defense lessons. I searched for the nastiest street-fighting teachers I could find."

"That's what you're teaching me."

"That and getting you strong enough to use it."

She pulled back, glancing around the weight room. "You work out almost every day. Does that mean you still feel guilty, like you let him down?"

He stiffened at her slicing accuracy. "Maybe." He hadn't been able to save, to protect. "Sí."

"You're such an idiot!" She shook him, actually shook him. "You were twelve. And outnumbered. Even if you'd been huge, could you really have won?"

Raoul frowned. Looking at the fight from a more experienced viewpoint, he knew there had been too many. No matter what he might have done, they'd have killed Manuel. "No."

She rubbed her cheek on his shoulder. "You know, if you'd been older, they'd probably have killed you. Your mom would have lost two sons."

A clever blow. His mamá—bearing the death of one child had been enough. Raoul sighed. He doubted the guilt would go away completely, but it had lightened. He stroked a finger down her cheek. "Thank you, gatita. For the hug...and the insight."

She smiled at him. The tears in her eyes were for him and Manuel.

Had he ever known anyone as sweet? However... "You still have to practice for another fifteen minutes."

Her sigh was expressive.

Trying not to grin, he kissed her pouting lips. "No more stalling."

BEFORE STARTING EACH set of blocks and strikes, Kim visualized her opponent. For the first time, Lord Greville and the Overseer had company, ugly street toughs who'd kicked a little twelve-year-old. Killed his brother. Who'd left him with so much guilt it radiated like heat waves from him. Scum-sucking jerkwads. She worked out silently, furiously, until she had to put her hands on her knees and pant to get her breath back.

A chuckle. Master R pointed to the bare floor around her. "I think they are all dead, gatita. Good job."

She grinned. "Thank you. I'm ready for a new set of—"

The doorbell rang.

Shaking his head at the way she'd frozen in place, Master R said, "Don't worry, cariño. It's only a special messenger delivering your clothes for this weekend." He pointed at the shorts and loose top she'd worn for Faith's visit. "Put those on and come out and meet him."

*Him.* "You're sure?" Her voice shook, and she bit her lip.

He didn't give her trouble over questioning him. "You've got two minutes to dress. We'll be in the great room." After tugging on her braid, he walked out.

Two minutes? She wiped down with a towel and dragged on her clothing, then hurried down the hall. Master R had taken his usual seat on the big leather sofa. A dark-haired man sat across from him. Expensively tailored black slacks and black silky shirt. A little older, maybe forties. He rose as she entered.

"Z, sit down," Master R chided. "She's in training."

"Indeed, I forgot." The man smiled and resumed his seat.

Staying well out of the stranger's reach, Kim sidled over to Master R. She knelt very, very gracefully at his feet and lowered her head. He made the tiny noise he used for approval, and she relaxed.

"Z, this is Kimberly." Master R stroked her hair. "Gatita, this is Master Z. He owns the Shadowlands and is Jessica's master."

Oooh, this was the creative dom who managed to keep feisty Jessica in line. She looked up and had to wonder if the silvering hair at his temples had been caused by his sub.

He studied her in turn, his gray eyes seeming to slide

into her soul. She pressed closer to Master R's legs. "You're doing very well," he told Master R, which seemed strange since she hadn't done anything to elicit his opinion.

"I hear you're visiting my Shadowlands this weekend, little one. I brought you a present." With a faint smile, he held a brown paper bag out to her.

A present? She started to reach for it, paused, and glanced at Master R first. He nodded permission, so she rose and brought the package back and then knelt again.

"Open it," Master R said.

*A present.* She gave the strange dom a suspicious look. *If this is a flogger, I'm heading for the bathroom and locking the door.*

It wasn't a flogger. She pulled out a very short silk satin dress, black with white lace at the bottom and top. A tiny heart-shaped white apron. *What the...?* Hey, he'd brought her a French maid's costume. A pricey one.

Master R checked the bag and removed white fishnet stockings. "Nice." His smile included her as he told Z, "Neither of us was comfortable with her being naked in front of the Overseer. This should work perfectly."

Her eyes stung, and she hastily lowered her head. She hadn't told Master R, but the dread of that had made her sick a couple of times. The maid's outfit was skimpy, but even a small amount of clothing made a difference. Master R had known. He'd felt that way too. *A breath. Two.* She managed to give her thanks to Master Z.

His gray eyes softened. "You're very welcome, Kimberly." He turned his gaze back to Master R. "I brought something else. I understand you might not be comfortable with this, but I believe it's necessary." He handed a second bag to Master R.

Master R opened it, and his jaw tightened until she could see the rigid tendon in his cheek. He stared at the other man.

*Oh boy.* Kim didn't move a muscle. If he turned that look on her, she'd melt into a terrified puddle on the floor.

Master Z merely chuckled. "It's just leather, Raoul. And if you're not going to go with a standard naked slave, you need to make your ownership very clear. Kimberly, what do you think?"

He'd asked her a question? She peeked at Master R.

His fury had disappeared, leaving weariness behind. He upended the bag over the coffee table and a variety of...of slave collars spilled out. Studded dog collars, ones with D-rings and chains, thinner ones with padlocks, a thick silver one that looked horribly uncomfortable, a dark red leather, a black leather with silver decorations.

*Never.* The thought of one going around her neck made her stomach turn over. Never. Absolutely never would she let... Her thoughts jerked to a halt. *"Make your ownership very clear,"* Master Z had said. The Overseer would be at the Shadowlands. Looking at her. But no one touched a collared master's slave.

She swallowed, straightened her shoulders, and faced Master R. "I think I'd like to make it obvious to everyone— to h-him—that you own me." She laid her fingers on the black leather collar, feeling as if she touched a snake. "This would go best with the outfit."

Master R watched her for a second, eyes dark and unreadable, then gave Master Z a cold look. *"Hijo de puta."*

"I know, Raoul." Z glanced at his watch and rose. "My time's up, and I have an appointment." He smiled at Master R. "As we tell our subs all too often, what you want and what you need aren't necessarily the same thing."

Master R walked him out and returned, the cold still in his eyes.

Kimberly tried not to flinch. If he was mad, she

wouldn't be able—

"I'm sorry," he said, looking down at her. "My anger is from the past and nothing to do with you. Why don't you run upstairs and shower? Take some time for yourself."

"I'd like that." She rose and bowed her head. "Thank you, Master, for your care."

He made a noise as if she'd slapped him instead of thanking him. Then he sighed and stroked her hair. "Go, sumisita."

# Chapter Eight

On Tuesday, muggy evening air formed a damp cloak over Raoul's skin as he took a seat on the patio. The outdoor lights flickered on, and the pool turned a clear blue around the young woman swimming laps. Kimberly looked strong and healthy. And she was never happier than when near the water. That was why he'd created erotic pool tag for her, and why their protracted make-out time last night had been on the beach.

He stretched his legs out. Aside from scenes in the club, how long had it been since he'd kissed and fondled a woman without making love to her later? Years? Even longer since he'd been so uncomfortable he had to jerk off in the shower. But his gatita had a stronger effect on him than any woman before.

She'd become nicely hot last night. He'd concentrated on her breasts, venturing lower at times. Over the past weeks, she'd become accustomed to his hands, but not to having him deliberately arousing her. When she'd started to panic, he'd stopped and held her, and she'd quieted. She looked to him for comfort now, and that pleased him...perhaps too much. He shouldn't get attached to this woman. When the slavers were no longer a threat, she'd return to her own life.

It would be difficult to let her go. He liked having her curled in his arms, showering with her, teaching her weight lifting and fighting. She was as affectionate and fun as the kitten he called her, and her need to give was spiced with a delightful temper.

She'd changed in her time with him. As she'd grown comfortable with his commands, she'd also acquired a submissive's trait of always being aware of her master, as he was aware of her. He'd forgotten the beauty of the constant perception between a dominant and his submissive.

Because of Alicia. His mouth flattened at the bitter taste brought by the memory of his marriage. He and Alicia had been happy at first, master and slave. Things had changed. Much was his fault. Having had a slave before, he knew—thought he knew—what a relationship required. Too in love to be cautious, he'd yielded to Alicia's pleas and jumped right in. Husband and master.

But he hadn't married a slave.

With one hand on the edge of the pool, Kimberly stopped to catch her breath. She saw him watching, waited a second in case he wanted her, then launched into another lap. Determined little submissive.

Alicia hadn't been submissive at all. New to BDSM, she hadn't realized that submission didn't punch her buttons; pain did. After they figured it out, he hadn't tried to continue as her master, but had hoped they could still have a good life together. *Foolish Sandoval.*

*And* when she'd betrayed him, she'd changed his memories of what had been good into something ugly. Then she'd gone one step further and turned his family against him by revealing his lifestyle.

Raoul tilted his head back. The setting sun was a red gleam along the horizon, disappearing as if washed away by the waves. A shame that memories didn't disappear so easily. Eventually...someday...he'd get into a Dominant/ submissive relationship, would love someone again. But, like a ripped muscle, his desire to launch into a new relationship had been weakened, wasn't ready to bear the burden. Until then, he was content with the casual relationships he had with various submissives.

The streak of light slowly disappeared, leaving only gray ocean meeting the dark sky.

A splash drew his gaze to where Kimberly had climbed out of the pool. She dried herself off and came over to kneel at his feet, cleverly bringing the towel to protect her knees from the concrete. Smart gatita. Her eyes were down, her body relaxed.

He smiled in satisfaction. Her first week she'd been constantly braced for a blow. Now her fears appeared in response to something new he proposed, but not until then. She trusted him.

Yes, he would miss her. It was good she wouldn't be with him much longer.

"There's a bottle of wine chilling in the refrigerator," he said. "Why don't you bring it into the living room? Two glasses. We'll watch a movie."

"Yes, Master."

When had her stutter disappeared? As she rose smoothly and headed for the kitchen, he remembered he wanted to add dance back to her day's routines. He'd enjoy watching her.

In the living room, he checked the end table drawer— no, the little minx hadn't found the toys he'd left there—and flipped off the lights except for the wall sconces.

Kimberly walked in a minute later. She set the tray on the coffee table, poured a glass of wine, then knelt and offered up the drink.

"Thank you, chiquita. That's beautifully done." He smoothed her hair, the ends damp from the pool, although she'd had it pinned on top of her head. Her skin was still glowing from her exercise. Her breasts were filling out, and her abs and thighs showed muscle definition. Pretty sumisa, now comfortable with her nakedness in his presence. "You may pour yourself a glass as well."

"Yes, Master. Thank you." She started to say something and hesitated.

"Go on. This is our room to relax together, so you may speak freely. Although respectfully would be in your best interests." He touched her nose, and she wrinkled it at him. "What were you going to say?"

"I haven't had wine since—since before."

"Well, I hope you like this one then." He took a sip and approved. "One of the Shadowlands' submissives became engaged last month, and her mother brought out a crate of California wines as a present for her son-in-law-to-be." A bribe to delay the wedding a month so she could help plan it. Nolan had been kind enough to share a couple of bottles.

Kimberly tried the wine, and a pleased smile lit her face. "It's really good."

Raoul walked over to the dark walnut entertainment center to decide on a movie. Just to get a reaction, he pulled out a World War II film. "Maybe some battles?"

"Ugh. How about *Runaway Bride?*" She burst into laughter at his expression. "*Miss Congeniality?* She's an FBI agent. You should like that."

When he shook his head in disgust, her giggles bubbled over like champagne. Was this what she had been like before her trauma? What kind of people would damage someone so bright? So sparkling with energy. He should have been there to protect her.

He cleared his throat. "Perhaps we should watch a Chuck Norris film. You can take notes and learn something of fighting?"

*FIGHTING? SUCH A typical man.* "Well, maybe we should watch chick flicks. You can learn more about women." Kim grinned. *That should get him.*

Master R raised his eyebrows and stepped close enough that her bare breasts rubbed on his shirt. Her nipples bunched in reaction.

"Do you feel my knowledge of women is lacking, gatita?" he asked softly. His dark eyes caught hers and held...held as every bone in her body turned into melted butter, and the promise in his gaze blanked her mind. When he cupped her chin and kissed her, so gently, lingering for a second before he retreated, her nerves started to fire in random bursts. "Kimberly? I asked you a question."

"Mmm?" *Question: Did she think he needed to know anything more about women? If he did, God help them all.* "Um." She shook her head, trying to throw off the sensual haze. Her nipples throbbed. "Perhaps not."

He chuckled and handed her a DVD. "How about this one? *Chocolat.*"

That was a strange choice. She blinked and nodded.

"Very good." He inserted the DVD, took his place on the leather sofa, and patted the cushion beside him.

Snuggling against him, as he liked—and she'd started to really like—she sipped her wine and watched the film.

"I know women go crazy over chocolate," Master R said after a bit, "almost as much as men obsess about sex." He pulled her onto his lap, leaning her back against his left arm. She stiffened, then relaxed. "Since you'll enjoy a chocolate movie more than me, I should get a treat for every time they eat candy."

"Your logic isn't—"

He cupped her face with his free hand, and his lips took hers, lightly in the way she'd grown used to. Then his tongue stroked insistently. He tasted of wine and of himself. Her hands curled around his forearm as heat rose inside her.

Lifting his head, he smiled down in her eyes. When he tried to move his hand, she realized she still clung to his arm and had to force her fingers open.

Shifting slightly, making her fully aware of the erection pressing against her bare bottom, he refilled her glass. She tried to check his, but it was behind her, on the end table. After handing over her drink, he resumed watching the movie. Jerk.

Before Kim had more than a few sips, the heroine talked someone into sampling her wares, and Master R kissed her again.

*How much chocolate do they eat in this movie?*

A lot. Each kiss grew more drugging, wetter, deeper. No longer teasing, he took her mouth hard, ravaging until her toes curled and heat flushed her skin.

She felt the wetness growing between her legs. Her fingers tangled in his black hair; her other hand pressed against his chest and the iron muscles that flexed as he lifted her closer.

When he raised his head, his eyes were half-lidded with his passion. He smiled slightly and paused the movie. "I have a couple of toys to add to the evening. Stand up, please."

Toys? When a man—a dom—said toys, he didn't mean stuffed animals or baseballs. A shiver ran through her. His eyes narrowed in warning. She jumped to her feet.

He pulled a package out of the end table's drawer. "Open." He patted her thighs lightly to have her widen her stance, but this time he kept tapping until her legs were so far apart that she rocked unsteadily. "You may hold on to my shoulders to keep your balance."

She rested her hands on his hard, hard shoulders, her loose hair falling over her arms. Her pussy felt open. Exposed. Oh God, what was he going to do? She bit her lip, trying to remember she'd asked for this. *"Touch me some,"* she'd said. *You're an idiot, Kim.* Her fingers dug into his skin.

"Good girl." The package held a small bullet vibrator. He slickened it in her wetness—and she realized she was very, very wet.

She had an instant of fear as his calloused fingers touched her so intimately, and then with a smooth move, he pushed the toy inside her vagina.

At her gasp, he looked up, studying her for a second, his hand still between her legs. His dark brown eyes held lust but also concern...for her. As he watched her, his finger traced through her folds, spreading the wetness, establishing that...that he could. Marking his ownership.

Her body tingled, top to bottom, with his slow stroking.

"Good sumisa," he murmured. He patted her thigh, indicating she could stand up straight. Her thighs closed over her swollen, throbbing labia.

"Now put these on." From the drawer, he brought out a black lace thong.

What an odd choice. As she pulled the thong on, she noticed something firm in the crotch. *What the?* She opened her mouth, and he shook his head no.

He set his glass of wine and two small boxes on the coffee table and pulled it closer. Resting his back against the sofa arm, he stretched out with his legs on the cushions. "Now sit here—silently—and we'll watch the rest of the movie."

She could feel the bullet inside her. The thing in the thong rubbed on her pussy as he took her hand and pulled her onto his lap. He leaned her shoulders against his chest, her legs between his. His thick erection pressed against her bottom, and her breath stopped. Then started. This was

Master R.

He put her glass of wine in her hand and resumed the movie.

Five minutes. As she relaxed, she found she liked leaning against him. A rather lumpy chair rest, but warm. He had his right arm around her waist, and the coffee table was close enough he could pick up his glass of wine with his other hand. She told herself she wasn't nervous—*I'm handling this quite well, really*—despite the quivers in her stomach and the way her mind kept replaying how he'd touched her pussy. After trying to sip, she realized her glass was empty. She frowned at it.

Even his chuckle seemed to have a Spanish accent. "You have no reason to be nervous...yet, sumisita," he whispered in her ear and filled her glass. As she took it, he kissed her ear, sending goose bumps racing down her arms. And she was feeling the effect of the wine—not drunk, but...comfortable.

As he leaned back again, somehow he'd moved so the dark hair on his forearm tickled the undersides of her breasts.

On the big-screen TV, a man saw his wife on her knees, scrubbing a bathroom. He looked at her butt in the air and walked forward, his intent very clear.

"Perhaps you should clean the bathroom on your knees," Master R murmured. The thought of him coming up behind her, bending over her... She took a slow breath.

He ran his finger over her naked stomach, making the muscles quiver, then reached sideways and picked up one of the little boxes.

The vibrator inside her came to life with a low buzz. She jumped at the weird sensation. Her wine sloshed in the glass, and his arm tightened around her ribs.

"It is not hurting you, gatita," he said soothingly.

"Relax and watch the movie. I will quiz you on the plot later."

"What?"

That earned her a nip on her ear. "Silence."

The vibrator buzzed inside her, making her...aware...but not rousing her nearly as much as the feeling of Master R's arm so close to her breasts, his cheek resting on her hair, the sensation of his chest moving under her with each breath.

The buzz stopped, and she relaxed. Johnny Depp appeared, and the movie revved up much like her arousal. What did Master R have planned? She'd probably be okay with it, but damn, she wished she knew.

He set his wine down on the coffee table, and a second later, the lump in her thong hummed. It was a vibrator too, and oh God, it was almost against her clit. Her muscles tensed.

She froze completely when he reached around her, traced his fingers up her pussy, and resettled the vibrator directly on her clit.

Oh God, she couldn't ignore that, not when he cupped her mound, pressing the vibrator into her. "Nooo." It hummed on her, tightening her muscles, sending panicky feelings running through her.

"Yes." He removed his hand from her pussy and took her wineglass before she spilled it. "Give me a number."

Number for what? *Fear.* She started to speak, then remembered to show it, like he'd ordered. Six fingers—no, not really. A slow breath. Three fingers.

"Very good. Are you watching the movie?"

The thong vibrator stopped, leaving her clit tight, hard, as if the vibrations still continued. "Y-yes, Sir."

His laugh rumbled in her ear. "Aren't you a good girl."

They were going to make love tonight. She knew it. Or

maybe not. He was devious. She'd expected him to take her in bed the last two nights, and he'd held off, teasing her in the pool one night, on the shore the next. Leaving her scared yet aching with need and wanting more of his touch.

*I want this from him. I want to move on—to get past being afraid.*

He stroked her stomach, brushed his hand against the undersides of her breasts, trailed down under the black lace to her mound. Then lower, his fingers touching the beginning of her cleft. "You're being very obedient, keeping yourself shaved for me. I like how nice and smooth you are, Kimberly." His finger never moved lower, just teased the top. Her clit seemed to throb as if begging for a touch. His touch.

He took a sip of wine and set the glass down on the coffee table. The vibrator inside her came on, jolting her hips up. With his hand on her mound, he pressed her back down. His palm was on her pubic bone, and he fanned his fingers out, tiny touches over her pussy. The vibrations weren't enough to get her off, but he'd turned the intensity higher.

"Ah, you feel it this time, don't you, gatita?" he murmured in her ear. "Look how pretty." His hand closed over her breast lightly, and she could feel the stiffness of her nipples. Bunched and aching. He ran his finger around each one.

"You are to be watching the movie, *mi pequeña sumisa.*"

Heat simmered under her skin as she tried to obey, but everything the actors did on the screen, even the way they bit into the chocolate pieces, made her hotter.

"Kissing you is difficult now," he murmured, "but this will serve instead." He rolled her right nipple between his fingers, and the edgy pain on the sensitive peak blazed fire straight to her pussy.

When Johnny Depp ate another candy, Master R rolled her left nipple. Kim moaned. Hunger pulsed in her bloodstream, and it sure wasn't for chocolate.

The inside vibrator turned off.

She sagged against him, let out a sigh, but the thong vibrator started. "Damn you!" *Oh, oh shit.* "I'm sorry, Sir. Master. Please..."

"You are certainly grumpy at being aroused, aren't you?" The amusement in his voice didn't help her nerves any. Not knowing what a wicked sense of humor he had. "How should I discipline you, gatita?" His fingers tightened on her nipple in a stinging pinch, then moved to the other. Pain...need shot straight to her pussy. Her hips tried to rise, but his right hand stayed firmly on her mound, just above the vibrator. He fondled each breast, making soft circles around the areolae and then squeezing her nipples. Tugging. Rolling. He had her trapped, leaving her no choice but to accept whatever he wanted to do.

The vibrator hummed against her, bringing her up, teasing her, never quite enough. Nothing was enough. She was in his arms, being touched, using vibrators, and still not getting off.

She'd probably never get off again. The thought dropped her mood, and she sagged against him, her arousal seeping away.

His hands stilled. He kissed her hair. "Well, since you don't like the thong, you may remove it."

Her lips quivered, and tears stung her eyes. He'd given up on her too. Because he knew how hopeless it was.

He pushed her to her feet, stood beside her, and waited until she set the thong on the coffee table.

As he studied her, his gaze lingering on her breasts, she felt naked, really naked, because he was looking at her not as a servant, but as a woman. She followed his gaze and saw her distended clit poked out from between her labia, glistening with her arousal. A flush crept up her face, and she shifted her weight, wanting to hide.

The sun lines at the corners of his eyes deepened. "Since I intend for you to come tonight—and I do—and the thong doesn't agree with you, I'm afraid you'll have to suffer from my personal attentions."

He hadn't given up at all. *Oh God.* Her eyes widened as he moved the wine and the remotes to one side, then lifted her and stood her in the middle of the walnut coffee table. "Master!"

"Yes, sumisa?" He sat in front of her, almost on her toes. "Open for me." He mercilessly pushed her legs apart until her feet were at the edges of the square table. He moved closer, his face right...oh God, right at her groin level. After pulling one of the remotes closer, he turned the bullet vibrator on. The buzz hit inside her, and she moaned.

"Master R, I don't think—" She bit her lip, feeling like an idiot, feeling the thing buzzing inside her. "I can't. This isn't going to work."

He laughed, actually laughed. "Then I'll simply enjoy myself with my little sumisa's body." His thumbs parted her labia as his fingers curled around her hips, anchoring his hands...and her as well. The feeling of his thumbs pulling her open sent heat spiraling through her again.

"If you start to lose your balance, you may put your hands on my shoulders as you did before." He looked up at her, his lips curving, "I thought of asking for a number, but I can see fear isn't what's on your mind at this moment. "

Fear? Embarrassment, maybe, but this was so far from what any of the slavers had done it held no comparison. It was Master R touching her.

As he leaned forward and blew a stream of warm air onto her exposed clit, the sensation shot across the nerve endings, making her toes curl. Before she got used to that, his mouth closed loosely over her.

"Oh, God." Hot, oh so very hot. His lips pressed and released, creating a circle of heat and pressure around the nub—so, so soft yet tightening more with each repetition until her clit was trapped. A flicker of his tongue over the top weakened her knees, and she grabbed his shoulders, bending over slightly to keep from falling.

"That's right, cariño, hang on tight." His breath teased her pussy, and then his tongue slid up and down one side of her clit, flickering over the very top, before moving to the other side. Blood swelled her tissues until they felt too tight. Bursting tight.

A whine escaped her, and his only response was to let go one hand and turn up the vibrator.

"No..." It shook her from deep inside. He put his hand back, fingers curving around her hip, thumb opening her labia even more firmly. As if trying to match the vibrator, his tongue rubbed at the edge of her clit, moving the looser hood back and forth, no longer teasing but demanding a response.

The pressure grew inside her, her climax approaching as inexorably as a rising tide. Her toes tingled, and the muscles of her thighs trembled until she wondered if she'd fall. She couldn't seem to care. Everything in her tuned to the movements of his tongue as it rubbed one side of the bundle of nerves, then the other. His lips closed around her, trapping her clit in heat, tightening.

Her fingernails dug into his shoulders, her hips giving little jerks, needing...more. She wanted to pull him closer, needed to, but he held her ruthlessly, doing exactly as he wanted.

Slowly his lips tightened, pinching the nub. He sucked lightly, and his tongue butterfly-winged over the very top, and everything in her tightened, tightened. The roaring of surf sounded in her ears.

He sucked—oh, God—sucked strongly, and sensation gripped her spine like a fist until it exploded; everything spasmed in massive waves around the humming thing at her center, shaking her in an earthquake of sensation.

His thumbs released her, and his hands curved under her ass, holding her up—holding her against his mouth as he flicked her gently again, making it last. Her legs gave out entirely, and his rumbling laugh against her clit made her come again. Without any effort at all, he lifted her. "Put your legs around me," he said in a firm voice. She was shaking too hard to fight him.

She'd had orgasms. She'd been afraid that part of her life was over. But he'd done what she asked and gone further even. Aroused her—pleasured her.

His eyes had darkened to almost black; satisfaction filled his smile. "You taste very nice, cariño. Since we've crossed over this bridge, and several days remain where you are still under my command, I will enjoy having my mouth on you often."

A shudder of anticipation ran through her, and his firm lips curved up.

As he set her on the sofa, pushing her back, she realized the vibrator inside her was off. He pushed her legs apart. She was so wet, his fingers slid inside easily, despite the way she clenched around him. He removed the bullet and laid it on the end table. Then he sat beside her, pulled her against his side, and kissed the top of her head. "You did very well, sumisita mía. I'm proud of you."

The joy of pleasing him mingled with her own satisfaction.

"Do you want to continue?" He moved to see her face, his eyes intent, waiting for her answer...and expecting an honest one.

*Continue. That meant he would...* Her mouth went dry. "No. Yes. I don't know."

"Do you trust me, Kimberly?" he asked softly.

She'd never trusted a man the way she trusted him. When had that happened? "Yes, Sir." She tilted her head up, reached to touch his stern jaw, feeling the slight scrape of his five o'clock shadow. "I do."

"Let's see how far we can go."

*Oh God. No.* Her breathing sped up, and then he asked, "What's your safe word?"

Safe word. He'd stop if she panicked. She swallowed and said firmly, "Cramp."

"Very good." He stood and started to unbuckle his belt.

Fear turned her cold as memories drowned her: men surrounding her, undoing their pants, pulling out... Her feet drew up, and she scrambled into a corner of the couch.

His hands stilled, and he watched her. So silent. After a long minute, he held his arms away from his sides. "I would like your pretty hands to unclothe me, gatita."

*Me?*

Not moving, he waited, his gaze never leaving her face. Patient. After a minute, he prompted, "*It will be my pleasure, Master.* Is this not what you say?"

He can hardly do anything with clothes on, she told herself, the sweet sense of satiation gone completely. *I wanted to do this. I can.* She swallowed and whispered, "It will be my pleasure, Master." *So, so not true.*

It felt as if it took her an hour to stand up, naked in front of him. Another hour before she touched him. She'd seen him before, she told herself. They showered together, after all.

His lips curved when her hand reached his belt. "You smell like flowers, cariño. I like the shampoo you brought with you. What do I smell like?"

She blinked, diverted from the icy terror surging up and down her spine. The end of his belt slipped loose. She unzipped his pants. "Um. Clean. Not flowery, more like a—the ocean. Not sweet."

His hand cupped her cheek; his thumb touched her lips lightly, a gentle kiss of skin. "And I am not sweet, mi pequeña sumisa." His eyes caught hers, dark and intent. Determined.

A shiver of fear—of heat—went through her at the thought of him inside her. His cock sprang free, and she realized he'd gone commando. This was it. She felt like a statue, frozen in stone.

"You have a choice, sumisa," he said gently. "We have both been tested, and your birth control is still active. Do you wish a condom or not?"

No longer a question of if they'd have sex, but just what way. It felt as if she was being pulled into a whirlpool. "Um." Memories spun into the circle with her...the plastic, slick horrible feel of the...others. They'd worn condoms. Their...they hadn't felt real, just evil. "No. No condom."

He looked surprised but simply took hold of her and moved her so he could sit in the center of the couch. "Kneel on the sofa. Straddle me, Kimberly," he said, his voice so very gentle.

Her hands had gone numb; her lips tingled like she'd been sucking on ice. She put a knee on each side of his thighs, trying to not see the thick erection raised between them, the piercing glinting in the light. He gripped her behind her thighs and pulled her forward until her pelvis pressed against his erection. "Look at me, little one," he said softly. "Who am I? My title, my name."

Her mind blanked, until his intent gaze captured hers again. "Master R."

"Bueno. Whose cock are you rubbing against?" A smile curved his lips. "Whose cock have you washed in the shower every morning?"

She had. She'd touched him, washed him. The words came easier under his dark brown gaze. "Master R's."

"Good. Kimberly, are you afraid of Master R?"

"Sometimes."

His laugh rang out, the darkly male one she loved that meant she'd surprised him—delighted him. His grin flashed at her. "There's an answer to warm a dom's heart." With his eyes still dancing with laughter, he nodded at her. "Time's up. Lower yourself on me, chiquita. You may go as slow as you want...as long as you don't stop."

His hands were still curled around her thighs, not moving except for his thumbs stroking her skin gently. She was shaking uncontrollably, but his laughter had freed her mind. He'd put her on top. Pulled her into position, because he'd known she wouldn't be able to force herself. But now, he'd let her set her own pace. Her fears of being held down, tearing, ripping—she shuddered.

"Eyes on me, Kimberly."

"Yes, Sir," she whispered. She reached down, between their bodies, and gripped his shaft, touched the piercing, and frowned. "Why couldn't you be little or without this...thing?"

His laugh burst out again, heartening her enough that she raised up and set him at her entrance. She was very slick, still sensitive from his mouth and lips, and a quiver ran through her...not of fear.

"As slow as you want—"

*As long as I don't stop.* She let herself down, feeling the stretch. His piercing caught for a second. Then he was in. The metal pressed on her as it passed in, the sensation strange, and the rest of him followed, hot, velvet covered, sliding into her, increment by increment. The stretch, the feeling was—she froze, skin going cold.

He cleared his throat, breaking into her thoughts, and

she nodded. Master R. She lowered farther. "You're so damn big," she whispered.

"Why, thank you, cariño," he said. He moved his hands then, massaging her bottom in a way that sent a quiver through her as it added to the sensations. She took more of him in.

Her mouth was even with his, and his hand curved over her nape, pulling her closer for a kiss. A real kiss, and he pushed his tongue inside as aggressive with his mouth as he wasn't with his cock.

Her head swirled, trying to take in everything: his hands on her bottom, his shaft in her, his mouth on hers. She lost focus and dropped down faster. Her cry of surprise let him deeper into her mouth, and he possessed it totally, then lifted his hips, filling her completely with his cock.

*No!* Tearing her mouth from his, she pulled up instinctively until she was almost off his shaft.

He gave her a half-lidded, lazy look. "That's very nice. You may continue doing that."

"You..." *Evil monster.* She held there, trembling. But it was impossible to hold her anger—or even her fear—when seeing the satisfaction in his face, the humor in his eyes. She gripped his shoulders and lowered herself down again. God, he was so big.

And she was very slick. Up and down, emptiness to overwhelmingly full, and about the third or fourth time, he felt...good. She went a little faster.

He hummed his approval and moved his hands between them to fondle her breasts and tease her nipples. A slow pinch sent a shock of heat to her pussy, and she clenched around him.

"Very nice. Do that—squeeze me—as you're lifting," he instructed. His resonant voice had slowed into a winding warm river of sound, smoothing the last jagged crests of fear.

She tightened herself around him and rose. Lowered slowly. God, she could feel the metal. The piercing slid over an area that made her shiver. Like it was rubbing at her clit from inside her.

"Again."

No pain, and the unexpected sensation of pleasure kept increasing.

"Slow up, faster coming down," he murmured. He leaned his head against the couch back, his gaze wandering over her eyes, her mouth, her body, the intent look at odds with his obvious enjoyment. He didn't want to lose control enough to stop caring for her well-being.

But he liked what she was doing. The realization thrilled through her. She had something to offer—something to give. And she wanted to. She lifted, then dropped onto him hard, the sudden penetration making her vagina spasm around him.

His pupils dilated, turning his eyes almost black. "Exactly that, cariño. Ride me."

Her voice came out husky. "Yes, Master." She gripped his shoulders and obeyed, working for his climax, wanting his pleasure, and with each slide down onto his shaft, arousal began unfurling again in her own body. That piercing was too...too... Her inner thighs quivered as heat punched low in her belly and sweat moistened her skin.

THE LITTLE SUB was incredibly tight, hot, and wet. Her small hands on his shoulders felt...just right. He saw how his orders took precedence over her fears and found the knowledge even more erotic than the way her pussy worked his cock with soft sucking sounds. She watched him with a woman's desire to share a connection during lovemaking, and her eyes held as much vulnerability and need to please as any submissive he'd met. She didn't serve from fear, but because the giving fulfilled her.

She'd grown wetter, and his groin hair was matted with her juices. Her face was flushed, and—so telling—an occasional shiver ran through her when her clit bumped against his pelvis.

He smiled slightly, pleased. "I didn't plan to push you, but if you want to join me..." *Then you're going to come again, gatita.*

She looked at him blankly, and he sighed. She was so out of touch with her own body.

Needing space in which to work, he slid down on the couch until he was half-lying, and she stayed upright. He released her ass and moved his fingers to her front, touching the wetness around the base of his shaft, then her swollen pussy. Her spine went rigid, as if he'd used electrostim on her rather than just his hand. With his fingers covered in her juices, he edged up toward her clit. The thickness of his erection had forced the nub completely out of hiding. He swirled one finger around it.

Her breathing stopped, then went totally erratic, and she dug tiny fingernails into his shoulders. Her trust in him—to let him rouse her at all—shook him to the bone...but he didn't stop the slow slide of his finger over her clit. Someday she might like erotic surprises, but today, she'd had enough. He stayed with a steady rhythm, rubbing the right side of her clit as she rose off his dick, the left when she lowered.

That worked well until she got too excited. Wiggling replaced the rise and fall as her rhythm totally disintegrated.

He grinned. But her squirming was making his balls feel as if they were going to explode, so he'd better stop stalling. With a palm under her ass, he raised her up, almost off him, then yanked her down as he thrust his hips up.

She moaned. Her breasts wobbled with the impact. And his cock hardened to the danger point.

The next time, he held her high, barely on his shaft, and used his fingers on her clit to push her toward her climax. She was panting with little moans. When she started to convulsively grip his shoulders, he dropped her down onto his shaft and had to grit his teeth as his own climax surged near breaking. She was right on the edge when he pushed her up and teased her clit with rhythmic strokes.

Then, tilting to get the most pressure on her G-spot from his piercing, he slammed her down.

Her back arched. Her head tipped. Her breathing stopped.

He murmured to her, "It's time to come, sumisita," and as if given permission, her cunt contracted around him like a hot fist; the walls battered at his cock as she climaxed violently. She didn't scream, not this little abused slave, but a tiny mewl escaped her as she rubbed harder against his fingers, took him deeper, obviously not wanting it to end.

He gave her more, until she loosened her hands on his shoulders, until she was gasping for breath. Por Dios, she was beautiful.

"My turn now, gatita." Her eyes were still glazed when he took her hips between his hands to lift her, then yank her down. Up, down. Her vagina contracted around him with each thrust, giving her aftershocks of pleasure that he saw reflected in her flushed face.

Up, down. His balls contracted against his groin; his erection swelled, ready to burst. He rode the edge, unwilling to release as the pressure at the base of his spine grew and then blasted out of his control, ripping through his cock in hard spasms. The feeling of his hot seed filling her soft cunt shook him.

When his mind cleared, he managed to move, lifting and turning on the couch so he could flatten out. He puffed a pillow under his head, brought his leg up onto the cushions. Still sitting on his dick, she sagged, her eyes closed, only her arms holding her upright as if she'd frozen into that position.

Or feared to lie on him?

"Come here, cariño," he murmured, pulling her hands from his shoulders and letting her drop down on his chest. She started to push up again.

"Shhh." He placed one hand on her ass, keeping them pinned together so his softening cock remained in her cunt as he coaxed her to put her legs between his. Finally she lay flat on top of him. Yes, he could have withdrawn and arranged them more easily, but he wanted to stay inside her, reminding her of their connection—one of pleasure, not pain.

He curved his hand at the back of her head, nudging it onto his shoulder. When he put his arms around her and held her firmly, her last bit of resistance fled, and she lay quietly. Hot and sweaty and slick, this soft woman whose curves fit him in all the right places. He couldn't have designed such a fine melding.

He lifted his head. Her eyes were closed, worries gone. "I like being in you, Kimberly," he said softly. "You're warm and soft, inside and out."

She stirred, and he saw the tiniest curve of her lips.

He stroked her hair, seeing the way the light glinted off it, dispelling the perception of complete black. Some strands were brown, some with a reddish tint. "You were afraid of having me on top of you, no?"

The instant tensing of her back muscles saddened him.

"Shhh." He kept the slow movement of his hand,

kissed the top of her head. "Now tell me."

"Yes." Her face pressed closer into the hollow of his shoulder as if she were a small animal needing shelter.

His arms tightened, reminding her that she had his protection. "Because of the way they took you?"

A tiny nod. "On my back or like a dog. Both…places."

Anal and vaginal. "In your mouth?"

Her snort of derision held tears as well. "I bit him." She tensed again. "And then he used…he…"

Raoul's jaw tightened until his teeth ground together. Of course. The asshole had strapped her in a device to hold her mouth open while he face-fucked her. Cabrón. "He is unworthy to call himself a man." Her shoulder muscles relaxed under his slow, careful massage. "If you might recall from your…excursion…into my toy cabinet, I do not own such a thing."

"Oh." More muscles went loose. Her breathing slowed, a small waft of warmth on his skin.

"But, although I like being inside you here"—he wiggled the soft remainder of his erection, and her responsive pussy clenched, pushing him all the way out. He grinned at her tiny sound of loss—"we might also have fun with my cock here." He squeezed an ass cheek, making her jump. "Will you trust me to take you carefully, Kimberly?"

This was why he'd decided to speak of such matters now—to prepare her for the next step while her body resonated with an orgasm, and while his so terrifying dick was soft and melting between her legs after having brought her only pleasure.

"I—" She sighed. "Okay."

He gave her the tiny growl he knew she'd recognize.

"Okay, Sir." A pause. "Master."

Satisfaction was a gentle evening rain, and headier than the wine they'd had earlier. "And?"

"I know." Her voice was husky. "You'll want my mouth too."

He snorted. "Only if you promise not to bite."

Her lips curved again, more this time. "Yes, Master."

# Chapter Nine

The next morning, Kim went down to the beach. The gulls cried overhead, and gray-brown willets foraged in the shallows. The tide was coming in, the waves slowly reclaiming the sand as she was reclaiming more of her life.

*I had sex.* She grinned at the sun. Its rays warmed her skin, and she bubbled with life, feeling as if she'd taken a huge step forward.

Heck, she had. She shook her head, unbraiding her hair so the wind could ruffle it with salty fingers. Master R liked her hair. Liked her skin. Said she was lovely, and his face held no untruth.

She rolled her eyes. He was her master. Why would he bother lying? It wasn't as if he had to talk her into bed, right?

He liked her. He'd taken more care with making sure she was satisfied than anyone ever had. And then at the very end, he hadn't stopped—he'd made her serve his own satisfaction, and that had been as fulfilling as getting off herself.

She headed for the Adirondack chair. Weathered white with age, it ruled over its section of sand like a beach throne. She dropped onto it, then squeaked. A little sore maybe?

God, she'd gotten off so thoroughly she still quaked inside. And she wanted to do it again. Wanted those strong hands on her, to feel his biceps bunching into concrete when he lifted her, to trace the ridges on his stomach. This morning, when he'd washed her—more intimately than ever before—he told her she was filling out and he liked her soft ass sized for his big hands.

He scared her and excited her and made her want him.

*Want him.* As the sun disappeared behind a cloud and shadows slid over the sand, a chill raised goose bumps on her arms. Life wasn't all sun and pretty waves. The clouds came, storms drowned ships, and people moved on.

*You realize he's just doing his job, right? Don't go all teenage-girl gaga over him.* Her inner cynic's interjection was like a cold dip in the water. And was right, unfortunately.

Master R liked her, but he was in this to shut down the slavers, not to start up a relationship with a messed-up woman. He'd never talked about being together after this was over.

She watched a tiny hermit crab peek out of its stolen shell and retreat again, hiding in the secure spiral. "Yeah, me too, little guy," she whispered. *Don't get too far from safety.* Falling head over heels in love with Master R would be...pretty much...the worst thing she could do.

He wanted a slave.

She hated even the word.

So. Once they pulled this off, she'd go home to Savannah. To her real life.

* * * *

Christopher Greville leaned back in his office chair as his majordomo entered.

"You rang for me, sir?"

"Dutton, when I was doing the accounts, I found a

large deposit into the Owner's account. It matches what I paid for a certain slave."

The majordomo's swarthy face flushed. One of the more satisfying retainers Greville employed, he handled the household accounts, which included the purchase of slaves and any equipment needed for them, like the heavy dog kennel, the whips, and gags…

Greville smiled. The new slave had arrived two days ago, a big-breasted blonde with such an ear-piercing scream that he'd been forced to gag her the first day to preserve his ears. After he and his staff had played for a while, her voice had changed to a pleasingly hoarse sound.

"I'm sorry, sir," Dutton said. "I forgot to mention it. After much stalling, the Overseer provided a refund for the black-haired slave. The one who—" He broke off.

The one who'd dared to attack her master. To stab him. Greville ran his fingers over his gray suit, feeling the lingering tenderness in his shoulder. The memory of pain as the knife punched through his skin still brought him up short on occasion. The little fuckhole had— *"Refund."* "What refund? Dahmer gave you a refund for a dead slave?"

"Oh, she didn't die, sir. She'd bled quite a bit but was still alive when we handed her over." Dutton's expression faltered into worry. "You did tell us to get rid of her, sir."

*Not dead.* She'd stabbed him, and she wasn't rotting in a grave? "I meant *kill* her. Fuck her to death or beat her to death." His temper surged; he forced himself to stay seated. "She's alive?"

Dutton's face paled, and he took a step back. "I'm sorry, sir. I didn't realize."

Greville stared at him and then smiled coldly. "Of course you didn't. I obviously wasn't clear." He nodded a dismissal and watched the majordomo quietly leave. Incompetent bastard. He'd be six feet down and feeding the worms before this week was out.

The fuckhole was alive. Greville turned to the computer and brought up the Association numbers shared with premium buyers. After using the code to get the right phone number for the current date, he punched it in.

"Yes." Dahmer's number. Dahmer was a typical flunky, but an efficient one. He'd definitely improved the quality of slaves in the Southeast quadrant.

"Greville. I just discovered I received a refund from you. When I questioned my staff, I found they hadn't disposed of the merchandise—as should have been done— but had returned it to you."

"That's right."

"Their actions were incorrect. Return the merchandise to me for proper handling." He would cut pieces from her body—a finger, an ear, a toe—and see how long he could keep her alive. Maybe let her choose which part she'd sacrifice each day. But he'd take her tongue first. And her teeth. Make a *real* fuckhole.

"I can't do that. It's been resold."

Greville's jaw clenched, and his voice came out raw. "Buy it back."

A pause. "I can try. As it happens, I'm scheduled for a follow-up with the buyer tomorrow." Dahmer sounded annoyed, as if Greville would give a damn. "But he won't hand her over for the same price. It'll cost you."

He'd hear her scream. See her eyes wide with agony, fighting to escape the pain, the dismemberment. *See the light go out.* "Do it."

\* \* \* \*

The day for their trip to the Shadowlands finally arrived.

Pity eating like a worm in his heart, Raoul kept his little submissive busy with cooking and cleaning. In the afternoon, he'd given her final instructions on high protocol and how an owned slave should behave in public. They'd practiced until he was satisfied, and she'd felt comfortable.

"Time to leave, Kimberly," he called. A minute later, he heard her footsteps on the stairs.

She looked adorable. The black dress laced tightly, pressing her breasts upward, her nipples barely hidden by a froth of white lace. The ruffles at the bottom came to the crease below her ass. The token white apron covered the front. Garters held up white fishnet stockings over her lovely legs, and she wore high-heeled fetish shoes. He knew her pussy was bare, and he had the urge to toss her onto the table and take her from the rear.

Maybe he'd buy the costume from Z. But, no. She wasn't his. The knowledge she'd be leaving soon didn't sit well in his gut. "You look beautiful, cariño."

An attempted smile was her response. He watched as she took the final few steps to stand in front of him. Body rigid. Cuffed wrists at her sides, hands fisted. Visibly fighting not to flee. It wasn't him she feared. "Kimberly."

"M-master?"

He sighed, hearing the return of the stuttered word. "Does the Overseer carry weapons?"

A blink of confusion. "No. I don't think he'd want anything a slave might grab and use against him."

"Will he have his guards at the Shadowlands?"

"You said only him."

"Then, chica, if for some reason you couldn't disable him—and you might do fairly well now—do you, by any stretch of the imagination, think he could beat me in a fight?"

"I—" Her gaze moved over him as if comparing their sizes, Raoul perhaps a couple of inches shorter, but far more muscular. A few lines eased from her face. "No. He couldn't, could he?"

"No, I think not. So…we must suffer his presence and be polite, but cariño, no matter what happens, he will leave by himself, and you will still be with me." Raoul tapped a finger on her chin. "I promise."

Her lower lip quivered. When she tried to smile, her courage broke his heart. "Thanks. Master."

He nodded. "Good. Now let's get this done." He picked up the black leather collar from the counter. The moment of revulsion and a memory of Alicia disappeared as he looked into Kimberly's clear blue eyes. The disconcerting desire to have her kneel, to request his collar, to kiss it, was so strong his hands shook slightly.

No, this was merely part of the costume. *Not real, Sandoval.*

Her big eyes fixed on his face as he buckled the leather around her throat. Z had even provided a tiny gold padlock. *Damn him.* It snicked shut, the heady sound of submission much louder in his head than in reality.

As he stepped back, he saw her hands trembling. Apparently the collaring affected her differently. "Ah, gatita." He tapped her nose, the teasing gesture enough to break her paralysis. He pressed the key into her cold little hand. "Your apron has a pocket. Put this inside it." He leaned forward and whispered, "But don't let Dahmer see it."

Her fingers closed, and she gave him a jerky nod, and then slowly, a real smile appeared, like the sun from behind the clouds.

Alas, the smile didn't last long, and the night drive to the Shadowlands seemed to drag as she became increasingly tense. All he could do was hold her hand and remind her of his presence.

In the parking lot, the headlights of Raoul's car

illuminated Dahmer. He stood beside his own vehicle, which was probably equipped with all the jammers that had frustrated the FBI. But the Feds would lie low now until the auction.

With an effort, Raoul pulled his emotions under control. He had a role to play: master of the slave who he would call girl and nothing else, reminding them both of their places.

He got out, nodding at Kimberly to follow. As he took his toy bag from the trunk, he worked a smile onto his face before turning. "Dahmer. Good to see you."

"Thank you." The man wore casual dom clothing. Black khakis, black T-shirt. He glanced up at the mansion. "Great place."

"It is." *And you taint it with your presence.* "Let's go on in."

Raoul headed for the building, glancing back once to check Kimberly. She followed a step behind him, eyes lowered, lovely in her silence and obedience. He could see the tiny tremor as she breathed. *Hang in there, sumisita.*

"No restraints or gags for your slave?"

"No need. She won't try to run." He gave Dahmer a cruel smile. "Not anymore."

"Ah, yes. I heard about your methods of control. I'm surprised she healed so quickly."

*What methods?* Raoul shrugged, not wanting to know. "I feed her well."

"That's a fine costume—although I'm surprised she's not naked."

"Only at home, not in public." Raoul walked beside Dahmer up to the front of the Shadowlands. "I keep my toys to myself. But when we're alone, I prefer naked—for the view, the access, and if disciplining is needed, it can be administered without any great effort."

The Overseer barked a laugh. "You're definitely experienced." He stopped and looked around at the dimly lit grounds. "I like the isolation here."

"No neighbors to complain about screaming." Raoul turned his palm toward the ground, and Kimberly sank to her knees. "Very pretty, girl."

She glanced up long enough to meet his eyes, his approval and acknowledgement lending her stability.

"You compliment her?"

"Of course." Raoul told the man the absolute truth. "The mark of a true slave is her desire to please her master. If I don't tell her when she's done well, then how does she know to repeat it? She works hard to earn a 'very good.'"

"I never thought of it that way. Then again, most buyers are into pain. They don't care to train a slave for more than sex and screaming."

"That's a shame."

WITH HER LEGS feeling as spongy as a jellyfish, Kim was grateful Master R had ordered her to kneel. She felt safer with his legs shielding her. She stayed rigidly in position, taking slow breaths, trying to conquer the nausea and panic from seeing the Overseer, from hearing his horrible voice.

God, she'd known she'd be scared. But she hadn't realized how her physical reactions—hands and legs shaking, cold sweat despite the muggy air—would somehow make her internal fear worse.

She sure hadn't expected the anger that beat like a red-hot hammer against her chest. She stared at a white jagged-edged rock, the focus of a landscaped garden plot. Her fingers curled as she saw herself picking it up, slamming it down on the monster's head. She tried to imagine how it would feel, the way he'd fall forward, the sound he'd make...

But then Master R would be furious she'd ruined everything, and—she sighed. *He wouldn't be furious, Kim.* He'd be disappointed in her, and the thought of seeing unhappiness in his eyes calmed the storm inside her. Eventually the Overseer would get his due, but first they needed to save the others. *Suck it up, wuss.*

*I want to go home.* She pushed the longing away and concentrated on breathing. The smooth concrete was warm against her legs and Master R's dark voice a calming touch on her fears. She kept her gaze down but her head angled so she'd see if he motioned for her to do something.

His tiny gesture had her standing before she even thought about it, and she realized the FBI agent had been correct. Anyone watching would notice how attuned she was to Master R. The time she'd lived with him, being corrected, learning to watch for the unobtrusive movements he used to direct her—none of it had been wasted.

As they took the last few steps to the Shadowlands, she chanced a reprimand and glanced around quickly, remembering the other submissives' intriguing stories.

The lights from the landscaping smoldered against the thick stone walls. The black ironwork on the doors and the heavy wall sconces didn't help lighten the effect.

Neither did the huge security guard inside the door, whose brutish features would be more suited to a medieval torturer. He glanced at her, then the Overseer. "Good evening, sir," he said, his voice a match for his size. "Are you lost?"

Master R moved into the room from behind them. "Not lost, Ben. These are my guests for tonight. I cleared it with Z."

"Master Raoul." The man's pleased smile turned him from terrifying to something entirely different, like a dog so ugly and sweet it was cute. "It's been a while since you were here."

Master R ran a finger along Kim's collar, brushing her skin. "I had someone keeping me at home."

"'Bout time." The pleased look she got from Ben made her smile, before she remembered her place. She dropped her gaze.

"Dahmer isn't participating, but Z wants them both to sign the papers." He glanced at the Overseer. "As a guest, you're not required to show ID, but you're not allowed to play either."

"Very cautious," Dahmer said. He glanced through the papers Ben handed him and signed with a scribble. Kim followed suit. The releases were much like other clubs', although more thorough, especially in the list of infractions and various punishments.

She looked up to see Ben studying her. "Great costume—and you may keep your shoes on too."

Master R told the Overseer, "The owner likes submissives barefoot or in blatant fuck-me stilettos."

No club she'd been to had been quite so strict. Then again, she'd never been in an exclusive club like this one.

They stepped through the inside door and into chaos. Kim froze at the sounds of pain and screaming and the slaps of implements on bare flesh. Perfumes had no chance against the scents of leather and sweat and sex.

A little ways into the room, a woman with her arms restrained over her head was being penetrated by two men. Kim swallowed. Oh God, obviously fucking was allowed in the club. The atmosphere thickened, affecting her air supply.

Master R wrapped his arm around her waist. "Relax, gatita," he murmured in her ear. "The last dom who tried to force a submissive against her will was tossed out the door. I think someone busted his fingers with a cane before that—

probably Z or Nolan. Everything here is consensual. Do you understand?"

Consensual. Not slavery. Only what both people agreed to. She nodded.

"Good. May I have my arm back?" His amusement tipped her fear onto the manageable side, and she realized her fingers were digging holes in his wrist. "Sorry, M-master," she whispered.

He winced and sighed. After glancing at the Overseer, who was a few feet away, watching a domme attach a chain between her submissive's hair and clit clamp, Master R said, "Give me a number, Kimberly."

Her anxiety went down a notch. He'd remember to check her fears. He hadn't forgotten. She opened her fingers on her bare thighs, showing six, then lowering it to five after another breath.

He smiled at her. "Brave sumisita." He nodded to tables of food and drinks in the left corner. "Munchies are there which we might enjoy later."

She doubted she'd ever be hungry again.

In the right corner was a tiny, crowded dance floor pulsing with the Sisters of Mercy gothic rock. An immense bar occupied the center of the room with a bartender equally as big. The roped-off scene areas ran down the left and right walls and across the back. The corners held fancy spiral staircases. "What's upstairs?"

"Private rooms for people who don't want to play in public—or who prefer somewhere quieter afterward." His chin tilted toward a domme helping a sweat-covered, lash-marked sub up the stairs. The man dwarfed the slender woman, but there was still no denying who was in charge. "Z and Jessica live on the third floor."

Wouldn't that be cramped? But the clubroom was huge, so the third floor was probably ten times the size of her duplex.

"I see Master Sam has already started," Master R said to Dahmer. "Why don't we get a drink and go watch? I can introduce you afterward."

"A fine idea." The Overseer glanced at her dismissively. "Do you need to gag her?"

"I have one if it becomes necessary," Master R said, patting the toy bag slung over his shoulder. "Will it be necessary, girl?"

She shook her head, her fear unfeigned.

"Let's keep it that way," he snapped, his voice cold enough to give her chills. To her dismay, he snapped her cuffs together in front of her. But when he clipped a leash to her collar, she felt disconcertingly better. A leash meant they were attached. He'd not be able to leave her.

"Thank you, Master," she whispered, and the crinkles at the corners of his eyes showed he understood.

Behind the bar, the craggy-faced bartender had his arms around a tall submissive whose golden brown latex dress matched her hair. He released her and grinned as they approached. "What can I get you, Raoul?"

"A glass of red for me and a bottle of water for the girl." Master R gestured to the Overseer. "And a martini for my guest. Dahmer, this is Cullen, one of the Masters here."

"Welcome to the Shadowlands," Cullen said and glanced at the submissive. "Andrea, see to it, please."

"Yes, Señor."

As the bartender engaged Master R and the Overseer in conversation about the local BDSM scene, the woman filled the men's orders. Then she set a bottled water in front of Kim.

"Thank—" Kim broke off quickly.

Master R glanced over. "You need to be gagged, girl?"

She shook her head frantically.

He ignored the big submissive's frown and turned back to the men.

Kim sagged against the bar. *How could I forget?* If she messed up again, he'd have to gag her. She stared at the bottle of water, knowing she'd heave if she tried to drink.

"Still got Glenlivet back there?"

Kim froze at the familiar voice. *Jessica.* Oh God. *Don't talk to me.*

She didn't. The little blonde gave Kim the polite nod of a stranger and climbed onto the adjacent barstool. "Hey, Andrea, Master Z sent me to get drinks." She scowled. "His usual, but I only get water."

The lady bartender sniffed. "You probably only deserve water." She leaned an elbow on the bar in front of Kim and faced Jessica, which turned her back to Master R and the Overseer. "Hi, Kim," she said in a very low voice, looking at Jessica.

Kim's eyes widened as she realized the submissive knew her name.

"Yeah, we know what's going on." Andrea laughed loudly and poked Jessica in the shoulder. "I don't believe you did that." Her voice dropped again. "The Masters found keeping secrets from their subs didn't work out." She and Jessica exchanged sardonic looks, and Kim remembered Gabi's hair-raising stories. "Anyway, just know we'll keep an eye on you."

Jessica nodded, her voice equally quiet. "One of us will stay beside you if for some reason Raoul can't."

That had been Kim's worst fear, to be left unprotected. Tears stung her eyes.

"Stop that," Jessica said, half an order and half in sympathy, then slapped the bartop, saying in a normal voice, "Hurry up, or Master Z will think I was gossiping."

Andrea smirked, setting a bottled water on the bar. "And you aren't?" She snagged a bottle of Glenlivet and poured a shot, saying quietly, "Master Nolan's sub, Beth, is here too."

Jessica opened the water. "Yeah. You're part of our club now. So you get supported whether you want it or not." She took a gulp of water, picked up Z's glass, and told Andrea, "Later, girlfriend," before swaggering across the room.

Andrea said, under her breath, "That's one soft-hearted bantam rooster."

The laugh Kim tried to suppress came out sounding like a sneeze.

Master R gave Andrea a frown. "Don't bother my girl."

"No, Sir," Andrea said. "Wouldn't dream of it, Sir."

The big bartender reached out a long arm and fisted her hair. "More respectful, love."

Andrea winced. "Yes, Señor." Her golden-brown eyes focused on Master R. "Please forgive my rudeness, Master Raoul."

Master R gave her a cold look. "Maybe add a reprimand from me to your next scene, Cullen."

"That'd be my pleasure, buddy," Cullen said with a grin. "I figure an extra-big anal plug would be appropriate."

Andrea's eyes turned anxious.

Master R led the way across the room toward the back. Kim was glad she'd left the cap on her drink, since the tugs on the leash made the water slosh in the bottle. She unobtrusively glanced around, trying not to wince at the sounds. Groans from the right where a slender domme in a red latex dress was dripping wax over a man's engorged cock. Farther away, the rhythmic whap of a cane, and then a woman's whimpers when her dom changed targets and slapped the cane lightly over her breasts.

Near the end of the room, Master R stopped where a silvery-haired man in well-worn leathers was flogging a sub on a St. Andrew's cross. "That's Sam."

"Very good. Let's watch him work." The Overseer took a chair close to the roped-off area, Master R the one next to him. Kim knelt at his feet, keeping her master between her and the Overseer.

Master R plucked the bottle from her hand, opened the top, and gave it back, all without looking at her. Or so it seemed.

She edged close enough to feel his leg against her shoulder and hip. Just the sensation of touching him eased the knot inside her that tightened every time she heard the Overseer's sleazy voice.

As the doms watched the scene in silence, Kim struggled to ignore the sound of the lash and the submissive's crying. *I'm not here. Open the throttle and hear the roar of the boat; feel the spray cooling my face, the wind whipping my hair.*

After a bit, she tilted her head, able to watch the scene out of the corner of her eye.

The slight movement drew the Overseer's attention. When he looked at her, the sensation was like foulness brushing against her skin. "She looks very good, Raoul. Good enough I'd like to buy her back from you. With the training you've done, she'd bring you a pretty profit."

He wanted her back? A tremor ran through Kim, and her mouth went dry. Auction her off... Her breathing started to increase despite her attempts to—

A jerk on her hair broke the pattern. Scalp stinging, Kim pursed her lips and exhaled. *Slow. Slow.* She sagged against Master R's leg. Somehow he'd seen her panic when he was paying her no attention.

A little pat on her head rewarded her. "Sorry, but I

spent too much time training this one. I'd hate to start over."

"But you could get a beauty of a slave with what you'd make on this one."

"Not interested," Master R said, an irritated snap in his voice. When he turned to watch the scene, the Overseer gave up and did the same.

Kim forced her fists to open so her hands would lie properly on her thighs.

The flogging lasted far too long, and the submissive's sobs turned to screams as she struggled to evade the pain. On and on. When the poor woman eventually hit subspace and no longer felt the pain, Kim could relax.

After freeing the glassy-eyed sub, the dom bundled her into a blanket and sat her on the floor. Unhurriedly, he gave her some water and fed her bites of chocolate before putting the candy in her hand. "You okay for a minute, girl?" Looking like an old cowboy, he had a voice as rough as his appearance.

"Yes. Thank you, Master Sam." The submissive kissed his hand. "That was wonderful. I feel all...open...again."

As she nibbled the chocolate, the dom wiped down the play area and packed away his tools.

Kim concentrated on him, trying to ignore the Overseer's discussion of the scene. Trying to ignore that it would soon be her turn to be watched. And Master R had never told her what he planned.

"All done?" Sam asked the submissive. He helped her to her feet, ran his hand over her abused back, and grinned at her flinch. "Off you go then."

She kissed his hand again and walked away, only a slight wobble in her gait.

"Will she be all right?" Master R asked, the concern obvious in his voice. Kim wanted to hug him. If he could,

Master R would probably take care of the whole world.

SAM LOOKED AT the pale man sitting next to his Raoul. Like a vampire, the asshole Overseer apparently didn't get out in the sun much. "She'll be fine. She likes to unwind in the sub's area, listening to the women chatter." He grinned. "She's a gay switch, so she'll probably end up taking one of them upstairs."

He spotted one of the Shadowlands trainees and held up a finger. The brunette nodded and reversed course to get him a drink from the bar.

Grabbing a towel from his toy bag, Sam wiped the sweat from his face and neck and dropped into a chair across from Raoul's guest.

"Sam, this is Dahmer," Raoul said.

The man leaned forward to shake hands and said, "You're quite skilled. That was a pleasure to watch."

Sam shrugged. "It was okay." He'd deliberately picked a real screamer. Although some tops preferred their subs to control themselves, his bottoms knew he enjoyed the sounds of pain. This time, he'd drawn as much noise as he could get out of her. "But the slut went into subspace too quickly. And if she doesn't, she'll safe-word out." He snorted. "They all do."

The Overseer nodded, as if he now understood why Sam might want a slave. "There are ways around the problem, you know."

"So I'm hearing." Sam glanced at his friend's little slave and caught a flicker of blue eyes before she looked back down. Brave woman, and pretty as hell in the French maid costume. "But I'm not interested in one like Sandoval's. I don't need someone to cook or clean, and with what I like to do to them, I wouldn't trust one wandering around."

"Actually, the majority of our...clients...have the same idea. Although Raoul's results with his slave are quite impressive, we have many satisfied sadists on our buyer list, and they tend to keep their toys locked up. Closet or spare rooms work if the windows and doors are remodeled." The man smiled and added, "Or even dog cages."

When the girl visibly flinched at the Overseer's words, Raoul put his hand on her head, and Sam noted a disturbing look in his eyes. The dom was too tenderhearted for his own good. Be hell of a thing if he got attached to an ex-slave. *Don't be an idiot, man. No kidnapped slave is going to want a master afterward.*

"Dahmer." Hoping to pull the asshole's attention from Raoul, Sam leaned back in his chair and said, "I'm rather interested. What's involved?"

The Overseer's smug expression would turn a man's stomach. "First—"

"Excuse me," Raoul interrupted. "I'll leave you two alone now. I reserved the office room for my scene and should get set up." He rose, picked up his toy bag, and tugged at the leash for his slave to follow.

The Overseer nodded. "I'll be along shortly to watch."

The girl cringed. When she bravely squared her shoulders and followed Raoul, Sam had to stomp on the urge to backhand Dahmer onto the ground.

The Overseer watched them walk away and commented, "She was a pleasure to fuck. Never stopped fighting, and I do enjoy a battle. The cage is what finally broke her to heel, no matter what your friend thinks."

"He's a fine trainer, but not particularly into pain... unlike me."

"So I understand." The Overseer went silent as Sally delivered Sam's drink.

"Thank you, girl," Sam said, smiling as the trainee

trotted away. Her short skirt bounced over her round ass with every step.

"We almost picked that one up"—the Overseer nodded toward Sally—"but she left town that week. May still get her later, but she's not suitable for this auction. Did I mention this one is for sadists? All the slaves offered will be masochists."

"Sounds perfect." Sam kept his voice level, although the thought of the bastards getting their hands on Sally was like hearing about a puppy being kicked to death. "I enjoy taking a masochist to her limits...and further."

Dahmer leaned forward and started outlining how the procedure worked.

Sam listened, his face calm, even as anger burned in his gut. When Raoul had asked for help, Sam had agreed simply because the idea of slavery offended him. Now, after meeting Dahmer, his interest had turned purely personal. He wanted to put the guy away for years. Better yet, he'd take a bullwhip to the asshole and leave only a pile of shredded flesh.

KIM OBEDIENTLY FOLLOWED Master R across the room, and the tiny tugs on her leash were a lifeline in a sea of fear. Yet the choppy waves quieted as the distance from the Overseer increased. She glanced back. People had obscured the sight of him.

If only his existence could be obscured as well. She sighed.

Somehow Master R heard her above the music, conversations, and sounds from the scenes. After setting his bag down, he tilted her face up and studied her for a minute, then unclipped her wrist cuffs. As he wrapped his arms around her, his faded leather vest was soft under her cheek, his body solid. Strong. He rested his chin on top of her head. "You did well, cariño. I'm proud of you."

Oh, the way her heart leaped at those simple words was worrisome. Very. Once this was over, she'd go back to her own life—yet how much would she be missing this man, this master who held her emotions in his grasp as easily as her body. *I don't care. Think about it later.*

Right now, she needed all her worry efforts for the scene. A real scene. In the last few days, he'd played with her in his dungeon, just a little, letting her get used to his style, to the feeling of helplessness, and to the sounds and scents again. Her panic attacks had eased off, so he could restrain her—usually—without her screaming and losing it. But he hadn't told her about this scene. "What are you planning, Master?"

"So nervous." The sound of his voice was sexy and low with her ear against his chest. He didn't seem worried at all, and his sheer self-confidence was something else she leaned on. "We're doing a fireplay scene, *gatita.*"

She stiffened. *No way. Absolutely not.* She realized with a sinking feeling that she hadn't added fire to her limit list as something to avoid. And she didn't really have a hang-up about it, just the normal dislike of getting *Set. On. Fire. Drown the man.*

He picked up his bag and started walking again, this time with his arm around her, which was good since her balance had gone somewhere. Probably back to Savannah. *I need to go there too.* Anywhere but here.

"It's what Dahmer wanted." He touched the end of her nose with his forefinger. "The good news is I won't restrain you."

"No restraints? Really?" A horrible fear tumbled off her chest. The thought of being helpless anywhere around the Overseer had...had been awful.

"Yes. Since this is the only scene we'll do in public"— he smiled at her—"you might as well have one you will enjoy."

*Enjoy*? "Um. Master. No restraints—that's good, but I'm not so sure about having you set me on fire."

He laughed. Hearing the rich sound was like being in an outside elevator, rising out of the building into the light. "I don't intend to scorch you, Kimberly." He continued walking toward the far end, exchanging greetings with the club members. Was there anyone who didn't know and like him?

Near the end of the room, Kim saw Master Z. His dark gaze met hers, and he smiled slightly, lifting his chin as if giving her courage.

He had. She took a breath and followed Master R down a hallway. Large glass windows on each side let people observe scenes in the various rooms. He pulled a reserved sign off a door on the left and walked in.

The room pretended to be an office with a six-feet-high filing cabinet on the near wall, a large oak desk in the center, and a couch and coffee table on the far side.

"Remove everything, including your cuffs, and kneel beside the desk, please," Master R said. He waited, eyes on her, overcoming her hesitation with his certainty she'd obey.

Her hands had gone numb, her mouth dry, but she did as he ordered, folding her apron and dress, removing her stockings, and setting them on the coffee table. She knelt on the glossy hardwood floor in his preferred position, hands behind her back, knees parted. She lowered her head reluctantly.

"You may watch, gatita," he said quietly.

He pulled a sturdy square table from the corner to beside the desk. Supplies came from the filing cabinet drawers. A wooden skewer with a ball of gauze wrapped around one end came from his bag. Three more followed. He poured a clear liquid into a high-sided metal bowl. A fat candle went into another heavy metal dish.

When he lit it, a shudder went through her. She gritted her teeth and looked down.

"Did you use lotion after showering as I asked?" His voice was casual, like checking if she'd added pepper to the seasonings.

"Yes, Sir."

"Excellent. It'll keep your skin nice and moist." He soaked a bath blanket in the sink and wrung it out. That, a pitcher of water, and a fire extinguisher went on the floor at the far end of the desk.

"You going to set the place on fire too?" *As well as me?* Her voice came out a high whine.

"It's a corollary to Murphy's law. If you're not prepared, bad things will happen. If you are, nothing goes wrong." He pulled a fabric-covered pad out of the cabinet. It was so thick it raised the top of the desk to his waist. He smiled at her. "And this material won't burn, gatita. Now come here."

*I'd rather not.* "Yes, Sir." She rose, striving for poise, since three people had already gathered outside the window. She'd never felt less like putting on a show.

He followed her gaze, then grasped her waist and set her on the desk. The material was cold against her butt, the foam soft. "People will watch, and it's nice to know they enjoy what we do, but this scene, Kimberly, is only between you and me." He kissed her lightly, and she inhaled the faint scent of his cologne, the one she thought of as sea mist and testosterone.

After walking behind her, he pulled her hair to the center of her back and...

"You know how to braid hair?" she asked, recognizing the tugging feeling.

"Mmmhmm. I used to brush and braid my mamá's hair." He was actually humming along with the music, and she realized it wasn't the Goth band playing on the dance floor. The room had its own sound system, and this was a Secret Garden album. One of her favorites. Soothing.

"You're trying to calm me down before setting me on fire."

A sharper tug on her hair. "This will not hurt you... unless I wish." He pinched her arm, a sharp nip. "That's as bad as it should get."

She breathed out. "You're sure?"

"I have been doing this for many years, sumisita." He tied a string around the end of her hair and stepped in front of her, taking her face between his hard palms. His eyes were so serious and caring and yet...stern. She might be afraid, but this was what they were going to do. He wouldn't back down—and why did that seem as reassuring as it did terrifying? Sometimes she didn't make any sense, even to herself.

"This is about trust, cariño, as so many scenes are. Human instinct is to fear the flame. Now we shall see if your trust in me can overcome it."

Oh, when he talked like that, she knew he'd never hurt her. "I trust you," she whispered.

"Brave gatita," he murmured. "I know you do. Now I want you on your knees, ass high, leaning on your forearms."

What? He planned to set her butt on fire first?

Once she was positioned, he ran his hands over her, rubbing firmly, waking her skin, waking her, darn him, as he moved from her shoulders, to her waist, and slowly down. He fondled her bottom for a long while, never touching anything, until all her *anythings* throbbed, needing to be touched. Her fingers tightened on the foam as she realized he was deliberately arousing her.

As he pushed her legs slightly apart, she felt her

wetness dampening her inner thighs. A second later, he pressed open her folds with his fingers, and he gave a satisfied hum.

Dammit, after the past few days, he knew just how to turn her on, and her body roused for him at a finger snap anyway. Too easily. Her head bowed, and she shut her eyes tightly. *Slut. I'm a dirty—*

The sound of a hand hitting flesh was simultaneous with the shocking sting on her bottom. "Ow!"

"You don't think those nasty thoughts about my sumisita, Kimberly." Another ruthless swat made her grimace as the pain shot through her.

His thick finger touched her pussy and pushed firmly into her. She gasped. Her need to wiggle was stopped by the heavy palm on her ass. He slid his finger in and out and chuckled. "I think if you stay with me much longer, we should have a few spanking sessions just for fun."

Her *no* was contradicted by the way her pussy contracted around him.

"Spread your legs more," he said, and as she opened, his other hand traced a path between her labia, spreading wetness upward. When one calloused finger grazed over her clit, slick and rough at the same time, she moaned at the excruciating jolt of pleasure.

"Feel, gatita. This is 'A.'" His finger slid up and around her clit in an odd pattern. "B." A different pattern. "C." Swirling touches over her clit. Never the same place twice. But with each new letter and the slow thrust of his finger, in and out, her need steadily increased.

"G..."

*No. Stop.* She could feel the blood swelling her tissue until her lower half pulsed in time with her heart.

Two fingers slid into her, filling and stretching. "L."

"I don't want to come. Please, Master. No. Not here."

"This time you don't have a choice, cariño," he said levelly. He never slowed, actually pressed deeper. "O... But since you don't want to share with our audience, then you will come without moving or making any noise...or I'll spank you some more."

Oh God, that just made her more frantic—and he knew it. *Drown him.* Her fingers gripped the edges of the foam pad as her willpower started to disintegrate, leaving her unmoored, floating away on the tide.

"R." After kissing the hollow of her back, he nipped her bottom, and the zing of pain sent a tremor through her.

*Don't move; don't make noise.* She trembled, trying to hold still, needing to wiggle, feeling how her vagina tightened around his fingers as she got closer. *No, I don't want to.* Her world narrowed to his slow tracing of the alphabet until each nerve around her clit quivered in anticipation of his touch. Oh God, she needed more. More. Her pulse hammered in her ears and between her legs. As her muscles tightened, her ass tilted just a little more.

"V." He chuckled, a low sound that almost sent her over. And then, to her shock, he added another finger, thrusting hard. She gasped as every muscle contracted around him, increasing the sense of fullness.

Her body gathered; her breathing slowed to nothing. *Almost. Oh please.*

"We should try clamping this someday." His words made no sense...until his fingers firmly pinched her clit.

*Oh oh oh. Explosion.* Mind-shattering pleasure blasted outward as every nerve in her body fired at once. She shuddered—*don't move*—and her immobility intensified everything until her skin itself pulsed with the sensations. She shoved her hand into her mouth, trying to stifle the cries.

"Pretty sumisita." As he chuckled and released her clit, the blood surged madly back into it, and the rush of sensation seized her body, shaking it out of her control.

He slid his fingers out and gripped her hips, holding her firmly. Her heart thudded against her ribs as she gasped for air.

"I heard too much noise, and you definitely moved," he said. Before she had a chance to regain her breath, four more stinging swats landed on her bottom.

Her insides clenched as the sting somehow engulfed her clit in another rolling wave of pleasure. She tried not to moan. Who knew what he'd do?

His sure hands rubbed her stinging cheeks, soothing the burn. Soothing her. Her breathing started to slow.

"Down you go," he said, pulling her legs out straight and flattening her, stomach-down, on the pad.

*Oh God.* Her butt throbbed, and her body still jerked from coming so fast and hard. Now more? *I don't want to do this.*

He dangled her braid off the side of the desk, laid a damp hand towel over her hair, and pulled the sturdy table of torture toys closer. When he lit the candle, it flamed up like a torch, scaring her spitless. With a grunt, he took something from his boot and snipped the wick. Making the flame shorter. *Flame.*

She closed her mouth over a whimper.

He returned the tool to his boot, then leaned over the table, his hand on her back. With a squeeze on her shoulder, he kissed her cheek. She saw the stern set of his jaw. His dark, dark brown eyes looked into hers. "Do you trust me, cariño?"

The question melted whatever resistance remained after his demonstration of how easily he could control her body. "I do," she whispered.

He waited.

"I do, Master." He'd showed he owned her body; now

he wanted her soul as well—and he had it. God help her, he did.

His knuckles grazed down her face, over her lips. "You please me very much, gatita," he said softly.

Oh, she wanted to, so very badly.

He moved away to lower the lighting in the room until it was like dusk after a sunset. Then he leaned on the desk, close enough she could feel his body brush against hers. "Breathe, Kimberly, and listen to the music. I picked this for you."

As his calloused hand stroked up and down her back, her muscles relaxed, flattening into the pad. Her breathing kept pace with the rhythm of the song, the slow sweep of his hand.

She felt something different—a cool streak and a flashing warmth almost simultaneously, and his hand slid over the same spot. Again, and again, and she realized there was no pain, just a touch of cool, then heat following and disappearing under the rough stroke of his hand. A circle around her bottom. Down her legs and up to her back. His rhythm was the lapping of water on the beach, not quite regular, but so natural. Warmth, stroke.

Her eyes were open, and she watched the shadows dance on the wall with the flash of flame, then die down to darkness again. She could hear, dimly, the sound of people outside the room, their voices like seagulls in the distance.

The heat intensified, nipping at her skin, yet her worry slid away as her body and her mind grew too heavy to stay focused.

His low baritone broke into her calm. "You're being such a good girl, mi pequeña sumisa. Time to turn over."

How did he make his voice tug at her like a strong current? His firm hands rolled her over, and cool air washed over her front. He arranged her arms at her sides and pulled her hair over the end of the desk again.

"Do you want to watch the flame, gatita?" he asked in that soft, smooth voice.

"I love your accent," she said, unsure if she was dreaming.

How strange a thing to say, but his eyes crinkled, and he simply repeated, "Do you want to watch?"

"Sure." Her back didn't hurt, not at all, except for her bottom where... "You spanked me," she told him.

"I did." He lifted her shoulders high enough to push a wedge pillow under the pad. "And I enjoyed it very much. You have a very spankable ass, no?"

Her giggle sounded odd. She felt like a bubble rising up out of the ocean, heading for the surface.

He turned, a little skewer with the white gauze burning like a minitorch. He ran it down her thigh, the streak of flame almost gone before the stroke of his hand erased it completely.

"Oooh, that's so pretty."

The flash of his smile was just as pretty. Then the rhythm came back, the blip of coolness, the flash of the flame, his big hand wiping it out so the touch of fire stayed only warm...or sometimes with little teeth.

He changed out the skewer thing for another, giving her a slow kiss between, making her happy that her mouth was available. He worked his way across her stomach, upward toward her breasts.

She knew she should worry, only her fear never quite surfaced before her breast lit with the dancing flame and, like magic, was gone. Her skin tingled, her nipple contracting as if unsure if it was supposed to get aroused. He held the torch away and stopped to lick that peak.

Then he closed his lips over her other nipple in a reversal of the order—hot mouth, cool air. The flame.

Around the outer sides of her breasts. Down the center. Flames danced across her body...

He smiled at her, his eyes holding the heat of the fire, and she realized the flickering was gone from the room and only his hands were left, his hands on her breasts, his mouth over her clit, and her arousal coming up and breaking over her like storm waves over a rocky shore.

# Chapter Ten

He'd never had a submissive climax so sweetly or trust him so completely. Raoul hadn't shaken off the exquisite ache of tenderness...until he turned and saw the window.

He'd been so far into topspace during the scene that he hadn't noticed when the Overseer had arrived, but the cabrón stood there now. Raoul nodded at him.

Dahmer tilted his head toward the clubroom, then strolled away. Displeased he'd had to share anything with the bastard, Raoul frowned. Time to finish talking and get Dahmer out of the Shadowlands, which meant subjecting Kimberly to his presence again.

Of course, without Dahmer, he and Kimberly wouldn't be here at all. Or together. She was worth it.

He smiled to see she hadn't roused, was still tranced out. He ran his fingers over her skin, feeling only a dry heat like a sunburn, but no blisters. Good. After using the damp blanket to wipe down her skin, he applied aloe lotion and tucked a fuzzy blanket around her. As he put the room to rights, he stopped every minute to stroke her gently as she slowly returned to the real world.

A tap on the door attracted his attention. The little cleaning woman waited in the doorway. She pointed to herself, then the room, indicating she'd take over the cleanup. Z had probably sent her.

Raoul nodded, wanting to have Kimberly in his arms. He wrapped her in the subbie blanket, picked her up, then glanced at her folded clothing.

Peggy whispered, "I'll leave them and your bag at the bar for you, Master Raoul."

"Thank you."

Kimberly's eyes opened, still a little glazed. She smiled at the woman, echoing his words, "Thank you."

Peggy beamed.

"Ah, you are coming back to me now, gatita?" Raoul kissed the top of her head.

She rubbed her cheek on his chest like a sleepy cat. "I like when you hold me."

Dios, she was going to break his heart. "I like when I hold you too."

He walked out the hallway and into the main clubroom, wincing as the music of Alice in Chains hammered into his head. Club members who'd watched the fireplay gave him a thumbs-up. A few started to talk, realized Kimberly's still sleepy state, and changed it to a quiet, "Great scene."

He nodded and smiled. Near the bar, he spotted Dahmer and Sam at a table, watching a suspension scene. Back to reality. But they looked engrossed enough that he could take time for Kimberly to rouse further. He caught Sam's eye, then chose a quieter area, knowing they'd join him when the scene wound down.

A pretty submissive appeared and set a beer and bottled water on the table. She murmured, "From my mistress."

Raoul saw that Olivia had taken over the bar. She gave him a small salute and returned to mixing drinks.

KIM FELT...WONDERFUL, everything open and loose and melty.

"Gatita." A deep, resonant voice sounded as strong as the arms around her.

She blinked and smiled up into dark chocolate eyes. Her heart swelled, filling with warmth, an infinitely stretchable balloon. Her arm didn't want to move, but the need to touch surged inside her, demanding action. She put her palm on his cheek and felt how it creased when he smiled.

"Are you with me here?"

*Always.* She opened her mouth to tell him how much she loved him, but a movement from the corner of her eyes silenced her. People. She stiffened, a shard of ice jabbing through her relaxed muscles.

"No, look at me, Kimberly," Master R murmured, pulling her gaze to him. "You were wonderful, sumisita, and I am very pleased with you."

Warmth flowed back into her, a returning tide. God she loved him so much.

"But we're not alone. We're still in the Shadowlands, and the other two men will join us shortly. You must stay very quiet." He nuzzled her cheek. "I hadn't intended to send you so deep, and I'm not going to leave you alone."

*Stay quiet.* "Yes, Master."

His lips curved. "Good girl."

As he held her, she rubbed her forehead against his muscular chest, wondering fuzzily when she'd come to feel so at home in his arms.

"That was an excellent scene, Raoul. Exactly what I need for the auction." The approaching voice was horrible, greasy, making her feel wrong…ugly…as if she wanted to run. Run and hide. *The Overseer.*

She made a sound, and Master R's arms tightened. He pulled her up slightly, setting his chin on the top of her hair. She pressed her face into his neck, breathing in his clean scent, like a wind off a stormy sea. Masculine. Safe.

The voices continued to talk around her. She turned her head, determinedly not looking at the slaver. Resting her cheek on Master R's shoulder, she watched the people and play areas.

In the closest one, an olive-skinned dom was caning his male sub. The next—a black domme used vampire claws on two subsmissives, male and female, who were wiggling with pain and pleasure.

Then a six-foot rope spiderweb had a pretty brunette sub tied to it. When she wiggled a foot loose, her face lit with laughter, and she said something—undoubtedly sassy—to her older dom. Without warning, he viciously slapped her face, snapping her head around. The sub turned back to him, her lip bleeding, expression holding pure, horrible shock. And she started crying.

Kim tried to sit up to go help, but Master R held her too firmly. "Shhh," he said under his breath.

Jessica stormed over to the scene. The short blonde walked right into the area, said something to the dom, and started to undo the submissive's restraints. The man, a lean English-looking type, shoved her away. She pushed him back, shouted something. And he grabbed her.

"No." Kim fought the arms around her.

"Stop. Now!" Master R growled in her ear.

She obeyed automatically, then was horrified at her idiocy. *What am I doing*? She went limp.

"I thought we'd taught her not to interfere," the Overseer said in a nasty voice.

"After a scene, the girl doesn't think too clearly." Master R added coldly, "She'll learn."

"I'm sorry, Master," she whispered against his neck.

A tiny pinch on her butt said he wasn't angry.

A hefty dom in a gold-trimmed vest walked over—

probably the dungeon monitor. The cruel dom scowled, talking to him. Jessica ignored them, busy trying to release the little submissive.

When Master Z showed up, all activity in that area came to a stop. Man, he was more effective than a police siren.

Relieved, Kim glanced around. Master Sam had left and was almost to the scene. The Overseer studied the commotion with an...odd...expression on his face.

Kim turned back. Nothing much different. The English-looking dom pointed at Jessica. Color darkening, she yelled back.

Master Z covered her mouth. A second later, he jerked his hand away, and his expression turned to granite. He moved, and Jessica landed hard on her knees. Fisting her hair, he ruthlessly trapped her head against his thigh. *Oh boy.* She'd actually bit Master Z? God, was she in trouble.

Master Z didn't look down. Face still frighteningly cold, he spoke to the jerk of a dom. The man took a step back.

"Appears the situation is under control," the Overseer said. When he glanced at Kim, she closed her eyes, burying her face back against Master R's neck and tuning everything out except the feeling of strength surrounding her. *Breath goes in. Breath goes out.*

"It's been an interesting visit," the Overseer said. "Especially seeing your slave so obedient. Really, Raoul, you'd net a handsome profit if you sold her back to me."

Master R laughed lightly. "Not worth the work it would take to start over again."

A pause, as if Dahmer wanted to keep trying; then he said, "Training is a bitch, isn't it? I've been doing some recently, since I still have one of the slaves you met. The redhead didn't get bought. Older slaves don't sell well, so I can only hope training will make her more enticing."

*Linda—going to auction? Oh God.* But maybe that was good. When the FBI took them down, she'd be rescued.

"Couldn't hurt," Master R said. "I take it the young one got sold?"

"More's the pity."

*Holly. He's talking about sweet, hopeful Holly.* Kim tried to sit up, and the arms around her contracted until she had trouble breathing.

"Oh?" Master R asked politely. "What happened to her?"

"Far as I can tell, the idiot owner got carried away with seeing blood. He beat her to death." The Overseer gave an exasperated sigh. "We made a profit, of course, but—"

"Yes, that's a waste." Master R sounded as if he didn't care at all, and Kim hated him. Tears spilled from under her eyelids. How could he be so cold?

She slowly realized his muscles under and around her were rigid. He was holding himself in check, holding her there as well. His anger was almost palpable.

"Until the auction then," the Overseer said. "I'll have an area set up to your specifications." A thump sounded as he set his drink down. "I'll call you a day or so before to give you the specific date and time. I look forward to seeing how impressed the buyers are with your scene."

Silence. She tried to hear if he'd moved away, but the room was too noisy. So she kept herself stiff and quiet. Waiting.

A minute later, Master R let loose, cursing long and low in a stream of Spanish.

She'd never heard him sound like that or seen him so furious.

When she moved, he stopped, and the fury faded from his face. "Gatita, I'm sorry about your friend." He wiped away the tears sliding silently down her cheeks.

The loosening of his grip released the sobs that had piled up inside her like a thunderstorm. *Oh God, Holly. Please God, not Holly.* She was too young. She'd told stories about the antics in her dorm at college. About her mother who lived in Alaska. She'd been so homesick and scared; she'd cried herself to sleep every night. How could she be dead?

Kim tried to curse like Master R but could only cry. She wanted to leave, to hide somewhere quiet, and he wouldn't let her go. Anger rose, engulfing her. He hadn't saved Holly; he was a man. *I hate you.* Her fists stung as she hit him, harder and harder. She choked on the names she called him. As he muffled her screams against his leather vest, she cried some more.

"What the hell happened?" A man's voice.

Kim tried to stop crying, to shut up, and couldn't.

Master R didn't tell her to be quiet, simply kept holding her. "The bastard told us a slave was whipped to death. The women were friends."

Kim shook, inside and outside. She knew how a whip felt, the tearing of skin, the slicing agony. How scared Holly must have been, pain and more pain. *Better it had been me.*

"Hell." The man paused. "You want to get her out of here?"

"No. I can't drive and hold her. She needs to be held right now."

Kim's crying slowed to hiccups, and she leaned against him, exhausted.

"Be careful, buddy. You look too concerned about a slave, and everyone nearby heard you swearing." His voice lowered. "Don't forget we still don't know who selected our subs for the Harvest Association. He might not be here tonight, but..."

"A good reminder," Master R said softly. "Thank you, my friend. I did forget."

Kim pulled a shuddering breath into her lungs and sat up.

The giant dom bartender was frowning down at them, heavy brows drawn together. He tossed Master's toy bag and her clothing onto a chair, then met her gaze. "Back with us, love? Good. Keep your master from letting his temper loose."

His conviction that she had that power was like a stepping stone away from her sorrow. She needed to stay in her slave character, and she had to look after her dom. "Yes, Sir," she whispered. As she wiped her eyes, she plainly saw Master R's rage.

The big dom was right. Master R wasn't keeping his face under control.

"Master," she said softly. "We should leave. Will you put my leash on and lead…so I can follow?"

He looked down. His fingers were infinitely gentle as he touched her cheek. "*Tesoro mío*," he said under his breath. "Yes, let us go home."

\* \* \* \*

"Did you get my goods back?" Christopher Greville spoke politely into his cell phone. It might be late to call, but he couldn't rest without knowing if Dahmer had succeeded.

Over the past day, he'd come to realize that he was pleased the cunt was still alive. This way, he could deal with her himself—could give her a very slow, excruciatingly painful death.

"No, the owner isn't interested in selling." Dahmer sounded irritated. "I thought he'd jump at making a profit."

A whip of rage struck. Greville's pulse throbbed painfully in his temple. Who was this fucking buyer? "In that case, just pick my merchandise up." *Kidnap the bitch.* "You're an expert at that kind of business."

"I will. But only if I can succeed without causing any...upset."

"I don't give a damn about—"

"Management reacts poorly to bad publicity."

Greville hesitated. Last month, when a naive buyer fell in *love* with his slave and tried to inform on the association, the Harvest Association's reaction had been...extreme. Removing them would have been adequate. A bullet. Simple enough. But no. Instead, the buyer and slave had been spread-eagled and restrained on the bed, one on top of the other; then the house was set on fire. Before the fire trucks arrived, the entire neighborhood heard them shrieking as they burned to death.

A bad way to go. He'd thought it funny at the time, but Dahmer's warning was...perhaps...valid. "Do what you can."

"I will. If I can't pick the goods up neatly, I do have another possibility to fall back on, if needed. Be patient, please."

*Patient!* Greville stabbed the Off button as fury seared his nerves. The need to hurt something was so strong he tasted it, but he forced himself to stay at his desk. If he started whipping the slave downstairs, he'd not stop until she was dead.

Since he was a premium buyer, the Harvest Association didn't enforce the delay when he killed a slave, but losing two within a short period wouldn't be wise.

He waited until his rage had died slightly. Enough, perhaps. Then he rose and headed to the basement. He needed to hurt her, to hear her screams rise to desperation, shriller and shriller.

\* \* \* \*

His gatita was exhausted. After carrying her into the house, Raoul tucked her into bed and then changed into regular clothes.

Looking down at the silky black hair surrounding her pale face, he felt the heavy foundations of...something settle slowly into place. He cared for her. Too much. With his history—with hers—this affection could only be a mistake, as foolish as building a bridge without considering the wind. He needed to back away while he still could.

Her eyes opened. She stared at his bedroom, her relief to be home obvious. Hearing about Holly had been too much, like stretching copper wire past the fracture point.

"How do you feel?" he asked, wanting to touch her. Comfort her. Yet hadn't he just told himself to pull away? *Stupid Sandoval.* She'd slipped past his defenses so easily.

"Okay." Her chin rose. "I'm fine."

As she attempted to appear strong, to lie to him with her body and her words, irritation scraped his already raw nerves. "Do you ever tell me the truth when you're not feeling well?"

"I—" Her brows drew together even as her arms wrapped around her waist, comforting herself as if she didn't believe he could do a good job. "I think I know myself."

"Why do you not trust me enough to be honest?" He set his jaw, knowing—knowing neither of them was thinking clearly—yet after what they'd shared, having her lie to him was like a stab in the back.

When her mouth firmed, he prepared himself for another untruth. Perhaps that was good; he'd have an excuse to leave her here with her dishonesty, her inability to be the submissive he wanted her to be—his inability to accept her even if she was. This was a way to pull away before they both got hurt. He started to turn—

"I—I'm sorry." Her fingers pushed the blanket into folds, straightened it out again. "Mom didn't—my father was cruel, made fun of her whenever she complained—so she stopped. And I learned—" She bit her lip and stared at the covers. Folding. Straightening. "I don't mean to lie to you. It just slips out."

*Dios.* Raoul took a step forward, even as his brain told him to leave. To back away before he had more cables binding him than he could escape. "Kimberly..."

"I'm not fine, Master. At all." She looked up finally, and her eyes swam with tears. "I'm scared to be alone. Only I'm going to cry some more, and I didn't want you to have to..."

"To get all wet?" Nothing in the world could have kept him from sitting on the bed and pulling her into his arms. "Sumisita—cry. I'll hold you."

Her shoulders were already shaking. So fragile to bear what she'd been through, and now to add grief to the mix. His own heart ached when he remembered the young victim, Holly. If he ever gained the opportunity to fight the slavers, some of them would die. But for now, his duty was to be a little subbie's support and comfort.

She cried for a long time, long enough to soak his T-shirt, and so violently that a couple of times she'd started to gag, and he'd shaken her out of it.

When her crying finally stilled and only an occasional shudder coursed through her body, Raoul's arms were still wrapped firmly around her. The tightness was gone from her muscles; the horror had faded from her eyes. "All right?"

"I'm fi—" She choked on a laugh and amended, "I'm better. Thank you."

"Good." He tilted her head up and kissed her, tasting the salt of her tears, the sweetness of her lips. She softened under his careful assault, then kissed him back, as if she needed the distraction—the affirmation of life—as much as he did.

He slid her off his lap, laid her against the pillows, and took her mouth again. His fingers tangled lightly in her hair, firmly enough to remind her who he was yet not rough enough to resurrect bad memories. He'd learned how to walk that tightrope over the past weeks. As he hardened, he deepened the kiss.

She wore nothing. The conviction that a submissive's body should be accessible to her master reverberated through him. For tonight at least, he would accept his role.

He ran his finger over the scar on her ribs, then up. Her breast fit into his palm, lush and soft. He pulled back far enough to watch her. He couldn't trust her to tell him if she was afraid or repelled, and he was no mind reader like Z. But when he studied her face, the changes of her muscles and her hands, he'd discover if she was fearful—or aroused.

Tonight, everything he saw spoke of desire: her lips and nipples reddening, the flush on her cheeks, the hitch in her breath when he cupped her breast. His gatita had responsive nipples, not overly sensitive, but sweetly erogenous zones. He licked a circle around one and then blew on it, smiling as it peaked.

"What are you smiling about?" she asked, her gaze on his face as soft as her hand in his hair.

"Women's breasts are fascinating. The way they wobble and move. How your nipples bunch up as if they had a mind of their own."

She rolled her eyes, then gasped as he pinched the neglected nipple into action.

"Of course, men have their own independently acting parts." He pressed his hard cock against her thigh.

She lightened his heart with a tiny snicker and stole it altogether when she set her hand on his cheek and asked, "Why can you make me laugh, even when I'm naked and a

little scared?" She pulled his tear-dampened shirt away
from his skin. "Seems like all you get from me is wet
clothes."

He abandoned her long enough to pull the shirt over
his head and toss it aside, then removed his pants. He put
her hand back on his shoulder. "Touch me, cariño."

Her soft palm ran over his chest, then paused when he
pushed her legs apart.

"Look at me." He'd been careful to avoid the
missionary position, never wanting to make her feel pinned
down or restrained by his size or body. Tonight—tonight,
with her emotions still high and the bond from their scene
strong between them, he'd push her further and try to
replace the sordid memories with brighter ones.

He moved his body over hers, staying poised above
her, but putting no weight on her. Fear widened her eyes.
Her hand flattened against his chest to push him away.

"Look at me, sumisita mía," he repeated softly.

Her gaze met his, and the tenseness slid from her
body. "Master R," she whispered, confirming what her sight
told her.

"Yes." He smiled and bit her chin, enjoying the sweet
gasp. "I want your hand on my cock. Touch me, gatita."

Still holding her eyes, he took her hand and put it on
him. At the sensation of her small fingers curling around
him, his shaft surged even fuller with blood. "You have a
soft touch. Stroke me," he directed.

Not looking away, she moved her grip up and set her
fingers on top of his piercing. Her thumb wiggled the part
on the underside.

The sensation was so heady, his eyes closed for a
moment as he fought himself. This one, the one woman who
needed his self-control the most, was the one who
challenged him more than any other. Pulling his attention

from the glide of her fingers around him, he balanced on one arm and his knees and reached down between her thighs. No weight on her yet—just his size looming over her was enough for the moment.

He smiled when his fingers touched her pussy. How she kept herself shaved bare for him, without him having to order it, was a delight. His voice came out low and ragged. "You're wet for me, gatita."

Her olive cheeks darkened with a flush, enough for keen eyes to note. Despite the slickness, her clit was still hidden in its hood, and he considered teasing her with a toy, then knew he wouldn't move from this spot. Tonight was for their bodies only, no ties or cuffs, no toys.

Of course, the lack of tools didn't mean he couldn't indulge in a little mental bondage. "Spread your legs farther apart," he said.

KIM STARED UP at Master R, a shiver running through her. He was so big, could easily hurt her. And now—

"Must I repeat myself?" he asked, his voice lowering to a smooth threat. His eyes were dark, dark brown.

Her knees separated more, her folds pulling apart, exposing her. He smiled and swirled his finger around her opening, spreading the wetness. So wet. She shivered as he dipped his head, taking one nipple into his mouth, even as his touch edged nearer her clit. Needed more. Her hips tilted up slightly.

His head lifted. He studied her for a long moment. "No, you get only what I choose to give you. I will not tie you tonight, sumisita mía, but you will put your left hand so..." He firmly curled her fingers around one of the metal swirls on the headboard. "Your legs stay open—no matter what I do." He smiled into her eyes. "Your other hand can continue to please me until I say otherwise."

Her pulse picked up.

"Do you understand?"

Mouth dry, she managed a nod.

"Kimberly?"

"Yes, Sir."

He shook his head no.

Her voice became huskier. "Yes, Master."

"Much better." He rewarded her with a slow kiss, a demanding one. When his tongue took possession, she could only think of the last time his cock pushed into her, filling her like that. He abandoned her mouth and inched down her body. A tiny bite on her nipple fragmented her mind. A light pinch on her clit made her gasp. Both pains, so similar, sent need streaming like a riptide between the two points. She was still tender from his attentions during the scene, and his fingers were slightly abrasive...and it only pushed her higher.

Keep arm over head, she told herself. Legs open. Her hips—the one wiggle that escaped her was rewarded with a nasty nip on the underside of her breast and made her gasp, increasing the feeling of being washed away in need.

His finger pressed into her entrance, a small stretch, then slid over her clit, repeating the motions. Her labia swelled and throbbed. Her clit tightened. Each time became more intense. The teasing hint of his finger in her vagina made her remember being filled completely, made her *need*... She wiggled again.

He lifted his head and gave her that unyielding dom look that melted her insides into a puddle. One corner of his mouth turned up. "Are you having problems, gatita?"

Her glare should have burned his eyelashes to stubby ash. "Would you just fuck me already?"

His dark sexy laugh burst out, so infectious, she couldn't keep a giggle back.

After pulling himself from her grip, he lowered his hips. His cock pressed on her open pussy; his pelvis touched hers; his chest touched her breasts. Fear slammed into her like someone had broken down a door, pushing all the—

"Look at me, Kimberly," he said ruthlessly.

She realized her eyes had shut. She opened them to meet his indomitable gaze.

"Keep your eyes open and on mine. And both hands on the headboard."

She realized she was pushing him away. *Oh.* She lifted her arm and grabbed another wire on the headboard. The position arched her breasts up and rubbed her nipples across the hair on his chest, making her toes curl with the sensation.

He positioned his cock and pressed into her, the metal piercing like a blunt finger inside on the front of her vagina, the sensation so intense her vision blurred.

"Open. Your. Eyes."

*Oh God.* He held her gaze as he was sliding in, stretching her, every inch setting new nerves into a clamor of need. Her hips gave the slightest wiggle.

"If you move again"—his whisper made the threat even more potent—"I will tie you up and leave you alone to suffer."

"Sorry. I'm trying. Masterrrr." The whine horrified her and made him smile. *Drown him.*

"So you are." He paused to lick her nipples, then rubbed his chest against her sideways, the abrasive feeling on her hard wet peaks mesmerizing.

He held his hips still, moving only his upper torso, and her insides throbbed with the need for more. She wanted to rub against him, all over, to push her hips up and... *Don't move.*

She forced her muscles to relax, to stillness, even as

everything burned, demanding action. The need to keep a portion of her mind separate to command her body distracted her, increased her arousal. Her clit felt the size of her fist, screaming for him to touch it.

He watched her, then smiled, easing out of her slowly. The metal ball rubbed against something sensitive inside her with an exquisite, almost painful pressure.

A slow push back in, and a shudder ran through her. *Don't move, don't move. Oh God, I'm going to die.* "Oh, please."

"Please is a nice word," he said agreeably. And he pushed in again, faster—just a little faster, his eyes intent on her, then flickering over her face, her arms and hands.

*More, more, more.* She wanted to lift her hips, make him go deeper, go faster.

"Speak to me, gatita. You need to work on communicating your emotions, and this is a good place to start." He slid out, tilting his hips so that damned ball scraped across something inside her, and the waves of her arousal turned into a heavy surf.

Boiling and churning. "Harder. More. God…"

The flash of his smile made her heart skip, and then he slammed into her.

Oh wonderful hardness. "More, more, more."

He laughed. "Very expressive." But he complied, hammering into her, and she knew somewhere it should be frightening, only she was so, so close that the driving rhythm only spiraled her up. *Up.* His big hand slid under her butt to lift her so every withdrawal rubbed his pelvis over her clit.

"Oh, oh—" Her breathing stopped. *More, please, more.* His cock slammed in, penetrating far inside her and scraping that damned piercing over her G-spot, and his groin rubbed her clit. He was so big, and everything she felt, everything he did expanded into pure sensation, and a depth charge of pleasure exploded, brilliant and hot, the fiery waves expanding everywhere.

She gasped for breath as another intense wave hit. Sparkles danced in front of her eyes. Her fingers and toes tingled.

Laughing slightly, he nuzzled her neck and shoved into her, deep, deep, hard, and his erection thickened, then was jerking inside her.

He was over her, surrounding her, filling her, his heat, his breath, his scent, drowning her in him.

Her heart turned over. "God, I love you."

*Silence.* Oh, a bad silence, growing worse the longer it lengthened. He lifted his head, and the languorous expression of satiation disappeared with his concern. Leaning on one arm, letting his hips pin her down, he pushed her hair from her damp face. "This is not...wise, gatita." He sighed, stroking her cheek with one finger. Not evading her eyes, not trying to pretend he hadn't heard her—not Master R.

"Why not?" she whispered, even knowing the answer. Some of it.

"You are not...healed, not ready to know your heart." His fleeting smile wasn't reflected in his eyes. "It would be wrong of me to permit this."

Could the master command her heart?

But he didn't want her. She heard that clearly. How could her body shimmer with satisfaction even as her emotions were disappearing into a hole of blackness? Her brief smile reflected his. "It's okay. Just the heat of the moment, you know."

"Of course." He kissed her lips gently, then rolled them both over, his hand curved over her bottom keeping them together with him still inside her. He settled her on top of him, guiding her head down into the curve of his shoulder. "Sleep. We'll discuss this in the morning."

*No. No, I don't think we will.* His skin was warm and damp under her cheek, and she inhaled the fragrance of him and sex. She'd survived kidnapping and slavery and the loss of friends. She'd survive this as well—but damned if she'd talk about it.

# Chapter Eleven

*"I love you."* Remembering Kimberly's soft avowal, Raoul abandoned the brewing coffee and walked outside to stare at the water. The brisk morning air ruffled his hair but didn't bring him any clarity of thought. How could he have let her get emotionally involved with him? This wasn't—she shouldn't love him. Dios, she should be running the other direction.

Only he knew better. She was tough, brave, and resilient. He'd known women who reacted with hysterics to a fender bender. Had her father taught her to be so durable? Or her mother? Had Kimberly lived with an example of how to survive abuse?

He rubbed his hand over his mouth. She was confusing emotional dependence and need with love. How should he handle this? *Carefully, Sandoval.* Like walking a girder with no safety line.

The problem was he cared for her, and he had no excuse that he'd been mistreated. No, his mistake was to have let her into his house, his life. His heart. He'd grown so fond of her that he had trouble imagining his home without her bubbly presence.

*Don't go there, Sandoval.* She'd leave as soon as the auction was over, and according to the Overseer, that might occur in a week or so.

The realization was like a gut shot from a steel rivet. He'd miss their showers. The workouts in the weight room.

The fighting as he taught her to cripple and maim, and the unholy light in her eyes when she'd mastered a technique. The evenings watching television, arguing over movies. Her snippy backtalk, and how she tried to hide her pleasure at serving him.

The way she softened under his hands when he kissed her. He felt himself harden. *Good job, Sandoval.*

Well, he'd see this through. And try to keep them both from being stupid.

As he turned to go back in, he wondered if she'd want to stay with him when this was over. *No.* She truly was submissive, but she'd made it clear, over and over, that she didn't want to live the lifestyle. And she needed to heal. Once her head was on straight, she wouldn't want a master. Not soon, probably never.

Even if miracles occurred, he wasn't ready for a relationship either. It was far too soon. And this time, he wouldn't settle for anything less than a full-time Dominant/submissive relationship with someone who wanted it as much as he did.

Over the waves, a gull gave a long screech as another stole its fish. He headed into the house. He'd need a massive amount of caffeine to figure out a way to pull back before he hurt her further.

KIM FROWNED AT the sunlight streaming in the balcony window, then glanced at the clock on the bedside table. Noon? No wonder Master R had already gotten up.

The empty space beside her in bed sent a pang through her. She'd come to like waking up with Master R's solid body next to hers, or for him to awaken her as he had almost every morning since they'd had real sex. His hands would caress her breasts, and his cock would ease between her legs from behind. He'd hold her in place, gently, firmly, and push into her. She'd start off groggy, but when his clever fingers would slide over her clit, she'd be right onboard with early morning sex. Who knew it could be so much fun?

Not this morning. She sighed and climbed out of bed,

But last night, she'd said she loved him, and he hadn't exactly looked thrilled to hear she cared.

With a frown, she stepped into the shower, missing his presence there too. The teasing, his laughter. The one morning he hadn't taken her in bed, he'd made up for it a few minutes later.

Her lips curved. That time she'd told him she wasn't interested in shower sex. *"Not today."* God, so not the thing to tell a dom.

*"Really,"* he'd said with that amused—stern—look in his eyes. *"Does a submissive have that choice?"*

Before she'd realized how much trouble she was in, he'd grasped her around the waist, walked out of the shower, and laid her on the cold counter. He pinned her legs to his shoulders, put his mouth on her pussy, and *forced* her to have an orgasm, waited a second, then did it again. She was dizzy when he pulled her back into the shower. And then, being the dom he was, he'd firmly bent her over and taken her from behind. Hard.

Why did she get off on that control? She soaped her body, snorting at how her nipples had bunched up. Yep, just thinking of him did it for her.

*But he doesn't want my love.*

Was he right about her? Did she imagine love when it was really only need? *Maybe.* She dried off. She didn't feel needy. Well, perhaps a little.

A pair of her jeans, underwear, and a tank top lay on the towel bar. Apparently Master R had decided she could wear clothes today. Her hand hesitated over the clothing. Today—or every day now? Her job was done, wasn't it? The entire charade had been to get Sam referred during the Overseer's follow-up visit.

Even if Sam failed and Master R had to attend the auction, he'd use an FBI agent as his submissive. *Not me.*

Her relief was balanced by the ugly vision of Master R with another woman. Would he spank the submissive? Make her come? *Of course he would.* The flood of sheer jealousy appalled her. *God, I need to get out of here.*

When she entered the kitchen a few minutes later, Master R sat on a bar stool at the island, newspapers and coffee before him. She started to speak, then saw the phone he held to his ear.

"That's right," he was saying. "Sam said Dahmer called a few minutes ago. His background check passed, and he should get an invitation to the auction sometime this week."

That meant the job was done. Kim hugged herself, trying to process her emotions. After her first scuba dive, she'd hauled herself up the boat's steps, shucked off the heavy air tank, and dropped the belt with twenty pounds of lead weights. She'd felt as if she might float away. Very much like now. *My part is over.*

Master R listened and then grinned. "Yes, he put on quite a show. Had one of the better screamers." He glanced at her, his eyes shadowed but approving. "Kimberly did her job perfectly."

A glow sparked to life and was snuffed out with his next words. "Since Sam is accepted, I think she should move to Gabi's house."

Kim stared at him. A slap in the face wouldn't have hurt as much. What had she done wrong?

"No, she didn't do anything wrong. But keeping her in a Master/slave relationship as she recovers from being kidnapped would be foolish. She's getting dependent on me,

Kouros." He met her eyes squarely, not trying to hide anything.

Anger started to overtake the pain. Yes, she could hate him.

"No, she doesn't need to stay here. Her job is finished. Even if Sam's invitation falls through, I'd use one of your people for the demo, not Kimberly. I would never take her to a slave auction. We discussed this already." His eyes turned cold. "Send her to Gabi's. She's done enough."

*Good to know.* Trying not to scowl, Kim poured herself some coffee.

Master R straightened suddenly. "When was this?"

The sharpness in his voice made Kim jump, and she hissed as coffee scalded her fingers. She set the cup down hastily, shaking her hand. *Ouch.*

"Kimberly!" Master R pointed to the faucet.

She hesitated. *But I want to hear.* Caving in, she ran the cold water over her reddened fingers. Over the noise of the water, she heard him say, "I'm putting you on speaker. She has a right to know." He set the phone on the island.

*Know what?*

"You're a stubborn bastard, Sandoval," came a man's sonorous voice with the broadened *A* sound of someone from Maine. "Miss Moore, I was telling your master why I don't want you to return to Gabi's house."

She swallowed. *I don't know this man.* "Why?"

"I don't know if Raoul ever told you, but we planted surveillance devices around the neighborhood. A simple precaution to keep you safe."

Her jaw dropped, and she stared at the walls. What had they seen?

"No, gatita," Master R said. "They're only outside—the front and sides of the house, and one on the patio pointing toward the beach."

The FBI agent snorted. "He wouldn't permit anything else. We've spotted a few people watching your house since Raoul bought you. Very casual. But earlier today, a private investigator checked you out and took pictures."

Kim wrapped her arms around herself, a chill running through her. The outside world wasn't safe. She already knew that.

"With the prior surveillance they did, they'd know you spend a lot of time outside. If you suddenly disappear, but Raoul is still in the house, they'd wonder why."

Watching the house. Ice crawled up her spine. "What if they try to take me back?" God, that was stupid. They wouldn't steal from their own buyer.

"Kidnapping a slave they'd sold wouldn't be good for business." The FBI agent paused. "If it helps your worries, though, the neighborhood is well policed and has a neighborhood watch. Raoul has a hell of a security system on both the house and grounds, much better than the one at Marcus's place. Nobody in their right minds would try to breech it."

Master R gave her a small smile and whispered, "I grew up on the streets, remember?"

*Huh.* She'd seen him making the rounds before bed, checking on stuff, and hadn't bothered to ask why. So she was safe here. But to stay?

Master R remained silent, obviously giving her the choice. *I hate making decisions.* She wanted to go to Gabi's...yet even if he didn't care for her, she wanted to be with him.

With an effort, she pushed her personal baggage to the side. Her wishes were irrelevant. No matter what she felt, she mustn't do anything to cause suspicions and blow the investigation. "I guess I'll be here for another few days."

"Thank you, Miss Moore. I look forward to meeting

you later this week."

With a low curse, Master R slid the phone shut; then his eyes narrowed on her. "Will you be all right with this?"

*I might never be right again.* "Of course." She winced when his brows drew together. *Telling the complete truth surely sucked at times.* "All right, it's difficult, being so unsettled. I want to go home and get on with my life. See my mom." *Stay with you. Run from you. Love you.*

"Of course." He took a sip of his coffee, and the release of his intent gaze was like escaping a riptide. "You must miss your mamá very much."

His voice held a wealth of understanding, and the tenderness with which he'd said "mamá" told her a lot. And left more unexplained. She frowned. "I thought your family lived in Tampa. Did you tell them not to visit?"

His mouth tightened. "We do not…speak."

"How come?"

"They don't approve of my BDSM lifestyle. At all. When they found out… They'd probably have reacted better if I'd been gay." He rubbed his face. He might have thought his expression unreadable, but it wasn't. Being alienated from his family hurt him.

"I'm sorry." He was so loving. To have his family push him away must have been terrible.

"It's not your problem, gatita."

"I s'pose not." She watched the coffee in her cup, making the black liquid swirl in circles. *Like my life.* He said she shouldn't be in a Master/slave relationship, and that she'd become dependent on him. Maybe he was right. "Master R?"

He tilted his head. "Yes?"

"Can we live together as…as friends? No more of the master—sumisita stuff?

His frown cleared. "We can. It's a good plan." He

tapped his fingers on his papers and then looked at her again. "You may have the guest bedroom as before."

No more being wrapped in his arms at night? The kitchen seemed to darken. "Great. I'll go move my stuff."

Her knees held up nicely all the way to Master's—no, *Raoul's*—bedroom. She bundled together the clothing Gabi had given her and left the French maid's costume in the closet for him to return to Z. After tossing everything on the bed in the guest room, she went back for her toiletries.

She turned her eyes away from the shower, refusing to remember how his big hands felt moving over her soap-slicked body. Warm and firm. *No.* One more week; then it was over. She'd go home and...do what? Aside from wanting to see her mom, she'd never thought about after that.

Her knees went weak, and she leaned on the counter, staring at herself in the mirror. *I should want to go home. To take up my life again.* Her friends would be overjoyed at her return.

Had her position at the marine lab been filled? Probably not—admin moved slowly. She'd go see them first thing and... A chill ran through her. What if she stepped out of the office or her house and...they took her again? *I have to go back to work. No choice.* She'd manage. She always did.

But she'd be so far from Tampa. How could she stand each day without Master R in it?

Her hands clenched. *Getting a little dependent, missy? Or a little in love?* Her inner cynic was so sarcastic that if it'd been a person, she'd have slapped its face. Because the answer to both questions was yes.

He...lifted her heart. She wanted to take care of him, put that special smile on his face, be there for him the way he'd been here for her. And why not? He obviously cared for her. *He did.*

Only...he hadn't exactly said "I love you" back to her.

Even if he did, they had differing goals. He was a master, and eventually he'd want a real slave, not a pretender. Cold seeped like a chill morning fog into her bones.

*I'm not a slave.* That wasn't the relationship she'd dreamed of—to kneel at a man's feet, to take his orders, to serve him. She hauled in a shuddering breath. *I don't belong here. Not really.*

She needed to not pine after something that would never work. They'd be friends like she said.

After she finished moving her stuff, she went back downstairs. Master R—*Raoul, dammit*—was still in the kitchen, making notes on a legal pad. Why did he have to be so...so wonderful? The broad shoulders, the strong hands, the stern jaw. Why wasn't life fair?

He looked up, and his smile faded as he got a *I-can-see-right-down-to-your-secrets* expression on his face. "Gatita, what is wrong?"

She shrugged. "Leftover nerves, I think." She rubbed at a smear on the floor with her shoe and asked casually, "Do we have any plans for this week?"

"Only one. To keep you safe until you go home."

*Go home.* How strange he'd mention that after she'd been thinking about it. Go home to what?

"For today, I thought we'd celebrate surviving our evening with the Overseer. I keep a sailboat at a marina nearby, and we can pick up a picnic lunch."

Be on the water again and be with Master R? Could anything be better? "Oh, yes. Please."

"Good enough. After I change, we'll head out. Meantime, can you get my toy bag out of the car?" He tossed his keys to her. "I don't like driving around with it...just in case of an accident or police. The car's parked in front."

She managed to stifle the *yes, Master* and said, "Sure,

I'll get it." Why hadn't he parked in the garage last night? Because he'd had to carry her upstairs. *Duh.* And the garage was on the opposite side of the house.

As she crossed the great room, Master R started up the stairs.

She stopped. *Wait. Go outside? By myself?* "Um. I'll... I'm not sure I know what your bag looks like." Her chest felt as if someone was wrapping ropes around her ribs and kept drawing them tighter.

He leaned one hip against the stair railing. "It's the only bag in the car."

"But—"

"Get the bag, gatita."

She didn't move.

His eyes narrowed, and then he came back down the stairs.

She relaxed. "You're going to escort me to your car?"

"No, I don't think so." His hand closed around her upper arm. He led her to the front and pushed her out the door.

She stood, stunned at his actions. Stood and stared down the curving drive. She could see the *street*—the street where anyone might wait. Where someone could shoot her and hurt her and cage her. "No!" *No no no.* She spun around and plowed into an immovable body.

He blocked the doorway, the light framing him, a dark angel. "Kimberly."

"No. No, I won't." She was trembling so violently that her knees buckled.

His arms closed around her, and he held her firmly. "Take a slow breath, gatita. Now."

She was cold, so cold. That was why she was shaking. Her fingers had even gone numb.

"Another breath. Let it out slowly." He made her take a few more.

Her heart slowed. And she realized she'd just had another damned panic attack for whatever reason.

"Now look at me."

The order couldn't be refused. She lifted her gaze to his intense dark brown eyes. His expression seemed strange. Concern and anger and...pity?

*How the hell dare he pity me?* She straightened in his arms and took a terrifying step away. "I'm just stressed from yesterday. Sorry."

"Then perhaps you should try again?"

*No!*

But he held his hand out, and she set her fingers in his.

He walked to the car, and she was all right. Yes, she was fine.

He released her hand. "Stay here for a moment, gatita."

When he started toward the house, somehow she was beside him, so close she was almost crawling into his clothes.

"Hmm." Without speaking further, he led her through the house, out the back onto the patio. He stopped by the pool, watching her closely. She wrapped her arms around herself, trying to figure out why she was still shaking and why she couldn't go outside. She'd been outside before.

He pointed to the beach ball on the other side of the pool. "Bring me that."

No problem. She'd only gone halfway when he called her back.

"You're afraid of being outside—on the street side—by yourself?"

"I-I—" She pulled in a breath of salt air, turned away from him. The waves rolled onto the shore; clouds puffed high in the sky. Normal world. *Abnormal Kim.* Her voice came out so tiny, he leaned forward to hear her. "When I went out to the front, I just knew they were there. They'd take me back. It's not safe outside." Everything inside told her that was truth.

"The patio is all right though? And the beach?" he asked softly, still holding her hand.

"I...guess so. It's got a fence. An ocean. No vehicles. They can't get me there." She blew a lock of hair away from her face. "It sounds stupid."

"Kimberly, where did they kidnap you?"

She remembered all too well. Every month, she'd drive from Savannah to Atlanta to spend the day with her mom. Then she'd spend the evening at the BDSM club. The highlight of her month. "Outside a club. When I reached for the handle of my car, I—I... The man Tasered me." Horrible pain, every muscle spasming, convulsing, screaming silently in agony. "They tossed me into a van."

He stroked her hair. "Now you figured out why you panic, does it help?"

"A little." Yet the thought of walking out a door again made her whole body tense in dread. She straightened her spine. "Try again?"

"Brave gatita." Hand on her arm, he led her to the front door as if she were a blind woman. "Let's see how far you can get."

She forced her feet to step outside. A long drive. The street. Something squeezed her chest, and black wavered like ghosts around the edges of her vision.

"Kimberly!" The command in his voice was as effective as a vicious slap.

She jolted and looked over her shoulder.

"I'm here. Nothing is going to happen to you." Fury came from him in waves, but it wasn't directed at her. "Take three steps. Then we'll go back in the house. Can you do that?"

She shook her head. Too far.

"Kimberly." He met her eyes, raised his chin. "Do it—for me."

For Master R. Her need to please warred with the fear. She eyed all the open space where she'd be exposed, the places someone could hide, and something tiny inside her quailed. Yet she took a step. Another. Her courage failed. She could only stand and shake.

"One more, gatita."

Her air was gone, and red streaked the lawn as she pushed a foot forward. One more.

"Good. Eyes on me." He was in front of her so quickly, she realized he'd been right behind her for each step. His face blocked the dangerous open lawn. "I'm very proud of you, Kimberly."

His praise released the last few bands around her chest, and she hauled in a breath.

"Next time you'll go four steps. In the meantime"—he held his hand out for hers—"we'll get my toy bag out of the car. Together."

* * * *

Three days of being friends wasn't all it was cracked up to be. With a silent sigh, Kim watched the morning sun move across the bedroom carpet, her hand over the wide palm cupping her breast. Contentment was being held in Master R's arms.

But...she wouldn't be here if she hadn't crawled into his bed in the middle of the night.

He'd made love to her. She grinned. She'd kinda started the process when she'd sneaked under the covers, run her hands up his thighs, and fondled his cock to hardness. At first, she'd thought he was asleep, but after a few minutes, she realized he'd been awake all along, waiting to discover how far she'd go.

*Far.* Giggling, she'd climbed on top of him, and it had been fun. He'd kissed her and stroked her. Sucked her nipples. But he hadn't taken control, hadn't demanded anything from her. His hands had been gentle, not firm. They'd both gotten off, but... She sighed. The sex hadn't been exciting at all. Kind of like piloting a motorboat instead of sailing in a strong wind. You'd get to your destination with the one; the other was sheer exhilaration.

*I want that kind of sex back.*

Master R was still asleep, one arm over her, spooned around her from behind. His morning erection pressed against her bottom. So...

They could have boring, we're-just-friends sex, but she wanted more. How far could a girl push a master before he lost his temper?

He didn't get angry easily. She bit her lip, unease quivering her nerves, and then rolled out of his arms. "No!" she snapped as his eyes opened. "No sex. You can't make me, and I don't want it."

When his darkly tanned face turned stern, her stomach spawned wiggly minnows. But then he relaxed. "No, I won't make you do anything you don't want, Kimberly." He put his hands behind his head, although his muscles were tight. "Go shower. I'll stay out of your way."

Dammit. After flipping her braid away, she poked his shoulder forcefully enough to hurt her finger. "You don't tell me what to do, *Ra-oool*. I'm not your property anymore." She'd expected the blaze in his eyes; she hadn't anticipated her regret at verbalizing the fact. *I'm not his.* She poked him harder to make the sense of loss go away.

He grabbed her hand, preventing more abuse, and sat up. "That's enough. Get out of the bed before I lose my patience with your rudeness." His voice had lowered, and excitement shimmered deep inside her.

She felt her nipples bunching into peaks, saw his gaze drop to her breasts, and her anticipation increased at the flare of heat in his eyes. "Stop bossing me around." She planted herself deliberately, kneeling with her butt on her feet. "I'm not going to do anything you say. Ever. Even if you beg me."

"And what if you beg me?" he asked softly, the increasing Spanish accent an obvious clue to his temper. "If you stay in this bed, I will take you, Kimberly, the way I want, as rough as I want, unless you scream your safe word."

His dark voice flipped a switch inside her, and she was suddenly very wet, her clit throbbing as if he'd stroked it with his tongue rather than his words.

But her mouth had gone dry at the threat in his voice. He would... He could hurt her. Only, she wanted that. Kind of. She took a breath. Besides, backing down would make her a coward. "Take me, *Ra-oool*? Pfft. You're all talk and no—"

He grabbed her. She squeaked as he flattened her on her belly, her face on the mattress inches from the ornate ironwork of the headboard. She felt a pull on her hair. Tugging.

"That should keep you out of trouble." He yanked her up, onto her hands and knees.

It was going too fast. Unable to help herself, she attempted to rear up and...couldn't. She tried to lift her head, but her braid was caught on something. She stared at the mattress, three inches from her nose, and fumbled at the headboard, trying to find what he'd hooked her braid on.

His ruthless hands closed on her wrists and secured them one-handed at the hollow of her back.

"Damn you!" She struggled, totally helpless, her head caught, her hands caught. He shoved his knees between her legs, pushing her legs apart, exposing her. With his free hand, he explored her intimately and hummed in interest. "You're puffy, gatita. And very wet."

His fingers moved over her clit, so very assured, touching her in the way he knew turned her on. Although she kept fighting, the more she fought, the more her need grew. His chuckle showed he realized exactly what was going on—and his ability to read her so easily increased her arousal as well. Dammit.

He positioned his cock at her entrance and swirled it in her wetness. His grip on her wrists tightened, warning her. He plunged into her, all the way to the hilt.

Her body froze in shock, and she gasped as her pussy strained to accommodate the invasion. *Yes, yes, yes.* Pushing her forehead onto the mattress, she let him take her over.

He did. He took her, roughly as he'd promised, slamming into her, thick and hard and uncomfortably long.

Not satisfied, he released her hands and gripped her hips, angling her for greater penetration until he nudged her womb with every thrust. Yet the roughness and discomfort increased her arousal, pushing her toward climax in a way she'd never felt before. He wasn't touching her clit, the stimulation only from his rigid erection. Everything inside her started to tighten, her entire lower half a fiery ball of nerves.

As he yanked her back onto his cock, over and over, her braid pulled at her scalp, reminding her she was restrained. Her hands fisted the covers as the pressure inside her grew. The air thickened until she cried out with each stroke, each demanding thrust wonderful, perfect, keeping her teetering right at the top.

And then he moved differently, his shaft circling her entrance, making her folds tug on her clit. The fire inside contracted into a whirlpool, blasting a tsunami of sheer sensation over her sea walls, flattening everything in front of it until an ocean of pleasure streamed to every far nerve. The room echoed back her scream, then her gasps for air.

He somehow hardened, thickened even more. Short, brutal thrusts sent more waves through her, and then he pressed, deep, deep, and the spasms of his cock made her insides clench over and over around him

His grip on her hips released—she'd have bruises there tomorrow, and she didn't mind in the least. No—she gloried in the thought of his marks on her. Every nerve in her body was singing, and satisfaction flowed with each beat of her pulse. And happiness. More than from her climax, but caused by the feel of his hands, demanding, controlling, merciless. Dammit, why?

She'd been dominated before; he gave her...more. Or she surrendered more. Anxiety rippled through her. How much would she surrender to him?

He ran his hands down her sides in long strokes, reached under to fondle her breasts, and chuckled when her vagina spasmed around him. When he finally pulled out, she moaned at the loss. Without speaking, he flattened her on the bed again to unhook her braid, then rolled her onto her back like a puppy.

Throat exposed, belly up. At his mercy. Her anxiety increased as she realized annoyance still tightened his jaw.

"Is this what they call friends with benefits?" he asked, holding her chin.

She felt her face heat and closed her eyes.

"Look at me," he growled.

Her gaze met his, and she couldn't escape from the anger in his eyes. She swallowed.

"If you wish rough sex or D/s sex, then tell me. I took you hard this time, so we could both discover your response." His gaze softened, his thumb stroking over her lower lip. "There's no question as to how you respond. You think about it and what you want."

He swung off the bed and turned, his expression dangerous. "And then you will talk to me honestly and openly."

*Dammit.*

* * * *

That afternoon, Raoul pushed back from his desk, rubbing his exhausted eyes. If he was going to continue designing at home, he needed a bigger screen.

On the left, Kimberly worked her way through the stacks of filing he'd accumulated. He hated paperwork. Normally, he'd summon his secretary to do the tedious business. But for now, it kept Kimberly occupied.

*My* friend, *Kimberly.* Smiling slightly, he watched her examine a paper and put it into a folder. Even lacking any power exchange, he liked having her in his house.

After she'd crawled into his bed last night, he'd discovered he still enjoyed making love to her. Then again, he was a man. Was fucking ever bad? Yes, the *normal* sex with Kimberly had been pleasant, although lacking any rich flavor or bite, as if someone had made tacos without adding cayenne or cumin.

She'd also felt the lack. He grinned, remembering how she'd goaded him, trying to make him lose his temper. He hadn't—barely—although he'd given her the roughness and control that she needed. She'd come like a dream.

He shook his head. It was amazing she tolerated sex at all after her experiences, let alone with a man dominating her. Would she admit she wanted his control in the bedroom? Could she be that honest with herself—and him?

For a minute, he simply studied her. Pretty gatita, her black, shiny hair loose over her shoulders, her curvy ass filling her shorts nicely, reminding him of the feel of her soft hips under his hands. His eyes narrowed as he looked more intently.

Pretty...but not happy. The quiet content she'd shown in the weeks prior to the Shadowlands had eroded away over the past three days. Her body now lacked...grace...as if she were no longer comfortable with herself. Tension simmered under her jerky movements and tensed muscles.

Yet she wasn't looking around nervously. He opened and shut a drawer loudly—no jumpiness. Not fear then.

He rested his elbow on the desk and leaned back in his chair, thinking. Serving her dom and others filled a need in her—whether she admitted it or not—but she was also more comfortable when she had rules. Boundaries. Consistency. Apparently, her erratic father had been loving, then not—stern when sober, nasty when drunk. She'd never known what to expect from minute to minute. Rules probably felt...safe.

When she'd requested that they be friends, she'd not only lost his domination, but the consistency that came with it.

She glanced over her shoulder, and his eyes met hers. He held her gaze, looking for—*Dios, stop it, Sandoval.* He turned away, disgusted with himself. Her need called to his, but she had said no. *No meant no.*

However, she wasn't happy or at peace, and he wasn't sure how to fix that. Not as *friends.* Hopefully, she'd discuss the problem with Gabi or Faith, but knowing Kim, she'd probably avoid discussions on dominance and submission.

He caught a movement out of the corner of his eye.

She was kneeling at his feet, head down, nape beautifully exposed. *Begging for a collar. No, stop dreaming.*

"You don't have to kneel to talk to me, Kimberly," he said. "We're friends, are we not?"

"Yes. Kind of." Rather than her hands resting open on her thighs, her fingers were laced and white-knuckled in front of her. "I…I don't know what's wrong with me, but being friends isn't working for me."

Well, apparently she was learning how to share her emotions. He smiled ruefully, then bent and tilted her chin up. "Do you have a request?" He winced, wanting to punch himself. Even when he told himself not to, he couldn't speak or touch without dominating someone, especially this little one.

"Can we go back to the way we were?"

He stiffened. "What way, gatita? Explain more clearly."

"I want…want to be your submissive again, like before. Until the FBI lets me go home or to Gabi's." Her blue eyes were earnest, without any apparent reservations.

The rising pleasure warred with his sinking feeling of dismay. How much more agonizing would it be to see her leave after she'd been his *willing* submissive? "Why?"

"I… It's silly, but I can't settle. It's like when I know I'm doing what you want, I relax and let you do the worrying. I can concentrate on the one thing you've told me to do." She shrugged. "I'm sure I'm just stressed over the past stuff and with not knowing what's going to happen. But…" She huffed out an unhappy breath. "I liked it better when you were in charge."

KIM STARED UP at Master R. His expression had changed to one of consideration. She loved how he'd take the time to think things through. Damn him. If he wasn't so very smart or if he made hasty decisions or bad ones, she wouldn't be here on her knees. But she trusted him to steer a straight path...as much as any human could.

She dared to lean forward, wrapping her arms around his legs and resting her cheek on his knees. A warm spring of contentment welled up in her heart. He could think as long as he wanted if he'd let her stay here, just like this. When he stroked her hair, she closed her eyes and enjoyed.

Sure, she still had a niggling worry that he or the slavers had brainwashed her into a weak-willed real slave, but right now she didn't care. Once this time was over and she went home, she'd get her life straightened out. And until then, well, she'd consider having a master to be a unique kind of pill—a tranquilizer or something.

"You need this?" he asked gently.

"Yes, please." She kept back the automatic *Master* because he hadn't agreed to assume the role again. But inside, she was whimpering, *Please, Master, yes, I do. Please.*

Would he agree? He liked being in charge. She bit her lip. Was she asking more than she should? The silence seemed to stretch, reaching to the horizon. *Please.*

"All right then." He paused. "I agree, sumisita, and I think you've overdressed for this house."

She smiled and rose. But the anxiety, the worries...didn't go away even with the relief rushing through her, and she still felt as if a rope was wrapped around her lungs, keeping her from taking a full breath. But, surely everything would settle down. Surely this was what she needed. "Yes, Master." She stripped her clothing off, folded it, and placed it on a chair.

He leaned back, one elbow on his desk. His fingers rubbed his lips as he studied her. She stood beside him, shifting her weight, and...if anything, feeling worse. *What have I done?* Maybe this was the wrong decision. She realized her hands were clasped in front of her. Should she—

"Kimberly, stop." He shoved his chair away from the desk and patted his knees. "Come."

Yes, she needed to be held. That was all. She started to sit on his lap, and he ruthlessly turned her and pulled her stomach-down over his thighs instead.

"Wait." She tried to push up. "No—I haven't been bad. What's *wrong* with you?"

His left hand pressed on her back, keeping her pinned down despite her struggles. "No, you haven't been bad, gatita. This isn't punishment." His right hand stroked over her bottom. "This is about a little submissive's needs." He smacked her, barely a sting, then gave her five more before pausing and rubbing her butt again.

She sucked in a breath as her insides started to shake. "Do you want me to count?"

"No. Since this is not punishment, there's no number, mi cariño. I continue until I decide to stop."

"But—"

The next set of swats hurt. He hit one cheek, then the other, waiting only for the stinging to die before giving another. She started to struggle again, trying to escape. Her eyes filled as the pain grew.

A pause, and he stroked over her bottom. Gently, not mean. How could he be loving and cruel at the same time? A gasping sob of frustration escaped her.

"Bueno," he said under his breath and started again. *Slap-slap, slap-slap,* and it hurt. It really hurt. Pain with each hit of his big hand, and then she was kicking and screaming as the wave of pain rolled over her. And continued. And continued.

When the nightmare didn't stop, sobbing tore through her. She beat on his legs and kicked, crying hysterically, until finally she went limp, unable to fight any longer, just taking the pain.

He stopped, oh God, he stopped and was stroking away the hurt, his hand tender on her burning flesh. "Very good, sumisa mía." As tears streamed down her face, he helped her to her feet and pulled her onto his lap. Pressing her face against his chest, he held her firmly, engulfing her in security.

Her pain had changed to mere throbbing, but she couldn't stop crying. What was wrong with her? Tears and choking and then...her worries dissolved. The noise and tension inside her receded with the tide, leaving only clean emptiness behind.

She lay still, lulled by his heartbeat, not wanting to move. After a while, she took a long breath. Another. The tight band around her chest had gone, washed away with the storm. She sniffled and lifted her head, felt the chair turning. A tissue was pressed into her hand.

She wiped her eyes, blew her nose, and with a sigh of regret, pushed to a sitting position to toss the Kleenex in the wastebasket. Her cheeks were probably all purple, her eyes puffy and red. "I'm sorry. I couldn't stop crying." Feeling humiliated, she dared a look.

"I know. That was the point."

She frowned at him. "You spanked me so I would cry?"

"Sí, sumisita." He kissed the top of her head. "Pain can be used for several purposes." She heard the note that came into his voice when he was instructing. Not like her pompous professors—*maybe this stupid person can be taught*—Master R had an undertone of gentle humor as if to lure a person into learning. "As you know from the clubs, pain can be erotic." He pulled her against his chest, and she snuggled closer with a sigh of content. Just listening to him and being held was sheer heaven.

"Or used to punish," he continued. "But some people

bottle up their feelings, their worries, fears, emotional pain. If they are physically hurt enough to make them cry, then sometimes the crying serves for the emotional pain as well. They can release it all."

*Bottle it up? Me? Well, maybe.* She lived enthusiastically, but her inside feelings were her own. Sharing emotional problems was...not her thing. The counseling sessions had been difficult, even with Gabi. She inhaled slowly, savoring the scent of soap and man. Maybe she did suppress things a bit. Her father had wanted perfection, not emotions. *"A Moore doesn't show fear." "Stop that bawling. It didn't hurt that bad." "That's lousy. It looks like a five-year-old did it." "You can do better than that."*

Like her mother, she'd learned to bury her feelings. The counselor had disapproved. Kim snickered.

"Share that thought."

"Faith told me I bottle stuff up and need to learn to let it out. Maybe I'll teach her to spank her clients."

He laughed. "This is, perhaps, more direct than she'd like." He sat Kim up so he could frown at her. "I expect you to learn how not to reach this point. And we, you and I, will work on you sharing those emotions before you need to be hurt to get them out."

His smile creased his cheek. "Write about it in your journal—and starting today, you will again fill a daily page to share with me."

*Hell, back to doing homework.* But, okay, so maybe she'd missed their bedtime chats when they'd talk about what she'd written for him to read. Long-term boyfriends, even her fiancé, had never known her as well as Master R did now.

"That reminds me—I want you to start practicing the dances you learned. Show me one before bed tonight." He nuzzled her hair and murmured, "If it is adequate, I will take you and please us both. If not, I'll beat on you first for a while and then take you anyway."

She gave a sigh of utter content and leaned back on his chest. "Yes, Master."

# Chapter Twelve

Black clouds blocked the late-afternoon sun as spatters of rain hit the windshield. Kim grabbed the seat belt as a gust shook the car, and debris swirled across the tiny country road. "I didn't notice how isolated the Shadowlands was last time."

"It was dark," Master R said. "And you were busy worrying."

"Well. Yeah." Her brows drew together as she stared through the rain at the palmettos and swamp. "How many members do you lose to alligators?"

"None, except for the occasional smart-ass subbie who we toss to them for their supper." He turned between open iron gates, drove up the long, palm-lined drive, and parked in the lot adjacent to a six-foot wooden fence. "Let's make a run for it, gatita."

An umbrella wouldn't have helped, considering half the rain was traveling sideways. They ran through the gate into a huge landscaped yard.

Ten or so people congregated under the covered, screened lanai, watching the storm. The FBI agent, Vance Buchanan, and a black-haired man with an olive complexion sat at a table. The rest were in chairs around a long oak coffee table.

"'Bout time you got here," came a yell from the giant bartender from the Shadowlands. More greetings followed, a hash of male and female voices.

When Kim stopped, overwhelmed at being the center of attention, Master R pulled her next to him as if to remind her she had support. After a second, she realized she'd met most of them. By the coffee table was the bartender, Cullen. Next to him were Gabi and Marcus. When Gabi tried to get out of Marcus's lap, he wrapped his arm around her, keeping her in place. She rolled her eyes and gave Kim a smile of welcome.

Kari sat beside her husband, looking even more pregnant than before. She grinned and waved, not attempting to get out of the chair. Next to her was Master Z and then the meanest-looking man Kim had ever seen.

Master R nodded toward the men at the table. "Do you remember Vance from the FBI?"

Her stomach tightened at the reminder of why they were meeting today. "Unfortunately, yes."

She got a nip on the neck. "Until you move from under my roof, sumisita mía, you will observe respect."

*His submissive.* An unsuspected knot in her stomach loosened. "I'm sorry, Master. Yes, Sir."

The stranger at the table regarded her with eyes even darker than Master R's. The man's white button-down shirt didn't hide his lean musculature, but he was smaller than the other FBI agent who was built like a Viking warrior. Yeah, she could see Vance leaping off a boat, heavy axe in his grip, or—with a name like Buchanan—maybe wearing a kilt and swinging a claymore.

The dark-haired man rose and walked over, leaning on a cane. "Ms. Moore, I'm Galen Kouros. We talked on the phone a few days ago, but it's nice to see you in person. Vance and I are in charge of this investigation." After a glance at Master R, he offered his hand.

"I'm glad to meet you, Agent Kouros."

"It's Galen." He kept her hand in his for a minute as

he studied her. "I can't tell you how sorry I am that you had to endure what you did, but I'm pleased you're looking so well."

"Thank you." Wow. Actual pleasantries. And everyone wore casual clothing with no collars, no BDSM equipment, no floggers in sight. Being in the normal world seemed unreal.

Galen gave her fingers a squeeze, smiled at Master R, and limped back to the table. Although polite, he was as intense in person as he'd been on the phone.

"Everyone here is either FBI or Shadowlands Masters and submissives," Master R said in her ear. "Since Kari's husband Dan is a cop, Galen asked him to help with coordinating the raid."

Dan's gaze moved over her in a lingering look, as if the cold-faced cop was memorizing her. He nodded but stayed beside his wife.

Master Z said something to the others and then crossed the patio. He glanced at Master R, then held his hand out to her.

Her fingers were in his before she had a second to think. Damn. Like Master R, the man simply exuded power.

"It's nice to see you again, Kimberly." His gray eyes held hers for a moment, then narrowed, and he gave Master R an unreadable look before smiling slightly. "I can tell you and Raoul are...getting along. You look good together."

"You're here!" Jessica trotted down the steps from the third floor, followed by Andrea and a slender redhead. The small blonde started toward Kim, then detoured to thump a tray of sandwich makings on the table by the FBI men.

Carrying a big bowl of chips, Andrea got snagged by the giant bartender who pointed at the coffee table in front of him. "Put it there, love. If anything's left when I'm through, the others can help themselves."

Andrea did exactly as he said and then pushed Cullen far enough sideways on the love seat to snuggle beside him.

The redhead added her bowls of dip before deliberately moving the chips to the center.

"Beth, those are mine!"

Grinning at the bartender's loud complaint, the slender woman knelt beside the mean-looking, scarred-up man. Kim's heart quailed as she waited for him to reprimand the woman. Instead he tugged Beth's red hair lightly. A smile lit his darkly tanned face when she kissed his wrist.

Kim relaxed.

"C'mere, girlfriend." Jessica pulled her away from Master R to give her a hug. "I wanted to visit you, but the feebies said I couldn't." She gave the FBI agents a disgusted look.

Galen frowned at her, although amusement turned his lips up. "New little slaves like Kim don't entertain friends," he said. "If Raoul didn't normally have employees coming to the house, Gabi wouldn't have been permitted there either."

"Pffft," Jessica said under her breath.

Master R grinned and murmured, "You may talk for a bit, Kimberly." He kissed the top of her head and joined the others.

Kim clasped her hands together, annoyed at how her anxiety rose without him beside her. *Dependent. You're getting as dependent as a clown fish needing an anemone to hide in.* She hauled in a breath. *I'm a strong, independent woman... At least, I'm getting back there.*

She deliberately turned away to talk with Jessica. "Hey, I saw you at the club when that dom slapped the brunette. I can't believe you actually broke into a scene."

"My bad. I should have called the dungeon monitor, but I was too mad." Jessica scowled. "Sally's one of the trainees, and when I saw her crying, I lost it. She's so not into the face-slapping stuff."

Kim understood completely. Being hit in the face was a shock. Horrifying in a way. Her stomach tightened as she remembered how Lord Greville had backhanded her. Unable to help herself, she glanced over her shoulder to check that Master R was close. Just the sight of him calmed her nerves. "What did Master Z do?"

"Oh, Master *Calm and Levelheaded.* He was mad at the dom, since Sally hadn't okayed face-slapping, but she hadn't used her safe word either. She said she was too weirded out, and I believe her. She'll sure be more careful with setting hard limits on her play next time. Z made the dom apologize, but he couldn't do much else."

"Uh...it looked like you bit Master Z. You didn't, did you?"

"Well." Red swept into the blonde's face. "Maybe a nip. It's not like I made him bleed or anything. I hate being gagged."

"God, Jessica. You need lessons in behavior." Kim bit the inside of her cheek to keep from laughing and glanced at Master Z. A little older than the others and with the elegant, pulled-together appearance of someone who was wealthy and accustomed to it. "What did he do to you?"

Jessica lowered her voice. "He made me strip and put me on my back at the end of the bar." She sent a fulminating glare across the patio at Z. "There I am, whining, '*We're engaged. You're not supposed to want to share me,*' and he laughs and says he's never minded sharing my beauty or even my punishments. God."

At Gabi's house, Jessica had mentioned Z's inventive discipline but always with a rueful expression, never like a woman who'd been brutalized. He couldn't have done anything too cruel. Could he? "Go on, before I burst."

"That's not sounding much like sympathy to me."

Jessica turned her frown on Kim. "You're supposed to feel sorry for me."

"Oh. Right. Lost my place for a moment." *Don't laugh.* Kim wrapped her arm around Jessica's shoulders. "Awww, you poor, poor baby. What evil things did your mean dom do to you?"

"That's much better. I knew I liked you." Jessica grinned. "So—the bar top has recessed rings here and there. He tied my hair to a couple, so I couldn't lift my head, blindfolded me, and used knee cuffs to spread me open for everyone to see."

Kim couldn't decide if she was horrified or turned on. She checked on Master R. He was talking to Z…and watching her and Jessica, his eyes filled with laughter. What was Z telling him? She turned back to Jessica. "Mmmhmm. Ah, go on."

"He has this miniflogger with three soft strands—a pussy whip. He lent it to every dom at the bar and let each one take five lashes at my pink bits."

"That douche bag," Kim snapped, her mood changing abruptly.

"No, it didn't hurt." Jessica pulled Kim farther away from the group. "Dammit, that was the problem. Getting lashed like that, off and on, got me hot. Really hot. God, I think it lasted an hour or more. He sat and lectured me on proper submissive behavior and calling dungeon monitors and not barging into scenes, and all the while the doms kept me right on the edge. I swear, he waved them off every time I got close."

Putting her hand to her throat, Kim tried to imagine being so exposed. Being excited and having something hitting her pussy. Oh boy.

"Look at those jerks," Jessica muttered. "He's sharing again, isn't he?"

Kim glanced over her shoulder. Master R was leaning back in his chair, studying her. He had an erection he didn't bother to hide, and he laughed when Z motioned like...like a whip. *Oh Lord, don't give my master ideas.* "Uh." What had she planned to say? *Right.* "Did one of them finally, um, ever...?"

"When I was a heartbeat away from a stroke, Z took over." Jessica shivered. "His other little flogger has a different leather. Not nearly so soft, and his aim—" Her color darkened. "I came so hard the entire room probably heard."

Even as heat flared through her body, and her clit throbbed in response, Kim choked with trying not to laugh.

"Oh, go ahead, everybody else laughs." Jessica scowled and giggled as well. But then her lips turned down. "Sometimes I wonder what kind of sleaze I am that I get off on something so public."

Kim blinked. She knew those self-doubts only too well. That this brightly intelligent and sweet woman also worried was incredibly reassuring. She gripped Jessica's shoulder. "You're no sleaze. Remember, before...this...I played in clubs a lot, and there's, like, an increased hotness, knowing people are watching."

"I guess so. Thanks." She tilted her head. "You know, at Gabi's, you'd never have said something like that. You'd have been too busy shivering. I think you're healing."

Kim's mouth dropped open. She hadn't paid attention to her progress recently. She still got uncomfortable at times but maybe because Master R kept increasing the stakes. But she was coming along. She'd had sex. Done a public scene. Could talk about stuff. Definitely improved. "You're right."

"Of course." Jessica gave her a smug look. "I'm always right. Ask anybody...well, anybody but Z." She wrinkled her nose at her dom and got a flashing grin that changed his lethal appearance into simply gorgeous. "So what do you and your lord and master want to drink?"

Easy answer. "Supposedly Z picked up some ale from someplace—the Swamp Head Brewery?"

"Oh, the 10-10-10. It's a malty brew. Be right back." Jessica grinned and headed up the steps to the third floor. The blonde might be fluffy, but her legs were in good shape. Shaking her head, Kim made a beeline for her lord and master.

He looked up, and his smile, just for her, made her spirits bubble like sea foam. *Oh, I'm in trouble.* God, she loved him. She walked over and waited, unsure if he wanted her to kneel or pull up a chair or—

He nodded at a large flat pillow lying between his feet.

When she knelt in perfect position, he leaned forward to murmur in her ear, "Be comfortable, cariño. You need not stay kneeling. Sam called to say he would be here in about ten minutes."

As she shifted to an easier sitting posture, his legs closed to rub against her shoulders, holding her in safety between them. She leaned on his thigh with a happy sigh.

And then, as if he did nothing unusual, he fed her chips and dip, alternating his and hers as they often did at home.

She whispered a thank-you, received a light kiss on top of her head.

Gabi's disbelieving look made Kim avert her gaze, only to see the slim redhead's dom feeding her little sandwich bites from his hand. The sub looked perfectly content.

Kim considered the woman. She didn't appear like a kick-me slave; in fact, she'd deprived the bartender of his chips.

After Jessica delivered their beers in frosty mugs, Master R handed one to Kim. Before she could drink, he leaned down to whisper in her ear. "What's wrong, gatita?"

How could she possibly say?

"Tell me."

The others were arguing over the benefits of involving the various law enforcement agencies. No one was paying attention to her. "Is the redhead a slave? A housewife?"

Master R rubbed his cheek, already slightly scratchy, against Kim's. "Beth isn't a slave, but she's definitely a submissive. I think they started in the bedroom, expanded outward, so to speak, and now they're probably living the lifestyle more often than not. She's not a housewife. She has a yard maintenance service and does landscape design. She did the grounds here for Z."

From her vantage point, Kim saw hints of flowerbeds, towering hedges, and tiny footpaths. The sound of at least one fountain. The place was as gorgeous as its owner. So this Beth owned her own company, had an independent life outside of serving her dom...like Master R's previous slaves had.

He turned her pillow—and her on it—to face him, then leaned his forearms on his thighs, ignoring everyone else to focus on her. "Does being at my feet in a gathering bother you?"

"I—" She bit her lip under the disconcerting weight of his regard. He was always aware of her, frequently watched her, but when he wanted an answer, an honest answer, his intensity changed. The pressure on her grew as well, like the difference in playing in the pool or diving down sixty feet. "No. It doesn't bother me," she whispered finally. "It's just confusing. I'm not like this. I'm *not*."

A shadow crossed his face. "I understand."

"Do I act this way because of my kidnapping? The slavery?"

He sighed. "We will talk about this more later. But,

Kimberly, dominance or submissiveness—or the need to serve—isn't typically created by circumstances. It's part of a person's personality.

She stiffened. Was he saying she had a slave's mentality?

Before Kim managed to phrase the question, Master Sam strode across the yard to the lanai, dressed in well-worn jeans, boots, and a pale blue cotton shirt the color of his eyes. He was older than everyone, with silvery hair and skin tanned to leather. He nodded to the men, smiled at the women, then looked at her.

"You two didn't get a chance to really meet the other night," Master R said to her as the man walked over. "Sam, this is Gabrielle's friend, Kim. Kimberly, this is Sam."

The sadist who'd flogged the sub so mercilessly that she'd screamed. Kim swallowed.

"Nice to meet you." Sam held his hand out, waited until she gave him hers, and squeezed gently. "You're a brave girl. Raoul is very proud of you, you know."

When her mouth dropped open, he winked at her and took the chair next to them.

"My friends," Master R said, stopping the various conversations. "Since Sam will attend the auction, I plan to tell Dahmer I'll be out of town this weekend.

"We did discuss that as a possibility." Galen's fingers made a staccato sound on the tabletop. His black gaze held hers for a moment. "Although I like some redundancy in an op in case of *oh-shit* moments, I'd as soon not put more civilians in harm's way." He glanced at Vance, who nodded.

Galen grinned and tapped the table with his knuckles. "Agreed."

Knowing she wouldn't be involved, Kim sipped her beer and paid intermittent attention to the talk around her. Various plans were discussed with the police dom, Dan,

contributing here and there. Outside the patio, the rain and
wind increased, shaking the palms and bushes, sending the
bright flowers to lie in soggy heaps in the grass. They hadn't
had their day in the sun. Their time had been cut short, she
thought. Like Holly. Her throat tightened, and she
concentrated on the conversation again.

"Can't you get there sooner?" Sam asked the FBI
agents in his sandpaper-rough voice. "Dahmer said the vans
deliver us buyers early, so we can check the *merchandise*, do
a miniscene, maybe even fu—" He bit off the word.

"You going to be able to do this?" Vance asked. "You
look more nauseated than Sandoval did."

"I have some lines I've never crossed," Sam snapped.
"So I'd like your raid to be sooner, not later."

"We'd prefer that too." Galen rubbed his face. "But
after you lead us to the place, we need time to set up
roadblocks."

Vance added, "A lot of the buyers will leave after their
purchase. Arresting them on the road means there'll be
fewer in the auction house—and less chance of the innocent
getting hurt."

"Except buyers will be hurting them while we're
*testing* the merchandise," Sam growled.

Master R's phone rang. He pulled it off his belt,
frowning at the display. "Private." He held up his finger for
silence. "Sandoval." He listened, then said, "Hold on—my
hands are wet. I need to put the cell down." He flicked the
setting to speaker.

"I'll wait, Raoul." The Overseer's voice bit into Kim
like fire coral yet made her think of rotting fish.

Nauseated, she silently set her beer down.

After positioning the phone on the coffee table, Master
leaned down and wrapped his arms around Kim, holding
her between his legs in a prison of security.

Every person on the patio had gone still, barely breathing.

"We're on for this Saturday," the Overseer said. "I'm looking forward to seeing your scene again. I think the buyers will be very pleased."

"Saturday?" Master R paused. "Dios, Dahmer. I'd hoped the auction would be Friday. I'm going to be out of town Saturday and Sunday. I have a consult in Venezuela."

Silence.

"I'm afraid your absence isn't acceptable, Raoul. It's too late to get another demonstration set up." Dahmer's voice had sharpened, sending a shudder through Kim. That was what he sounded like when he'd ordered a slave to be whipped. *Oh God.*

Master R's arms tightened. "I'm sorry, but I don't have a choice. Business must come before pleasure."

"I see." More silence. "Well, I do understand how inconvenient it can be to rearrange appointments. Let me sweeten the pot, starting with your friend."

Galen's eyes narrowed.

"Go on," Master R said.

"One of the...shipments...fell through, which means less merchandise available this week. So the last batch of buyers—including Sam—will have to wait for another auction. But since I believe in a favor for a favor... If you do the demonstration, I'll put your pal back on the list so he can attend. Hell, I'll even give you both a twenty percent discount on anything you buy."

Master R inhaled slowly. After a second, he said, "That's tempting, Dahmer. I might manage, but my timing would be extremely tight. After I fly in, I won't have time to fetch my...pet...from...storage. So if I do rearrange my schedule, I'll have a different pet with me."

"Absolutely     not.     Only     previously     purchased

merchandise can be brought into an auction."

Kim put her hands over her mouth. He'd have to take her? Not the FBI agent? A chill ran up her spine.

Master R started to speak, but Galen made a cutting-the-throat motion.

"Well, that complicates matters. Give me a second to figure out if I can juggle things," Master R said. He set the phone to mute.

A violent tremor shook Kim's body.

Galen's eyes turned to her, but he didn't say anything.

"I'll have to go," she whispered.

Master R growled something foul in Spanish. "No. No, you will not do this. You've done enough. *No más.*"

*If he really loses his temper, will he shift completely to Spanish?*

Why couldn't she think of anything to say in any language? Needing not to think, Kim stared at the ground. An ant was trying to drag a fragment of chip to its home. The piece was too big, but it tugged and tugged. So stubborn.

Sam broke the silence. "Galen, I think this would destroy the girl." His pale eyes were cold as ice, but he gave Kim a small smile. "I'm rather fond of this one, even if she does reduce Raoul to swearing in Spanish."

"I don't understand why Dahmer's so adamant about Sandoval doing this demo," Vance muttered.

Galen didn't speak.

"No." Master R said, although no one had asked anything. "Dan, you know how often something goes wrong. I will risk my life. Not Kimberly's—or her freedom or her well-being. Would you take Kari to such a thing?"

Dan's hand opened, conceding him the point.

An auction, filled with slavers, filled with women

being sold. *I'll never escape, will I?* Kim leaned her forehead against Master R's thigh. Everything in her was struggling, drowning in fear, sinking. Deep in the ocean, colors would fade away until everything turned gray. Turned cold. Like death.

*I can't.* But could she sleep at night, live with herself if her absence meant a woman would get bought by another Lord Greville? She lifted her head; it felt too heavy to support.

Master R looked directly across the table. "Z?"

Z had a low voice, as smooth as Master R's, but without the spine-tingling accent. "No, Raoul, I wouldn't agree." His arms tightened around Jessica, and his brows drew together. "But I've discovered some foolhardy submissives have steel spines."


RAOUL REMEMBERED TOO well how Gabi had forced the FBI agents to let her work undercover, trying to catch the slavers. Although Kimberly might be terrified, she was no less brave than her friend. But surely she wouldn't push to do this.

Rising onto her knees, she twisted around to face him, her hands on his thighs.

Her wide blue eyes could pretzel a man's heart. "Gatita, no."

She swallowed. "Sam called me brave. It's not brave to hide, knowing that if you do, other women will suffer. Might die." Her lips trembled. "Linda will be at the auction. When she's sold, she might never get free." Her cold hands tightened on his legs.

Raoul shook his head. "No." When her lips pressed together, he shook her. He didn't care if every slave in the world died. She wouldn't—couldn't do this. "*No.*"

Her arms closed around herself at the loss of his

support, and he grunted and pulled her onto his lap. He'd worked all his life to be strong and powerful so he could guard the ones he loved—yet he couldn't keep this little bit of female safe?

She buried her face in his neck. "We must," she whispered.

Kouros cleared his throat. Raoul would have punched him if he hadn't seen the pain in the man's eyes. The agent didn't want to ask this either, but he would, just like he'd allowed Gabi to go undercover in the Shadowlands.

Raoul held Kimberly against his chest, wanting only to shelter her. But he remembered what his mother had said when he'd tried to keep his younger sister, Lucia, from going to the mall...starting to date...driving a car. *You can't protect her against her will, Raoul. It's her life; you don't own her.* He didn't own Kimberly.

"Gatita mía, are you sure?" he whispered.

"Yes." Shivers ran through her soft body.

"You still there, Raoul?" Dahmer's voice came from the phone.

Kouros looked as if he wanted to kill something. But he nodded.

Raoul pushed the Mute button. "I'm here. If I move some appointments, I can attend," Raoul said, unable to manage a friendly tone. "I hope you make it worth the inconvenience."

"Oh, you'll be pleased. You have my word." Dahmer chuckled. "So I'll be in contact sometime on Saturday night."

"Until then." Raoul snapped the phone shut, barely managing to keep from throwing it across the patio.

* * * *

Kimberly was very quiet that evening, pulling away

from him as if she couldn't bear to be close. Yet when she moved away, she'd watch as if afraid she'd lose him. He finally took her to the tower room to see the stars appear in the darkness of the sky.

"I'm sorry, sumisita. This was not how it should have gone," he murmured into her hair. Dread had lodged in his bones, yet he wanted nothing more than to sit here with her in his arms. Soft and fragrant and warm, and appallingly brave.

"It's not your fault. Sorry I'm being weird." She rubbed her cheek on his shirt. "I keep remembering how helpless I felt. How trapped. I wish Saturday came faster. Can you keep me busy tomorrow?"

"I can, yes."

Her eyes started to drift shut. "I hope Gabi comes over tomorrow. Some noise would be good. She's like a one-woman party."

*A party*. As he held his little sumisa, Raoul considered possibilities. At the auction, Kimberly might have to endure another public demonstration. If she felt more comfortable with being exhibited, her concentration might stay on him, not on the slavers.

A party would be a good idea.

# Chapter Thirteen

Raoul strolled out to the kitchen, carrying a bunch of beach towels, and spotted Kimberly looking at the filled ice chest, arms crossed over her naked breasts.

She scowled. "Did you forget to tell me something? Are we going somewhere?"

"Kimberly."

"What?"

He kept his gaze on her, waiting her out.

Silence. "I'm sorry, Master," she muttered after far too long.

"Do you feel in need of being punished then?" he asked softly.

A step back. "No. No, Master."

Did she have any idea why she was coming across with the attitude? His pity for her made him want to ignore it, but she needed consistency and rules more than sympathy right now. Since nothing else in her world remained stable, he must. He moved into her personal space, not touching, letting the size of his body add to the intimidation. "Then perhaps you would explain?"

"I—" Her fingers tightened on her mug. "I… It's wrong. Those monsters buy women to be slaves, and here I am, volunteering to be your slave. But I'm not really, and I don't want to behave like one." Her chin jerked higher…and then her gaze dropped. "Only, then sometimes I do."

*Most of the time, you do, little sumisa.* He cupped her cheek, and his thumb under her chin kept her face raised to him. The shiver running through her at his care and his control reinforced her words. She was in conflict, and he knew the feeling well, especially when it came to her. "Any decent human, master or slave, is revolted at kidnapping and brutality and rape." He rubbed his thumb over her soft lips. "Aside from the fact that the slavers' crimes brought us together and into these roles, they have nothing to do with what is between us."

Her mouth opened.

He shook his head, pleased when she obeyed. "You are not my slave, Kimberly. Although definitions vary, in my mind, a *slave* gives up the ability to say no, something like if she'd enlisted in the army. She deliberately places her life under someone else's authority, often because her need to belong is so profound that she *wants* to be owned. Are you with me so far?"

Under his restraining hand, Kimberly nodded.

"Now a submissive gives up power, but not as much. Perhaps like a job instead of the military. A submissive wants more than an arranged scene, but that can be erotic domination all the way to serving full-time. Each relationship balances how those needs and wants are worked out."

He pressed his thumb between her lips in an imitation of a cock. Her breathing increased as her soft mouth closed around him, holding him within. "You are submissive, Kimberly. You knew that even before you met Gabi, years ago." He smiled. "And you require more than bedroom domination. Serving a master fills a need in you as great as the need to be dominated to truly enjoy sex."

She glared at him.

"Oh, it is true, gatita. You're not a slave who wants all your choices taken away, but you may very well be a full-time submissive." He stepped even closer, holding her gaze. "Now use your tongue on my thumb the way you would on my cock."

Redness streaked her cheeks as she ran her tongue over him, butterfly light.

"Suck."

Her pupils dilated as she sucked.

He hardened. "Good. I'll give you the real thing later."

Her lips were wet, and he could see how they'd look around his shaft.

After replacing his thumb with his lips in a slow, drugging kiss, he said, "It's a good day to remind you of the pleasures of domination—the fun of it—so we're joining some people in a bit."

Her face paled, and she took a step back.

"No, gatita. Nothing to do with the slavers. This is Marcus and Gabi. Andrea and Cullen. Each dom plays with his own sub." He ran his knuckles over the outside of her bare breast. "And I will play with you."

"Oh." The way heat replaced the fear in her eyes pleased him. She trusted him. "Do you want me to prepare anything?" she asked.

Raoul shook his head. "Put on a suit and cover-up. We're taking the sailboat out."

When her face lit up, he knew he'd chosen wisely. Water always calmed her. As he watched her run upstairs, he smiled at how trepidation had glimmered in her eyes, the knowledge that today would be different.

Although they'd had sex frequently, he hadn't pushed her, knowing the encounter with the Overseer needed to fade. But she'd worked through those fears, and now he could introduce something new. Something to take her mind off the auction and remind her BDSM could be fun as well as terrifying.

ON THE thirty-two-foot catamaran, Kim sprawled on the forward trampoline with Gabi and Andrea. The cool spray sprinkled over her skin as the boat slid through the water with a swishing sound and an occasional snap of the sails. Lovely. So different from the motorized boats she'd grown up with. Clean and quiet.

She could even hear the murmur of the guys' talking in the cockpit. She smiled, thinking of how they harassed each other in that weird guy fashion.

Watching Master R interact with his buddies was interesting. Sometimes when around other men, a guy would behave as if his girlfriend was unimportant, as if showing a woman affection would make him less macho.

But Master R stayed the same in public as in private. And his concern and affection for his friends was clear. Dammit, why did she have to like him so much? *I need to go home. Soon.*

Gabi bumped shoulders with her. "You holding up all right?"

"Oh sure. I just want it over, you know?"

Andrea tipped her face up, and the sun glinted off her golden brown hair. "I bet." A big woman with a full figure, her size was perfect for Cullen.

Kim smiled at her. "Thanks for the support at the Shadowlands the other night. It helped to know people were keeping an eye on things. On me."

Andrea nudged her arm in the same way Gabi had. "No problem. Shadowlands subs watch out for each other. It took me a while to really get that."

"No kidding." Gabi sneered amiably at Andrea and then glanced at Kim. "When Ms. Call-me-independent here actually asked Beth to help her with planting a garden, I thought the entire group would drop dead in shock." Gabi tilted her head back, letting the breeze rumple her shaggy hair. "I'm glad Raoul invited us today. Marcus prosecuted a really nasty murder case, and it was bothering him. It's good to get away."

Kim smiled, enjoying how normal the day had been. Blue sky with puffy clouds, ocean mist, light conversation. The nightmares seemed to belong to someone else. She glanced up as the sails spilled air, and the boat slowed.

"We're going to hang out here for lunch and swimming," Cullen called.

"Good plan," Andrea yelled back. "You two hungry? What comes first—food or swim?"

With the boat stopped, the sultry heat increased quickly. "Swim," Kim decided. She stripped down to her two-piece pink suit and jumped off the back. Bubbles frothed around her, and the cool, silky ocean enfolded her.

A whoop sounded, and Andrea hit the water, creating a tidal wave.

Gabi jumped in on Kim's other side. "That feels perfect."

They played for a while, splashing and gossiping, sharing recipes and dom tales, television shows, and Tampa gossip.

"Aren't the guys going to get in the water?" Kim asked finally.

"They're male. The only thing men are fast at is sex." Andrea grinned. "Want to try getting them in sooner?"

HALF-LISTENING AS Marcus and Cullen discussed an arson case, Raoul sipped his iced tea and thought about Kimberly. He'd enjoyed seeing her relax, talking and laughing with the other two women. Unlike some of the submissives he'd brought on outings, she fit nicely with the others, adding to the pleasure of the day.

Raoul set his drink down and listened, hoping to hear her infectious giggle again. He heard only the men's voices, the clanking of the lines and muted flap of sail, and the waves lapping at the boat. No women's voices. Not even any splashing. He rose to check forward where the women had been sunning. No one. "Why is there no noise? Where are the women?"

Cullen paused in his story, then set down his soft drink. He peered over the starboard side and shook his head.

"What—" Marcus strode to the port side. "Nothing."

A quiver of worry stabbed at Raoul. The area had no strong currents—and the subs would have shouted if they'd had problems. *I should have watched more closely.* "I'll take this side." Already shirtless, he balanced for a second and dived off.

Nothing.

Still no noise. No one could be that quiet in the water...unless they wanted to. *Ah.* He frowned at the boat, at waves too small to conceal a person. Surely they would not be so foolish... He swam forward and rounded the port hull.

The three women were silently hiding under the trampoline section. Kimberly's hands were over her mouth to suppress her laughter.

He flattened his smile and frowned at them. "You are all in so much trouble." With a yell, he summoned the other two doms.

Cullen swam around the side, saw them, and cursed. "Sneaky little pet, aren't you?" He reached out and snagged Andrea.

She yelped and kicked, her foot connecting with Cullen's gut. He sucked water, and she got loose, swimming past him.

As Marcus rounded the hull, Gabi fled.

Kimberly followed right in her wake, and Raoul chased after.

His little sub could swim—better than he could, in fact. He finally caught her, partly because she couldn't stop laughing, and he enjoyed the sound too much to want it to end.

KIM GRINNED, FEELING the way Master R crowded her as she climbed the ladder. Maybe because she'd knocked him back in the water last time? God, he was so going to kill her. Her sides ached from laughing as she joined the others.

The flat trampoline area between the catamaran hulls where Kim and the other women had lounged had grown crowded with the addition of pissed-off men.

Trying to stop giggling, Kim leaned on the railing and watched her master step from the ladder. *Oh my God, just look at him.* Water ran down the center of his chest between solid muscles that looked as if they'd been carved from cedar. His soaked shorts sagged on his hips, displaying his ridged abdomen. When he folded his arms, she couldn't look away from the rock-hard muscles of his biceps. The other men had great builds, but Master R looked like a god of war.

And, uh-oh, he looked as angry as one. When his dark eyes focused on her, her laughter died, and her mouth went dry.

"Kimberly. I am displeased."

Her throat clogged at the thought that she might have really upset him, and she dropped to her knees on the mesh without thinking. Her head bowed. "I'm sorry, Master."

Silence.

She glanced up through her lashes and saw laughter in his eyes. He wasn't really mad, drown him. "It isn't nice to lie. Master," she muttered. What had happened to honesty?

A warm hand cupped her sea-cooled chin, and he lifted her face. "You're right, gatita. I shouldn't make you think I'm angry when I'm not." His lips curved into a devilish smile. "I'd planned to say you were disobedient and punish you, but that would be wrong."

Oh, good. She gave a sigh of relief.

"However, I still plan to punish you...just because I want to. I'm your master, and that's all the reason I need."

Her mouth dropped open. "You're going to hurt me...for fun?"

"Most definitely." He gripped her upper arms and pulled her to her feet.

Kim looked around, starting to realize what had happened—their little game had transformed easygoing men into doms, and the atmosphere of the simple boat outing had changed.

Cullen had already dragged Andrea back to the cockpit. She could hear the smack of his huge hand hitting bare flesh, and the sound was distracting. Erotic.

Marcus had pushed Gabi on her knees. Kim stared at him. This wasn't the ever so polite Southerner she'd stayed with. His blue eyes were icy as he told Gabi her diversion had caused his beer to get warm, and that was simply unacceptable.

"Your beer got warm?" Scowling up at her dom, Gabi pushed her hair out of her eyes. "God, you're uptight. Did the aliens maybe forget to remove your anal probe?"

"That does it." He grabbed her hair and pushed her toward the cockpit.

Kim grinned. The pampered doms wanted a comfortable bench to sit on to punish their subs.

Still smiling, she looked at Master R. He was studying her with a speculative look in his eyes as if assessing how much she could take. She swallowed. "What are you going to do, Master?"

"Strip for me, please."

*Oh boy.* He might be enjoying himself, but his tone said she'd better watch her step. The first tiny flare of arousal sparked to life in her belly. She pulled off the top and stepped out of the skimpy bottom. When he put his hands behind his back, she knew what he wanted and assumed the inspect position he'd taught her. Legs apart, hands behind head, breasts elevated. Cold dribbles of water ran down her back from her tangled hair. The mesh was warm under her bare feet, the breeze cool on her damp body.

He walked around her slowly, his gaze warmer than the sun against her shoulders. "I prefer your nipples to be more colorful," he said finally. "The water turned them blue."

What kind of complaint was that?

He shook his head at her when she tried to say something. "Stay in position, sumisita." He went into the salon and returned with the picnic basket and some cushions, which he tossed around the area. After rummaging in the basket, he pulled out...a packet of wooden skewers? Rubber bands? And a brown lunch sack.

What the heck?

He opened the packet, removing two of the skewers. She eyed them with a frown. They looked awfully pointy.

"You think they're sharp?" he asked in a mild tone as he broke them in half, making them a few inches long. He lined up the pointed ends, wrapped his fingers around all four...and pressed them gently on her upper breast. "Are they sharp?" he asked, as if merely curious.

The sensation, just short of pain, took her breath. "Um. I guess."

"Good." He tapped them against her skin, lightly in a circle around her breasts, leaving marks like mouse prints behind. She stiffened at the tiny stinging—arousing—pains. Her nipples couldn't get any tighter, and her clit poked out as if wanting attention as well.

Master R worked his way to the edge of her nipple, then ran his free hand between her legs. He slid his fingers easily through her wet folds and caressed her hard nub to urgency.

Her hips tilted forward as his middle finger penetrated her to the knuckle. Then the second knuckle.

"I think we'll explore pain more today," he said, his soft voice curling across her nerves. "You seem to be ready."

*Pain.* Her pussy clenched, and his finger was right there to tell. Dammit. The thought of pain terrified her...and turned her on at the same time.

And he knew. The little sharp sticks worked in toward her left breast and back out, not quite touching the areola. Teasing her. She could feel her breasts growing heavier, more swollen. Aching.

He tapped the sharp, sharp points right on top of her nipple.

The sudden bite of pain sent carnal electricity ripping from her sensitive peak straight to her clit.

When she tried to step back, he pushed his finger deeper in her pussy in an intimate anchoring. The sticks moved to her other breast. Oh God, knowing how it felt increased her anticipation. Her left nipple still stung as he circled her right breast.

Her clit throbbed wildly, and when the points jabbed ever so lightly into her right nipple, she almost came.

But not quite. Her whole body flamed with need. She whimpered when he pulled back, leaving her empty inside.

His firm lips curved into a smile. "I love the sounds

you make, cariño." He kissed her sweetly, then tugged on one nipple, mercilessly pulling it into a point.

*Sweet kisses. Mean fingers.* Her brain spun.

He placed a skewer horizontally above and below the peak, pinching it between them. Her mouth dropped open as he put rubber bands on each end. Homemade nipple clamps.

Her nipple flattened as he increased the tension with the rubber bands, and the pain grew. "Mmm," she protested, afraid to yell, "ow."

"Breathe through the pain. One breath. Another." He held her chin, forcing her to look at him. "Take the pain—for your master."

For Master R. She sucked air in through her nose, her teeth gritted.

"Good gatita." The tenderness in his voice increased her determination to endure.

The pain eased into a mild pinching sensation, but one that didn't stop, keeping her constantly aware of the discomfort.

He did her other nipple the same way, watching her expectantly as her teeth ground together, before the bite let her catch her breath.

"Such a good sumisa." Taking a step back, he surveyed his work. "Very nice. You may relax now."

She put her hands down at her sides, hissing when the movement jostled her breasts.

"Hey, that's a great look." Cullen's rough voice. He and Andrea had returned. His sub was stripped as bare as Kim. Andrea's eyes went wide when she saw what Master R had done. She glanced warily at Cullen.

He grinned. "Those big nipples of yours will squash and look great." As Andrea sputtered something in Spanish, he asked Raoul, "Got any more of them, buddy?"

Master R set the package and the bag of tiny rubber

bands in Kim's hands. "Take them to Master Cullen," he said.

Kim crossed the trampoline and dropped the evil things into his big palm.

"Thanks, pet. Now go on back to Master Raoul."

*I'm not sure I want to.* Kim eyed the water. Escape again? No, he'd catch her and probably be truly upset. With a sigh, she returned and knelt in front of Master R.

The trampoline vibrated as Marcus returned, followed by a dutiful-looking Gabi. He pointed to his feet, and Gabi went to her knees.

Kim exchanged a rueful glance with her friend, feeling how things had changed. When they'd visited BDSM clubs together, the scenes had been just erotic fun.

Today was more. Under Master R's teasing, Kim heard a serious note, the undeniable will of a master. Perhaps this was the difference between a dom who didn't really know her and one who knew exactly where her limits lay...and intended to push them.

Feeling herself sway with more than the movement of the boat, she met his contemplative gaze.

"Raoul." Marcus was studying Kim's breasts, laughter in his sharp blue eyes. "Might I ask if you happen to have anything else interesting?"

"If I'd known the submissives would become so unruly, I'd have brought my toy bag. But there are a few more pervertables in the picnic basket."

Marcus patted Gabi's head. "Well, we just see what I can find, won't we, sugar?" He stepped around her and lifted the lid.

Kim bit her lip, trying not to laugh as Gabi's eyes started to spark. *Temper, temper, Gabrielle.*

"Cullen, the man's got rope." Marcus tossed a handful of precut ropes and a pair of heavy scissors into the middle of the area and dug farther. "Ah, here we go." He straightened, holding rubber bands and two plastic clamps, about three inches long with serrated edges.

Gabi's eyes shot fire. "You are *not* putting those on me. You dumbass, those are for potato chip bags, not for breasts."

"Hands behind your back."

She looked at the set of his jaw, and her hands laced together behind her back.

"Very nice, sugar."

With the first clamp, Gabi yelped, hissing as he wound a rubber band on the handle part to lessen the pressure.

Kim's eyes narrowed when she realized the clamps had chunks chipped from the handles so the rubber bands wouldn't slip. Master R had used them before, hadn't he? She gave her master a scowl. Tricksy dom.

Grinning, he bent and whispered, "She'll have a tantrum any minute now."

Kim smothered a laugh. When staying with the couple, she'd heard some pretty creative insults. Gabi's voice did carry a ways.

Marcus put the second clamp on, and Gabi made a sound like a teakettle.

Smiling, he held her upper arms, keeping her from moving. After minute, he asked, "Better?"

Gabi glared. "If you want to add some variety to your sex life, why don't you just use your other hand?"

Marcus barked a laugh. Pushing her legs apart, he cupped her pussy, then held his glistening palm up to show her. "You seem to like this kind of variety, darlin'." He smiled as she turned red and sputtered, obviously searching for an insult potent enough.

Kim's eyes stung with tears.

Master R turned her face toward him, frowning. "He won't hurt her, chiquita. I promise. This is how they like to play."

"It's not that." Kim blinked and smiled at him. "I'm so happy for her. I always wanted her to find someone who'd push her to be herself and not some perfect person like her parents wanted."

"Sweet gatita." Master R kissed the top of her head. He glanced at the other couple, snorted at another Gabi insult, then shot Kim a warning look. "Just in case you think to imitate your friend, I do not permit such disrespect."

She already knew that. He gave her a lot of leeway, but she'd learned how far she could go with mouthing off. If she'd said what Gabi had, she'd have had her butt blistered, and that certainty actually felt reassuring, like when winds stop veering and blow straight and true. "Yes, Master."

"Now, you will please me with your soft mouth, and if you do well, your punishment won't be…too bad."

"What's my punishment, Master?"

The corners of his eyes crinkled, but he didn't answer, just unzipped his shorts and took out his cock. The piercing glinted in the light. Oh God, she hadn't done this since…since Lord Greville and… A shudder ran through her.

"Easy, gatita." He held his hands out to her, and she put hers in his. He squeezed reassurance, then curled her fingers around his erection. Hotter than the sun with steel under the velvety skin.

She opened her mouth to take him in—and froze. *They'd tied her hands behind her back; that device had held her mouth open. Pushing into her throat, choking, no air.*

"Kimberly." A sharp tug on her hair reminded her of where she was. "Watch me, not the past."

She pulled her thoughts together, thought through the fear the way Faith had taught her, knowing he would let her take as long as she needed. After a minute, she nodded. *Ready.* And reminded herself, This is Master R.

"Use your hands."

She smiled, remembering the first time they'd made love, how he let her go as slow as she wanted as long as she kept advancing. So patient and calm. He might know her well, but she knew him too, and God, it really, really helped.

He made a noise in the back of his throat, a dom-style sound of encouragement and prodding.

*Stop thinking.* "Yes, Master." She slid her hands up and down his cock. It was so engorged that the skin was taut, the veins distended. Men's equipment never seemed particularly attractive, but Master R was so devastatingly, potently male. She ran a finger around the head, touched the piercing, cupped his heavy balls, and felt the light hair tickle her palm. She nuzzled his groin and inhaled. His own masculine scent mingled with that of the ocean. Her muscles loosened.

"Now your tongue," he murmured.

She leaned forward and ran her tongue up his length, getting him wet. He hummed his enjoyment, and warmth filled her. God, she loved that sound he'd make. She licked until his shaft was wet and she'd traced every vein. Then she looked up.

When he nodded permission, she took him into her mouth, trying to go deep as—

"No, *tesoro mío*." He wrapped her hands around the base of his shaft, preventing her from taking him in fully. "If I wanted to fuck your throat, I'd remove the piercing first, at least until you have more experience. For today, play with what I've given you. And be careful—metal is unforgiving on teeth."

*Oooh.* She ran her tongue over her teeth. *Avoid the piercing, Kim.* He was still worried, she could tell, but actually, she'd daydreamed about having his cock in her mouth. She was ready. *Really.* She took him in carefully, making sure her teeth went past the piercing...and then *played*, as he'd instructed. Tracing her tongue around him, then sucking vigorously enough to get a low moan of approval.

She cupped his testicles with one hand, enjoying the weight and size. Mmm. And he'd probably smack her if she called him Master Bull.

Lifting her head, she took the top of his erection between her lips and teased the piercing with her tongue. By carefully tugging on the metal ball with her teeth, she won herself a growly groan.

His hand fisted in her hair, and she froze; when he didn't do anything further, she continued. He grew harder, and she gloried in it.

"All right, little torturer." Using her hair, he pulled gently her away. "Now for the punishment I promised you a while back."

"What one?"

His evil grin wasn't reassuring in the least. "Ass in the air, please."

A spanking? She positioned herself, careful of her breasts, which still burned and ached every time she jostled his strange nipple clamps. After putting her head on her forearms, she arched her bottom up.

He picked up the sack and removed... Oh, holy hell, the anal plug she'd chosen from the ones she'd hidden. She'd really hoped he'd forgotten. She closed her eyes, wanting to whine. The plug was shaped like a plump, round goldfish...on steroids. Too big. He'd used his fingers in her a time or two and once put in a smaller plug during a shower, but this...

He trickled lube over it and between her cheeks. The muscles of her vulnerable hole puckered more tightly, and she tried to twist her bottom away.

A stinging slap made her jump. "You do not move."

"I'm sorry, Master."

"Gatita." His voice was so soothing she wanted to crawl into his lap. "I think you will like this once it's in. Until then, you will take the discomfort for me, will you not?" His hand stroked the place he'd slapped, turning the sting into pleasure.

Her arousal dampened the insides of her thighs, and she wanted to beg him to just fuck her instead. But his calloused hand on her bottom—so determined, so careful—made her tongue tangle.

"Now push back against my finger." He circled the rim with a slick finger, then firmly penetrated her.

She whined at the stretching feeling. Not painful. Uncomfortable.

He added another finger, slowly thrusting in and out. "Such a pretty asshole. Maybe we'll go to bed early tonight, no? I would enjoy being there."

A shudder of nerves and arousal ran through her. He pulled out and pressed the slick anal plug against her. He pushed the tip in and out, farther each time. It was bigger—more than the size of his fingers, stretching and burning. His grip on her hip kept her from moving away again as he eased it slowly inside. Wider and wider.

She groaned and pushed her forehead against her arms, trying not to remember...them. The pain. She tensed.

"Ssssh. Almost there, chiquita." And then with a soundless *pop*, it was in, and her muscles settled into the tail part that was smaller than the rest.

She stayed in position, panting, feeling his strong hand rubbing her bottom reassuringly. Her memories faded under his touch. Never before had anything back there also aroused her. How could something so uncomfortable make her clit throb demandingly?

"You were very good. I'm proud of you," he murmured, rubbing her back and her bottom, and she realized she'd endure much more to win that note of approval in his voice.

"You won't hide toys anymore, will you, chiquita?"

"Next time, I'll hide only the small ones."

A second, and then he laughed, the sexy, delighted sound that always made her grin. He said sternly, "Bad gatita. No hiding toys." The light smack on her ass shoved the plug in farther, zinging against unfamiliar nerves.

"No, Master. Never." She turned her head, eyeing the sack lying on its side. It wasn't empty. What else had he brought?

He helped her to her feet, and the nasty thing he'd stuck up her backside felt huge as her cheeks closed around it. She shifted her weight, trying to find a comfortable position.

Master R grinned. "Don't worry; you won't be thinking about it in a bit." He pointed to a corner of the trampoline. "Lie down there, on your back."

Each step moved the thing inside her, and the discomfort made her aware of how wet she was and how swollen her pussy had gotten. Her clit begged in heavy throbs to be touched. But touching herself was a spanking offense. Being spanked with an anal plug in? *So not my choice of fun ways to spend the afternoon.* She carefully lay down where he'd directed.

He picked up some rope from the pile and tied her wrists together, then over her head to an upright on the railing. A cushion went under her hips so her pelvis arched up in the air. After restraining her legs widely apart, he sat back on his heels, his gaze running over her, head to toes, lingering on her breasts and then her pussy.

She'd never felt so exposed. So available.

"You're beautiful, Kimberly."

*Uh-huh.* She knew full well, she was only passably pretty, but when he said that, looked at her like that, she felt absolutely hot. And totally ready for him to pull his cock out and have at it. *Now now now.* She squirmed.

"No, you will not entice me to move faster." His eyes were heavy lidded as he trickled his fingers over her mound, then traced her labia down. He gave the anal plug a wiggle that sparked shots of electricity straight to her clit. Her hips pushed up uncontrollably, and a crease appeared in his cheek. "I thought you might like the plug."

His smile grew. "Now you get a new toy as well." He pulled the hidden thing out of the bag. Soft-looking and the size of a couple of fingers and thumb forming a C curve. "I don't think you need lube for this." He pushed one end of the C into her slick pussy and angled the other part over her clit, letting it rest there. Not doing anything, dammit, but with that monster anal plug, even the small part inside her seemed excessively tight. Too much.

Her heart rate increased as her body shivered with the sensation of being tied down. Penetrated. With a whimper she closed her eyes and tried to relax. Waves splashed on the boat, the sound of a distant motor mingled with the pants of one of the other women and the low growl of a man's voice. The sun shone down on her, heating her skin to almost the temperature she was inside.

Pulling on the restraints, she found no give and could feel the last remnants of control slipping away. Helpless. Vulnerable. She opened her eyes and looked up.

He stood beside her, watching her squirm and fight, his silent regard reinforcing his obvious determination that she be open to him emotionally as well as physically. That she surrender.

Under the power of his gaze, his authority, she felt her muscles go limp. And she gave up.

His eyes warmed with approval. "Sumisita mía," he said softly. Down on one knee, he ran his knuckles tenderly over her cheek.

She turned her head and kissed his fingers, the action just so...right.

So was his kiss that followed.

After a minute, he sat back, and his expression changed. Heat. Anticipation. "I like that position. You look like a pagan sacrifice, all stretched out, just waiting to be served up to a god."

Sacrifice didn't sound good. "Master R." She'd attempted a teacher's stern tone, but her voice sounded more like a nervous first-grader who'd wet her pants. What could he be planning? He didn't have any whips or floggers aboard, and no toys were left in the sack.

His expression had a little of the sternness she'd seen when she messed up. He was definitely aroused—his erection still tented the front of his shorts. And his eyes held amusement. That worried her the most.

She licked her lips, tasting him.

He straddled her hips, keeping all his weight on his knees. Softly, he ran his fingers down the insides of her arms, over her armpits, which made her jump, and down her ribs. His touch was light, almost too light. Back up.

Her skin grew more sensitive. He stopped below her armpits, stroking higher, and...it tickled. She tried to shift away, but he had her strung to immobility. He teased his fingers under her arms.

Giggles broke from her, and she squirmed. "Stop it. That tickles!"

His smile was white against his tanned skin. "Cariño, I know." He did it again, making her laugh uncontrollably, not stopping even when she started to curse.

"Damn you," she gasped when he sat back. "Stop it. I don't like that."

"I said you'd be punished, mi pequeña sumisa. Did you think I was joking?"

"But not this way." *Good God.* "I'd rather be spanked."

He grinned and said softly, "I know."

She glared at him. "Are you done?"

"Oh no. I'm still exploring."

She moaned.

"But I'm going to mix some sensations together to see how you do." He reached down to the part of the toy that lay over her clit and clicked something. A buzz started both inside her and over her clit. Too light, too slow to do much, but...distracting. Just enough vibration to frustrate her, as if she were riding a Harley, but not enough to get her off.

Master R watched, his hand rubbing her arm, letting her need grow. Letting her stew. "Take a breath, chiquita. You're not quite through being punished"—he grinned— "although you're sweating enough, yes?"

God, sweat trickled between her breasts and down her face. "Please stop now." Her hips wiggled uncontrollably.

"Ah, but I like watching you squirm. And laugh. You don't laugh enough." He clicked the vibrator through several cycles, settling on an odd erratic rhythm, fast, then slow. Bringing her close to orgasm, then retreating too soon. Driving her up. *God, he's going to kill me.*

He moved between her legs, his knees pressing on the insides of her thighs. As the vibrations increased and she stiffened with the approaching climax, his fingers brushed down the insides of her forearms again to the tender area under her arms, teasing her with feathery touches. She gasped, jerking helplessly. Laughing, then moaning, then laughing as his fingers grazed over the increasingly sensitized skin.

He eased off, his fingers moving just enough to keep her aware, to keep her whole body tensed as the vibrator ruthlessly brought her back the brink.

*Oh God, I need to come.* Her lower half coiled, the feeling strangely intense. With the humming on her G-spot from inside, the flickering over her clit from outside, the entire area of nerves between them tightened. The pressure inside her built higher...higher...

Everything clenched for a long, impossible second, and she exploded. *God, God, God.* Even as she bucked under the climax, Master R drew his fingernails lightly over her ribs. She arched as new sensations blasted through her, making her laugh, making her scream, sending the entire world into a blaze of sensation, buffeting her between pleasure and torture and more pleasure.

She shuddered to a halt finally, slowly realizing he'd stopped tickling and even removed the vibrator. Grinning, he nuzzled her cheek.

"You bastard," she gasped.

"No, Mamá insists I am born of a marriage," he protested and claimed a hot, wet kiss, pulling her under his spell again.

Okay, she hated him, but she loved him, even if he was a sadistic scumbag asshole.

Sitting back, he ran his hands over her thighs, stroking gently, making her feel cherished and beautiful, even as shudders still ran through her body.

"You know, buddy," Cullen said a minute later. "I've never seen a tickling session quite so hot. I'm not sure it was much of a punishment, but damn." He eyed Andrea speculatively.

She shook her head frantically. "No. Absolutely no. I hate being tickled. Don't you even think about it."

Master R whispered in Kim's ear, "There's a lesson for you. That is never a smart thing to say to your dom."

Kim choked on a laugh. From the half leer on Cullen's face, he'd just hopped onboard with the tickling idea. He'd already had Andrea's hands bound in front of her, and now he hefted her to her feet. Turning her toward the ocean, he lashed her hands to the railing, forcing her to bend at the waist, and roped her ankles widely apart to the uprights.

"No, Cullen. Please, no, Señor."

"I don't have a vibrator, but we'll manage, little tiger." His laugh rang out, and he stepped out of his shorts, completely comfortable being stark naked. "Toss me that lube, Raoul." He caught the lube and drizzled some between his sub's buttocks and more on his very erect cock.

"Oh, God, you wouldn't," Andrea gasped.

He contemplated the body stretched out before him, then frowned. "I need to heat you up first, right?" His fingers teased from her armpits down to her clit and back up.

Once he had Andrea cursing and laughing and wiggling uncontrollably, he worked his cock into her anus, a little at first, then pushing all the way in. She groaned and groaned again as he started to thrust. His hand disappeared around her front, and from the way Andrea moaned, he was playing with her clit.

"That sounds pretty good, love." Cullen wrapped his free arm under her stomach, stabilizing them both, and changed from her clit to tickling under her arms. Giggles and groans filled the air.

God, if they did this in town, Kim thought, the cops would be pounding down the door.

Andrea was begging and cursing, mostly in Spanish.

Kim smiled. Here was someone she could ask to translate Master R's swearwords.

From the sound of rhythmic thumping on the side of the sailboat, Marcus had taken Gabi back into the water and was enjoying himself. A string of insults was abruptly cut off, and then a minute later, Gabi sputtered. A very calm Southern voice said, "Sugar, you're fixin' to drown if you keep that up. Now suck."

*God, these doms.* Kim shook her head and looked up. Master R's expression was tender as he ran his finger over her lips. "You're still smiling, mi tesoro," he murmured. "I like seeing you happy." He kissed her gently, lingeringly, in a way that had her heart turning over.

"I think these have been on long enough, so off they come." He leaned over and snagged the scissors from the deck.

*These?*

When his fingers touched her left breast, she realized. The clamps. *Oh no.* He snipped through the rubber bands. As the wooden skewers fell away, blood surged back into her left nipple.

She gritted her teeth together as fire bloomed in her breast, and only a whimper escaped, changing to a high whine when Master R's tongue stroked over the throbbing peak. The pain grew worse, then turned erotic as he continued to lick circles around the nipple and blow on it.

Her clit started to throb in response, and then Master R undid the other clamp.

"Ow ow ow, dammit, ow."

He chuckled and licked over the burning, making her shudder, making sensations stream like a marching band straight to her clit. He moved down, nipped her side, licked her belly button, and ran his tongue over her clit.

Hot and wet, and the shock arched her back. His tongue circled, teased the hood, waking her whole pussy as if he'd hit her with a jolt of electricity.

Her insides clenched, making her too aware he hadn't removed the anal plug yet. Maybe she could ask?

He lifted his head long enough to smile at her. "You're being a good girl, Kimberly. I think you deserve a reward." He licked over her clit, up and down, slowly but deliberately, bringing her right to the edge. Every firm rub made her insides tighten more.

Totally aroused, and damn him, he made her feel as if she had no control over anything, not even her body. Tied up, couldn't move, a giant plug in her, she'd already climaxed, and now he was—easily—showing he could bring her off again.

"Let's see how tight you are with your favorite toy still in," Master R said. He sat up and unzipped his shorts. Her eyes widened as he pressed his erection against her entrance and started to inch in.

*Oh no.* Too big. Much too big. "Wait. No."

His piercing hit, stopped him. He moved to a new angle, and the metal went in, a firm pressure sliding along her insides.

"You won't fit, dammit. You're too big."

"No, Kimberly. The toy you hid is big. I'm just right." He leaned forward onto his forearms and kissed her, teasing her lips. Holding steady inside her for a minute.

His broad hand fondled her breasts. Pinches on her abused nipples arched her spine.

And then he resumed pushing his shaft in, inexorably, like a tanker forging through the ocean. He watched her face, smiling a little when she'd tried to wiggle free. "Does it really hurt, sumisita?"

"Yes!" Under his steady gaze, she amended grumpily, "Kind of. No. But it's not comfortable."

The corners of his eyes crinkled, and he whispered, "I didn't think it would be." And he kept going until he was finally, completely in. His balls touched her ass. God, she was so full it was impossible to breathe. Stretched, aching, throbbing.

She closed her eyes and shivered. He was on top of her, inside her, and the feeling of being taken—being helpless—was frightening, and yet not, because he was watching her so closely that she felt the heat of his gaze.

"Look at me, gatita." His voice had roughened.

Her eyes opened and were trapped by his. Intense.

Then he pulled back, and every inch of movement somehow transmuted into exquisite pleasure. She gasped as her insides tried to clench and spasmed over the fullness. His eyes on her, he slid slowly back in, then out, totally in control. In and out, rocking slowly as she adjusted to the feeling.

"Bueno," he murmured, and his strokes changed as he drove into her in short thrusts, only partly in. With the anal plug, his piercing rubbed even more firmly over that sensitive place inside her. Stroke after stroke.

The pressure in her lower half grew into a shivery, desperate fullness. "I need to stop. I need the bathroom."

"Oh, I think this is something else, mi tesoro." He reached down, slickening his fingers, and stroking over her clit, without ever losing the determined thrusting.

Too much. The anal plug sent odd zinging sensations through her. His ruthless finger rubbed on her from outside, his pierced cock from inside as if they'd trapped her sensitive clit between them, mercilessly pushing her until everything inside her gathered, whirling her senses like a massive hurricane.

No pause. No teasing now. Faster, faster, and then everything spun completely out of control. She broke, shattering, her entire body having the orgasm as she screamed and bucked and shattered some more. She felt wetness everywhere, and Master R chuckled and pounded into her deep and hard, and she just kept coming, unable to stop.

Finally he tensed into rigidity, pressing in until she could feel the distinctive jerking of his shaft against her cervix as he gave a low rumble of pleasure.

His weight pressed her against the mesh as he lay on her, radiating such satisfaction that it made tears prickle in her eyes. Then, with a groan, he reached up to work at the ropes around her wrists.

She swallowed, tried to speak, and nothing came out. Swallowed again. "You're evil." Her voice was hoarse from laughter, from screams.

"Sí." He kissed her ear, then nipped her shoulder and laughed when her vagina clenched around him.

Her arms came free, her wrists still tied together, so she encircled his neck and leaned up to kiss him.

He kissed her back, taking her mouth to please himself until she felt like melted wax on the floor. As if she hadn't before. *God.*

Eventually, he sighed and pulled out of her, making her aware how wet she was. After he'd released her legs, he helped her sit up, then steadied her as her head spun.

She realized she was drenched, way past normal, and a flush heated her face. Talk about a wet spot. At least it was mesh under her. Still... "I...I'm sorry." Darn it, she'd said she needed the bathroom.

"Ah, Kimberly, it's not urine, chiquita." He cupped her cheek, forcing her to look at him. "You did what is called squirting, although that's an entirely inadequate word for something so very erotic. So hot. You women climax in many different ways—this is just one of them." He kissed her teasingly, his eyes lit with laughter. "Did you enjoy it?"

She leaned her head against him. "I wasn't sure if I'd

survive it, but...yeah."

"Then I will strive to give you more of them."

As he rose, she frowned. "Um, Master? Without the tickling next time?" Yeah, maybe it made her whole body more sensitive and gave her a great climax, but still... *Please God, let's skip the tickling stuff.*

He touched the tip of her nose. "That, mi pequeña sumisa, will depend on how obedient you are, no?"

# Chapter Fourteen

The time had come.

Kimberly stared at her reflection in the bedroom mirror and ran a finger over her new collar. Master R had obviously ordered this one especially for her. It was very soft on the inside. On the outside, the black leather boasted a silver engraving: *Master Raoul's gatita.* He hadn't added a padlock, saying she'd feel better if she knew she could remove the collar, and the engraving would make it clear she was owned. She touched the leather. Reassuring.

*I'm Master R's cat. I've got claws, and I know how to use them. Look out, you bastards.*

As for the rest of her outfit... *Ugh.* A leather micromini for the bottom, so short that if she bent over, they'd see her tonsils. The top was even worse since the decorative leather harness left her breasts totally exposed.

She'd applied makeup with a heavy hand, hoping to disguise the fear in her eyes. Fear of the auction, of the Overseer, of the slavers.

Not Master R. After yesterday on the boat, she felt closer to him than ever before. He was her security, a lifeboat in a horizon-to-horizon ocean.

He came up behind her in the floor-length mirror, wearing skintight leather pants and a matching black vest. His face was set, his eyes remote. He'd looked like that on the night he'd bought her, but not here...never in his bedroom before.

His gaze took her in, and his whole demeanor softened. "You're beautiful, gatita. The outfit should keep their attention nicely." He laid a cape over her shoulders. "They called and are only a few minutes away. We need to go down to the street now. Remember your part?"

"Yes, Master." *Oh God.*

\* \* \* \*

The black, windowless van pulled in front of the house where Raoul waited, his arm around his brave submissive. She suffered an occasional shiver but was holding up better than he'd thought.

A Harvest Association hireling hopped out, slid open the side door, and let the built-in steps down. "If you would, sir." He gestured to the door.

Raoul climbed the shaky steps and glanced at Kimberly in blatant irritation. "Come, girl. Stop lollygagging."

She wore the fetish shoes, tall with spike heels, and as she hurried forward, she stumbled and fell to her knees. With a loud impatient sigh, Raoul put his arm on the top of the van for balance and motioned to the attendant. "Help the clumsy bitch."

As the man assisted Kimberly to her feet, Raoul crushed the vial he'd concealed in his hand and smeared the exposed swab in long streaks across the roof of the van. To his satisfaction, nothing showed. Kouros had said only special glasses could see paint glowing. Since the slavers used GPS jammers in their homes and vehicles, the FBI's tracking devices had been useless. But now, hopefully, a helicopter could follow them. When picked up, Sam would perform the same swabbing maneuver.

Raoul covertly flicked the empty applicator high in the air to land in the bushes and with an annoyed sound, helped

Kimberly up the last step. In the van, three unaccompanied men occupied the luxury seating near the door, watching small DVD displays. Two turned avid gazes toward Kimberly, and Raoul wrapped her cape more firmly around her.

She took a breath and stood straight. *Brave gatita.*

"May I have your personal items, please, sir?" the attendant said, waiting on the steps.

Raoul handed over his wallet and phone and keys to be sealed away, then suffered a pat down. The multitool in his boot was checked for sharp points and replaced when he mentioned he'd be doing a demonstration.

The light flashed toward Kimberly. She opened her covering, and everyone could see she wasn't hiding a thing.

As the man jumped out and closed the door, Raoul chose a seat in the back, far from the others. He pulled Kimberly onto his lap, snaked his hand under her cape and over her breast.

Her startled gaze met his, and he kissed her lightly, murmuring into her ear, "If I play with you, I have a reason to hold you on my lap, but if you would prefer to kneel at my feet, you may."

Her head gave a little shake. At home, she'd have given him a laughing look and shown her pleasure at being in his arms. Not here.

"Stay beside me at all times, Kimberly. We'll use the leash again, but even so, I want you close enough to feel you. Is that clear?"

"Yes, Master."

He cupped her face in his hand, ran his thumb over her lips. "I am very proud of you, cariño," he murmured.

She burrowed into his arms in a very unslavelike manner, and he couldn't find it in his heart to deny her the comfort.

An unknowable time later, they emerged from the dark van and walked up the sidewalk to a mansion blazing with lights. Raoul strained his ears, thought he heard a faint whisper of helicopter blades, and hoped it wasn't his imagination.

As they approached the door where the guards were matching photos to arriving buyers, Raoul attached his leash to her collar. "Stay beside me now, Kimberly."

"Yes, Master," she whispered. "Thank you." In the glare of the outside lights, her face appeared gray.

He lifted her chin and forced her to meet his gaze. "You are *mine*, Kimberly. No one will touch you."

Under his fingers, the muscles of her jaw loosened. She gave him a jerky nod.

He ran his finger around the edge, touching her soft neck. "I like seeing my collar on you," he murmured.

Her smile of agreement was followed by confusion. He understood. She didn't want to be a slave—anyone's slave.

He stroked her hair once, then strolled arrogantly to the door. She remained to his right and half a pace behind. Closer than normal, but he needed her close for his own peace of mind as well as hers.

The two bulky guards at the door scanned a list of photos and stopped at one. "Master R?"

Raoul nodded.

The guard triggered a house intercom. "Tell the Overseer Master R has arrived."

A slave hurried over to take Raoul's coat and Kimberly's cape as Dahmer strode up.

"Welcome to the auction, Raoul." When the man turned his gaze on Kimberly, Raoul had to force his muscles to stay relaxed. "Very nice. I like the harness. You'll probably receive requests for her company tonight."

"I don't share." Raoul buried his hand in Kimberly's

hair, using the rough move to pull her closer to his side. "My mother thought I was quite selfish."

"Of course." The Overseer gave him a thin smile. "While your area is being prepared, can I show you the merchandise? We have some lovely showpieces this time. I daresay you'll find one or two you'd enjoy far more than this damaged one."

*What the hell does that mean?* Raoul tugged on Kimberly's leash and followed Dahmer, thinking of how a bridge would oscillate prior to collapse. Something in Dahmer's behavior was giving Raoul the same sense of impending disaster. His grip tightened on the leash.

The marble-floored foyer held a wide staircase that looked straight out of *Gone with the Wind.* Rather than ascending, Dahmer led them into an antebellum ballroom on the right. Textured wallpaper in red and gold warmed the room, and ornate crystal chandeliers attempted to convey a feeling of romance. But there was nothing romantic about the sound of sobbing and screams drowning out the classical music from hidden speakers.

Raoul stopped, too angry to move. This was a slave market, no matter the attempt to render it *high class.* Small café tables and chairs filled the center of the room. The slaves to be sold lined the walls. A heavy cable ran the perimeter, and each slave wore an ankle cuff and a chain securing her to the cable. Raoul nodded in understanding. According to Buchanan, the slavers changed locations with every auction, and a rental agency would take a dim view of someone putting heavy bolts in the walls to serve as restraints.

Buyers wandered the side aisles between the slaves and the tables, marking the notepads they'd been given. A small pedestal in front of each girl held a large number—the sale item—as well as her biographical and physical information for the buyers to peruse. When Raoul heard the smack of a hand against flesh, he didn't turn. He was far too close to using his fists on the man beside him. "This is very impressive, Dahmer."

"Thank you. I have things to do, so go ahead and walk around. Pick out a couple of slaves you like and remember their numbers. You'll understand why in a bit."

The hair on the back of Raoul's neck lifted. Yes, something was definitely going on.

As Dahmer headed out of the ballroom, Raoul glanced at Kimberly. Fast respirations. Hands clenched. He wanted to sweep her up in his arms, hotwire a van, and get her the hell out of this nightmare. Instead he squeezed her shoulder. "You're doing very well, gatita. I'm proud of the bravery you're showing."

A glimmer of tears showed for a second. Then she lifted her chin and gave him a firm nod. "Thank you, Master. Your words mean a lot to this slave."

*This slave?* She'd referred to herself in third person, undoubtedly trying to be even more obviously a slave for the evening. She'd gone one step too far.


KIM SAW THE way anger lit Master R's face, eroding the control in it.

"I realize you meant that for the best, but do not ever refer to yourself in third person. *You are not an object.* Try it again."

She took an involuntary step back at the violence in his voice, yet...the anger was on her behalf. The reassurance that he was the total opposite of the leering buyers dimmed her fears. "Yes, Sir. That's good to hear, Master."

His lips curved, making her heart swell.

Pleasing him felt...right. Too right. Flattening her mouth into a line, she turned and stared at the chained women. *He wants me to be like that.* Only he didn't. He treated her as someone he cherished, someone he found sexy, but not a *nothing.* He was more aware of her feelings than she was—and had been pushing her to recover.

But he wanted to take the decisions away from her, make them for her. *I'm so confused.*

The leash tugged. He'd taken a step and waited for her to pay attention. His eyes were gentle, as if he knew her struggles.

*Get out of your head, Kim.* Time to do the job. She followed him obediently, eyes on the ground at first and then not. Instead she looked at the women, memorizing their faces. If the operation failed, at least their families would know where to start looking. She met their eyes, willing strength into them. *Hang on. The nightmare might be over soon.* Let Galen and Vance show up like they'd planned. *Oh God, please.*

A shrill scream lifted over the rest of the noise, and Kim turned. A woman restrained to a cross. A red mark marred her white back. The buyer swung a short whip. A cracking sound. A terrified, pain-ridden scream. Another bloody stripe.

Kim tried to look away and couldn't.

An attendant in a red uniform hurried over to the buyer. "You must not mark the merchandise, please, sir," he scolded with the utmost of deference.

The buyer, an obese man, red-faced from the effort of using a whip, laughed. "I'm done. She'll do great for what I have in mind." He checked the number on the metal pedestal. "Slave number eighteen."

Kim could hear the woman whimper. Farther away, another whip cracked. Sobbing. Men's voices thick with lust. A shriek of terror. Heat swept over her, then a clammy cold. Even as her breathing increased, she couldn't seem to get enough air.

"Kimberly?" Master R's voice sounded over the roaring in her ears.

She opened her fingers, all ten for a panic attack, knowing it wouldn't matter. He couldn't show her—

He wrapped her in his arms, surrounding her with his strength, his clean scent. His dark voice murmured in her ears, blocking the other sounds. Anchoring her.

On her first trip to a beach, she'd toddled into the water. A wave knocked her sprawling, and as she tried to stand, another hit, and another. Her world turned to churning sand and water and choking—and then her mother carried her up the beach to safety.

As Master R had done over and over.

She sagged against him, the tight band across her chest easing, her lungs able to draw air again. "Okay," she whispered. "I'm sorry."

"No *problema*." He kissed her hair, not releasing her. "But I'm going to paw you a little so it looks better to the cabrones, sí?"

Oh, his temper was definitely up, the way he'd slid into Spanish.

"Sí, Señor," she whispered back, getting a huffed laugh in return.

His powerful hands closed on her bottom under her tiny skirt. He gripped her bare cheeks, traced the crack, holding her firmly against him. Oh God, she loved his touch, and it didn't matter where or when. An arm around her, he tipped her back so he could tease her breasts. Her knees wobbled, and his arm tightened. He yanked her hair, pulling her head back, and kissed her, deliberately rough, biting her lips.

When he released her, she knew her mouth was swollen and red, and her breasts and butt carried red hand marks. His lips curved. "You look nicely used now, mi pequeña sumisa."

She flashed him a nasty look that made him laugh, and then lowered her head properly. He tugged on the leash, and they moved down the room. She returned to watching the slaves. A blonde with terrified blue eyes, surely too young to be here. Two cringing brunettes, one already bearing whip marks. One woman unable to stop crying was next to an older woman, standing straight and defiant, who—

"Linda." Kim halted, jerking the leash from Master R's hands.

"Bad girl!" He pointed to the floor.

*But...* Her training took over, and she sank to her knees. Knowing she'd screwed up royally, she bent completely, arms above her head, wrists crossed, forehead on the floor. The surrender position.

He left her for long minutes.

A guard appeared, asking if there was a problem. Master R admitted she was still being trained, but he'd needed her for the demonstration the Overseer had asked for him to do. The guard's voice acquired more deference, and he lingered to exchange gossip and admire her harness.

The polished wood floor was cool against her forehead, and she wished she could stay in the position for the remainder of the evening. *I don't know how much more I can stand.*

When the attendant finally walked away, Master R snapped his fingers, and Kim rose to her feet, keeping her gaze on the floor, knowing if she saw Linda's face, she'd give herself away.

"I recognized her, gatita," Master R said in a low voice. "If we see Sam, we'll ask him to keep an eye on her if he's able." His concern for both her and Linda was clear.

God, she loved him. When he tugged on her leash, her

heart as well as her body followed.

They passed a woman in hysterics. When the attendant slapped her and she started to sob, Kim's hands fisted. *God, get me out of here. Get us all out of here. And home to our mommies and husbands and friends.*

"Raoul." Sam's rough voice. "Hell of a place, isn't it? I already got my eye on three of the beauties."

"You're a lucky guy," Master R said casually. "Maybe after I train this one, I'll come back and buy another." He dropped his voice. "One of Kimberly's fellow slaves is here. We'd appreciate it if you could...keep an eye on her. Especially when things get interesting."

Kim dared to look up through her eyelashes to see his reaction. Would he agree?

"Yeah, I like them spirited too." Sam laughed loudly and pointed to a nearby slave. "That one got a good beating for her attitude. Makes me think I'd better test the goods before I plunk down my cash."

Master R grinned. "You try out enough merchandise, and you'll crawl out of here." He pointed down toward Linda. "There's an older one on that aisle who might give you a challenge." His voice dropped. "Number ten. Redhead. Linda."

"Got it." Sam glanced at Kim, and his light blue eyes were the color of ice on a lake. "I like the harness, girl." He walked down the aisle, pausing for a moment as an attendant offered a buyer a selection of canes.

When Sam stopped in front of Linda's spot, hands in his pockets, obviously checking her out, Kim let out a breath of relief.

WELL, HOW WAS he to be about this business? Sam wondered, studying Kimberly's friend. Number ten was an older woman, probably midforties, but one of those who only got lusher—erotically softer—as she aged. Her chin-length red hair had been curled back in a smart style, showing some silvering in front of her ears. Freckles up her forearms, lightly tanned legs, the rest of her body a pure white that made the sadist in his soul salivate. She was like a blank canvas for a painter. Think of the marks he could put on her.

Her rich brown eyes had a few wrinkles fanning out from the edges. Would those deepen as she forced herself to take the pain? Was she truly a masochist as her information said?

As with all the slaves, she was naked, her wrists cuffed together in front, one leg shackled to a heavy cable running along the wall. She gave him a calm stare that made his cock sit up and take notice. He could see her terror. Despite the way she'd laced her fingers together, her hands still trembled. She'd start to pant, her gaze would dart around, and then she'd catch herself. Slow her breathing, lower her eyes. So lovely in her control.

Using pain, he could take her deep, make her give up that control—and then he could care for her. His sadistic and dominant sides both yelled for him to move forward.

Now he knew how Raoul had felt when he'd bought his slave. How he must have wanted to explain he wasn't like the others, didn't want any of this nonconsensual bullshit.

But a man had to play the cards he'd been dealt. He stepped forward. "Girl."

Her head stayed bowed. "Yes, Sir?" Her voice was that of a woman, low and resonant. No shrill screaming would come from this one.

"Look at me."

She lifted her gaze, and he looked into her brown eyes. Soft. She probably didn't have anything hard about her, not her body, her eyes, her voice. The thought of burying himself in all that softness... His dick had hardened enough to count the teeth on his jeans zipper.

"Are you a masochist?" he asked, more to determine her honesty than to get the facts. The sign posted on the pedestal gave her specifics, including her experience and preferences. Not that any slaver would care, except to design something to rip her to pieces more quickly.

"Yes, Sir," she said quietly and dropped her gaze, a slight flush on her cheeks. Didn't like admitting to that need?

"Keep your eyes on mine, girl." He moved forward, close enough to smell the light scent of soap from her body, to see tiny golden specks in her brown pupils. Her heavy breasts brushed against his shirt.

He'd positioned himself directly in front of her so he could speak freely, and she could react without being observed. Not that he'd reveal anything past the bounds of good judgment. But this would be easier if she didn't think of him as a total enemy. "Your friend, Kim, suggested I visit you." He nodded toward the front of the room.

Her eyes followed his.

Kim, Raoul, and the Overseer stood by the stage where the women would be auctioned off. The auctioneer was already tapping the microphone, and two attendants bracketed the first slave. A sign to the right announced SLAVE # 30.

Selling women. Sam's gut felt as if he'd swallowed a field of thistles.

While Raoul was talking to the Overseer bastard, Kim caught Linda's gaze and then nodded slightly at Sam.

Damndest referral he'd ever gotten. But the redhead released a slow breath. Her muscles relaxed slightly. Better.

He figured the Feds might take another hour before they got their crap set up. At number ten, this woman would be among the last to be auctioned off. Unfortunately, buyers could abuse her that entire time...unless Sam monopolized her. How many minutes could he waste?

Would she want him to? "I can play with you until"— *the Feds arrive, but I can't say that*—"until you're sold, or you can take your chances with the other buyers. It's up to you, girl."

"You'll hurt me," she stated.

Keeping his eyes on hers, he nodded. "That's right. That's what I do." He paused a second. "It's what you need— although this isn't the place. But I won't hurt you past your limits."

Her mouth twisted slightly. "And you would know those how?" She winced and lowered her head. "Forgive me, please, Master."

He barked a laugh that had her eyes jerking up to his. "I like plain speech. Honesty." He pinched her chin roughly enough to keep her attention focused on him completely and saw—felt—the smallest of easing in her muscles. Yes, she was a masochist and submissive as well. His favorite combination. If she responded to pain and domination sexually, well, hell, she'd be perfect.

*Use your brains, Davies. You're in the middle of a bunch of slaves. This one would knife you and spit in the hole given half the chance.* "I know this because I can read you, little girl. Right down to your toenails." He leaned forward, still holding her chin, keeping her mouth available for his use, and he took her lips with no teasing, just sheer domination.

Forcing her response and feeling her response before pulling back.

Without Kim's okay and if he hadn't given her the choice of being with him, he knew this self-possessed woman wouldn't respond to him at all. But she did.

"I won't scar you. I won't go past what you can take. If

you can trust me that far, this will be much easier for you."
He met her eyes straight on, letting her read his body, hear
the truth, and see it in his face. "But, Linda, I'm going to
hurt you. You'll hate me when I make you take it, and you'll
hate even more that you need it. That it fills that hole inside
you and cleans away the clutter."

The shudder ran through her, telling him she'd heard
him on all levels. Her muscles were still tight, her eyes
blazing, yet he could almost smell the subtle perfume of
submission.

She yielded. Now he would give her what she wanted
and finish that surrender.

# Chapter Fifteen

Raoul was grateful when Dahmer finally showed up in the ballroom. Following the Overseer, he steered Kimberly toward the doors. She didn't need to see any more. Bidding had started on the third woman whose screaming and fighting caught the buyers' attention like bloody flesh attracting sharks. As he walked into the quiet foyer, Raoul gave a silent sigh of relief. The crying slaves had kept him tensed with the need to protect.

"Before you set up for your scene, I need you for a moment upstairs." The look in Dahmer's eyes was still...off.

Raoul tightened his hand on Kimberly's leash, pulling her closer. "Is there a problem?"

"No. Well, yes, in a way there is." Dahmer led them up the wide stairs, the dark red carpeting like a waterfall of blood. He opened a door directly across from the staircase and motioned them inside.

Raoul glanced around at the richly furnished sitting room. To the right was a small table and chairs on an Oriental rug. Against the far wall was a hand-carved buffet with a serving tray and the remains of a meal. Oddly enough, the corner held a portable dog kennel. On the left...*ah-hah.* A lean man waited in an armchair by the window, the lamplight glinting off styled light brown hair. Two men—bodyguard types—stood behind him. He would be the reason for Dahmer's detour.

As Kimberly stepped into the room, she gasped and

gave a thin moan.

Raoul spun, grasping her shoulders. "What?"

"Lord Greville," she whispered, her eyes going glassy with panic, her breathing like a steam engine.

Raoul slapped her sharply across the face, rocking her back on her heels. Fisting her hair, he pulled her head back so the only person she could see was him. "You are mine. You do not react to any other master," he told her through gritted teeth...and saw reason return to her eyes.

She blinked tears of pain away, and he let her lower her head. "I'm sorry, Master."

"Better," he grunted. He glanced at Dahmer, letting his irritation show. "What's this about—aside from trying to destroy the work I've put into this slave?"

"I apologize for not explaining earlier, but I wanted you to view the undamaged beauties downstairs first." Dahmer's gaze lingered on the scar visible beneath Kimberly's harness. "Which ones did you find interesting?"

"I have a slave, thank you." This wasn't going well at all. Kimberly's former owner had given Raoul a dismissing look, then hadn't taken his eyes off her. From the hand-tailored suit, the Italian shoes, the sheer pampered posture, Greville wasn't used to being denied anything. And he wanted Kimberly.

The hatred burning in his blue eyes sent cold streaming up Raoul's spine. He saw murder in that gaze.

Raoul took a firm grip of Kimberly's arm and whispered in her ear, "He seems a little angry. Some people are poor sports about being poked with a knife, no?"

Her shocked laugh lightened his spirit. Brave, brave Kimberly. "Dios, I love you," he said under his breath, not realizing he'd spoken until he saw her face. The dawning glow outweighed her fear.

When she looked down hastily, he squeezed her arm

lightly. She needed to hold up awhile longer. Somehow.

And he had to keep her away from Greville. The FBI would arrive eventually, but if her previous owner got his hands on her, she might not survive that long. *Stall. Stall and stall.*

Dahmer took a seat on the couch and motioned to the chair across from Greville. "Please sit. I'm sure we can reach a meeting of the minds. Raoul, this is—"

"Greville, I assume." Raoul assessed the bodyguards with a glance. One had puckered scars across his face and neck. The other had a shaved head with a death's head skull tattoo on one side of his neck, a swastika on the other. They wore white shirts, dark slacks. No weapons visible. They'd probably received the same pat down as the buyers—so weaponless—but from their stances, they were well trained.

Not good odds. He was no Chuck Norris. *Stall.* He took the chair, caught Kimberly's gaze, and glanced at the floor beside him.

She knelt at his feet and kept her eyes lowered.

"Hello, fuckhole." Greville spoke directly to her, trying to get her to meet his gaze.

"You do not address my slave without permission," Raoul snapped.

Greville's face reddened with rage.

"Raoul." Dahmer held up a hand.

"This is not the professional standards I was led to expect from the Harvest Association. What kind of shoddy scam are you running here?"

Dahmer drew himself up. "Not a scam. Lord Greville simply wishes to repurchase his slave. During his...illness, his staff returned the slave for a refund. He wasn't aware and had no intention of returning her to us."

Raoul forced himself to lean back in his chair. "Perhaps he should keep closer track of his staff. They sound incompetent." *This is not going to end well.* If he got Kimberly out of the room, could she hide until the FBI arrived?

\* \* \* \*

The attendants were too damned efficient, Sam thought. In answer to his request, one had quickly wheeled a mobile St. Andrew's cross into Linda's slave space. So much for his attempt at stalling.

After turning the woman to face the X shape, he secured her wrist cuffs to the upper rings. The other blank-faced attendant handed him a cane and dragon's tongue whip.

He set them down, out of his working area, and considered how to go about wasting time until the FBI arrived. Unfortunately, anything he did would have to be genuine. The assistant had positioned the cross so bystanders could see the marks he'd put on the slave's back.

*Well, then.* He had a masochist who preferred him to the others, he had equipment, and he obviously had time. Apparently he had a scene to do.

His concentration narrowed.

He stepped behind the woman and ran his fingers over the pretty spattering of freckles on her shoulders. "Linda," he said quietly. "Are you ready to begin?"

Under the freckles, her muscles tensed. She nodded.

"When I ask you a question, I want to hear your voice, girl," he said in an even tone, setting up the rules of the game. His hands curved around her wrists, adding to her sensation of restraint as he pressed his groin into her from behind, then let his whole body meld with hers, pushing her ribs against the wood in the middle. "You can call me Master if you need to beg."

He threaded his fingers into her short hair, tugging

her head to one side so he could close his teeth on the curve between her neck and shoulder. He bit down firmly, enough to hurt. Waking her to her helplessness and his intent. The beast inside him moved forward; his body felt larger, stronger.

"If you yell, 'Mercy, Master,' I will...perhaps...give you a break," he growled, sickened and aroused at the same time. He never worked without a safe word, without consent, but to save her from worse, he'd have to do so—or at least appear to do so. "Say it now."

"Mercy, Master," she whispered. Even her lips looked soft, slightly puffy. Kissable and damn fuckable.

"Good," he grunted. He rubbed his hands over her arms and shoulders and down her back, pleased with the gentle hollow at the base of her spine. A big-arsed woman, his British friends would say. His favorite kind. He slapped that white ass, one cheek, then the other. Not hard, just enough to warm the skin, stroking the sting away before striking again. He hadn't bothered with trying to fasten her ankles to the legs of the cross, not with one shackled, but he set one boot between her feet and shoved them roughly apart.

"I want you open to me," he said in a raw voice and was hell of pleased to see a flush rise into her face. His eyes narrowed, meeting hers, and she flinched and dropped her gaze. Submissive. God, she was a beauty.

Pushing the noise of the auction from his mind, he filled his thoughts with only this woman. He slid his hands over her ample curves, over her rounded stomach to her God-be-thanked breasts. Heavy in his cupped palms, spilling over the sides. Fucking her would be like burying himself in a down quilt, surrounded by feminine softness.

He pressed his chest against her back, delightfully surprised when she didn't cringe away. When he rubbed his erection on her reddened ass, he heard the smallest moan—

and hell with it, he needed to know. He put his hand on her pussy, unsurprised to find she'd begun to dampen. "You're wet, girl."

"I'm a slut." The self-loathing and misery in her voice pissed him off considerably. Raoul had mentioned something about this.

He growled in her ear and pressed his cock between her buttocks. "Feel that, missy? A man's dick rises with the smell of a female, with the sound of a woman's voice, with the dawn, at the sight of pretty tits, at the touch of...anything. No one calls us names because our cocks aren't under our control." He cupped his hand over her—nicely—bare cunt, playing in the dampness. "So when a woman's pussy reacts on its own, why would I call her a name?" He sucked on her earlobe, surprising a shudder out of her, then ran his scratchy cheek over hers, giving the so-sensitive nerves there a hint of pain. And her juices responded.

"I've been doing this a long time, girl," he said, using her own arousal to slicken her vulnerable clit. "And I'm not only good at it, but we—you and me—we have something between us."

"No," she whispered.

"Yes, missy." When she tried to pull her legs together, he kicked them open again and felt her tightening nipple press into his palm. The beast inside him said, *Hurt this one and make her mine.*

*Dammit, not mine. I'm here to stall.* Dragging his brains up from where they'd lodged in his balls, he diverted himself with a quick check of the restraints. Hands were pink, cuffs not too tight. Then to please himself, he cupped both of her breasts again, hearing her inhale, feeling her heat against his body.

"I'm going to make you hurt now, girl," he whispered. Her breasts were heavy in his hands, and he tightened his grip until he heard her breath catch. "I'm going to whip you until you dance the dance, until your screaming wakes God himself." He pulled her nipples, pinching cruelly.

Tears stood in her eyes—and her ass pushed back against his shaft. "No, please." Her head whipped back and forth as she moved her body, trying to evade his grip.

He wanted to see her face. A shame he couldn't walk around the cross and simply look at her; he preferred a chain station for that reason. But this was what he had. He grabbed her chin and turned her face toward him. Her eyes held the pain he'd given her, showing some fear—and more heat. Just right.

"Eyes on me," he snapped. "And don't look away." He took one nipple, rolling it between his fingers. Damn, he wished the slavers provided breast clamps as well as impact toys. He squeezed harder, enjoying the whine in her throat. Pulled and pinched, studying her eyes to judge the right amount, and savored the blossoming of fresh pain in her eyes, her face, the way her body stiffened, muscles tensing here and there.

Sweat started to bead on her upper lip.

He smiled at her. "That's a good girl. Let's do the other side."

"Master, please. My breasts are sensitive."

He paused, knowing even now that she wouldn't safeword out, that this was the beginning of the dance, and he answered the need under her words. "I know they are, Linda. That's why I'm doing this." And he squeezed her other nipple.

"Eeeeee." Her scream caught between her teeth as she shut it down. Her arms jerked with her efforts to escape. To push him away. Her knees sagged.

He stroked her damp face. "Those screams in there aren't going to be buried very long," he whispered into her ear. Her hair was silky, and he rubbed his cheek over it. "If we were somewhere else, afterward I'd fuck you hard...and pull on your nipples every time you came."

The tremor ran from her breasts all the way to her fingers, and he smiled.

Stepping back, he ran his fingers down her ass, between her legs, to the dampness on her inner thighs. He teased the folds between her legs, nice fat labia—perfectly designed for clamps. His finger slid into her, earning a low moan and wiggle. Very wet. She'd be a joy to fuck. He played with her clit and cunt, the scent and little noises she gave upping his own desire.

She'd take more pain and last longer if he could keep her arousal high. Fucking slavers—he damn well didn't want to be here.

He wiped her juices off on her leg and felt her flinch, remembered her word. *Slut.* He gripped her hair, pulled her head back. "I like you wet, Linda," he growled. "And what *I* want is all you have to worry about right now. Clear?"

The way she moistened her lips to speak... The way her response flowed to him was getting to him. Hell. He took advantage of how he'd made her arch, and shoved his hand between her legs again—forcefully this time—pushing into her in a manner that showed exactly what he wanted to do to her.

A tremor ran through her as she clenched around him. More moisture wet his fingers.

She liked rough. Hell, maybe he'd add a little pussy pain while he was at it. Drive her high before endorphins shoved her head into the clouds.

He barely glanced at the two buyers who stood nearby as he strolled to his spot. Even turned away from her, he could almost feel her breathing. Feel how the ache in her breasts receded, but the memory lingered. Feel how she craved more.

After a second, he picked up the cane. Time to warm her up. A slow, slow warm-up. Damn them for not having his favorite toys available. But a light application would work well enough.

He started by sliding the rattan over her legs, letting her enjoy the smoothness of it, the hardness, before running it up her front.

She stiffened.

*That's right, girl. This is a cane.* But pain wouldn't come from it. It was just for warm-up to the whip.

Tapping lightly, occasionally giving her a feather-stroke touch, he woke up the flesh on her back, butt, and thighs. He followed the path of the cane with his free hand as her muscles gradually lost their tension.

Her breathing slowed.

He increased the intensity, keeping to the sting rather than the blow. Her body was still relaxed, and from the tiny curve of her lips, he knew the small smacking sounds of the cane pleased them both.

Her ass was turning a pretty pinkish red, a color that made a dom want to use his hand to see if he could darken it. Light play just didn't do it for him. He glanced at his watch. How long could he drag this out? He saw an attendant talking to a buyer and frowning in his direction. Not long.

He tossed the cane off to one side and picked up the whip. A dragon's tail—not his favorite but a good choice in tight quarters. About three feet of rolled leather opening into a swordlike shape and ending in the distinctive point. At least the leather on this was thin enough to give a whippy sensation. After rolling his shoulders, loosening his arm, he snapped the tail a few times, getting the feel, gauging his accuracy, smiling each time she flinched at the light crack. Hell of a lot lighter than a flogger—he could do this all day.

Then he let the end strike, enjoying the slapping sound, up and down her back, her ass, her upper thighs, finishing the warm-up in the medium range of pain. He moved into a good rhythm, watching her start to fog over. Her breathing deepened as he slowed his strikes.

He stopped and stepped forward quickly so the loss of the whip was balanced by his hand on her shoulder, the pressure of his body against her back. Rubbing his chest and groin on her reddened skin should give her a rush of pain from everywhere, different from the individual slaps of a whip. Her gasp felt as if it gripped his balls.

After checking her restraints and circulation, he turned her head, looked into her eyes. "You still with me here, Linda?"

She blinked and actually smiled at him. "That's my name. You used my name."

This one could tear a man's heart right out of his chest. "That's who you are. Linda." He kissed her cheek and brought her back to the scene by taking her lips, taking her from lightness to hard and demanding. Her body melted into his, then revved with arousal when he cupped her breasts and teased her puckered nipples into jutting points—velvet softness, the bigger size said she'd nursed her babies. He wanted his mouth on them.

Instead, he ran his hand down to her pussy, beautifully wet and puffy. Her instinctive pulling away from the intimacy rubbed her soft ass right on his cock, forcing her forward again and onto his fingers. A nice predicament for a little sub.

But he solved it for her, removing her choices by leaning forward, trapping her even as he penetrated her with a finger. Hot, wet sheath.

He felt how her arousal, her need, vied with her wish to move away from him, to keep herself hidden from him. She made a sound he couldn't interpret, then whispered,

"No. Don't." Her words were negated by the low moan she gave.

"Are you asking for mercy, girl?" he whispered, pinching her clit lightly and sliding back in.

Panting, she hesitated. "Yes." She shook her head. "No."

"Then we continue. You ready for some real pain now?"

Her cunt clenched around his fingers, and he grinned.

After picking up the dragon whip, he did a set, up and down her body, bringing her pain level back to where she'd been before. Then he held the tip of the tail in his free hand and snapped it at her ass like a rolled towel. The end hit. Her skin jumped a split second before her jerk. A sob came from her, and he smiled.

"Not the same sensation, is it, missy?" *Snap, snap, snap.* "Feel a little like a whip?" *Snap, snap, snap.* Her first tear splattered onto the floor, then more. The dragon's tail flicked its way down the backs of her thighs in pretty red streaks, the narrow leather giving barely satisfying cracks.

And up her legs, her ass, her back. Her first gasping scream.

"That's a good girl. Give me more." After easing up for a moment, not too long, he worked her into pain, into screams that satisfied his soul and squeezed his cock. By the time she tipped into a truly deep subspace, she'd stopped holding anything from him.

Her husky scream resonated in his balls.

He continued a little longer, watching closely now. A safe word wasn't worth shit if a sub's brain wasn't awake enough to use it. He lightened up, finishing what they'd both wanted. Needed. Then even slower, gentling the strikes. Bringing her down.

Sweat made her skin gleam as if covered in oil. Her

head sagged against her upraised arm although her legs still held most of her weight. Yes, she was no stranger to bondage and pain. He set the whip down and moved forward, feeling like a predator stalking his prey but also a man wanting to please a woman. Sadistic. Dominant.

He ran his hands over her, pleased with his handiwork, even more pleased with her gasp as his thick calluses scraped her abused skin. Her ass pushed back as if begging. He straightened and turned her head. Still mostly in subspace. Aroused and needy.

Damned if he'd fuck her here, treat her like that, but he could at least ease her, give her relief. And if he walked around with a boner for a while, it wouldn't be the first or last time. He bit her neck, reminding her of his presence, emotionally ground-tying her so she didn't detach entirely.

"You gave me your pain." His voice came out raspy. "Now give me your pleasure." His rough fondling of her breasts brought forth a moan, and when he reached down to her swollen, wet pussy, she was right with him. Her body showed her need; her eyes showed her submission.

Surrounding her with his body, reading the tightening of her muscles, hearing the faint noises in her throat, he stroked over her engorged clit, working her up and up. Was there anything more satisfying than moans after screams? He kept her on the edge, savoring the quivers of her inner thighs around his big wrist, then stroked firmly.

When she came—her hips bucking, her pussy creaming over his hand—her wailing moan ran down his spine.

He leaned against her curvy back and her lush ass, pressing her into the cross as he nuzzled her neck, adding sweetness to the ending.

\* \* \* \*

*Don't look at the cage in the corner. Don't look at Lord Greville.* Kim stared at her knees, controlling her breathing. Controlling the panic was like piloting a boat in a tropical storm, trying to keep the bow headed into the seas. The counselor's suggestion of imagining Greville with a rabbit-sized dick, whiskers, and a fuzzy tail didn't help at all.

The men talked. Lord Greville had a voice like his whip, cutting and ripping, leaving bloody flesh behind.

The Overseer's voice was an oil film on water, suffocating all life beneath. Her chest tightened.

When Master R spoke, the sound washed her clean, let her breathe. His knee pressed against her shoulder, bumping her now and then as if to keep her in the present. Her shoulders straightened. *Pay attention. He'll need your help.*

"You'd said that buying damaged merchandise might have been a mistake, so this is your opportunity to find a slave more suited to your needs," the Overseer said, still trying to arbitrate.

"I see. I did complain about the damage, didn't I?" Master R sounded so reasonable, they probably didn't hear the tight thread of anger underlying his words. "You're offering to buy me a different slave?" She felt the vibration as his fingers tapped on her leash. "I wouldn't mind owning one with a curvier figure. Big breasts appeal to me."

*What?* After a moment of fear—then a sense of insult—she understood he was stalling for time. He could do no less, although all she wanted was out of here. The sickly sweet scent of Lord Greville's cologne filled the air, and she breathed through her mouth, trying not to gag. The sounds of screaming came faintly past the closed door. The auction was going on.

"Well then, we should be able to work something out." The Overseer sounded relieved.

"Perhaps.   Unfortunately,   the   slaves   here   are

masochists—not anything I'm interested in. What other auctions do you have coming up?"

"I—Well, the next will be in October. The black-and-white affair, featuring blondes and brunettes, with a sampling of black women as well."

"I definitely like blondes. That might work out quite well." Master R rose. "In October then. And Greville there will buy whatever slave I wish in return for the girl."

The leash tightened; Kim started to rise.

"Unacceptable. I'll take possession of her now." Lord Greville's voice was flat.

"Leave me without a slave? I think not. October."

"I'll buy her outright then. How much?"

"Still leaves me without a slave." Master R pulled, and Kim rose to her feet, staying a step behind him.

"The hell with this. Just take her." Lord Greville motioned to his men.

Master R dropped the leash and shoved her toward the door. "Run!"

She scrambled away, expecting him behind her—only he wasn't. He'd charged the bodyguards. She hesitated and—

The Overseer slammed into her, knocking her into the wall. He grabbed her hair and yanked her back against his body.

*No*! She jammed her elbow into his gut.

He folded over but still clung to her hair.

Screaming, she ignored his grip, curling her fingers into claws.

*TWO AGAINST ONE. Dios.* A big fist grazed Raoul's face, leaving a burn in its wake. He spun and kicked the other guard in the gut, knocking him on his ass. Spin back, block another fist, try for a knee. Missed. The guards were both damn good fighters. Scarface's return punch nailed him in the jaw, stunning him.

Raoul shook his head and half-blindly punched back, feeling the impact and crunch as his fist hit a nose. A bellow. Hot spray of blood. He twisted to check the other.

And then something punched him from behind, high on the right shoulder. He jerked around to see the Greville bastard jump away.

The skinhead swung. When Raoul blocked with his right arm, pain sheeted into him like all of hell had opened. He grunted and continued, but his block held no power, and the man knocked him into the wall. As he hit, fire ripped through his shoulder. His knees gave, dropping him to the floor.

"You knifed him good, Lord Greville." Scarface stepped sideways as Raoul pushed to his feet.

*Greville.* He'd attacked from behind like a feral cur.

The two guards had him bracketed, his back to the wall. He could feel the knife, still stuck in his shoulder. Pain shot through him with every movement.

As the two glanced at each other, trying to synchronize their attack, Raoul darted a look across the room. Dammit, Kimberly hadn't run, and Dahmer had grabbed her.

Still looking, he faked a grin, and Skinhead fell for it, glancing over his shoulder at Kimberly. Raoul stabbed rigid fingers straight into the bastard's throat and felt the cartilage break.

Scarface yelled and lunged. Raoul tried to block, but his right arm failed—*fucking knife*—and a roundhouse knocked him sideways. He staggered, fell onto his hands and knees.

"Use the knife and just kill him, you incompetent

turd," Greville said coldly. "I've got better things to do."

When two more men ran into the room, Raoul knew his—and Kimberly's—chances of survival had just died. *Run, gatita, dammit, run.*

Scarface jumped forward and ripped the knife from Raoul's shoulder. Pain burst like fireworks. Before the guard could step back, Raoul slammed his fist straight up into his balls.

With a choking gasp, Scarface fell to his knees, grabbing his groin. The knife clattered to the floor. A fucking steak knife from the dinner tray.

Raoul tried to snatch it and got kicked in the ribs. New guards. His hand skidded on the blood on the floor.

HEART BATTERING AT the inside of her ribs, Kim stared across the room at the group of men.

Lord Greville's bodyguards were down, one on his knees moaning. Between two new men, Master R pushed partway up and dived at Greville, hitting him in the stomach, knocking him down.

Swearing, the new men grabbed his arms, tearing him off Greville, holding him between them.

Face dark with rage, Greville staggered to his feet. Using a handkerchief, he wiped blood from his mouth, looked at it. He bent and picked the knife up. "Hold him good—I'm going to gut him like a trout."

"Nooo!" Her shriek stopped everything.

Lord Greville turned, taking his time, Kim could tell. Playing her. He glanced at the Overseer who lay a few feet away, moaning, hands over his face. "Worthless bastard."

She didn't look, wouldn't look at the Overseer or her bloody fingers. Could only think of Master R. He'd die because of her, because he'd tried to save her. *My fault.* "Please, don't kill him. Please!"

Lord Greville tilted his head. "You *care* for him?" A cruel smile twisted his lips. "Oh, I like that. Yes." He pointed his knife at her, then the cage in the corner. "In."

*A cage.* Her breath stopped. *Darkness, no light at all, the scent of a basement, excrement, urine, blood. Wire under her fingers, around her, she couldn't stand, couldn't straighten her legs.* An ocean pressed on her chest, flattening her lungs. Air gone. *No...* She felt a breeze from the open doorway behind her—she could run. *Run.*

She edged toward the opening.

Master R was fighting madly, drawing everyone's attention. His gaze caught hers, and he jerked his head toward the door. An order matching the one that every nerve in her body was screaming. *Run.*

"Hold him, dammit." Lord Greville sliced at Master R with the knife—the blade scraped over the leather vest on the left, then cut viciously over his right ribs. A huge, long gash.

He made no sound, but Kim saw him jerk. A trickle of red spilled over the edge of the gaping flesh; then blood flowed.

Sobs choked her; tears blinded her. He'd die; he was dying. "No, no please, oh God, no. Please."

Lord Greville glanced over his shoulder. "The cage or I cut him into little pieces in front of you. Crawl, fuckhole."

She did, her hands numb, her heart hammering too violently. None of it mattered. The cage surrounded her.

Lord Greville laughed, jagged and cold like a saw blade. He turned back to Master R and scowled at how the two men had to hold him up. "Hell, he's out cold. That's no fun." He glanced at the water pitcher, hesitated, then motioned toward the cage. "Toss him in."

As the guards dragged Master R over, Greville's eyes met Kim's. "If he's still breathing when we get home, you can show me just how far you'll go to keep him alive."

She'd do anything, and her stomach tried to empty as she thought of the perversions Greville would demand.

The guards heaved Master R into the cage. She pressed against the wire, feeling the wire sides closing in on her. Just as small as the one in Lord Greville's basement.

"Get that collar off her," Lord Greville said.

One man grabbed her hair, yanking her far enough forward to unbuckle the collar with one hand. The feel of air against her bare neck was horrible—not like being stripped, but like seeing her house burn to the ground.

The guard stepped back; the other closed the door and snapped the heavy padlock, removing the key.

"Look, fuckhole." Lord Greville waggled her collar and threw it out the door.

Kim stared after it, her life tumbling down the stairs with it. *Dreams die before people do.*

Greville accepted the padlock key from the guard and put it in his pocket. "You're mine, cunt, for as long as I let you live."

No matter how many hours or days, it would be too long. Kim couldn't stop shaking, her chest so tight no air seemed to get through. Red and black wavered in her vision—blood and death—and she wanted it, wanted the oblivion.

Lord Greville pointed to the moaning Overseer. "Haul him downstairs and have someone see to him. I need him able to sign the papers." He turned to check his bodyguards. One had managed to stand. The other was...was dead.

Kim stared at Master R. He'd killed. And he was dying.

Her hands shook; her body shook. *Don't die.* She tried to turn him. *Stop the bleeding.* No room to move him, no room. Her hands clamped into fists.

"I'll clear us leaving with the front door attendants," Greville said to the guard. "Get three more men to carry the crate—and something to cover it." He laughed. "Good deal. Two slaves for the price of none."

The door closed behind them with a solid thump.

A hand gripped on Kim's arm, and she jumped.

"Cariño." Master R looked up at her, brown eyes completely alert.

"Master R?" she whispered and stared at him. *The scum-sucking bottom-feeder... He'd been faking it.*

His eyes were filled with laughter. With pride. "So, gatita with sharp claws, what did you do to Dahmer?"

* * * *

Sam knelt beside Linda. He'd released her, lowered her to a sitting position despite her groggy protest.

The scrawny attendant pulled the portable St. Andrews into the aisle and frowned at Sam. "Please step out of the display area, sir."

"She needs a blanket and some water." Abandon a sub who was coming out of subspace?

"She's up for sale, sir. Your time to sample the merchandise is over."

"I get it." God blast these bastards. He couldn't leave her so vulnerable. Sam slapped her face lightly. "Wake up, girl. Now."

She blinked, eyes focusing on him, then looked around the room, and her fear yanked her out of comfort faster than anything he could do.

"That's right. Come on back," he said, smoothing her hair.

She pulled away from his hand, and her expression held...revulsion. Anger. "Damn you," she whispered and shuddered.

Sam frowned. *What—why?* "Linda, what—" He saw the attendant signal for a guard and stopped. *Can't draw that kind of attention. Or be forced from the vicinity.* He rose to his feet, bent, and patted her shoulder. "Hang in there, girl."

She cringed away...from him.

He hesitated, then withdrew to outside the display area. That hadn't been fear she showed, but anger. Disgust. His lips tightened. He'd stay close. She might not want help, but too bad.

Another buyer approached, looking almost mesmerized. No question as to why. The redhead might be older, but after taking what Sam had given, she had a...glow. Her lips were swollen, her face abraded, her breasts marked by his hands. Her eyes were heavy from how intensely she'd come. She looked like a wet dream in chains.

The buyer, middle-aged with a hefty paunch, stared at Linda and started to signal to an attendant. Leaning an elbow on the pedestal, Sam said quietly, "I'm buying that one. You can play, but if I find one mark on her body that I didn't put there, I'll take that whip and knot it around your neck."

The man puffed up, trying to look bigger, and then yellow-dogged out. "Fine. If you're going to purchase her, no need to waste my time." He walked away, his attempt at dignity spoiled by a nervous glance over his shoulder.

Sam half-smiled, then looked over at Linda in satisfaction.

She stared back. Coldly.

He winced inside. Dammit, she hadn't acted like that before he'd whipped her. Or when he'd been getting her off. She begged—he closed his eyes as the pieces started to fit.

Dignified. Older. Not letting fear show in her manner. Controlled. Embarrassed by her own needs.

And he'd taken those needs and reduced her to begging—in front of others. The slavers who called her a slut.

*Hell.* He should have stopped at the whipping. Getting her off had been a fucking major mistake. It had seemed like a gift he could give, to help her escape her awareness of this place for a bit, but...females were odd creatures. Emotional. Rather than a gift, he'd shown her how easily her own body would betray her.

He rubbed his hand over his mouth, wanting to swear up a storm. He'd sliced into her defenses with less finesse than a baby dom with a new whip. After a glance at the attendant who still hovered nearby, Sam knew he couldn't explain to her, to apologize—not here—but when this was over, they'd talk. Damn straight, they would.

\* \* \* \*

Raoul struggled to reach down his leg but failed. With both of them stuffed in the cage, there wasn't enough room. "Chiquita, get the tool out of my right boot. On the outside."

"But I need to stop the bleeding."

"Now."

With her mouth set in protest, she squirmed around and did as he asked, his sweet, sweet sumisa.

She frowned at it. "What is this?"

"Safety tool. I always carry it if I'm doing a scene." He twisted onto his right side. The pain ripped through him as his weight came onto his stabbed shoulder—*that knife-happy cabrón.* Sweat broke out on his forehead as tiny lights blurred his vision. "Madre de Dios."

She examined the tool, opened the handles. "Like scissors?"

"Mini bolt cutter," he said, taking them from her hand. Good for rope, wire, leather...

"But the lock's too big." The hope in her eyes died as she stared at the thickness of the steel padlock.

"It is, yes." Raoul snipped the wire above the lock. Then the one to the side. She gasped as she understood—the lock need not be open if the wires around the latch were gone.

He clipped the last wire and shoved the door open, then pulled back. She scrambled out. He followed, muffling his groan as his back grazed the door frame. After a second, he pushed to his feet, her hand under his arm lending support.

Slow breath. He brought his body back under his control and then frowned at the unoccupied cage. "I was going to leave you in there for him to see, but I need your help out here. If you would—"

"You're bleeding like a stuck pig, you idiot," she said in a furious low voice. Such a temper, his tesoro. "Don't move."

GOD, HE WAS going to bleed to death in front of her eyes. Swearing under her breath, she used his bolt cutters to cut up her leather harness. Linen napkins made an adequate crappy dressing, and she secured it all in place by knotting a long leather strap tightly around his chest. The wound on his shoulder—she couldn't figure out how to contrive something for that.

He ignored her, studying the room. "We're directly across the hall from the top of the stairs. And there's a chair right outside. I should be able to get rid of one or two that way."

By sitting in a chair? How much blood had he lost?

"We don't want to get trapped in here." He eyed the door, then made Kimberly push and angle the couch so someone entering wouldn't see the emptiness of the cage until they were well into the room.

"Now what?" she asked. There were going to be too many men for them. She knew it.

He pointed to the heavy ironwork lamp on the end table. "Get that, gatita."

After she'd unplugged and carried it back, he motioned for her to keep it. "Use it on the first man through the door—unless he's FBI, of course. Hit him in the head as hard as you can. I'll go after the others, and we will party." He waited a beat, then teased her, "This is when you say, 'It will be my pleasure, Master.'"

Master R's grin made her feel better, and how dumb was that? *We're going to die here.* Her chin came up. But she'd do it fighting and not dying little by little in a cage. "I always liked to party."

"Tesoro mío," he murmured. Andrea had said the words meant "my treasure." The approval in his eyes made her insides tremble—and strengthened her legs. He needed her to be strong; she'd give him anything he needed.

He tilted his head to listen, then pointed for her to stand behind the door and took the other side for himself.

*Footsteps.* Many. Men's voices. The horrible sharpness of Lord Greville's voice. *No.* She lifted the lamp over her head and braced her legs. Her hands shook, almost dislodging her grip, and she growled and steadied them. Master R nodded approval, increasing her determination. She'd hold up her part. See if she didn't.

The door opened. "Cover the cage—I don't want extra witnesses," Lord Greville said.

Her heart was hammering, pounding, hitting her lungs. She couldn't—couldn't move.

Someone walked into the room, the open door hiding him from her. "Yes, sir," the man said. One step past the door's edge, he spotted the empty cage.

She saw—actually *saw*—his mouth open, but the buzzing in her ears drowned out his yell. With a death grip on the base, she swung the heavily decorated solid iron lamp down onto his head. He fell like a rock.

She almost dropped the lamp. Blood streaked the back of his head. She stared, waited. His chest rose—he was breathing, thank heavens.

As she started around him, the smooth iron base of the lamp slipped from her sweaty hands. *My only weapon.* She snatched it up, curling her fingers into the fancy ironwork on the top. The balance was poor, but at least she wouldn't drop it.

She heard grunts and shouts outside the door. *Master R.* Fighting all the rest. By himself. *Damn you, Kim. Move!* She lurched into the hall and almost tripped on a man on the floor. Eyes open, chest caved in. A buzzing started in her ears. She edged past him and stopped, trying to see. So many men.

With a roar, Master R swung the chair that had been outside the door and knocked a man down the wide, steep stairs. Then he spun, bending forward, kicking backward to catch another in the groin. The man staggered, lost his footing, and yelled as he went over and down the stairs.

Off balance, Master R dropped the chair, staggering a few steps until he caught himself on the banister. Two more guards moved in.

*And Lord Greville.* Kim's blood turned cold. He'd grabbed the chair. Master R's back was to him as he pulled the chair back like a bat.

"No!" Kim yelled.

Greville's head turned. His cold gaze stopped her...held her...

*No.* Screaming her fear, her fury, she swung the lamp

with all her strength. The heavy base hit Greville in the side of the head, and she felt something break as if the light bulb had shattered.

He fell, and his head... *His head.* The lamp dropped from numb fingers. The floor whirled under her feet: *red carpet, red blood, red carpet...*

She was on her hands and knees, choking, trying not to throw up. Cold sweat ran down her face. *God, God, God.*

*Don't look.* As the ringing in her ears subsided, she heard a low groan. *Master R.* She pushed up on trembling legs and turned. Still alive. Fighting. A man at his feet. More men ran up the stairs.

\* \* \* \*

Raoul and Kim had disappeared to an unknown location, and Sam was ready to kill someone. No buyer was allowed outside of the ballroom unescorted, so he couldn't wander through the place, yelling for his pal. As the auction continued, less than a third of the buyers and slaves remained.

The FBI hadn't shown up. *What did they do, stop for a beer first?*

Finally, he spotted a dark jacket, another; then a steady flow of them streamed in under the arched ballroom door. *About time.* Vance followed. He exchanged glances with Sam and stopped nearby as his men moved up the aisle. Their presence was masked by the screaming and sobbing of slaves, the auctioneer's sick humor, and the perverted display on the stage.

In the front of the room, a door opened, revealing more men. Sam would give odds that they also surrounded the house. He wished he could see the Overseer's face right now...and where was he, anyway?

A buyer jumped to his feet. *"Cops!"*

"So observant." Vance lifted a bullhorn. "This is the FBI. You will kneel on the floor, hands laced behind your heads. Any resistance will be met with deadly force." He lowered the bullhorn and added under his breath, "You fucking assholes."

No one moved.

Vance put the bullhorn to his lips again. "Sit!" His voice whipped across the room with the authority of a hardened cop—and a dom. Most of the slaves dropped instinctively to their knees, and a lot of buyers did as well.

Sam grinned and glanced at Linda, who was still on her feet. His slave was made of tough material. *Mine.* She studied Vance—frowned at Sam, who wasn't moving either—then knelt as well.

Galen limped up to Sam and gave him an assessing look before asking, "Where's Raoul and his sub?"

"Don't know." Sam scowled. "The Overseer took them somewhere outside the ballroom."

\* \* \* \*

Kim screamed as a guard hit Master R from the side, slamming him into the wall. He grunted in pain, started to fall, then caught himself.

Another headed for him.

Kim lurched for the guard, turning at the last minute to kick the side of his knee. Pain shot up her ankle, but as Master R had promised, the guy went down, bellowing curses. She jumped for another—spoiling his blow at Master R—and punched the side of his neck, even as he backhanded her. Her butt hit the floor, her head a second later with a cracking blast of pain. The lights dimmed, turned black. She moaned. *No. Can't.*

"FBI. Freeze!"

Through unfocused eyes, Kim stared up at the slaver

over her, at his furious eyes. She braced for his kick... Then he raised his hands and stepped back.

She lay for a second, pain ripping through her head with each pulse beat, then managed to sit up. Her stomach lurched, nausea churning, making her swallow and swallow again. The room whirled, a merry-go-round of lights. And finally slowed to a stop.

Vance was at the top of the stairs, several uniformed police coming up behind him. Unable to stand, Kim watched as two uniforms dealt with the men Master R had knocked down the steps. One was handcuffed and taken away. The other didn't move. The remaining officer checked for a pulse and left him there.

*Master R.* Where was he? Dread clawing at her, Kim turned the other way. *Thank you, God.*

Still standing, Master R was propped up by the wall as he gasped for air. The white napkins she'd used on his wound were soaked with blood.

Kim moaned.

He glanced at Vance and Dan, then looked around and spotted her. His intent gaze ran over her body, returned to her face, and he actually smiled. "Bueno."

"Raoul," Vance said. "You're a mess."

"And you're late." Master R winced and put his hand over the linen napkins.

"Asshole. Where're you hurt?"

"In the back," Kim said, talking right over her master. "And over his ribs, and he's been bleeding forever." She tried to stand, but the world started to disappear halfway up.

"No, gatita!" Master R took a step toward her. His knees buckled, and he fell back against the wall. He slid down, leaving a bloody trail on the wallpaper.

*Oh God.* Kim crawled frantically. "No no no."

"Medic!" Vance yelled. He pulled Master R forward,

netting himself a foul curse in Spanish. "That's a knife wound. Thought they couldn't have weapons," Vance growled, easing the leather vest off Master R's shoulders.

*Still alive. He's alive.* "It's from a dinner tray," Kim said.

"Ugly hole," Vance muttered. He pulled off his black jacket and ripped the sleeve from his white shirt. After shoving it against the bleeding shoulder wound and getting cursed again, he looked at Kim. "You able to keep pressure on this?"

She nodded, ignoring the pain in her head. *Just watch me.*

"Good enough."

Galen appeared, leaning heavily on his cane. He had jackets under his arm and tossed one over Kim's shoulders and another over Master R's legs. "That might keep you from being dumped into the slammer."

"Whoa!" A yell came from nearby. "Looks like this mother's not going anywhere. His skull's cracked like an eggshell."

A younger deputy at the top of the stairs reversed course, his face green. *I know the feeling,* Kim thought. Along with the painful throbbing, her head kept replaying that shattering sound. She tried to swallow.

A firm grip on her knee got her attention. "Cariño? Are you all right?"

She smiled down into Master R's worried brown eyes. "I love you."

* * * *

With an FBI jacket over his shoulders, Sam worked his way back into the ballroom, shoving past a cop and the buyer he'd threatened earlier.

"Hey! Arrest him too. He was whipping a slave," the asshole shouted.

The police officer frowned at Sam, then the jacket he wore. "Wait one minute, please." He pulled a notepad from his pocket, flipped to a set of thumbnail photos. Sam saw his own face, Kim's, and Raoul's. The cop nodded politely at him and gave the slaver a push. "Let's go, you."

Sam shook his head. The two feebies had definitely tried to make sure their civilian undercover people were safe. Holding the blanket he'd found, he headed back to Linda. An FBI agent with a bolt cutter had just gotten her unchained from the long cable.

Sam scowled. That was inefficient at best. "You know," he told the agent, "if you could locate the asshole called the Overseer or Dahmer, he'd probably have master keys."

"You seen him?"

"Maybe the kitchen or upstairs. He's not in the ballroom."

The feebie motioned for a uniform. "Get a description from this man and find the Overseer guy. Try the kitchen first, then upstairs."

Sam filled the cop in and turned to his woman. "Linda." He kept his eyes on her.

She stiffened, her gaze on the floor. Embarrassed. *Hell.*

He stepped forward and wrapped her in the blanket.

The agent with the bolt cutters was working on the next woman's chain. He looked up. "Hey, where'd the blanket come from?"

"There's a stack in the closet by the front door." Sam pulled the blanket more securely around Linda.

Streaks of red appeared on her cheeks. She stared stubbornly at the floor. Dammit.

"Look at me," he growled.

Her eyes lifted. Pretty, pretty brown, then down again.

"They're going to take you all to a ward in the hospital where the docs can check you out. The feebies will be doing interviews. I doubt they'll let me in to see you." His jaw hardened when she didn't answer. Unease tightened his gut, flattened his voice. "Give me a way to contact you."

Her chin jerked up, and she gave him a stunned look of revulsion. "No. Never." She took a step back from him. "I never want to see you again." Another step back. Her lush mouth had flattened in a tight line.

He saw her shiver and knew she feared reprisal for the rudeness, but her determination to keep him away had been enough to risk it. He could read her as clearly as if he'd been in her head.

The agent dealing with the next slave over frowned.

This wasn't the time to push. He'd made a hell of a mistake with her, going with the scene dynamics, and not taking into account the rest of the world. "All right. My name is Sam. When... If you want to reach me, ask at the Shadowlands here in Tampa." He hesitated. "Be well, Linda."

She looked away.

* * * *

They'd taken Master R from her, said they were airlifting him to a hospital. Kim had watched, still unable to stand, unable to do anything except shiver.

He was gone. She was alone. The memories of shattering, blood, and screaming kept surging forward in waves, twisting her stomach. If she could manage to get to her feet, maybe she could... Where would she go?

"Hey, what're you doing here?" a cop asked brusquely and tried to yank her up.

She yelped and grabbed her ribs. The Overseer had

gotten in a good punch.

He stopped pulling but didn't let go. "You slaves are supposed to all be in the ballroom until—"

"They're not slaves, now are they?" A cold, gravelly voice. Kim looked up as Master Sam walked over. "Last time I looked, slavery was outlawed in this country."

"Sorry. I'm sorry, sir." The cop released her and took a step away. "Um—"

Sam moved in front of the officer and knelt. "Are you all right, Kim?"

"My master." Her mind blanked on the name. "My...my Master R. I need to go there." *Where he is.* "He's hurt. I need to go there."

Sam didn't answer, just wrapped the blanket he held around her and over the black jacket she wore. When did she get a jacket? Her thoughts stuttered, started forward again. If her head would just stop *hurting...* She pulled the covering closer. "Thank you."

"That's better." His hand cupped her chin before she could dodge. After turning her face to each side, he examined the lump at the back of her head. Pain burst behind her eyeballs. He frowned at the blood on his fingers. "You're banged up, girl."

"My master. I need to go to—"

"Stop." He made an exasperated sound. "Dan arranged for us to go to the hospital with the first bunch of women. We'll get you seen by a doc, and you can see Raoul."

She nodded, taking it in, although her mind seemed to be awfully slow.

Maybe he realized, since he didn't move. "You're not tracking too good, are you?"

He'd take her to Master R. "I'm fine." The floor insisted on moving in waves, upsetting her balance. *Wait. Something else. Someone.* "Linda?"

"She's okay. She'll get processed with the rest. Galen wouldn't make an exception in her case." Sam wrapped an arm around her.

She tried to jerk away, and he waited, not releasing her. As she saw his pale blue eyes, she remembered. Master R's friend. "Sorry, Sir."

He simply smiled and lifted her to her feet. "Let's go."

Halfway down, she saw... She fought from Sam's grip, bent, and picked up a black collar. And fell forward.

With a curse, Sam grabbed her and yanked her back upright. "What the hell are you doing, girl?"

She ran her fingers over the leather, the silver engraving. Her grip tightened when he tried to take it. "Mine."

Instead of fighting her, he turned the collar in her hands so he could read the writing. *Master Raoul's gatita.* "Yours."

# Chapter Sixteen

Raoul opened his eyes and frowned. Bed with shiny metal railings, white walls, Marcus sitting in a chair. *Auction, fight.* As his memory returned, he tried to sit up and grunted at the flare of pain in his shoulder and ribs. He remembered the ER crew checking his back. He'd only cursed once. Then they'd moved to his front. Carajo, he hadn't liked seeing the white flashes of his rib cage when they'd checked to see how deep it was.

"When my sister was ten, she got a sewing kit," Marcus said in his easy Southern drawl. He pulled his chair closer and used the controls to raise the head of Raoul's bed. "You look like one of the stuffed bears she...mended. Stitches everywhere."

Friends were a joy to the heart, Raoul reminded himself. "Thank you." *The auction.* Anxiety welled inside him. "Where's Kimberly?"

Marcus gave an exaggerated sigh. "She's in the ER being checked over, but she's all right. Sam is with her. They should never have doped you up to give you stitches."

Raoul relaxed. "Why?"

"A pleasant dopehead you're not. Every time your eyes open, you ask about Kim...then try to get down to the ER. You punched an orderly, by the way. The nurses dragged me in here to reassure you she's alive." Marcus grinned. "And I've been telling you that every five minutes since."

"Sorry. And thank you." Raoul frowned. "Have you

checked on her recently?" Sam was good. He'd watch out for her. Wouldn't he? Scowling, Raoul looked up at the IV bag hanging on a pole, traced the plastic tubing to the needle in the back of his hand. He could yank it out.

"Don't try it," Marcus said, his Southern accent not covering up the steel beneath. "I'd sit on you, and then they'd put it back in. You lost enough blood to worry them. And me."

Giving up for the moment, Raoul asked, "Did they catch everyone?"

"We did," Galen Kouros said from the doorway. Weariness lined his face as he walked into the room, leaning heavily on his cane. "I am very tired of visiting you pushy bastards in the hospital after you get damaged in my operations."

Raoul snorted and had to suck in against the groan. The skin on his ribs felt as if it wanted to split open again. "No jokes," he gritted out.

From behind Kouros, Z appeared. He pointed to the pain-control device. "Use that, Raoul."

Raoul scowled. "I will wait to see my sumi—see Kimberly."

"I'll have her wake you up if you're asleep." Z picked up the remote and pushed the button, smiling at Raoul's curse. "Don't get into a pissing contest with me when you're flat on your back. You'll just get wet."

"Cabrón."

Z grinned. "You can stop worrying about her, you know. I stopped in the ER and sent Sam home. Kim is getting X-rays. Then Jessica and Gabi will bring her up." He glanced at Marcus. "I don't think the doctors stand a chance against the three of them."

The pain medicine hit. It felt as if the bed dropped away a couple of feet, but the burning in his shoulder and ribs eased to a mild smolder. Z was still a bastard. "What else?" he asked Kouros.

"The upstairs looked like a war zone. One man had his skull smashed in—which Kim said was her work."

Raoul winced. He'd glimpsed the end of Greville. She should not have had to do that. "Is she—you made her *talk* about that?"

"Since you weren't available, yes. She held together until she finished...then spent the next ten minutes throwing up. Dammit." Kouros gave him a level stare. "From what I know of your background, you've seen your share of violence. She'll be all right, but you know it takes a while."

Raoul nodded.

"For you, you caved in one man's chest, one died going headfirst down the steps, one from a crushed trachea. Most of the rest are in a world of hurt. Nice job." Kouros thought for a moment. "The Overseer is in surgery right now—and he talked quite a bit while we were waiting for his transport."

"I didn't think he'd change sides so quickly," Raoul said.

"If he doesn't end up completely blinded, he'd have such poor vision that"—Kouros had a grim smile—"he'd make an excellent fucktoy for some big joe in prison. He didn't like the idea."

"I rather do." Marcus's eyes were cold. "Gabi still has nightmares from being kidnapped."

"And Jessica," Z said.

"Yes," Kouros said heavily. "But on the bright side, the Harvest Association has lost this quadrant. And with the personnel and the buyers, we've got enough information to dig out the ringleaders."

"And the kidnapped women?" Z asked.

"Can go home," Kouros said. "The Association is going to be too busy looking for caves to indulge in any reprisals."

Kimberly could return to her family. "That—that is good." She'd leave. He felt as if someone was ripping out his stitches one by one.

Women's laughter came from the hall, warming the sterility of the room. Gabi and Jessica walked in, followed by Kimberly.

*Alive. On her feet.* The knot of worry in his chest loosened; the ache of loss didn't.

She limped to the bed and smiled down at him. "You look horrible—and so much better than I thought you would."

She had a bruised face, split lip. Her leg had been hurt somehow. Her body moved...stiffly, as if to guard from pain. She had lines of strain around her eyes and mouth, but she could smile. Such an indomitable spirit.

He opened his palm, giving her the choice, and the world turned brighter when her small hand slid into his. "What did the doctor say, gatita?"

"You have a thousand or so stitches in your—"

He narrowed his eyes. "About you." Thinking more clearly, he turned to Jessica, defender of the subbies. "What did her doctor say?"

Ignoring Kimberly's glare, Jessica glanced at Z, received a quick smile and nod, and reported, "Aside from the damage to her face, she's got an ugly bruise over her ribs—but nothing broken—and a twisted ankle. Nothing broken there either. A concussion, and they want her to spend the night." Jessica grinned at her friend. "She got out of the wheelchair just outside this room, 'cause you might worry. 'Bout as stubborn as you are."

As Jessica finished, Raoul used Kimberly's arm as a leash to pull her down. He needed her lips, her fragrance, her gentleness, and he savored them all as her soft mouth moved over his. They would have to talk soon but...not yet.

\* \* \* \*

Right after Z and Jessica left, a nurse showed up for Kim—and Master R ordered her to be an obedient patient. The obstinate blowfish. God, she didn't want to leave him.

The hospital staff and FBI had talked about splitting the rescued women into different hospitals and rooms, but Gabi'd taken charge, and they discovered the women preferred to stay together, at least for now. Kim understood completely. Safety in numbers, others who comprehended what had happened, friendships formed in suffering. Until their families arrived, each other was all these women had.

In the big room filled with ex-slaves, the nurse tucked Kim into a bed next to Linda, took her vital signs, and increased her headache by shining a light in her eyes.

But she was a nice nurse and showed up a few minutes later with pain medication in repayment for the flashlight torture. For a while, Kim talked with Linda, sharing tears and comfort over Holly's death, and relief that the slavery nightmare was over.

Linda told Kim not to be mad at Sam for whipping her, that he'd had no choice. He'd given her a safe word, and she'd agreed. But...then she wouldn't talk about it anymore. Something was wrong.

Linda's eyes were drooping, and she drifted off before Kim could think of a tactful question.

All around the room, women were sleeping, crying quietly, and talking to the counselors who'd arrived with Gabi. Thanks to the Overseer's care of the "merchandise," most weren't hurt badly—at least not physically. And they'd be able to go home.

As Kim looked around, her anxiety kept increasing.

The shaking had started deep inside while she talked with Linda, slowly expanding. Her hands were quivering like a palm in high winds. *Dammit, everyone else can get to sleep. Why not me?*

*Maybe I should have talked to someone.* She hadn't told Linda about Lord Greville or about the fight. She'd fended Gabi off too, saying she wasn't ready to discuss anything yet. There would be time later since as an FBI victim specialist, Gabi would be here every day until the kidnapped women went home.

Kim wrapped her arms around her waist, feeling hollow. Empty. After this was over, would there be anything left of her? *I need to move, to do something.* She slid out of the bed, her hospital gown flapping, but at least the ER nurses had given her matching pajama bottoms. She wouldn't forget their little kindnesses.

Only slightly dizzy, she walked the halls, holding the railing along the walls. The scents varied as she moved past the doors: disinfectant, sickness, excrement. Her muscles tired; her feet started to drag. Go back to bed, she told herself.

But the numbers were familiar, and then she knew. She'd thought she was wandering at random, but…somehow she ended up at Master R's room.

As she peeked in, her heart did a slow tumble. Not everything inside her was hollow.

He was still awake, scowling at a small dish on the tray table. A middle-of-the-night snack?

"Do you need help eating?" she asked, walking over.

"What kind of a meal is Jell-O? And it's green. Food shouldn't be green." He frowned at her, his eyes turning intent, although his voice stayed easy. "A beer would be more welcome. Come here, gatita." He held his hand out.

She put her fingers in his, feeling the calluses, the

careful strength. But seeing him didn't help. Nothing would help her, she realized, and tried to pull back. "You need sleep."

"And you should be in your bed as well." He smiled at her. "Put the side rail down and sit beside me."

"No. It'll hurt you."

"Now, sumisita."

God, when he used that tone, sometimes—rarely—she could disobey him. Not today.

As she slid the rail down, he lowered the head of the bed, then took her forearm and pulled her to sit on the edge. She knew moving and being jostled must hurt him, but nothing showed on his face.

"All right, I'm here. Are you happy?" Sitting stiffly upright, she scowled at him.

"Not yet. Galen said you told him what had happened. Did you tell him how you felt as well?"

She tried to rise, and his grip tightened. "I don't want to talk about it."

"But you will." The corner of his mouth tipped up. "As will I, and then we'll hold each other."

"No."

His chin tilted up slightly, and she discovered she'd used up all the defiance in her soul. Her gaze dropped.

"Bueno. I'll begin. When you said the person in the room was Greville, I was angry. And scared that we'd been set up."

He'd never shown any of that. She looked up. "Really?"

"I was very afraid, Kimberly." His fingers curled around her hand, and his thumb stroked circles on the back. "And you? You didn't seem angry," he prompted after a second of silence.

"I-I was so"—her eyes filled as the memory swamped

her—"so scared. I knew I'd die."

His eyes narrowed. "You thought I'd leave you?"

The trembling spread until she could feel the whole bed shake. "I knew he'd make you go. He wouldn't give you a choice, and..." And she'd be alone and screaming as she died.

He sighed and pulled her down onto him. She struggled. "No, I'll hurt you."

He huffed a pained laugh. "If you fight me, yes. I feel stitches popping already."

She froze, staring at the white gauze dressings on his bare chest.

"Lie beside me, gatita." As she complied, he gave a grunt of satisfaction, settling her with her head in the hollow of his unhurt shoulder. Warmth streamed from him like sunlight, and her coldness receded. Her sigh shuddered her whole body.

"Good." His big hand stroked her hair; his other arm curled around her back, holding her securely against him. "Gatita, don't you realize I need you in my arms as much as you need to be here."

She closed her eyes at the reassurance. "Thank you."

His low baritone laugh was as intimate as being held. "Now we must talk about what happened so our memories process correctly, no?" He'd had a fascination for her counseling sessions, studying PTSD as if he were a researcher. "My turn. I knew it was all going to hell. I wanted you to run—but you came back. I've never been so scared." He inhaled and growled. "I am very proud of you, sumisita mía, but I intend to beat you for disobeying me."

She giggled into his shoulder, knowing he'd do no such thing. "I'm very proud of you too, but I should smack you for not letting me fight beside you."

He grunted. "You did well with the Overseer and the

guards. And Greville."

Her breath hitched. *Swinging the heavy lamp, fury and terror filling her, feeling the shattering sensation. The indescribable sound he made, the thump of his body hitting the floor.* Her eyes welled with tears, and she let them this time. "I killed him."

Master R's hand stroked down her arm. "I know." Another stroke. "The only choice was his death or ours. Galen says I killed several as well."

She sniffled, her tears dampening his chest. He was a man. He probably—

"I have killed before, and it's never grown easier to handle afterward. There will always be a part of you that feels guilty. Blackened."

"You too?"

His bitter laugh teased her hair. "I'm not God, and killing another is wrong. We will both mourn the deaths we gave and be angry and want to yell at the bastards for forcing us to it." He nuzzled the top of her head. "And since I am a man, I would appreciate it if you would cry for us both, gatita."

*Wrong. Mourn. Anger. Grief.* A sob choked her, and then it all spilled out, just tears after all, in safety with someone who could take comfort from her in return.

* * * *

Sunday afternoon, Kim sat beside the hospital bed and watched Master R's face as he slept. His color had improved, and the frown had disappeared from his forehead. The nurse had given him a gown this morning, and again, he'd tossed it at the foot of the bed. But this way, Kim could see the bandages on his bare chest. The white gauze showed only a few red splotches rather than being blood-soaked.

She grinned. He'd be growly when he woke and

realized the pain meds had knocked him into sleeping again. And he'd blame her, since she'd gotten good at detecting when he was hurting, and cajoling him into using the button. A shame she didn't have the nerve to push it herself like Master Z would.

Earlier she'd sent Gabi and Marcus home since her so very polite master wouldn't let himself fall asleep if he had visitors. Obviously he didn't consider her company. The thought set up a glow inside her. And he slept better if he was holding her hand. She'd pulled away a few times, and he'd awoken within a minute. Some sort of dom radar, maybe.

She slept better beside him too. After returning to the room full of women, she'd spent a sleepless night and sneaked back here before dawn. Master R had been reading. She'd pulled up a chair and rested her head beside his hand...just for a second...and had woken up a couple of hours later when Cullen and Andrea arrived. He'd been sleeping too, his fingers tangled in her hair.

God, she loved him.

He'd risked his life for hers. *"Run,"* he'd said and taken on everyone to let her get away. He could have let Lord Greville have her, but he wouldn't. Not her master.

*Master.* Dammit. Every time she thought about staying—if he even wanted her to stay—the word bubbled up inside her with its sweet, terrifying sound. *Master.* And she was a slave.

Only he'd said she wasn't. Submissive. She still didn't want him to take her decisions away, to control her. *Why didn't I ever ask him what he wanted from a...person? A lover?* Would he be happy with her love and what she would give him? How much of her, of her life and her soul, would he demand?

They'd lived like Master/slave, but that was to get her ready for the slavers. And yeah, she'd begged for him to continue as her master. He had. She'd knelt at his feet. He'd fed her from his hand, even during the briefing.

She scowled. Surely she'd just needed that extra week of security because of her kidnapping.

He didn't seem to think so.

Could she be happy living the lifestyle? *God, I don't know.* She stared at him. When he looked at her in a certain way, she'd do anything. His voice could take her anywhere.

He had powerful hands, gentle and unyielding, the same as he was himself, compassionate with a solid core of...honor. Like her mother would say, *"This man has character."* She could lean on him; he'd keep her safe. How could she leave?

"Here, Mamá." A female voice with a light Spanish accent.

Kim turned as two women entered the room. One older and slightly stooped in a floral dress. Her face was wrinkled with age, hands gnarled with arthritis, and she possessed the dignity of someone who'd worked all her life.

The other was around Kim's age, an attractive woman with a sturdy, big-boned body in jeans and a loose top. She appeared familiar... Black hair, chocolate brown eyes, Hispanic coloring, and Master R's strong jaw in feminine form.

"Are you Mas—Raoul's family?" Kim asked, flushing at her wayward tongue.

The older woman hadn't seen her, her gaze only on Master R, and she jumped. As the two women turned toward Kim, horror filled their faces.

What? Then she remembered her banged-up face. "Sorry about the—"

"We shouldn't have come," the younger one interrupted and walked out of the room.

What the heck was that about? "Wait," Kim said. The

older one hesitated, and Master R awoke.

"Mamá," he said, his voice more of a rasp than smooth. "What are you doing here?"

The old woman took a step forward, wringing her hands. "The hospital called. I am listed as your family."

How could a mother be so stiff with her son? With Master R, who was never cold with his friends?

"Ah. I'm sorry, Mamá. I didn't realize you were—" He broke off, his jaw tightening. "Mamá, this is Kim. Kimberly, my mother, Anna Sandoval."

"Are you all right?" Mrs. Sandoval asked Kim.

"I'm fine, thank you." Why didn't she ask Master R how he was? No one could miss the bulky bandages taped to his ribs. This was too awkward. Kim squeezed Master R's hand. "I'm going to get some coffee. I'll be back in a bit."

She stepped out of the room and came face-to-face with the other woman.

"Uh, hi." God, no two strangers looked that much alike. "Are you his sister?" Kim asked.

When the woman's mouth tightened, she looked so much like Master R that Kim almost laughed.

"Yes, I'm Lucia. Are you his slave?"

*What the*—Kim felt the flush run up into her face. "Ah, not really. I'm Kim."

"He is my brother, but I cannot let him…" The woman straightened her shoulders. "Maybe you think it's all fun, but it's not. It isn't safe to be with him. He'll hurt you, beat you so badly you cannot walk. Don't stay with him."

"*What?*"

His sister nodded, her mouth tight. "He likes to hurt women. To make them scream. To keep them as slaves and not let them leave."

His mother walked out of the room, closing the door

behind her. She'd obviously heard the last part of the sentence. Tears filled her eyes. She nodded.

Kim stared. The two women believed that garbage. A shiver ran through her as her own nagging fears stepped into the light. Not Master R. "Why would you say such a thing?"

"It's true," his mother said. She looked at her daughter helplessly.

"His wife," Lucia said. "They broke up so suddenly. Got a divorce."

The mother touched her lips. "Raoul would not talk about it."

"Alicia told me"—Lucia nodded at her mother—"showed us both what he had done to her. She had welts and bruises and bleeding places all over her body. Her wrists were ripped from being chained to a wall." Her gaze fell on Kim's wrists, which bore the light abrasions from the rope Master R had used on the sailboat.

"What they did, was...something they both wanted," Kim said, trying to think of Master R hurting someone so badly. His wife. "It's called consensual."

"No," his mother said sharply. "No consent. Alicia said she screamed and begged, and he wouldn't let her go. He made her his slave, and she didn't want that. She hated him."

"When she got free, she ran away. Divorced him," Lucia said. "She lives somewhere else now."

His mother turned her face toward the wall and whispered, "Alicia said he let others...have her. Abuse her. I love him, but I cannot act as if he is my son."

"No—"

"He admitted it. Leave him while he's here in the hospital," Lucia urged.

His mother touched the bruise on Kim's cheek and

shook her head. The two women walked away, the younger supporting the older.

"No," Kim whispered. "He didn't. He couldn't."

\* \* \* \*

Raoul closed his eyes, grief filling him faster than the returning pain. *Mamá.* He hadn't seen her in almost three years. She'd come because he was hurt, but had taken one look at Kimberly and known he was still in the lifestyle.

Raoul tipped his head back and stared at the ceiling, the taste of bitterness familiar.

Why hadn't Alicia settled for being unfaithful? That had been enough of a blow. A horrible one—coming home early to find his wife tied to a sawhorse bench, covered in welts and stripes, her brother-in-law fucking her in the ass.

Raoul had taken a step forward, thinking Randolph had whipped her, was raping her—he'd kill the man. But he heard Alicia demanding for more pain, for him to fuck her harder.

He hadn't killed either of them. Maybe he should have. He'd filed for divorce...and in revenge, she'd told Mamá about her son, the dom. The *master.* Raoul had tried to explain the BDSM lifestyle to Mamá. All she saw was that her son was a pervert. Sick. An abuser.

Raoul sighed, his throat tight. Her eyes used to light up when he came home. She'd scold him in Spanish for being so long away. Now her gaze held revulsion.

The phone on the bedside table rang, and Raoul grunted in pain as he stretched to answer it. "Sandoval."

"Hey, buddy." Cullen's hearty voice blasted through the phone. "Galen sent me to pick up Kim's mom at the airport. We're downstairs. Can you tell Kim she has company?"

Her mother. "Is she a good woman? Able to care for

her daughter?" Raoul asked slowly, trying not to let his growing loss show in his voice.

He didn't succeed, for Cullen's voice turned cautious. "Seems to be. She's been in tears half the time and furious at the slavers the rest. Good thing none of them are within her reach. Reminds me of Jessica. And your Kim."

"Bueno." Blackness welled inside him, until the air itself seemed to darken. The time had come. "Bring her to the waiting room at the end of my hallway. I will meet you there."

Kimberly should not remain with him longer. She needed to heal, and once she did, he doubted he'd ever see her again. To step back into a D/s relationship would be more than she could tolerate, no matter how brave she was.

And she was so very courageous. She'd tried to protect him, had crawled into a cage to save him, had killed a man.

Last night, in his lightless room, she'd sat on the foot of his bed, and the hall light had haloed her small figure as if her soul had turned luminous. Her spirit, despite all the hurt, remained beautiful and giving.

But she'd given enough. He swallowed the tightness in his throat away. The next meeting would play out as it should, and then it would all be over. As would the dreams he hadn't realized he'd held. *Foolish Sandoval.* She'd made no secret of the fact that she didn't want a Master/slave relationship or to be a full-time submissive. Even if she hadn't lived through what she had, she still wouldn't have wanted it.

Yes, before the auction, she'd asked him to continue as her master, but she'd only needed someone to cling to.

He scowled. Yet she'd been happy with him. Content. Fulfilled. He hadn't imagined that. He should give her a choice.

First, he'd meet her mother. Make sure his gatita

would be cared for if she went home. He glanced at the IV bag and started undoing the tape holding the needle in his arm.

* * * *

Kim sat on a chair in the cafeteria, watching the torrents of rain outside the hospital, listening to the bone-shaking thunder. Thunderstorms, waves... No matter what stupid things humans did, the universe continued. The tides rose and fell; storms rolled in off the ocean; the sun came up every morning.

Life went on.

*What about my life?* Galen said she could go home now.

*Home.* She frowned as lightning flashed from cloud to cloud, and a few seconds later, thunder rumbled.

Go back to Savannah? To what was familiar. Away from slavers and FBI and kidnapped women. Homesickness surged in her, pushing her like the gusts of wind outside. She needed to return to her own life, her work, her duplex, her friends. Her mom.

Time to go home. But...Master R? The thought of leaving him made her chest ache as if the lightning had hit it. She pushed to her feet and headed back to his room.

Could she bear to not see him anymore? To never again feel his hand on her head, or kneel at his feet, or hear the warm pleasure in his voice when she anticipated his needs. But then other memories oozed up, nauseating her: the Overseer stomping on her foot, Lord Greville whipping her until blood ran down her legs, the cage trapping her.

She froze in the center of the hall and concentrated on breathing. *I can't go through that again.* Master R's mother said he was an abuser...but he wasn't. He couldn't be. But Mrs. Sandoval was so sure. *What am I going to do?*

She stopped in his doorway.

He looked exhausted. Pale. Hurting. Had he tried to get up to use the bathroom? Stubborn dom. "I think you need to push the button for your pain medication," she said sternly.

He glanced at the IV, his expression odd. Then he looked at her. His gaze was intent, as if memorizing her face, lingering on the puffy bruise on her left cheek, the tender split in her lip. His mouth tightened. "I did not care for you very well, did I?"

"I'm alive. Not a slave. We took down a slave ring." The expressionless look on his face sent warnings shooting through her in small unsettling flashes. "What's wrong, Ma—Raoul?"

His muscles tensed, as if she'd hit him. He looked at her with a shadowed gaze. "Nothing is wrong. You have a visitor."

"Who? More cops?"

"Not this time." His smile didn't reach his eyes. "They're done with us—at least until they start the legal maneuvering." He lifted his hand as if to touch her. "You can go home now."

"I can?" He was sending her away. The realization felt like a blow, crueler than the Overseer's fist into her ribs, solid enough to force her a step back.

He hesitated, and then asked slowly, "What do want to do, Kimberly?"

A surge of hope shivered through her body. He was giving her the choice. She wouldn't have to leave him.

Only she wanted to go home. Didn't she? *No, I love him.*

But was that enough? She wasn't any blind romantic child. Love didn't mean a person could live with someone or that the other person was trustworthy. Didn't guarantee happiness. She knew she couldn't stay—it wouldn't work—yet the thought that he wouldn't be there to hold her in the night, to greet her in the morning with heavy-lidded eyes as he rolled on top of her and pinned her hands over her head...

"I..." Her heart slowly split into two pieces.

His eyes closed, and his jaw tightened. "Your mother is here, sumis—Kimberly."

"Mom?"

"Sí. She's in the waiting room down the hall."

*Mom.* Kim stared at Raoul, hearing his mother's words. Thinking of her own. Her mother had loved her father in the beginning—she'd said so—and he'd loved her. But that hadn't mattered. He'd ground her into the dirt with his demands. Made her a slave.

*I don't want to be that kind of a person. I'm not like my mother.* Aside from sex, she'd never wanted to be subservient to a man. She'd only done it to trap the slavers, not to...to stay. *I have a life.* "I need to go home."

The brown eyes watching her seemed to darken.

"Yes, I think you do," he said, no doubt in his voice. Dominant. Master.

Her flare of anger was welcome. She stiffened her spine—*look, I still have a spine*—walked over to the bed, and held out her hand. "Thank you for...everything." For the tenderness and firmness, for the understanding and the sex and the...love. She wanted to say more, but her throat closed, preventing words and tears.

His head bowed as he took her hand, kissed her fingers, and opened his hand. Releasing her. "*Adios*, gatita."

The words echoed over and over as she walked away.

# Chapter Seventeen

*"Adios, gatita."* No more, Kim told herself. Stop hearing those damned words. Stop feeling abandoned.

When the hell would she be able to forget about slavers, horrors, and fear?

And love?

Damn Master R anyway. He should have pushed her more, done something—anything—so she could have walked farther than fifteen feet from the door. Fifteen feet wasn't enough. Kim stood in the doorway of her duplex, staring out at her car. Parked at the curb, as always. So far, far away. Her hands fisted. *I can do this, dammit.*

Over the past week or so, she'd managed everything else. Her nightmares were helped by lights staying on—although nothing was as effective as a slow, dark voice and solid body pulling her into his safety. *"Adios, gatita."* Drown him.

Work kept her busy, especially when she got out on the water. Her friends and coworkers had welcomed her back with joy. And worry over what to say, what to avoid. She missed the understanding of Gabi and the other Shadowlands subs.

But she was getting better, although every single day she ached inside from the loss of...

She shook her head. *That's in the past. This is now, and the task right now is to reach the car.* She'd managed the first few days—and sat in the car shaking afterward—

but her fear was getting worse every day.

She'd better find a place with a garage and an automatic door. Of course a garage wouldn't rescue her in other locations, but at least she could leave her own house.

She sniffled a little, trying to steel her nerves. Steel, ha. Her nerves were pretty much frayed twine that snapped under tension, like a couple of nights ago. She'd stood in the door for twenty minutes, trying to go out for groceries. When she'd answered the phone and heard Gabi's voice, that had done it. Hysteria city. Embarrassing as hell.

Time to try again. Kim made it three steps and froze at the sight of a van coming closer. It pulled up behind her car. Her skin chilled as she tried not to run into the house.

*I hate vans.* But it wasn't black; it was a cheerful pale yellow with hand-painted dogs decorating the sides. Really, no self-respecting kidnapper would drive a vehicle like that. Right?

The woman driver jumped out and rather than approaching, she opened the back. Unable to master her fear, Kim retreated until she stood in the entrance, ready to slam the door shut.

The woman called something, and a dog jumped out. Brown with a darker muzzle, pointed ears upright. A big dog. A German shepherd?

Curiosity greater than nerves, Kim waited.

The short gray-haired woman walked up the sidewalk, carrying a thick envelope. "Well, you make it easy. Would you be Miss Kimberly Moore?"

Fears sliding away, Kim smiled. "I am." Unable to resist, she knelt and held her hand out to the dog. "Aren't you a pretty boy? Aren't you sweet?"

With a low whine, he waited until the woman said, "It's okay, Ari. This is your person."

The dog gave a bark and lunged forward, tail wagging,

taking all of Kim's petting and responding with nuzzles and quick swipes of his tongue.

The older woman sighed. "He just won't learn the no-licking rule." She held out the envelope. "Let's take a few minutes to go through this before I leave. Of course, you can always call if you have questions."

Kim frowned. "Questions?" Was this some new religious technique? Use a dog to get the sinners to let you in the door? "About what?"

"About Ari—it's short for Ariel, by the way, after the archangel." She smiled at the dog's whine. "I think your friend was correct. You two seem quite suited for each other."

*Friend. Suited.* "I'm not following this. Are you saying you're leaving the dog—Ari—here?"

"Well, yes." The woman's brows drew together. "He didn't call you?"

"Who?"

"Oh my." With a sound of exasperation, the woman held out her hand. "I'm Maggie Jenkins, and I train guard dogs for women. Only for women. A man named Raoul Sandoval called earlier and kept me on the phone for a good hour, making me describe every dog available. And then he bought Ari for you and asked me to deliver him today. He said you, especially, needed one trained to be an escort, a dog to either accompany you into stores or wait outside."

"An escort?" Kim stared at Ari, seeing the large fangs, the strong body, the sheer threat of him. "He'll go with me—everywhere? And wait outside if he can't come in?"

"Absolutely. That's his job."

"But—for how long do I have him?" God, if she could only keep him a month, long enough to get past her fears.

"Child, the dog is yours. Mr. Sandoval didn't hire him. He bought Ari outright, which is good." Maggie smiled. "Ari isn't happy being hired out. He wants his own person. In fact, I think you've bonded, and he'd already be unhappy to leave you."

Kim realized the dog was completely in her arms, leaning against her until his top half sprawled over her legs. She gave a laugh, felt him licking the tears from her cheeks, and buried her face in the thick fur.

Three hundred miles away, and Master R still protected her. How could she not love him?

\* \* \* \*

Her mother's kitchen hadn't changed, Kim thought as she filled the dishwasher from the stacked plates on the counter. Such a cheerful room with white cupboards and ruffled curtains, dark blue countertops, and cows frolicking on the fridge and canisters. *Grinning cows. That's just wrong.*

"So, this person—man—you were living with…" Kim's mother plunged a pot into the dishwater.

"Raoul." Saying his name still sent a shiver up her spine. Ari, who'd stationed himself nearby in case of appetizing accidents, whined slightly.

"Yes, that one. He seemed very nice."

Startled, Kim glanced over. "Wait—you met him? When?"

"He came into the waiting room a little before you did. Said he wanted to meet me."

"How did he get there? He wasn't supposed to get out of bed." Kim stared at a picture on the wall, her as a child, arm in a cast, face tight as she tried not to cry from the pain. The last time she saw Master R, he'd worn the same strained expression. He'd taken her hand in his, kissed her fingers, and now she realized the IV needle had been missing from the back of his hand.

"That idiot." He'd walked down the hall to meet her mom. "God, no wonder he looked like he hurt." She wanted to hit him for being so stupid. So damned macho.

"He wanted to make sure I'd take care of you. Asked me many questions."

He'd met her mom. "Really?"

Her mother laughed. "Yes. He was very worried about you."

Kim smiled at her mother, who looked so much younger these days. They'd celebrated Kim's return at a day spa, Kim with a manicure and pedicure, and her mother had her hair restored to a light brown. With highlights, no less. *Who is this woman, and what have you done with my mom?*

But she knew. Before the kidnapping, her mother had met a man. During the time Kim had been missing, he'd apparently been a rock of comfort. "Kind of like how Greg worries about you?"

Her mother flushed and glanced toward the living room where Greg and one of his younger colleagues were cheering a touchdown. "He does, doesn't he? Kim, I'm so happy to have found him. To know that all men aren't like your father. To be respected."

"How can you tell? You're still cooking. Cleaning. Working." Kim frowned. "In fact, we're in here washing dishes while they watch television. I'm not sure there's any difference."

"It's...even now. Balanced. Inside the house is my area. Outside is his. Remember how he mowed the lawn and trimmed the bushes when you came, so we could girl-talk?"

"True." Mom and Greg both worked and weren't living together yet, although that was undoubtedly coming. "I've never seen the yard looking so nice." Or the house in such repair. Nothing squeaked. No paint was scraped. Greg had laughed when she complimented him and said he enjoyed working outside after a day on the computer.

Her mother dried her hands on the towel. "But it's not just the fairness, honey. It's the way he...appreciates...anything I do. Who I am." She sighed. "I wonder sometimes if I might have managed to leave your father if my sense of self-worth hadn't been so ground down. When someone tells you that you're worthless and stupid and ugly, eventually you start to believe it."

"It's another kind of abuse," Kim said. How strange to see her mother as another female, subject to all the problems women had. And to be proud of how she'd grown and moved on.

"Yes, it is. And I'm sorry, baby, you had to see it. I worry that it gave you a warped view of marriage. Of loving."

It had. Her mother'd been a slave as much as any woman with a collar around her neck. How strange that a housewife could have fewer rights than a submissive. And Mom had been much, much less cherished. "Maybe a little. I'm still working it out."

No need to make Mom feel guiltier though. She bit her lip, thinking to change the subject, and the one topic she didn't want to talk about—and couldn't forget—slipped out. "So what did you think of Raoul?"

"How could I not like a man who would take a knife for my daughter?" Mom sniffed and wiped her eyes. "Or one who sent you home although anyone with a brain in her head would see that it tore him up to let you go."

It did? As Kim's aching for Master R intensified, Ari rose, pushing his muzzle into her hands. She kissed the top of his furry head. "I can't be with him though. He wants to make all the decisions, to have me serve him—wants a slave."

"You wouldn't work outside the home?"

Kim remembered what he'd said about his former slaves. "I don't think that's a problem. It's what would happen the rest of the time."

"Well." Her mother shook her head. "That's odd to think about, and yet how is that different from being a housewife? A marriage is... Each person serves the other, and from what I saw of your Raoul, he would care for you as much as you cared for him. So perhaps it comes down to who makes the decisions. Do you want him to do that?"

Kim opened her mouth, prepared to say, *Of course not.*

But her mother held up her hand. "If you really knew the answer, you wouldn't seem so unhappy. You're not forging ahead to deal with your choice, because you haven't made one."

"I haven't? I thought I had."

Her mother shook her head. "You look lost, baby."

"Yeah, well, that's how I feel."

"Think about it until you're sure, then let it go. Whichever way you choose, I'll support you."

\* \* \* \*

After letting her inner cynic and inner coward battle it out, Kim had phoned Raoul. She'd thank him for Ari and then...talk. But his secretary picked up the call. Master R was overseeing a project in Costa Rica.

So much for that. As she put together a salad, she averted her gaze from the phone on the counter. No. Getting dependent on Gabi wasn't a good idea either. But she missed her company. And that of the other Shadowlands subs as well.

Gabi had described Beth and Nolan's outdoor wedding. Master Z had volunteered his gardens, so it must have been beautiful.

And Kari'd had her baby. *I wish I'd been there for that.* Gabi had snapped a shot with her cell, and Kim had cooed over the tiny, scrunched-up face. A baby boy with Master Dan's dark hair in a fine fuzz. *Why do I feel like my life should be there?*

Kim carried her salad to the couch and turned on the television. Not much on, although face it, she mostly wanted the noise.

Ari stuck his head in her lap, sniffing the bowl to check out the prospects for tidbits. With a whine of disgust, he lay down at her feet. He loathed salads.

So did Master R.

Kim smiled, remembering the lecture she'd gotten: *"If God wanted humans to eat vegetables, he wouldn't have colored them green. Green things are moldy."* Despite his opinion, he'd always helped her cut up the ingredients and dutifully eaten a portion. She felt wonderful when he ate food she'd prepared, and even more so when she knew it was good for him.

When she'd teased him that it was her job to keep him healthy, he'd smiled, his expression approving and pleased, although all he'd said was yes.

Was that how he felt about her? It was his job to keep her healthy? Happy?

She liked that. *But what about him making the decisions for me?* The times when he told her to do something and she didn't agree. She bit her lip. There had been quite a few instances like that, actually. But she'd complied, because it had mattered enough to him to order it, and...she wanted to give him that pleasure, to receive his smile of approval.

*I am so confused.*

Returning home was supposed to have put her life back on track, but the track seemed to have turned into a rut. Had it been this lonely before? Maybe she should get a roommate. She wiggled her toes in Ari's fur, and he rolled so she'd rub his side as well. A roommate who could talk. And argue, even if it was about the merits of action movies over chick flicks.

She'd actually watched a Chuck Norris movie last night. How weird was that?

"What am I going to do, Ari? Should I try to visit Master R while I'm there?" She glanced at the boarding pass on the coffee table. She had a flight to Tampa on Friday. In the hospital, Galen and Vance had warned her she'd be called back, off and on, for some of the legal stuff. Ugh. The thought of talking about her slavery again made her sick. Then again... She smiled. Partly because of her, the buyers and slavers were imprisoned. In cages. *Go me.*

What about Master R?

"I miss him, you know. I really do love him, and I think he loves me too. Maybe." She frowned. How many times had she wondered? He'd only said it that once. *What if he didn't mean it?*

She took a bite of her salad, chomping determinedly. "And I miss..." She sighed. "Belonging. Maybe that's what it's all about." She pointed her fork at Ari. "Take you, for example. You know I own you, but you also know that I'm yours. I'm your person, and I take care of you. I feed you and brush you. But you guard me and feel important because you do. Part of it's serving and giving, and part of it's belonging, and part of it's being dominated. I see the pattern, but it's sure confusing.

"I don't think I'd love him as much if he weren't dominant, because that's who he is. But just because I like some of his control, do I want it all the time?"

*Dammit, why isn't there a book with the answers in it?*

# Chapter Eighteen

The US District courthouse was intimidating, and the quizzing Kim had gone through hadn't helped her nerves any. She sat on a bench in the long hallway, trying to make her insides stop shaking as she waited for Vance to return. She'd done her duty, given her information. With Lord Greville dead and the Overseer cooperating, she was mostly filling in the gaps.

She'd been able to identify the photo of the man who'd tried to buy her before Lord Greville had, and the two buyers at the sale house. The one who'd taken Holly. Her heart twisted. Beaten to death.

"There's a pretty girl." The rough voice brought her head up, and she checked the hall. *Sam.*

*And Master R.*

Every tiny cell in her body yearned toward him so violently it was a wonder she didn't fly down the hall.

He just looked at her with his dark eyes. He looked tired—deep lines beside his mouth, his color almost muddy.

*Are you all right?* she wanted to ask but didn't. "Hi guys," she managed. "Are you here for FBI stuff too?"

Master R didn't speak.

Sam frowned and then nodded his head. "The place is filled with witnesses. But we're done now."

"Yeah, me too."

"Can we take you somewhere?" Master R asked

finally, and the wonderful sound of his rich baritone had her eyes filling with tears.

Behind the men, the door opened. Two uniformed police walked out, escorting...the Overseer. His tone, sharp and oily, struck her like a blow, the unexpected sound making her guts twist. He wore patches over his eyes, and the memory of her thumbs, the squishing—his scream...

Her stomach turned over. Gagging, she ran for the bathroom down the hall.

RAOUL WATCHED HER flee and closed his eyes, despair washing over him. To have her run from him...

His heart had stopped when he'd seen her sitting on a bench near the end of the tiled hall. He'd given a bitter laugh and started to turn away—every dark-haired woman made him think of her—but it really *was* her. His Kimberly. He'd headed straight for her, leaving his brains—and Sam—behind him.

Sam had caught up after a step, seen where Raoul was looking, and given a grunt of...satisfaction?

The distance had seemed interminable, almost as long as the preceding weeks.

When he'd been released from the hospital, he'd returned to a house as empty and cold as if in the far north. He tried watching the waves, searching for the solace she'd always received from her time on the beach. All he found were memories of her hair streaming back in the wind, her little toes wrinkled from walking barefoot in the surf, her skin smelling of salt air as if he'd caught a mermaid.

He abandoned the shore after a couple of days, the tower room soon after. The dungeon he couldn't face at all. The kitchen had echoed with her laughter and the memories of sharing meals, her kneeling at his feet to take food from his fingers, pulling her into his lap to get her closer.

He started avoiding his kitchen as well.

When Z and Cullen had showed up unexpectedly and discovered that he'd forgotten to eat that day, Z had been...blunt.

Raoul had flown to a job site in Costa Rica, returning only a couple of days ago. He was doing better. He could get past this and move on.

He frowned at the restroom door. She didn't look healthy, with dark circles under her eyes and gaunt cheeks. And when they'd seen her, she'd had her arms around her knees, holding herself in a tight ball. She must have talked to the Feds. He hadn't been there to hold her, to give her a feeling of safety. Anger sparked in him, that Kouros hadn't told him that she'd be coming.

If she'd wanted him to know she was in Tampa, she knew his phone number.

And seeing him nauseated her. His body felt like a lead robot as he turned to Sam. "I'd better go before she comes back out."

Sam said a foul word, then nodded reluctantly. "Maybe so. Is tomorrow still on?"

Raoul hesitated, then nodded. He couldn't cancel the party without hurting little Kari's feelings. That would be unworthy of a man. "Sí."

On Sunday, he'd return to Costa Rica.

* * * *

Sam watched his friend bow his head and walk away. Tenderhearted bastard. The girl's reaction had ripped his guts right out. After all Raoul had suffered, he didn't deserve that crap. What the hell was she thinking?

He stalked over to the women's restroom, shoved the door open, and walked in.

A woman stood at the sink, decorating her face—and doing a lousy job of it.

"Out," Sam snapped.

With a squeak, she fled, leaving her lipstick behind. Sam shook his head. *Coward.* He had a feeling his redheaded Linda wouldn't have run. The thought only made him more furious. She *had* run, in a way. No call. He'd asked Galen about her and seen the answer in the agent's face. She'd requested no contact from him.

*Fine.*

The sound of jagged breathing came from the end stall, and Sam pushed the unlatched door open. One little subbie, on her knees, half in tears. Served her right. Trying to ignore the welling of pity, Sam wet a few paper towels. "Wipe your face."

She jerked at the sound of his voice and obeyed, tried to stand, and failed.

Sam took her arm and yanked her to her feet. Not politely. "Clean up, and I'll see you in the hallway."

"I'm fine," she said. Her voice was hoarse, and she was muddy white.

He frowned as he stepped into the hall. Odd she'd react so violently to Raoul when she'd worried so much about him after he'd been knifed. Had something ugly happened in the hospital?

Unfortunately, she was in no shape to get back to wherever she was staying. Why the hell was she here by herself anyway?

That was his first question when she came out.

"Gabi has appointments," she answered, looking up and down the hall. "Marcus was in court. They wanted Jessica or one of the others to come with me, but I thought I'd be all right." She straightened her shoulders. "Vance is planning to return and escort me out. I'm fine now."

"Sure you are, girl." He flipped open his phone, called the FBI agent, said, "I'm taking Kim home," and shut it without waiting for an answer. He took her arm, ignored her trembling, and led her out to the parking lot. She tried to pull away at the taxi stop, and he gave her a stare that stopped her right fast. There were benefits to escorting submissives.

Once he got her in his truck and was safely on the freeway, he asked her the question that had been bothering him. "Did something happen the last time you saw Raoul?"

She looked up from her hands, her brows together. "N-no. He handed me over to my mom and said good-bye."

"So what the hell happened that the sight of him makes you upchuck?"

"The sight...? You think I was sick because of Master R?" She stared at him.

WAS THE MAN insane? Kim's hand curled around the strap of the seatbelt as she frowned at him. How could he think...?

Maybe they hadn't seen the people leaving the courtroom behind them. Probably hadn't even heard that oily voice—it wasn't as if they'd painfully learned to pay attention to every nuance in it. "The Overseer came out of a room behind you. He spoke." She shuddered, and her stomach roiled queasily. "I saw him." Bandages...because his eyes... She tried to swallow.

"Hell no. Take a breath, girl." Sam flipped the air-conditioning to high. "You puke in my truck, and I'll wallop your hide, no matter what Raoul says."

The air—and the snap in his voice—wiped away the memories and settled her stomach. Her hands unclenched. Then her brain kicked in. "You thought seeing Master R made me sick? God, Sam, did he think that too?"

"Yep."

"Oh no."

"You planning to see him while you're here?" Sam asked, his fingers tapping impatiently on the wheel as the traffic slowed, horns blaring.

"I..." She sighed. Her flight out on Saturday had been a compromise. Rather than leaving today, she'd left herself time to call him this evening...if she decided to. "I've changed my mind so many times I'm dizzy. I want to see him so...so..." So badly that her insides went all quivery at the thought. "Then I remember he wants a-a"—not a slave, he'd said—"a full-time submissive. Not me."

"You didn't like serving him?" Sam asked easily, as if his question was no more important than asking if she liked Chinese food.

"I..." *Yes.* "Dammit, no. I was pretending." *I'm a bedroom submissive. No more.* She stared out the window at the cars in the next lane. Old man—probably retired here. A married couple with young children—vacationers.

"Pretty good pretense, subbie," he said, his voice level. "You looked contented as a cat in cream sitting at his feet."

The stab slashed painfully, and she scowled. "Well, I lo—like him. A lot. That doesn't mean I want to...to slave for him."

Sam snorted. "Missy, when I pick a woman to scene with, I don't choose a lightweight who enjoys a widdle spanking. I pick a masochist who wants what I can give her. I look for someone whose need for pain matches my need to give it."

"I—"

"Shut up, girl." He switched to the fast lane to get around a slow semi and returned to the middle lane. "A master like Raoul looks for a woman whose need to serve and submit matches his need to protect and take command.

It's a balancing act, missy, and in the best relationships, the master is as involved as the submissive. If you hadn't loved being at his feet, neither one of you would have looked happy."

Had Master R been content?

"So you ask yourself this: being under Raoul's command and serving him, did it fill a need inside you? Make you feel whole when you might have not even realized something was lacking until then?"

"I—"

"Did I say you could speak?" The chill in his voice kept her silent, and in silence, he finished the drive, then escorted her to Marcus's house.

Marcus let her in. "Sam, what are you doing here?"

"Met her at the courthouse." His light blue gaze pinned her in place. "Do yourself some thinking, girl. And you call Raoul and explain why you ran, or I'll beat your ass myself." He gave her another hard look and stalked away.

* * * *

After refusing to join Marcus and Gabi for supper, Kimberly did what Sam had ordered. At least the thinking part.

God, she'd loved seeing Master R. Had wanted to throw herself in his arms. Damn the Overseer for messing everything up. Master R might have hugged her, held her, kissed her. She sighed. But would that have answered her questions?

Kim scrunched down farther on the patio chair and watched the giant inflated swan drift aimlessly in the pool, batted by the tiny breeze. Just like me, she decided. Unable to make a decision at all.

She sighed and started thinking, trying to discard the past bullshit and her preconceived notions of how the world should be. *I love Master R.* That was a given.

Did she want to live with him? *God, yes.*

Did she want him in charge? Because he would be. He couldn't help it. And okay, she liked it. Mostly. No matter how much she'd told herself otherwise, when she'd asked him to be her master again, it hadn't been totally because of the slavers and her recovery. She wanted him in charge more than just in the bedroom. The acknowledgement made her wince. How much more?

Would he try to make her into something she didn't want to be?

*Do I trust him?*

How could she not? Like her mom said, he'd taken a knife for her. But risking your life to save a person was very different from being in command over them in all the day-to-day stuff. She put her feet on the chair and laid her head on her knees.

The memory of his family's accusations was like sand in her shoes. She could walk, but it abraded her nerves. She didn't believe them, yet she needed to find out what had happened with Master R's wife before she could resolve any of the other questions.

Her plane left tomorrow morning.

She returned to the living room where Gabi was playing with her cats, Hamlet and Horatio. "Where's Marcus?"

"He had to run back to his office for something. Did you finish your thinking about Raoul?"

Kim gave her a rueful smile. There was nothing like a girlfriend to know what was going on without explanations. "Mostly. But I need some help. I met Raoul's family in the hospital. He'd told me his family doesn't talk to him because of his lifestyle, but they said he was abusing his ex-wife. I... It's been bothering me."

"Damn, I bet. But Raoul? Abuse someone. No way."

"That's what I told them. But, Gabi, I need to know."

"Mmm. I get that." Gabi tossed the fuzzy mouse, and the two cats gave chase. "He was already divorced before I met him. Before Marcus and Jessica too. But I bet Jessica can tell us who to ask."

\* \* \* \*

One phone call and a nice drive later, they met Jessica at the door of the Shadowlands. Despite her nerves, Kim laughed at the look on the guard's face when he saw them. Ben didn't approve of their casual shorts and T-shirts and had made them remove their sandals and sneakers. He also carefully explained that Z, Marcus, and Master Raoul weren't present...as if the knowledge would give them second thoughts. *Not.*

This early on a Friday night, the Shadowlands was just revving up, and only a few stations were occupied. Cullen manned the bar, his back to them, and from the way Gabi and Jessica headed for the nearest, darkest sitting area, Kim started to worry. "You aren't going to get in trouble, are you?"

The two exchanged glances and snickered. Jessica said, "I'm not allowed to be here without Z. Ever. If he sees us, Master Tattletale Cullen will be sure to tell him—if he doesn't toss me out all by himself."

Gabi gave Kim a rueful grin. "Same here. Marcus'll throw a fit. See how much I love you?"

"Oh God, I'm sorry. Just point the trainee out and leave before anyone sees you. I can—"

Jessica shook her head no. "Sally doesn't know you. She might be gossip girl, but she's really discreet who she shares with."

"Kim, we love our doms, but there's times when a girl's

got to do what a girl's got to do." Gabi grinned at Jessica. "Besides, we've been so angelic lately, we're in danger of losing our official 'brat' status."

"Can't have that," Jessica agreed. "And there's our target." She pointed to the food tables and waved, catching the eye of a pretty brunette who grinned and headed over.

She had an energy that reminded Kim of a child, all enthusiasm, no worries about dignity. Then Kim frowned. Wasn't this the submissive who that nasty dom had slapped?

"Hey, guys." The brunette glanced around. "Where're your masters?"

"You don't want to know," Jessica said firmly. "Sally, this is Kim, who is—"

"Master Raoul's submissive." Sally's eyes widened. "I didn't see your fireplay scene, but I saw you together afterward. God, he really dotes on you, doesn't he?" Her envy was obvious and heartening.

"I—" Kim sighed. "Maybe. But I have a question about his past. Can you help?"

"Sure. If Jessica says it's okay, then I figure it's okay." Sally nodded to a group of chairs by the munchie tables. "Sit and I'll get provisions. Gossip is hungry work."

"She's so cute," Kim whispered to Jessica as they sat down, and Gabi headed for the bottled water. "I can't believe she doesn't have a dom of her own."

Jessica grinned. "She's totally sweet and fun, but during a scene, usually some poor sucker of a dom finds out she's also incredibly smart. She's had a couple of relationships, but she can't give up control unless a guy is sharper and stronger than she is."

Gabi set down bottles of water, giving the bar a wistful look. "I sure could use a drink."

Sally brought over a plate of tiny egg rolls and another

of minipizzas, then dropped into a chair. "Okay, what information do you need?"

Kim hesitated. This felt like a betrayal, poking into Master R's business, but—

"Raoul's ex," Gabi said firmly, winking at Kim. "Something ugly happened with her, and Kim needs to find out what."

"Oooh," Sally waved her hand in the air. "Pick me, teacher. I know the answer."

Jessica and Gabi laughed.

*Oh God, there really was something.* Kim's stomach clenched.

Sally sobered and said slowly, "There's like two parts to this, and I shouldn't know this first part, right? But it's not like I snooped or anything. See, Master Raoul had just filed for divorce, and he was here real late with Master Dan, and they'd both been drinking more than normal." She grimaced. "Um, I'd rather they not find out I spilled. I got the impression Dan's the only person who knows."

"I won't tell him," Kim promised firmly.

"Dan drinks?" Jessica asked.

"He stopped a while back." Sally munched down an egg roll. "It boils down to this: Master Raoul came home, went into his dungeon, and found his wife screwing her sister's husband. Very willingly."

"Holy shit," Gabi said. "Poor Raoul."

"Yeah." Sally opened a bottle of water. "It gets worse. The bro-in-law had whipped the hell out of her first."

Kim frowned. "She made love to the guy after he hurt her? That doesn't make sense."

"Oh, it does. See, she was a serious pain slut—even kinda warped about it, you know? Into scars and blood, anything. I'm not sure she even had limits, but Raoul—well, you know him—he's got a line he doesn't cross. He'd deal out bruises and welts and stuff, but not permanent damage. They were definitely mismatched."

Alicia's injuries hadn't come from Raoul? Kim frowned.

"God, this is good gossip," Jessica said. "I mean, it's horrible of us to share, but..." She wiggled. "Go on."

"So there I was, carrying over their drinks with Raoul talking about it. Just totally wrecked."

"God, that must have hurt him bad." Kim felt the ache deep in her bones. Master R was so careful of everyone and so insistent on honesty. To have his wife cheat on him—and in his home. "But didn't he have a clue? He always knows if I'm lying."

Jessica wrapped an arm around Kim and squeezed gently. "Even the Shadowlands Masters are only human— although it's not easy to remember sometimes. When they're in dom mode, they're really, really perceptive, but they can't stay that way all the time."

"You could see their marriage had problems. Raoul, he's so honorable, he wouldn't give up, but Alicia—" Sally shrugged. "She was nice enough, and everybody liked her, and she had this great sarcastic sense of humor, but she was...hmm...maybe not all that honest."

Adultery wasn't exactly honest, no. But why had Alicia gone to Master R's family with that bullshit story? It wasn't like he'd been the one screwing around on *her*. "So she divorced Master R, and they went their separate ways? I heard..." How could she put this? "I heard she said some stuff about him."

Sally popped an egg roll in her mouth, holding up her hand for them to wait. "Okay, this is the second part of the story. I got it from Vanessa, who got it from Alicia since they were BFFs back then. And it's not a big secret. See, Alicia demanded a prenup 'cause Master Raoul had just started his company not long before, and she was making the big bucks. She didn't want to share, you know?"

The woman sounded like a cast-iron bitch, Kim decided.

"What a loser," Gabi muttered.

Sally continued, "But then Raoul's company takes off, and he's mad at her cheating, and he sticks to the prenup—*yours is yours and mine is mine*. Even worse, he filed for divorce the day after he found them. So she goes ballistic, saying he'd screwed her over."

"Only she was the one doing the screwing." Gabi shook her head. "Poor Raoul."

"Yeah. She came here after she'd gotten the papers and was screaming her head off in the dressing rooms. She stripped to show off all the damage—and the bro-in-law had really messed her up. But she was saying Raoul did it."

"Oh my God," Gabi said. "I bet people believed her too."

"Not for long." Sally grinned. "This was before Raoul was a master, so Z hadn't a clue about what had really happened, but you know how Z is. Superpsychologist-plus and a layer of dom on top?"

Jessica snickered. "That's him, all right."

"Anyway, he, like, stalks into the women's room—and really flusters some naked women too—and Alicia has her back to him. He listens to the bullshit."

Kim realized she was holding her breath. "Were you there?"

"Yeah, all us trainees were getting dressed." Sally gave a mock shiver. "Z was—God, he listened, and his face got that really pissed-off, cold expression of his, the one that can shrivel everything up inside you? And he says right to her face that she's lying."

"Oooh," Jessica said. "Z never makes a mistake about liars."

"What happened?" Gabi grabbed Kim's hand.

"She didn't even try to deny it. Not to Master Z." Sally waggled her water bottle. "He told her she had one minute to put her clothes on. Then he booted her out and canceled her membership."

That explained why Master R's ex had been out for revenge. But what about the other part? That he hadn't let her leave. "And was she his s-slave?"

Gabi said, "Kim—"

"I need to know."

Jessica frowned. "He and Z and I were talking one night. Z'd swatted my butt for being impertinent, and he told Raoul about how we'd started off keeping the D/s stuff to scenes and bedrooms, but how it had edged out into our lifestyle." She shrugged. "It really has. Knowing Z might pick up the reins at any minute means it's always simmering under the surface—and I love it."

Sally gave an audible sigh.

Jessica grinned at her. "Anyway, Raoul said his went the other way. He and Alicia started off in a Master/slave relationship, but it had died away." She bit her lip. "He looked, I don't know, empty."

Kim could feel the ache in her chest. "So—why start and then stop?"

Sally shook her head and said slowly, "I think new love makes you crazy, and if you're new to BDSM, maybe it's difficult to tell what's what. But if you don't have that need to serve or submit, then a power exchange won't work very long. On the other end, there's solid M/s and D/s relationships where the people aren't in love, but they're both fulfilled."

"That's pretty convoluted, but I almost understand what you're saying," Gabi said.

Sally grinned. "Anyway, Alicia wasn't into service or

even submission. Straight-shot masochist. And it was obvious. But it was hard on Master Raoul. He's dominant right down to his bones."

*Could I keep Master R happy?* Kim frowned. *Do I want to serve him just because I love him?* Oh, wonderful. More questions. But for right now... "What time is it?"

"A little after nine. Why?" Jessica asked.

"I have a visit to make." She rummaged in her purse and pulled out the note she'd made earlier. It was downright scary how easy it was to use the Internet to get a person's address.

She started to ask Gabi to lend her the car, then rethought. Panicking on someone's doorstep wouldn't be smart—she should have brought her escort dog. "Gabi, can you come with me?"

# Chapter Nineteen

Her plane would be leaving right about now. Raoul frowned at the design for a cable bridge on his computer and shut the program down. If he continued in this half-assed fashion, he'd end up redoing all the work. He leaned back in his chair and stared at the ceiling.

*Time to get your life in order, Sandoval.* Truly, he should be grateful for yesterday, for seeing how she reacted to him. His last doubt had been resolved, and he no longer had to argue with himself whether he wanted her to return. He rubbed his cheek, scowling at the scratchiness. Forgot to shave again. He needed to clean up before the party.

If she showed up and dropped to her knees and begged him to make her his slave, he wouldn't agree. He closed his eyes and hauled in a painful breath. *No.* Over the past weeks, he'd realized he couldn't take that step. Not now. Especially not with a woman who'd steal his heart, his life, and then decide she'd made a mistake.

He glanced around the house he'd built in an attempt to eradicate his wife from his memories.

Now Kimberly's presence infused it instead. So many memories just from the few weeks they'd been together, and even though he'd known she'd leave.

How much worse would it be if they tried to build a future together? And then she'd tell him she didn't want a master, didn't want to serve him—or love him either. Would he have to build a new house again?

He tried to laugh, but it sounded more like a response to a gut shot. His love for Alicia bore no resemblance to the overwhelming way he felt about Kimberly. She was warmth and laughter and hopes he should never have harbored.

If he really thought she'd stay with him, accept him, that might be different. If he'd met her before her slavery, maybe...maybe he would have risked trying to teach her about her own needs.

She was brave, so very resilient, but that would ask too much.

He'd tried living a vanilla life. He couldn't do it again. He'd unconsciously take the control from a little sub, and she would resent it. And leave him.

No. Maybe in a few years, he'd be willing to open himself up to the potential for pain. Kimberly would have married some nice normal man, probably have some children by then. The thought stabbed into his heart like a rapier.

He swallowed and forced a smile. He would wish her well.

Mouth tight, he sat back down at his computer and brought up the program. He'd work. Period.

An hour later, the sound of the doorbell ran through Raoul's empty house. He glanced at the clock—only ten in the morning. The party for Kari and Dan didn't start until one, and the caterers had already arrived and filled the fridge. Who would this be? Kimberly? The momentary hope lit his heart and died as quickly. Long gone.

He saved his design and headed for the front, actually a bit pleased at the interruption. Anything was better than the hollow feeling of his home. *Pitiful, Sandoval.* But he'd be happy to leave again.

He pulled open the door, assuming he'd be buying some Girl Scout cookies or a magazine subscription he didn't need. The neighborhood children had him figured for a soft touch. But no child waited in the entry.

He stared for a second before his voice would work. "Mamá?"

"*Mijo*." His mother had tears in her eyes. Lucia stood a pace behind, openly crying.

Had one of his nephews been hurt? Raoul took his mother's frail hands. "Mamá, what has happened? What is wrong?"

"Raoul, I was so cruel. I didn't know." His mother wrapped her arms around him, weeping as if her heart were breaking.

"Please, please, don't cry. Whatever is wrong, I will fix it."

A second later, his sister attached herself like a burr to his side.

Carajo, this looked bad. "Has something happened to the boys?" More sobbing. He clamped a hand on his sister's arm and gave it a shake. "Lucia, talk to me."

His sister gave a shuddering laugh and wiped her face, then rubbed her mother's back. "Shhh, Mamá, we're scaring him."

Raoul growled. "Lucia, you will tell me what is wrong. Now."

They exchanged glances and smiled. *Smiled?*

"Dominant, yes, you are surely that," his mother said. "You sound like your papá did."

He winced and tried to step back. "I just—"

"'Mano, we found last night that your wife lied to us that day. The day you filed for divorce," Lucia said. Her voice turned icy. "Alicia said you whipped her until she bled, that you hit her over and over. You forced her to be a slave and gave her to other men. She said she had to run to get away from you."

"We didn't believe her." His mother wiped her face with the tiny handkerchief she always tucked under her belt. "But she showed us horrible bloody marks and bruises everywhere."

Raoul stared at them. "But... I didn't."

"No, you didn't." Lucia's eyes flashed black with anger. "But when Mamá asked you if you ever hit Alicia and if you ever had put a collar on her, you said yes." She held her hand up to stop him from speaking. "You thought we were talking about how you lived. Raoul, we thought you were admitting to beating her and forcing her to be a slave."

Someone had jammed a lead pipe into his chest. Pain with every pulse. "All these years, and you thought—"

"Mijo, I am sorry," his mamá whispered. "I should have known you would never do such a thing. Only you said you had. But you didn't."

"Then—" Why didn't his brain work? "How did you find out—"

Both women smiled at him, and Lucia said sweetly, "It's not important, 'mano."

The hell it wasn't. His mouth tightened. He'd find out, damned if he wouldn't. But for now... "Come in, Mamá. Lucia. I have coffee made." As they walked inside, his heart swelled. His family was in his home.

"Raoul, this is beautiful," his mother said as she walked through the great room, and his throat tightened when he saw his mother's eyes. Love. Pride. How long since she'd looked at him that way? "We will not stay long, but...we couldn't wait any longer."

"I wouldn't let her call. I wasn't sure you'd talk to us," Lucia admitted. "I've been horrible to you."

He shook his head, remembering the marks on Alicia's body. He pulled cups from the cupboard and set them on the island. "You thought I'd abused her. I would have reacted the same way."

The time passed quickly as they sat in the kitchen, eating cookies and drinking coffee and catching up.

Too soon for his taste, Lucia stood, saying, "The boys will be home soon." She gave him the mischievous smile he remembered from childhood and hadn't seen in three long years. "But we expect to see you for Sunday dinner tomorrow. I have a feeling Mamá will fix all your favorites."

His mother looked up at him, and his heart caught at the pleading look in her eyes. Begging forgiveness.

"Of course I'll be there," he said gently and kissed his mother's cheek. He walked them to their car and helped his mother in.

"Raoul." His sister waited beside the driver's door. Pleased, he walked around to give her a final hug.

She returned it, then took an unhappy breath, one that made him tense. "One more unpleasantness; then we'll put it behind us. This morning, I called Alicia's sister. Penny's been divorced for a while, ever since she found out Randolph was cheating on her." Her mouth thinned. "She hadn't known that the *other* woman was her own sister."

"How did you hear that?" Raoul's fingers clamped on her shoulders. Somehow they had the whole story—all of it. And to call Penny. "Lucia, that wasn't—"

"Yes, it was necessary. I know you protect women, *mi hermano*. But, speaking as a woman, there are certain things I would want to know. A man's cheating is..." She shrugged, having survived her own divorce. "But such a betrayal from a sister? There is no excuse under heaven. Alicia will find her family—and friends—to be less welcoming, I think." Lucia patted his cheek. She'd worn the same smug smile after he'd used her Barbie dolls in his war games and she'd turned his prized comic books into cat litter in revenge. A firm believer in retribution was Lucia.

She added, "I felt much better after the call." Another kiss on the cheek, and his sister slid into the car.

Women could be much crueler than men. Smiling a little, Raoul watched the sedan move down his long driveway. As he walked back into his house, his brows drew together. But he still wanted to know—how had they found out all the details of his divorce?

* * * *

By one thirty that afternoon, the doorbell in Raoul's house rang incessantly as people arrived for the barbecue. He shook his head, still amazed at how easily Z had manipulated him.

Everyone had wanted to celebrate Dan and Kari's new baby. In many ways, it felt like the first for the Shadowlands Masters, even if some had children from previous marriages. Marcus and Gabi would have given the party, but Gabi wasn't sure she'd be in town. Cullen's home wasn't large enough. Sam's house was isolated in the country. Neither of the dommes could host the party. Z liked to entertain, but this time, he'd given an excuse and said Raoul had the space, a big patio and the beach, and was convenient to everyone.

Yes, the cabrón had set him up.

At least Jessica and her friends had taken over answering the door. Raoul concentrated on the barbecue, needing to stay occupied. Although his family's visit had lightened his heart, the sight of so many couples in the lifestyle rubbed his nose in the fact that he had no one.

Mistress Anne walked out on the patio, her favorite submissive trailing behind her. She patted the pretty young man's face. "Joey, look lively and help the others set up the tables."

The redhead gave his mistress a meltingly sweet smile

and moved stiffly toward the kitchen. Considering Anne's sadistic streak, she'd probably shoved an overly large anal plug up the poor sub's ass. Oddly enough, Jessica was moving in the same fashion. What had the little blonde done to get herself in trouble with Z this time?

The subs trotted back and forth, carrying platters, covering the long patio tables with food. A hum of conversation came from the guests sitting on the patio, splashing and squeals from those in the pool. Some had taken the chance to walk on the beach and enjoy the bright afternoon sun.

Sam walked over with a cold beer. Raoul took a small drink before putting the bottle down. The way he felt, the alcohol looked too appealing, and he didn't drink for escape.

"I took her home," Sam said, as if continuing a conversation.

"I know. Thank you for caring for her." Hoping Sam wouldn't continue, Raoul turned the chicken, the scent of the sizzling meat filling the air.

"She call you?"

"No."

"Hell. She was—"

"I checked with Marcus yesterday to make sure she'd gotten home." And heard about her flight time. He glanced at his watch. Her plane would have left a while back. *Gone.* That was good. It was good.

"You going to let her just go?" Sam asked, his gaze on the ocean. "After what she's been through, you figure she won't get over it?"

Raoul sighed and shut the grill top. After wiping his hands, he picked up his beer again. "At one time, I thought she might be willing to try. But it is better this way. She's been hurt, and to be with me in...in the type of relationship I want is more than she could take." *More uncertainty than*

*I'm willing to risk.* When had he turned so cautious?

"Pretty much the conclusion I'd come to," Sam muttered, and Raoul decided he wasn't talking about Kimberly but about Linda. Sam had kept the redheaded slave safe, as Kimberly had asked, but apparently something else had happened.

Not that Sam would confide in Raoul. A man wouldn't...not unless drunk. He winced. The last time he'd drunk that much was three years ago, after Alicia's betrayal.

"You know, about Kim," Sam started. "At the courthouse, she didn't—" His voice was drowned out by the arrival of the Shadowlands trainees, all dressed in civilian clothing. Sam turned away at a hail from Cullen.

Raoul almost didn't recognize the trainees: Uzuri in a pale yellow halter-top and shorts that accented her dark chocolate skin and with her kinky hair in dreadlocks. Dara's blonde spiked hair was tinted purple. In a pink sundress, Maxie looked cheerful and sweet.

Pretty Sally brought up the rear, in short shorts and three tank tops layered in the odd female way. After exchanging greetings with the milling submissive group, she leaned over to Jessica and whispered something, receiving a smile and a big hug in return.

Both women turned to look at him...and saw him watching them. Color rose in Sally's cheeks, and she shifted so her back was toward him.

Raoul took a sip of his beer, his interest aroused at the un-Sallylike behavior. No greeting. No hug. Was something wrong?

When Sally said something, Jessica glanced at him and met his eyes. She whispered to Sally, and the trainee's spine grew stiffer.

Raoul's suspicions started to rise. He hadn't lived with

slaves and submissives without learning a few things—like the ability to detect body language that sang of a guilty conscience.

None of the other doms received the darting looks. So whatever they'd done had something to do with him. And Kimberly? No. She'd been home with Gabi yesterday evening. As a trainee, Sally would have been at the Shadowlands last night. His eyes narrowed.

Sally was a bubbly, talkative little submissive who'd been part of the club for maybe five years. None of the other trainees had been around as long. Raoul rubbed his chin. Ever since his mamá and sister's visit this morning, he'd wondered how they'd learned about Alicia's betrayal. The only person he'd told had been Dan, and his friend never revealed a confidence.

But no one paid attention to the submissives in the club. They'd been trained to be invisible. *Perhaps too invisible.* Could she have overheard something when he'd been talking with Dan?

Sally peeked over her shoulder, saw him watching her, and jerked back around.

*Hmm.* Not looking away, he drank his beer.

"Sandoval, how are you doing?" Vance Buchanan walked out the door onto the patio, Kouros beside him. "Who're you staring at?"

Raoul nodded toward the group of submissives. "The little brunette."

The two FBI agents turned. Sally darted a look at Raoul and saw all three men looking at her. The color flared in her cheeks. She edged closer to Jessica.

"If she was my sub," Kouros said, "I be wondering what she'd been up to."

Buchanan grinned. "Yep, looks guilty as hell, but she's the prettiest little perp I've ever seen."

Raoul considered. If Sally had been the one to tell his family about Alicia, she'd done him a favor. Yet a submissive should know better than to divulge a dom's private affairs. As a trainee in the Shadowlands, she fell under the authority of all the Masters—including him. He didn't have the heart to punish her but was obligated to teach her discretion. "I think I know what's up, and a bit of intimidation would be appropriate," he said. "Want to interrogate her while I watch?"

Kouros leaned on his cane. "It would be a pleasure." He waited until Sally turned, then gestured. *Come here.*

The color drained from her face, and Buchanan covered his laugh with a cough.

She crossed to them, all bounce gone, her gaze down. Across the patio, Z looked up, studied the situation for a second, grinned, and returned to talking with Olivia and Sam.

Jessica was watching, her brows drawn together. Definitely worried. Raoul leaned over to Kouros. "Better hurry, or Z's sub will spoil the fun with either a confession or a tantrum."

Kouros followed his gaze, and his lips quirked. "Got it."

Sally stopped in front of the men and lifted her chin. "Did you need something, Sirs?"

Raoul smiled at her. "Trainee, these two doms want to speak with you." His use of the word *trainee* put her on notice that she was expected to obey.

"Yes, Master Raoul."

Buchanan moved behind her, blocking the sight of her from the other submissives.

Kouros stepped forward. Big men, both doms, intimidating in size and personality. "What we need from you is the truth," Kouros said, his clipped New England accent striking the sub like sparks from a low burning fire.

Sally tried to back up and bumped into Buchanan. He grinned at Raoul over her head. "But—"

"We'll start with something easy," Kouros purred, setting his hand under her chin. "What is your name?"

"Sally, Sir." She made an obvious effort to stand straight, but Raoul could see her melting under the force of Kouros's personality. Experienced doms, years as FBI agents—the girl didn't have a chance.

"Very nice, Sally. You can tell the truth, see?" His voice turned silky with approval. His free hand stroked her hair back behind her ear, both a caress—and exposing her face more.

She stared up at him like a cornered mouse, an unusual change in the spirited sub.

Buchanan stroked her bare arms, adding to the sense of reward.

"Now tell me what you did to Master Raoul," Kouros demanded, his voice as cold as a New England winter.

She moaned, her hands rubbing on her hips in a self-comforting motion. She tried to look at Raoul, but Kouros shifted, keeping her gaze on his face.

Raoul smothered a smile, making mental notes. He rather liked interrogation scenes, and this one was pretty lightweight...except for Sally's obvious guilt and the agent's undeniable experience with breaking down hardened criminals.

"N-nothing." She pulled in a breath, lifted her chin. "I haven't even seen him for a long time."

"Oh, you definitely did something, little one," Kouros said softly. "I don't want to get angry with you, sweetheart." He moved closer until she could probably feel his body heat, until she had to tilt her head back to stare up at him. "There are other things Vance and I would rather do...to you."

Her eyes got bigger, and the combination of anxiety and sudden arousal was a fine sight.

"What are you doing?" Jessica stepped around Buchanan. She actually shoved Kouros back a step and pulled Sally out from between the two agents. "Leave her alone!"

As Buchanan and Kouros moved back, Sally recovered her spirit. Her spine straightened, although she quickly edged out of grabbing distance.

"Ah well." Ignoring glares that should have fried his ass, Buchanan grinned at Raoul. "How about drinks for two hard-working agents?"

"It would be my pleasure." Raoul looked for the other agent.

Using his cane to block Jessica, Kouros cornered Sally again. When his eyes met hers, she froze. "We'll continue this at another time, pet," he murmured. "And I assure you, you *will* tell us everything we want to know." He ran a finger down her flushed cheek and smiled.

As the Fed turned away, Raoul saw Sally shiver. Then her hands fisted. "Not until hell freezes over," she muttered, just loudly enough to hear.

As Jessica slung an arm around her waist and escorted her friend back to the safety of the submissive group, Kouros joined Buchanan.

Raoul grinned at him. He had a feeling Sally would probably disappear into the bathroom the next time she spotted the agents. "Let me get you a beer, Kouros."

After Raoul had taken care of his guests and introduced them to a couple of the doms they hadn't met, he returned to check the barbecue. He loaded up a platter with chicken and handed it to Joey to put on the table.

"Hey, Raoul," Gabi called from the back door. Her hand was in her dom's in the way they had of walking with fingers laced, and Raoul firmly stomped on his envy. As she and Marcus crossed the patio, Raoul frowned at how stiffly she moved. Had she been spanked? No, it was the more gingerly movement of a submissive unaccustomed to walking around with an anal plug. Both her *and* Jessica? He'd think they'd been up to something together, but Marcus had said they weren't going to the Shadowlands last night.

Raoul shook his head in confusion and kissed Gabi's cheek. After dutifully admiring her current arm tattoos of SpongeBob—the same yellow as her halter top—he slapped Marcus's arm. "Welcome, my friends. There is beer in the dark coolers and wine in the light cooler."

"You look like *hell*," Marcus said, his accent making the word sound like hey-all.

"Geez, Marcus, were you raised in a barn?" Gabi frowned, then looked over her dom's shoulder and grinned, bouncing once on her toes.

Raoul followed her gaze, and his muscles went rigid. *Kimberly?*

Dios, she was a vision in the afternoon sunlight, wearing a pretty strapless sundress, the blue the color of her eyes. Her black hair shone like a raven's wing, rippling over her tanned shoulders. He walked forward a few steps, then had second thoughts. *Not your woman, Sandoval. Don't want a woman. Be polite, then keep your distance.*

Uncertainty crossed her face as she stared at him, and his hand went out before he knew, offering anything she needed from him. If she ran from him again, he wouldn't be able to bear it. His mouth tightened. *No.* He did not want to walk this path.

Before he could withdraw his gesture, she crossed the last few steps and set her small hand into his. Unable to help himself, he drank in the sight of her, feeling as if the empty places in his heart were filling. Her hand in his trembled slightly, and he told himself to release her, but his fingers wouldn't open.

"Kimberly." His voice came out ragged. But at least she wasn't throwing up at the sight of him, although it might be easier on him if she did. "I'm sorry about yesterday."

"Yesterday?" Her gaze moved over his face, and she seemed as hungry for him as he was for her. "Yesterday. Oh…right. The courthouse," she said. "God, I'm sorry, M— Raoul. Sam said you thought you'd made me sick, but that wasn't it. I saw the Overseer. He came out of the courtroom right behind you, and when I heard his voice…" Her color faded.

*She hadn't been reacting to me.* The blast of relief was like having his chest cracked open. His mouth tightened. He didn't want to feel like this.

"Well." He needed to stop this now, not lead her on. Not encourage her. He pulled his hand back. "It's good to see you again. You're looking well."


KIM'S HAND FELT empty, as if yearning to take his again. She stared up at him. He looked tired, but oh, his face was even more darkly tanned, his black hair shaggy, brushing the collar of his blue short-sleeved shirt. The touch of his hand—just the damned touch—had sent a thrill through her.

For a moment, his eyes had started to smolder, but now he looked remote. Cold. Like he'd been at the auction. But that expression had been for the slavers—never for her. Did he no longer…?

She swallowed. "I—"

"They're here!" Jessica yelled. People turned to look.

Dan walked out and held the door for Kari, who held a tiny bundle in her arms.

*The baby.* "Oh, look how little," Kim whispered.

Master R tilted his head. "You haven't seen the child yet, have you?"

"But..." *I want to stay with you.*

"Go see the baby, Kimberly."

An order. A definite *go away.* A frozen ball took up residence in the pit of her stomach. She shouldn't have come. Why had she been so silly, building a castle of dreams made of sand? It only took a wave to wash it away.

She made her feet cross the patio and joined the women surrounding Dan, Kari, and the baby. Beth frowned, cast a quick look at Master R, and put an arm around Kim's waist. Andrea stepped to her other side, her brows pulling together.

Kari smiled a welcome and glanced in Master R's direction. "It's about time you came back, Kim. He's been a bear."

"No kidding," Dan muttered.

Why did hearing that make her feel better? Not that it changed anything. *Accept it, Kim. He's made the decision for you.* And she needed to concentrate on her friends now. Not spoil Kari's moment with unhappiness. She forced a smile "Let's see this new baby."

Kari flipped back the light blanket to reveal the baby's face and grinned at the "Awwws" and "Oooos." "Meet Zane." Black hair, blue eyes like Dan's, a little chin and nose like Kari's.

Grumbling, Dan retreated from the crowd of women, casting a glance over his shoulder as if checking to be sure his two charges were safe.

Unable to resist, Kim reached out. *Look at the tiny hand.* His fingers closed around her thumb. "He's precious, Kari."

Kari grinned. "He really is." The tenderness in her

eyes as she stared at her baby, then across to Dan, matched the way Dan's face softened, showing his pride and...love.

Kim swallowed, her throat clogging with envy, then said, "I missed the baby shower, but Gabi told me this is a baby celebration, so I got you a present this morning. Got him a present, I mean." She dug into the canvas bag she had over her shoulder and handed over the gaily wrapped package.

Jessica took Zane as Kari opened the gift, then laughed and held up the blue onesie to show the writing on the front: *I give the orders around here*, then the back: *Master Zane*. Kari gurgled a laugh. "Oh, it's true. He's totally in charge. When Zane cries, even the big dom of the house comes running." She touched the baby's hair. "And I love it. It's just so..." Kari smiled down at her son.

Satisfying, Kim filled in. Up at all hours of the night, tending to every need. And Kari was happy.

Was that what a master got back from a relationship?

Kim shook her head. She'd never tended much except boats—then again, even boats need care. Patching and cleaning, oiling and barnacle scraping, doing all the tedious things that kept it running well. She never begrudged the chores, because a sturdy vessel would hold up in a storm, would bring you back to shore, would never let you down. She looked over at Master R. He was her boat.

Dan worked his way to Kari and kissed her. "I set up the carrier and monitor in the little living room for when you're ready to feed him and put him down for his nap." Grinning, he took the baby. "My turn to show him off before he decides he's starving." He snuggled his son against him and headed toward the doms.

Andrea grinned. "He's so proud, it's cute."

Kari snickered. "Don't be a smarty. Can you imagine how your Cullen would act?"

"Pretty much like that. Wouldn't they all?" Andrea's smile softened as Cullen touched Zane's cheek, pleasure filling his face. "He wants children, so we'll be locking up the dungeon furniture sooner or later."

"Hiding the equipment?" Beth stared at her scar-faced dom and the gentle way he'd taken the baby's fingers as if marveling at how small next to his big hand. Beth's eyes narrowed. "That's what Nolan was drawing last night—dungeon furniture that converts into bedroom furniture."

"If he sells it, he'll get rich. Richer." Jessica grinned. "Dan and Kari have started a trend. Look at those so-called hard-asses."

Kim sighed. The doms' faces turned gentle when they looked at the baby. Then each would gaze over at his submissive as if imagining her with his child. "I bet some birth control pills are going to get dumped in the next few months."

"Dios, after seeing the baby, I might not protest too much," Andrea muttered. "Maybe I'll let Cullen marry me after all."

"Respectability sucks." Jessica pouted. "Z said no babies until we get married, and Mom's insisting on a church wedding. You know how long those take to plan?"

"I know the feeling," Beth grumbled. "I still can't believe mine bribed Nolan to delay our wedding. With wine, no less. Men are so easy."

Kari laughed. "I can't believe you took less than two weeks for a honeymoon."

Beth colored. "It wasn't as if I got to see much of anything besides the bed anyway."

Smiling, Kim watched as Dan and his son got to Sam. Sam already had grown children, didn't he? He smiled at the baby and said something to Dan that made him laugh.

Then Master R reached out, and Dan actually put the

baby in his arms. He held the little bundle easily, and a smile flashed in his dark face as tiny fists appeared out of the blanket. He rubbed his knuckles over the baby's cheek, and Kim remembered how he'd do that with her when he was especially pleased or tender.

As he passed the baby to Dan, he smiled, and maybe only Kim saw the touch of envy. Her heart wrenched when, as the other men had done, his gaze came to rest on her, the heat, the sheer desire so potent that her feet started across the patio. Just because he'd shown her his need.

But he shook his head and turned away, checking the food he was cooking on the giant barbecue.

She halted. *He doesn't want me. Or he doesn't want to.* She wanted to give him everything. Starting with herself. But he didn't feel the same. She stood in the center of the patio. Needing to retreat. Needing to go forward. Still as torn as she'd been since the night he bought her.

Sam had been talking with Cullen, but he paused. He stared at her for a minute, his face expressionless, then leaned over and spoke to Master R.

Master R's muscles contracted beneath his thin cotton shirt before he slowly turned. With an unreadable expression, he walked over and stood beside her, pretending to watch Kari. "He's a pretty baby, no?" He didn't touch her. Didn't smile.

"Yes." She stared at her feet. He'd only said he loved her that one time. Dammit, she shouldn't have come. This was unbearable. She glanced up and saw the smoldering need in his gaze, like a surge of electricity to her own desire. And then he buried it again.

"Damn you," she whispered.

He frowned. "Chiquita, what is wrong?" He touched her, the graze of his knuckles, the tenderness exactly as with the baby. This man would never take his loved ones for granted; she knew that right down to the bottom of her heart. He'd cherish and protect, care for with everything in him.

*He doesn't want me though.* But she wanted him. And she was tired of trying to make a decision. *Let him decide for both of us—hey, that's what he wants, right? To be in charge?*

And suddenly, it was so easy after all. Turning her head, she kissed his fingers and saw him freeze. She let her bag drop to the pavement and slipped down to her knees.

Over the pounding of her heart, she heard a squeak. Jessica.

She pulled her bag closer. It held something she'd cried over, thrown across the room, kissed, hated and cursed, and then cuddled at night. The concrete was hot against her legs. The scent of the ocean hung in the air as she took out the collar he'd given her, the one she'd found on the stairs the night of the auction. The leather was smooth, and she traced her fingers over the words *Master Raoul's gatita.*

*Am I still?*

She laid it over her palms, trying to bow her head but failing. She needed to see his face or she might die. She raised it up. "May I wear your collar, Master?" she asked and heard no sound on the patio at all except the surging of the ocean and the hammering of her heart.

His silence terrified her. For a moment, his eyes kindled as if a fire had lit behind them, and his breath ran ragged. Then his face grew remote... Her Master R had stepped behind his walls. His voice was gentle but firm. "No. I'm sorry, Kimberly. I cannot be your master."

Like a knife wound, his words sliced through her, cutting open her flesh, driving ruthlessly into her chest. The pain arrived a second later. Her protest escaped before she could think. "But... You wanted this. Wanted me."

He rubbed his palm over his mouth, his eyes unhappy. "I did," he said so softly she barely heard him. His voice strengthened. "But it cannot work between us. You don't want a master. You never did and even less now, after what you've been through."

"I do."

"Can you be that sure, cariño?" he asked so softly.

She started to say yes, then caught his intent look. "No," she said honestly and blinked back the tears. "But I'll regret it all my life if we don't try. I want to try." She swallowed. "Master, please."

He just looked at her, and his gaze filled with pain. "I...can't. No."

She bowed her head, trying not to give in to tears. She'd promised herself she wouldn't cry, no matter what happened.

Master R hadn't moved. It was up to her to get out of here. Out of his way. Out of his party and his life. Her chest had hollowed out, an aching hole where her heart had been. This was far worse than leaving him before. At least then, she'd had hope.

She put the collar back in her bag, touching it like a tiny being that had died. Her legs didn't cooperate when she tried to stand.

A hand appeared in front of her face. Not Master R's thick-boned, powerful hand. This was lean, fingernails groomed, a dark watch on the wrist. She wrapped her fingers around his palm, and the man pulled her to her feet with a graceful strength.

Master Z. When he tucked her into his side, she leaned against him. "Don't quit yet, little one," he whispered in her ear.

"Can you see she gets home, Z?" Master R asked. The smoothness and lilt had fled his voice, adding to her sorrow.

"No, I don't think so, Raoul."

She started to say she'd get herself home, but Z's arm around her squeezed the air from her lungs.

Master R's face tightened, anger shadowing his eyes. "Don't interfere in what you don't understand, my friend," he said, a threat hanging in the air.

"I think I understand quite well," Z said mildly. "Your marriage left scars. And you don't want to be hurt again, but this little one keeps doing it. She's finally made up her mind, but you can't be sure and aren't about to risk it again. Unfortunately, she can't give you a guarantee, especially after everything she's been through. Do I have it about right?"

She'd hurt him when she'd left? Oh God, she really had. She'd been so stupidly focused on herself, thinking he was self-sufficient. She hadn't looked at what she was doing to him. "I'm so, so sorry," she whispered, wincing at the misery flickering across his face.

"This is not the place to discuss this," Master R said tightly. "Take her ho—"

Z smiled faintly. "This is exactly the place. Nothing in life is guaranteed, Raoul."

"I know that." Master R's gaze dropped to her face, unyielding. Unhappy. "Kimberly, I tried living in a relationship without...being who I am. I can't do that again. And you cannot submit to a master, not after what you've been through."

"But I did. I can." Yet she wasn't totally sure herself. This wouldn't be a limited few days, and she'd already capsized on him once. Why should he trust her? How could he trust her? "Is there," she said slowly, "a test? A shakedown cruise? Something to prove to us both that it can work?"

She saw his spark of hope flare, then die. He smiled

ruefully. "There's no—"

"Traditionally," Z said casually, "a submissive is whipped when receiving her collar as a way of showing her submission, her trust in her master."

Whipped? Her mind went blank, and she tried to pull away from Z.

The iron bar of his arm didn't release. "You've been whipped in front of strangers, little one. Would you like to enjoy one in front of friends—given by your master?"

*Whip.* A shiver ran through her, and Master R growled, his hand fisting. "Damn you. She can't—"

So many *she can'ts* coming from him. *I can do anything if I want it enough.* Maybe she did want it. Just as Master R had replaced her horrible nightmares of other men by making love to her, now she could replace memories of cruelty with his care. And perhaps create something for them both to fall back on. She'd never trusted him more or felt so close to him as after the fireplay scene. If he wanted her to do this, then she knew she could…and it might help her doubts as well. "Yes, please, Master R," she whispered. "Yes."

Silence. "No."

Catch-22. If she accepted his mastery, then he had the right to say no, but if he said no, then she had no master. She bent her head. "I want the tradition if it pleases Master. I will take any pain you want to give me, take anything you do. We both need an answer."

Silence. Then a heavy sigh. "This master is going to kill Z."

Z chuckled. His arm dropped from her, and he simply walked away.

Master R laid his hand against Kim's face. He studied her, seeing her in the way no one else had ever done. "You would face your fears—bear pain for me—just for a chance to be together?"

She nodded.

He looked away, brows drawn. Thinking.

Hope started to tap-dance over her heart. She held so, so still, not wanting to interrupt his thoughts.

"Yes." His expression changed. His shoulders straightened. His mouth firmed. Everything about him coalesced into the master she loved. "Then, gatita, it would please me to test your submission in front of our friends."

HOW HAD THIS happened? Raoul stared down at Kimberly, trying to batter down the hope rising inside him. She couldn't do this, couldn't truly submit.

And, if she could, what would it prove? Really?

But if she could face her worst fears for him, how could he not do as much for her?

If she could submit to him, here, in fear and in public, he'd know that she'd work as hard as he would to make a D/s relationship succeed.

A shiver ran through her, and he pulled her into his arms, giving her comfort. Whether she succeeded or not, he would withhold nothing. She needed to trust him, to want to please him. After so long apart, to do this now was foolish— yet neither of them could tolerate waiting. He knew that as well.

He rested his cheek on the top of her head, inhaling her light fragrance. He'd forgotten—tried to forget—how she fit against him, how her strong arms would hold him as tightly as he held her.

After a minute, Raoul lifted his head and motioned for Cullen. "You know where the dungeon is. Can you get the box labeled *patio* and set it up at the archway? Bring wrist and ankle cuffs as well."

"Got it, buddy." Cullen grinned at Kimberly and

tugged her hair. "Welcome home, pet. Why didn't you come over and say hi last night?"

She gave him a shrug, looking away, her body stiff.

Raoul frowned. She wasn't usually rude. She relaxed when Cullen moved away.

*Last night.* Cullen would have been playing bartender at the Shadowlands all evening. *"Come over and say hi."*

Obviously, Kim had been at the club, probably with Gabi. Maybe conversing with guilty little Sally. Kim had met his family in the hospital; he'd heard them talking in the hall. It didn't take a calculus formula to figure out the answer. But this was not the time to deal with family issues. Instead... He rubbed his cheek on her silky hair and asked, "Did you get the furry present I sent you?"

Her laugh—how long had it been since he'd heard her soft laugh. "My Ari. He's wonderful and..."

Contently, Raoul held her, ignoring the conversations around them, and listened to her telling of returning to work, of the big dog, of her life. As Cullen and Nolan set up chains from the bolts in the patio cover beams, he answered her questions about Costa Rica.

She'd missed him and tried to call him. The knowledge was far too pleasing. "I missed you, sumisita," he admitted in return. She was being gut-wrenchingly honest and more courageous than he was. "My home is empty without you, and I couldn't bear the silence."

Her arms tightened around him, and he bent down and took her lips. Soft and welcoming as she molded against him, keeping nothing of herself in return. Her body was fragrant and even lusher than when she'd left. He wanted to explore, to fill his palms with her breasts.

When he lifted his head, she made a tiny sound of protest. One a man should not make, but a man might feel. After a slow breath, he noticed Cullen had set cuffs on the table nearby.

Time to start. One by one, he slowly fastened the cuffs on his sumisa, cherishing the way she held out an ankle, her wrist, offering herself. Her pleasure was obvious in her open stance and her curving lips. She wanted his cuffs.

He ran his finger around the insides to ensure they weren't too tight, then rose and checked the setup at the edge of his patio. Chains dangled from rings he'd installed in the support beam. Two more chains lay at the base of the four-by-four posts. Ready.

Was Kimberly? Her breathing had sped up, and she was biting her lip. But she nodded firmly. "I'm ready, Master."

He'd always known she'd break his heart. His hand slipped down under the hem of her sundress and between her legs. Small panties, already damp. Her muscles were tensed with anxiety, but her pussy showed her arousal. Maybe, maybe she could do this. His hopes flared. "Remove your clothing."

Her breath hitched, and a flush grew in her cheeks. But she pulled the sundress over her head in one smooth move. The sight of her breasts—yes, fuller than before— sent a bolt of lust through him.

She pushed down her tiny panties—the ruffles matched the ones on the dress, he noticed appreciatively.

"Are you still ready?"

"Yes, Master." Her lips formed around the word as if she liked the taste of it in her mouth, and he was grateful she hadn't hated it like she had the word *slave*—he enjoyed very much the sound of his title when she said it.

*Mine.* His heart uttered the word again and again. Submitting to him. Nothing could give a dom more of a rush in a scene. In life? Nothing filled a dom's heart so fully.

Unable to resist, he pulled her against him, curved his

fingers around her nape, and plundered her sweet lips. He ran his hand over her ass, massaging the roundness, still cool, but soon to be glowing with heat.

He held her eyes, rejoicing to see them so clear and free of fear. "I love you, gatita."

HER HEART MELTED right down into a puddle. Never, ever would she tire of hearing that. "I love you, Master."

When she finally looked away from him, she saw the tables and chairs on the patio had been moved to form a semicircle, leaving a large open area. For a whip.

"Master Raoul." Z stood a few feet away. His dark gray eyes held hers as he said, "Tell your submissive what you wish to use so she might bring you the proper tools."

*Tools?* Things he'd use on her. To hurt her… She wrenched her gaze away and realized people had congregated around the patio. Watching. Like at an exhibit or a slavers' stage. Her horrified gaze fell on Gabi.

Gabi jerked her chin up and then deliberately made a fist, arcing it in the tugboat hand signal for *full speed ahead.*

Kim blinked. *Well.*

Next to her hard-faced dom, Beth had her hands clasped together, and her lips moved, *You can do it.*

Andrea gave her a firm nod of encouragement.

Kari's eyes had tears in them, but she waggled a baby monitor emphatically and mouthed, "Yes. Do it."

Jessica was alternating glaring at Z and nodding vigorously at Kim.

*Not an exhibit. I have my own set of cheerleaders.*

"I think you agreed on whips?" Z asked, as if deliberately rubbing her fears raw.

A shudder ran through her, but she forced steel into her spine. *I fought the Overseer and Greville and won. Can I be less brave in going after my dreams?*

Master R's face held only fury as he stared at Z, but then he sighed and smiled. "Remind me to hurt Z after this."

*Master R is on my side. He always is.* But she could…almost…understand the pressure Z was putting on her. This was her opportunity to prove herself to them both, and Master Z would make it a proper test. She raised her chin. "Can Master describe his wishes?"

His hand touched her cheek gently, his gaze intensifying, as if he assessed her determination, and his lips curved with approval. "My gatita makes me proud."

God, everything in her melted, and she felt as if she'd drown in his eyes.

Master R thought a minute. "I want you to bring me the flogger with a faint yellow stripe on the handle, a crop—one with soft leather—and the bullwhip on the leftmost side. You will do this to please me, Kimberly."

The bullwhip. Her mouth was too dry, so she gave him a jerky nod and walked off the patio. Her legs didn't seem to belong to her, but they were moving, and that was all she could ask.

The dungeon was cool. Quiet. And, oddly, held no fears, just memories of Master R: Leaning against a wall and counting with his fingers as she walked around the room. Massaging her on the bondage table. *"You're not going to fall into pieces if I touch your breasts."*

He'd led her out of panic each time—her wish to please him would work that magic again. It must.

The crop was easy and she picked one with the softest leather. The flogger he'd actually teased her with once and let her play with. The bullwhip…

She got near and couldn't touch it. Had to circle to get

close. Another circle. Did he even know how to use a whip? What if he—No, this was Master R. If he used something, he'd be superb. She'd never seen him practice though.

That was scary. During the next detour, she frowned at the empty space on one side of the room. She'd never wondered why it was there. A newspaper was clamped chest-high on the wall, thin strips of it dangling like streamers. She shivered. Maybe he did practice.

Another circle.

*Enough stalling. I will do this.* She brought up in her memory the approval on Master R's face. *"You will do this to please me."* The need to see that approval again grew, slowly outweighing her fear.

Her fingers closed on the whip, and she whispered a vow to herself. "I'm going to learn to use this damned thing. Rip up some newspapers myself. See if I don't." Her hand tightened on the leather.

As she stepped out onto the patio in the bright sun, she saw Master R in the middle. He'd taken his shirt off to get ready for the scene, obviously never doubting her courage. The sight of the contoured muscles on his chest and arms made her stop. So powerful. She smiled, remembering when she'd said that to him. He'd laughed and picked her up so, so easily, murmuring into her hair, *"The better to hold you with."*

A thin pink ridge ran across his left ribs where Greville's knife had cut, an atrocity on his beautiful, tan skin, and anger flared in her. Then she huffed a laugh, glancing down at her own scar. They were definitely a matched set now.

The people around the patio went completely silent as she crossed to him. She knelt at his feet. "I brought your tools as you asked, Master."

"You did very, very well." He took everything from her, setting it all on the ground off to one side. His stride was as she'd remembered in her dreams—unhurried, steady, and solid.

With an easy yank, he lifted her to her feet, then rested his hands on her shoulders, massaging lightly. "You will take everything I give you today," he said, holding her gaze. His eyes were filled with a dark promise of pain and pleasure.

A thrill of anticipation went through her. He'd never pushed her in the dungeon, but now, now his eyes promised he would today. *Oh God.* "I will, Master." It was a vow for both of them. *I will.*

He guided her under the chains, facing her toward the ocean and away from the audience. After restraining her arms over her head, he secured her legs apart, opening them widely, before tightening the chains to her arms. He circled her slowly, looking her over, his gaze like a caress on her bare skin. He stopped in front of her, cupping her chin in his palm. "I've dreamed of seeing you here, like this," he said, his voice a little rough. "Open to me, wanting what I can give you."

"I want that," she whispered, every cell in her needing to please him. And she'd take whatever he asked so he'd be proud, would know how much she loved him. The need to give, to accept, filled her.

He kissed her, his tongue taking her, his lips demanding but so, so sweet. When he lifted his head, her breath came thick and hot. Obviously someone had turned the humidity up on the patio.

His hand glided over her shoulder, then her back, as he walked around her, and then lower: her bottom, her legs...

When he stroked up her inner thighs, she jerked.

"Be still, gatita." Warm hands. Firm touch.

Just like her dreams. She realized her pussy was wet

with her arousal.

"Very nice, Kimberly. I like this." His fingers slid through her folds, making her shiver. The murmur of conversation came to her, then disappeared under the rush of heat as his fingers pressed her labia open and ran over her clit. She bit her lip as electricity sizzled through her.

He teased her clit and then eased a finger inside her and out.

Legs wide apart, she was exposed to anything he wanted to do, and…it was the most erotic thing she'd ever felt in her life, knowing she'd willingly given him the power.

He rose to his feet.

*Oh no.* Her thoughts stuttered at the memory of the *tools.* "Wait."

The smack on her ass stung. "Who?"

"Master R. Master, what are you going to do?"

"Whatever I want to, sumisita mía." His voice wasn't mean, just that firmness that sent quivers into her stomach and more wetness between her legs.

He chuckled and pressed his body against hers from behind, his erection pushing on her buttocks, his muscular chest heating her back, his arms surrounding her. "Pretty gatita, are you ready?" His fingers tweaked her nipples, and his touch sent streaks of pain straight down to her clit.

He gathered her hair and moved it forward over her shoulder. Baring her back. She tensed, but he only ran his hands up and down, waking her skin, making her breasts sway.

He slapped her bottom lightly, a tiny sting, then harder, and more, until she wanted to move away from the burning. She arched away—uselessly.

"Sí, I like knowing you have to stay put to take what I give you," he murmured and walked around to face her, his hand always on her, stroking from her back to her shoulder.

Her bottom burned, and her skin was so sensitive that even the touch of the sea breeze felt like an icy kiss.

His lips brushed hers. Then he captured her mouth with hungry urgency. "I've missed kissing you. So...you will tell me if the pain becomes too much, no? What is your safe word?"

"Cramp."

"Very good." His grin flashed at her. "Which will make you scream first, gatita—the sting of the lash or the fury of your orgasm?"

Oh boy, how could he terrify her and turn her on at the same time? Sensuality darkened his face as he regarded her, not hiding the pleasure he got from playing with her. Not hiding his intention to exercise his power as her master.

*I can't believe I'm here. Doing this...wanting this.* Yet the more she surrendered, the more she felt a part of him.

He knew. He touched her cheek, his gaze softening.

She stared at him helplessly, bound with more than physical restraints.

The flogger he used next didn't hurt. Like a million elves drumming on her skin, the strands of the flogger moved from her back to her front.

She stared at him, almost mesmerized. So big, shoulders broad, his chest and arm muscles rippled with each movement. His control was absolute, his focus totally on her and the flogger as if it connected them like an umbilical cord.

He lightened the strokes over her stomach and thighs, even lighter over her breasts, making them swell and throb. The very lightest flick between her legs sent her up onto her toes with surprise, followed by a hot rush of pleasure.

He saw, and a smile softened his stern features. As he circled her, her skin grew more sensitive, started to burn. And somehow her pussy throbbed as if it had swollen too much.

A pause. His hands stroked her body, soothing the ache. He moved in front of her and studied her for a silent moment. Then the corners of his eyes crinkled. "You are very beautiful, all aroused and ready for the bite of the lash." His palms covered her breasts, and he watched her intently as he pinched her nipples lightly, then harder, rolling the peaks between his fingers.

She closed her eyes as pleasure washed through her.

"Look at me."

She forced her eyes open, stiffening as his hand moved to her pussy, sliding through her folds. The streak of sharp pleasure was almost painful, unexpected, and she made a protesting sound.

"Shhh, gatita. You want this—there is no shame in it, in being a woman. In letting your master rouse your body." He smiled, fingers pushing intimately inside her, then out and over her clit. Over and in, repeating until her hips pressed forward into each movement.

*Oh God, I need more.* She hadn't dreamed she could get so hot, so needy.

Then he smiled. "Very good. You're ready." His gaze was level, direct, utterly in control and confident.

And she nodded. She could handle pain if he was in charge.

He kissed her slowly and then ravenously. "Sumisita mía," he said, tipping her chin up. "After this, I intend to take you." He shifted uncomfortably. "Hard."

Her vagina clenched. As her gaze dropped to his groin, delight rose inside her. "As Master wishes."

"Yes, my gatita's submission—and body—makes me needy." He touched his nose to hers, took in her breath. "I've missed taking you every morning before breakfast."

She closed her eyes and breathed, "Me too." Waking

alone, wanting him so much she'd slept with an extra pillow to have something to hold.

He pressed another kiss to her lips, then walked away. A second later, she heard the crack of a whip.

Panic rolled over her, drowning her in memories. Slicing pain after pain, screaming. She pulled frantically at the chains, her breathing a tropical storm turning into a hurricane.

"Kimberly." His voice cut through the winds. "You will take this for me."

Silence grew around her, the fears held at bay with just his voice...and her need to please him. Master R, not Greville. Master R would stop if she needed him to...and so she could go on. "Yes, Master. I will."

The first touch of the whip was a flicker: here, there, up, and down. A little sting, the rhythm almost soothing. A brush over her skin like a rough kiss. More. She'd never watched whipping scenes. Who knew it could be so...sensuous?

After a while, he walked forward to rub her back. Played with her breasts, sending new sparks of arousal flickering through her body. His erection pressed into her from behind, and he ground it against her bottom, making her feel the lingering burn from her spanking. His fist closed in her hair, tugging her head to the side. His voice was low and ruthless, sending a thrill through her. "Now, I'm going to push you, Kimberly. And you will take it—for me."

He obviously felt her shiver; his laugh was guttural. Terrifying. *Hot.* He moved away, but she could hear him. "That's my good girl."

A crack, a tiny whoosh, then the sting, pain blooming beneath her skin. She gasped, a little shocked. *That hurt.* He kept on, over and over, like the bite of flame from the fireplay, the whip was a flash of pain that almost seemed to light her up inside.

Down her ass, a few touches on her thighs that zapped straight to her clit until—oh, God, she was shaking with the need to come.

The intensity increased. More. Sharper. She sucked in her breath to keep from yelling. He eased off to the sweet brushing strokes. Harder again. Stinging, shocking, burning...*pain.*

Nothing moved, but she fell backward, tumbling into the ocean, surrounded by softness. Her eyes half-focused on the tide rolling in on the white shore, and she realized his strokes were timed to the ocean waves. The pain hit and rolled over her, flowing back out before the next one. So wonderful yet so arousing. The whip strokes slowly moved down her ass, her thighs, and back up.

His body was against hers again, warm, holding her.

"Eyes on me," he said, turning her head. Brown gaze, calm and wonderful.

She smiled at him and savored his grin.

"Look at you. Even under a whip, you trusted me enough to hit subspace," he murmured, kissing her until the ground disappeared from under her. "I'm very proud of you, gatita." He pulled back. "Tell me your safe word."

"Cramp. Only I don't need it," she confided.

His eyes crinkled. "I'm going to give you five more, and they will hurt."

A worry started to rise in her. She heard the sharp crack behind her, but nothing hit.

"Take a breath, gatita." Firm. Her master.

An orgasm seemed to be floating inside, waiting, as she inhaled.

"Let it out."

She breathed out and heard a crack and razor-sharp

pain shot across her right buttock. She sucked in a breath, feeling her body jerk, and as she exhaled, another line of fire hit. Yet it was Master R doing it, expecting her to handle it, making her take it, and that sent her even deeper. Tears rolled down her cheeks. Another razor cut of pain jolted her to her core and another—white-hot pain—and another.

Through the surging of the blood in her head, she heard his footsteps. His arms surrounded her, pulled her into his warmth. "I'm so proud of you. You have pleased me very much," he murmured into her hair.

She blinked at him. "I will take more if you need me to, Master."

He frowned. "Do you want more?"

"No. But if you—"

"No, gatita. You're not a masochist." He kissed her cheek. "For which I am very happy. You have had enough."

She sighed, still half in the clouds, and when he kissed her long and slow, her whole body reminded her of what she wanted. "Can we go somewhere and…?"

His head lifted, brown eyes keen. Hot.

"And make love," she finished. It would be love. She knew that.

His grin flashed. "Are you saying, *'Just fuck me already?'*"

She choked, but the throbbing of her lower half wouldn't be denied. "Yes, Master. If Master pleases."

"Oh, that will please Master," he said, gripping her hair. "But we aren't going inside, Kimberly."

*Out here?* Her eyes rounded.

Laughing softly, he unsnapped the chains holding her legs apart and then reached up to the panic snaps above. Two clicks, and she was free. She groaned as she lowered her arms, her shoulders aching. Her knees wobbling.

He picked her up, snuggling her against his bare chest. His clean, masculine scent surrounded her, musky from the exercise, making her want to rub her skin over his. She felt small in his arms, delicate and cherished.

He crossed the patio and sat her on the unused wooden table. "Lie on your back, sumisa," he said and folded his arms over his chest.

Even though sweat covered her body, she felt the flush rising in her face.

When he lifted his eyebrows slightly, she knew she didn't want to let him down. Never. She lay back.

"Such a good girl," he murmured, the heat in his eyes scorching across her skin. "When we met, you preferred pain to sharing the intimacy of your orgasm in front of others," he said, running his hands over her breasts. "Will you offer it to me now?"

Make love here? In front of...everyone?

His eyes held hers. Demanding...more. That she surrender everything. And she wanted to. "I will do whatever Master wants," she said. "Yes."

His gaze softened. "You took pain for me, Kimberly," he said soberly. "Now can you take being restrained—and then pleasure?"

Shivers ran over her body. "Yes, Master."

His hand stroked over her leg, warming her flesh for a moment. Then he pushed her legs against her chest and slid her down the table until her bottom was just over the edge. A tremor ran through her. The drifty feeling hadn't quite disappeared, but she rapidly returned to the real world as he hooked her wrist cuffs to the edges of the table even with her waist. He moved her left leg so he could clip the ankle cuff to her wrist cuff and did the same on her right, spreading her legs widely.

Her pussy was exposed. Very exposed. He stood back

as she conquered the first shudder of fear. She stared at him, using him as her anchor, knowing he'd keep her safe.

His broad hands ran over her body. "I've missed having a little submissive bound and open before me," he said softly. His knuckles trailed down her cheek. "To have one that loves me and tries so hard to please me is an even better feeling."

Everything inside her melted.

"But this is a test for you. Will you yield me everything?" He unhooked a wide canvas strap from under the table and pulled it across her low stomach, just above her mound. "Even when I take the last few bits of movement from you?" He secured it tightly, pinning her hips against the smooth table.

"Yes, Master." She tried not to wiggle, to test the restraints, and couldn't help herself. But her hips wouldn't move at all. Panic rose and fell like the tide.

"And a test for me as well. Do I trust your surrender enough that I will push you as I should and give us both what we need?" The ruthless determination in his gaze shook her to the core. "I trust you more than I thought I could. Are you all right, gatita?"

Fear didn't stand a chance next to Raoul Sandoval, her master. She smiled at him.

"Beautiful Kimberly." He leaned an arm on the table, filling her vision.

His lips brushed over hers, and he kissed her, severing the current of fear, replacing it with need. His warm hand closed over her breast, cupping it, teasing the nipple to a point even as he stroked his tongue over hers, as he reminded her of his taste, his scent, his possession.

"Mmm." He lifted his head and smiled, whispering, "You look like you need to be fucked, sumisa."

And everybody probably saw that. She glared at him

and earned a pinch on her nipple that made her gasp. Her breasts were swollen, as if they'd grown a cup size, leaving the skin too tight. Her nipples throbbed, and she could feel the odd stings from where he'd lashed her lightly. He bent down and licked over each nipple, circling them, leaving them wet so the breeze cooled them, tightening them further.

*More.* Her back arched.

"Too much movement." Straps went across her, above and below her breasts, constricting everything between until the mounds were pushed up tightly.

And she really couldn't move.

"Sí, I like that." He smiled and closed his big hands over her aching breasts, fondling with calloused palms and pinching her nipples lightly. Her clit started throbbing to match the ache in her breasts.

She wanted to beg for more and knew he'd just laugh and do whatever he wanted in his own time. God, why did being naked and exposed, restrained and unable to stop him, make her so, so hot?

He stepped back, regarding her...as if considering all the dirty, dark things he could do to her. Her insides clenched with desire.

What would he do? His hands? Mouth? Toys? But she hadn't fetched up any plugs or clamps or... Her breath stopped as he walked out of sight. *I brought him a crop.*

*Oh no. No no no.*

Master R strolled back into her field of vision, tapping the long, thin rod on his palm. Oh God, he was going to. Her breasts were pointing up like two targets, her legs wide, her labia gaping open. He wouldn't...would he? She felt the trickle of her own moisture from her pussy down to her asshole.

"Look at that," he said softly. He rubbed the crop's

leather flap over her breasts, teasing her nipples. "All excited. Not a hint of fear in you."

She realized it was true. The anticipation of pain seemed to just turn her on further.

"I was watching when Jessica told you about how Z restrained her on the Shadowlands bar." The crop trailed down her stomach, flickered over her labia.

Oh God. Just the touch of it, the teasing. She felt swollen, tight. Desperate.

His fingers followed the leather. The contrast between cool and warm, smooth and rough, inanimate and alive, made her body pulse with need.

At the foot of the table, he smiled slightly as he traced her folds with one finger, up and over her clit. Deliberately, mercilessly increasing her arousal.

He pushed a finger into her, sliding easily, his thick knuckles adding to the swelling sensation. Two fingers, and his tongue licked over her clit, bringing her higher. Her thighs quivered as she tried to raise her pussy higher, to get more. Nothing—absolutely nothing—moved. She was pinned, completely immobile.

Master R pulled his fingers out of her vagina slowly and ran his slick hand over her leg. "She told you how he used a whip on her pussy."

He hit her inner thigh with the crop—the very tip of the leather flap. The sting made her gasp.

"I saw how much it excited you, gatita. To think of having your pussy whipped." The crop made its way up the inside of her thigh to the top of her mound. Each flick of the leather against her skin stung.

Her entire body tensed in anticipation of that small pain landing on her throbbing clit, but he continued up, hitting her lightly across her stomach.

She jumped when the crop hit the underside of her

right breast. He circled, once, twice, around her breast. It was so tight, each sting reverberated through the whole mound. Her breathing was like a boat tossing in the waves, finding and losing its rhythm.

He stroked her hair away from her face, studying her carefully, his eyes intent and hot...very hot. Without speaking, he moved to her left breast. Around and around. How could they possibly feel tighter? she wondered, hearing a low whine escape her.

"Yes, give me the sounds." The leather flicked sharply over her peaked left nipple.

The sudden sting bit like sharp teeth into the sensitive tip and felt as if he'd also struck her clit. "Ah!" Her spine tried to arch; her hands jerked; nothing moved. The feeling of being trapped passing into complete heat as he flicked her right nipple.

Back and forth, leaving only enough time for the bite of pain to dissipate before hitting the other nipple. Her breasts felt as if they were on fire yet so very, very swollen and needy.

He bent and pulled a peak into his mouth, gentle lips, heat, but when he sucked, pulling strongly, her whole body shook like a leaf. *Oh God.*

As he changed to the other nipple, hot, sucking, her insides started to coil, pressure building inside.

His brown eyes met hers as he lifted his head. "You're very close to coming, gatita."

She swallowed, wanting to beg. *Please, please, now.* He wouldn't, she knew. The knowledge that he had control, everything was up to him, and she could do nothing about it increased her need as if someone had opened her motor to full throttle, sending excitement humming through her.

He trailed his hand down her body, soothing the little bites the crop had left over her breasts, her stomach, her thighs.

The crop smacked her thigh again. Slightly harder, like a kitten with sharp milk teeth. Up toward her pussy, over her mound, down her leg. Aching. She could feel her engorged clit trying to extend, trying for attention, and she shuddered with fearful anticipation.

Up her leg again, only this time, the flicks hit her outer labia. Pinpricks of pain, up and down her newly shaved, tender flesh, each time closer to the apex. To her clit.

Her breath hitched as he almost...

The crop lifted. Everything inside her tightened. Her inner folds were swollen, wet, as a cool breeze washed over her. Her vulnerable clit pulsed, filling her world. She stared at the crop, in the air, as her muscles pulled against the restraints.

His eyes met hers.

The crop hit directly on her clit. *Pain. Pleasure.* The sensations mixed, raw and brutal, exploding up and out. Her body tried to shake itself free as the waves of pleasure ripped through her. The scream turned to gasping wails as her pussy contracted over and over.

She pulled in a breath.

The only warning was a touch at her entrance, and then he sheathed his cock in her with one merciless thrust. She gasped in shock. He was too big, her tissues too swollen.

His groin brushed over her abused clit, sending waves and waves of pleasure and pain ripping through her again. He held still for a second, letting her adjust, then looked her in the eyes. "I'm going to take you hard now."

He didn't ask permission. God, he felt so huge inside her. She tried to move, and the straps held her in place. Open. She felt possessed, taken. Owned.

Leaning forward onto one forearm, he pushed in

deeper. "Look at me, gatita." His voice was rougher, lower. "Keep your eyes on me." His free hand curled under her ass, making the stripes there burn as he pulled back. And then he drove into her, using his legs, his hips. The piercing was like a solid finger rubbing her right...right on that inside spot. *God.*

KIMBERLY'S PUSSY CONTRACTED around Raoul, hot and slick, battering at his dick. Dios, he'd missed being inside her, missed the connection. In his mind, this was the proper way to end a scene between a couple. Making love confirmed the bonds they'd built.

He squeezed his little sub's ass, knowing it would hurt, seeing her response in the quivering of her thighs, feeling the way her cunt clutched him.

The legs-high position made her extremely tight, the tugging of the piercing waking every nerve in his cock. He thrust hard again, letting his body tell her, show her, what he would soon say to her. *Mine.* Mine to possess, to protect, to push, to cherish. *To love.*

He pounded into her, slowing to run his hands over her breasts, the nipples puffy now, and each tiny pinch on a peak made her pussy tighten. Her blue, blue eyes stayed on his as he picked up the pace. He wasn't trying to last. She'd had enough, but they both needed this to complete what they had done here.

And she felt so hot, so wet, her cunt was still pulsing around him in a lingering orgasm. He pushed in harder, feeling her cervix against the head of his shaft. His balls pulled up tighter, contracting. *Just. One. More. Thrust.* And then the heat flowed through his shaft so violently, in such intense pleasure, that his hand tightened on her ass, and she squeaked.

He pulled out and pushed back in, his climax not ending, as if his cock wanted to hold out, to stay inside her.

His chest heaved as he fought for air. Sweat trickled down the hollow of his back.

He looked into her eyes, seeing her utter submission, her joy in giving him pleasure, in giving herself. The tie between them was almost palpable, and he wanted her in his arms so badly he almost shook with the need.

He kissed her softly and then pulled out with a pang of regret that matched her soft sigh. Moving back, he pressed a quick kiss to her stomach and smiled against the quivering softness.

Dios, he loved her. And her courage. He hadn't pulled back. He'd demanded from her what they both needed, and she'd given him...everything. The scene, the sex... Both had answered his worries, made her sure of herself. The connection between them was stronger than ever.

He smiled. The bridge was built, was open, and ready for traffic.

After doing up his jeans, he moved to give her a long, long kiss. "I love you, sumisita mía" he whispered and was surprised when her eyes pooled with tears despite her smile.

Always touching her, he released the straps, rubbing her skin lightly to help the blood return, massaging her shoulders and hip joints. Finally she struggled to a sitting position.

The people on the patio were silent, not wanting to interrupt. Raoul glanced their way. Cullen grinned, his little sub obviously riding him; Marcus had Gabi in front of him and his hand in her shorts. Raoul's lips twitched. Must have been as hot from the outside as it was from the inside.

Z moved Jessica off his own lap, picked up a tightly rolled blanket from the table beside him, and walked over to hand it to Kimberly.

She started to unfold it, and Z shook his head, so she wrapped her arms around the bundle. He touched her cheek lightly with his fingertips, smiled at Raoul, and returned to his sub.

With a sigh of pleasure, Raoul gathered up his woman, soft and warm and fragrant, fitting…just right…in his arms. After kissing the top of her head, he carried her across the patio, down the steps, and onto the beach.

He went to her favorite spot, the weathered white Adirondack chair. As he settled her against him with a sigh of contentment, she buried her face in his neck, starting to tremble.

The aftermath was catching up with her.

With his arms around her, he awkwardly unfolded the blanket Z had given her and found a bottle of water, a tube of ointment…and his collar. Clever dom. After setting everything to the side of the chair, he wrapped her in the thin blanket then pulled her closer. He still felt so in tune with her that he knew when she started to unravel.

She looked up at him, her expression vulnerable, everything open to his gaze. "I missed you so much," she whispered. "And I was lonely." Her eyes filled with tears.

He stroked her cheek, recognizing her need. "Cry for me now, Kimberly."

*"CRY FOR ME."* A dom's command. Kim stared into his face. He was here, really here, and she hurt, and everything inside her felt as if he'd ripped away all the bandages over her emotions, and he was really here. A sob wrenched out of her, a belated sound since tears already streamed down her face. She buried her face in his neck, breathed him in, and cried.

Cried for the weeks apart and for missing him and for his gift of a furry protector. For him losing his family and finding them again, and for her fear of today and the whip, and because her back hurt like hell, and eventually, she realized she was telling him all that in between her sobs.

He'd laid his cheek on top of her head and was murmuring encouragement, Spanish mingling with English.

After a shuddering breath, she looked up. His eyes crinkled, and he dug a cotton handkerchief from his jeans pocket. *A handkerchief.*

As she wiped her face, she muttered, "You knew this would happen. I cry way too much around you. I never used to cry at all, so this is all your fault."

He laughed, low and pleased, knocking her heart over as if it had tripped. "But no, gatita, I think you're making up for lost time. Eventually it will settle down."

"One can only hope." She gave him a soft kiss, enjoying the slow movement of his mouth on hers. "I love you."

He rubbed his nose against hers and then resettled her on his lap before holding a bottle of water to her lips. After she'd finished most of it, he wrapped the blanket back around her.

With a finger under her chin, he asked, "Kimberly, did you have anything to do with my mother and sister visiting me this morning?"

She jerked and realized she'd given herself away. Oh damn. Her turn.

Gabi and Jessica had already gotten in trouble. That nasty Cullen had called Z and Marcus and told on them. Talk about pissed-off doms.

But how would Master R react? His expression didn't tell her anything. She bit her lip. "Um."

He nodded as if her hesitance totally confirmed his suspicions. "Why?"

She huffed out a breath. Dammit. "In the hospital, your family warned me about you, saying what you'd supposedly done to your ex, only...that's just not you. It bothered me. Worried me. Last night, I, uh, checked around."

"You asked Sally."

*Whip or not, I'm not going to confirm that.* "After I finished my research"—that sounded nicely vague—"I talked with your mom and sister, and now they know Alicia is a liar and a bottom-feeding, skanky bilge rat who slept with her—"

"Kimberly."

Kimberly broke it off—*the scum-sucking bitch*—and sweetly added, "I simply explained what consensual means."

RAOUL SHOOK HIS head. It had been the gatita who'd fixed everything.

All these years, alienated from his family because of a vindictive woman's lies. He frowned. "I wonder if Alicia spread those lies in the BDSM community." Not in the Shadowlands, since Z was a walking lie detector, but elsewhere.

"She sounds like she's enough of a blowfish." Kimberly frowned. "The Overseer always acted like he thought you were like him."

"It's probably why I was accepted as a buyer so quickly. And why I was there to buy you that night." His arms tightened. Kimberly might have been bought and disappeared forever. Any buyers not picked up at the auction would hide their slaves forever...or dispose of them.

One little submissive in exchange for three years of not speaking to his family. His lips curved. Maybe he'd send his ex a thank-you note.

Kimberly was biting her lip again, still worried about her interference in his life, his generous-hearted gatita who had healed a wound that had lasted far too long. He ran his finger over her cheek. "Thank you, mi amor."

Her soft lips turned up in a happy smile. "You're welcome." She gave him a mischievous look. "Your sister called before we left Gabi's house—I'm supposed to come to Sunday dinner with you."

AS MASTER R laughed and hugged her, Kim sighed in relief. In perfect contentment, she lay in his arms, listening to the waves roll in and the sound of gulls in the distance. Even the voices from the party up the shore didn't disturb her—she was part of them. "So did I pass the test?"

He ran his finger over her lips. "You know you did. Before we go further, do you have questions, some negotiating?"

*Oh. Hmm.* She'd worried over so many things, and somehow most of them no longer seemed that important. "Will I live with you?"

"You will."

"So I'd move here and get a job?"

"Do you want to keep working?" He kissed her. "You don't have to, you know."

"I want to." She wrinkled her nose. "Housework is past boring."

His laugh bounced her head on his chest. "This is your decision, gatita. And, before you ask, your money is also your own. I have enough trouble with my own finances."

Her breath eased out. "You're being awfully easygoing." Disappointment, worry tightened her chest. Wasn't he going to stay in charge?

"Now and then. I'm also making one very big concession, chiquita," he murmured. "You will have a small part of the day to call your own...although I may take that away eventually." Master R considered her, his eyes narrowing. "You like rules and schedules, so...in the morning, from arising until noon—or at your job—you are in charge of yourself."

One worry...of being constantly monitored ...disappeared. *But...I want him in charge.*

"The rest of the time, you submit *completely* to me," Master R said. He leaned forward, holding her eyes. "For sex, for clothing, for food and exercise. As we lived before. You are *mine*."

Her breath huffed out as the tightness in her chest eased into warmth.

His hand fisted in her hair, pulling her head back so she stared up at him. The love in his eyes did not conceal the determination, the sheer steel of his character. "That is the point, is it not, chiquita?"

"Oh yes."

He kissed her so thoroughly that she felt owned right down to her soul and beyond, then smiled, a wicked gleam in his eyes. "Lunch has been and gone, so this is my time, no?"

A tremor went through her as amusement lit his eyes. *Uh-oh.* "Yes, Master R."

"Lie across my knees."

A spanking. Her back and bottom still burned from the whipping and flogging. *But...but.* From the look on his face, she knew better than to beg for lenience. "Yes, Master." Slowly, as if maybe he'd change his mind—had that happened yet?—she went stomach down over his lap.

"Good girl. Now hold still."

She tensed. Something cold drizzled over her skin.

Ointment, she realized, and then his ruthless, hard hand rubbed it over her back and bottom. *Ouch, ouch, ouch.* Unable to help herself, she squirmed.

"Stay still." He set a heavy hand on her lower back to pin her like a bug as he treated every stripe and welt and sore spot. Every damned one. He ignored her wiggling and whimpers—and actually laughed a few times. Sadistic bastard dom.

When he *finally* finished, everything throbbed with pain. He set her on her feet, rose, and with a grin, lifted her chin to kiss her sullen lips. "I take good care of this little body that is mine, no?"

His good humor was contagious, and her mouth curved up as she grumbled out, "Thank you, Master."

He picked something up, then turned toward the patio and gave a shrill whistle.

She saw he held the collar in his hand. *Oh my God.* He was really going to do it.

The Shadowlands people gathered quietly along the edge of the patio. Kim saw a teary-eyed Gabi holding Marcus's hand. Jessica was tucked under Z's arm, and the Shadowlands owner was smiling. Andrea and Cullen had equally big grins. Dan with Kari wiping tears from her cheeks. On left end of the line, Sally beamed. On the right of line, the FBI agents had satisfaction in their faces. Sam's eyes met hers. He nodded, his expression pleased and a little haunted.

And the rest of the people... She knew she'd have time to get to know them all. Unable to show how happy she was, she could only grin up at everyone.

Then she turned to Master R. Her heart hammered in her chest as it had done so often this past month, only her hands were warm, her lips were curved in a smile, and her body wasn't filled with fear, but joy.

He glanced at the ground.

She knelt with perfect grace and bowed her head.

He raised his voice. "Kimberly, I promise to hold you and keep you safe, to support you and guide you, to be honest and open with you. You have trusted me to tend to your happiness, health, and well-being. I will never break that trust." His voice was rough, his eyes so, so warm. He held up the collar, the engraving gleaming in the sunlight. "Do you accept this collar as a symbol of your submission and devotion?"

She wanted special words to give him back but could only manage, "I will wear it proudly."

He touched the buckle. "The lock is missing. At the beginning of the new year, if we are of the same mind, then we will have a formal collaring—and locking—ceremony."

Under the murmuring of approval, he whispered in an amused voice, "That means I'll get to whip you again."

She choked, trying not to laugh. Relief mingled with joy. He understood that her mind and emotions weren't as yet all her own, and would give her time to finish healing, to let her enter into a formal relationship with a whole heart.

He fastened the collar around her neck, checking that it was loose enough, and the feeling of belonging shook her whole body. His eyes crinkled. "That's exactly the right reaction, sumisita mía," he murmured.

When tipping over backward into the ocean during a scuba dive, she'd always have a moment of disorientation before everything turned clear and the ocean turned to an embrace. She'd plunged, and now here she was, right where she wanted to be. "Master, have I mentioned how much I love you?"

To the sound of applause, he lifted Kim to her feet, his hands warm and firm on her arms. His eyes met hers, serious, burning with his own love. "Not nearly often enough. Please work on that, sumisita mía. "

"It will be my pleasure, Master."

# THE END

# Cherise Sinclair

Now everyone thinks summer romances never go anywhere, right? Well...that's not always true.

I met my dearheart when vacationing in the Caribbean. Now I won't say it was love at first sight. Actually, since he was standing over me, enjoying the view down my swimsuit top, I might even have been a tad peeved—as well as attracted. But although our time together there was less than two days, and although we lived in opposite sides of the country, love can't be corralled by time or space.

We've now been married for many, many years. (And he still looks down my swimsuit tops.)

Nowadays, I live in the west with this obnoxious, beloved husband, two children, and various animals, including three cats who rule the household. I'm a gardener, and I love nurturing small plants until they're big and healthy and productive...and ripping defenseless weeds out by the roots when I'm angry. I enjoy thunderstorms, playing Scrabble and Risk, and being a soccer mom. My favorite way to spend an evening is curled up on a couch next to the master of my heart, watching the fire, reading, and...well...if you're reading this book, you obviously know what else happens in front of fires. :)

—*Cherise*

http://www.cherisesinclair.com

# Loose Id® Titles by Cherise Sinclair

*Available in digital format and print from your favorite retailer*

*Master of the Abyss*
*Master of the Mountain*
*The Dom's Dungeon*
*The Starlight Rite*

\* \* \* \*

## The MASTERS OF THE SHADOWLANDS Series

*Club Shadowlands*
*Dark Citadel*
*Breaking Free*
*Lean on Me*
*Make Me, Sir*
*To Command and Collar*

\* \* \* \*

"Simon Says: Mine"
Part of the anthology *Doms of Dark Haven*
With Sierra Cartwright and Belinda McBride

\* \* \* \*

"Welcome to the Dark Side"
Part of the anthology *Doms of Dark Haven 2:*
*Western Night*
With Sierra Cartwright and Belinda McBride

CPSIA information can be obtained at www.ICGtesting.com
Printed in the USA
BVOW080510241012

303797BV00001B/82/P